Jill Mansell worked for many years at the Burden Neurological Hospital, Bristol, and now writes full-time. Amongst her many *Sunday Times* bestsellers are NADIA KNOWS BEST, FALLING FOR YOU, THE ONE YOU REALLY WANT and MAKING YOUR MIND UP; a full list of her books appears on page ii.

Also by Jill Mansell

Making Your Mind Up
The One You Really Want
Falling For You
Nadia Knows Best
Staying At Daisy's
Good At Games
Millie's Fling
Miranda's Big Mistake
Head Over Heels
Mixed Doubles
Perfect Timing
Fast Friends
Solo
Sheer Mischief
Open House
Two's Company

Jill Mansell

kiss

First published in 1993 by Bantam Press, a division of Transworld Publishers Ltd

This edition published in paperback in 2006 by
HEADLINE REVIEW
An imprint of HEADLINE BOOK PUBLISHING

25

A format 0 7472 6846 0 (ISBN-10)
A format 978 0 7472 6846 8 (ISBN-13)
B format 0 7553 3255 5 (ISBN-10)
B format 978 0 7553 3255 7 (ISBN-13)

Typeset in Plantin by Avon DataSet Ltd, Bidford on Avon, Warwickshire

Printed and bound in the UK by
CPI Mackays, Chatham ME5 8TD

Headline's policy is to use papers that are natural, renewable and recyclable products and made from wood grown in sustainable forests. The logging and manufacturing processes are expected to conform to the environmental regulations of the country of origin.

HEADLINE BOOK PUBLISHING
A division of Hodder Headline
338 Euston Road
LONDON NW1 3BH

www.reviewbooks.co.uk
www.hodderheadline.com

For Cino and Lydia
With all my love

Chapter 1

'I just want to know,' Katerina said slowly, 'whether your intentions towards my mother are honourable.'

And despite the fact that it was snowing hard, she stood her ground in the doorway, refusing to allow Ralph inside.

'What a little darling you are.' He grinned and ruffled her hair, because he knew how much it annoyed her. 'And whatever did your disgraceful mother ever do to deserve such a daughter? If you were a few years older, Kat, I swear I'd whisk you off to Gretna Green myself.'

'Ah, but would I be silly enough to go? Besides, we aren't talking about my marital prospects,' she continued, her expression stern. 'I asked you a question and I'm still waiting for an answer.'

'Of course. Are my intentions honourable?' Frowning, he paused for a second to consider his reply. Snowflakes, melting in his hair, were sliding down his neck. It was very cold. 'No, sorry,' he said finally. 'Absolutely not.'

Katerina shrugged. 'That's all right, then,' she replied cheerfully, stepping to one side and waving him through. 'Mum can't stand honourable men. She's in the kitchen, by the way, dyeing her hair.'

'Go away,' grumbled Izzy, her voice muffled, her head plunged upside down in the sink. 'You're early.'

'No, I'm not.' Ralph pinched her bottom, denim-clad

and excitingly stuck out. 'You're late. What colour is it going to be, anyway?' Peering more closely at the mass of curling, dripping hair, he saw that the rinsed-off water in the washing-up bowl was an ominous shade of indigo.

The final jug of hot water cascaded down, splashing into the sink and on to the floor. When Izzy had wrung out her hair and wrapped an enormous pink towel turban-style around her head she resumed vertical posture and planted a wet kiss on Ralph's cheek before he could dodge out of the way.

'Glossy Blackberry. It'll be irresistible, darling.'

She was already irresistible, he thought as he followed her through to the cluttered living room – untidy, but irresistible. And although they were supposed to be going to a party in Hampstead he was beginning to have second thoughts about it now, despite the fact that an extremely useful film producer was rumoured to be attending. It would take Izzy at least an hour to get herself done up and it was arctic outside. The prospect of a quiet night in – just the two of them in front of the fire – was becoming increasingly inviting.

'Going out?' he asked hopefully, addressing Katerina. Stretched out across the entire length of the cushion-strewn sofa with her bare legs dangling over the arm, she was engrossed in a book.

She didn't even bother to look up. 'No.'

Why couldn't Katerina be like normal teenagers, he thought with a trace of exasperation, and go out on a Friday night? The mother-daughter package might have its small advantages – and the fact that Katerina was able to *organise* Izzy was an undoubted plus – but her total disinterest in the social whirl, at times, could be a distinct pain.

He seriously doubted whether Katerina even knew the meaning of the word enjoyment in its generally accepted sense. At seventeen, she didn't have a boyfriend, didn't like discos or parties and deplored teenage magazines. She never gossiped. Her idea of a really good time, it seemed, was to hog the sofa and devour a few chapters of *Gray's Anatomy*. God knows, she was a *nice* enough girl, well mannered and charming, funny when she wanted to be and undoubtedly beautiful. Why she wasn't out every night making the most of it he simply couldn't imagine.

But the fact remained that she wasn't, and since she didn't appear to be showing any sign of moving from the sofa either, Ralph reconciled himself to the idea that they may as well go to the party after all.

'I'll be five minutes,' lied Izzy, heading towards her bedroom with the pink towel trailing damply behind her like a matador's cape.

'Mum, your hair's blue.' Katerina, who failed to understand why anyone should even *want* to change the colour of their hair, let alone practise it on a monthly basis, gazed after her mother with a mixture of exasperation and tolerance.

'No, it isn't,' replied Izzy loftily over her shoulder. 'It's Glossy Blackberry. It'll be irresistible. When it's finished.'

There really weren't many greater luxuries in life than this, Izzy decided. Chronic lack of money, the frustration of being wildly talented and as yet undiscovered, the sheer *bother* of having to wonder how much longer their revolting landlord was going to allow them to stay in their less-than-luxurious flat . . . these problems simply faded into insignificance when one was lying in a warm bed with a gorgeous man, caressing deliciously warm flesh and knowing that one didn't have to get up for hours. It was positively blissful.

'Skin contact,' she announced, pleased with herself for having recognised its importance.

'Hmmm?'

'The three most pleasurable experiences known to man.' She smiled, sliding closer still and plastering the entire length of her body against his side. 'Sex, sneezing and skin contact. No, make that sex, skin contact and sneezing. Touching skin is the second greatest pleasure. And it's certainly more fun than a cold.'

A foot brushed against her shin, moving experimentally up and down. 'Only if the other person remembers to shave her legs.'

Izzy raked her fingernails down his chest in protest. 'I did remember! I did them the other night.'

'While you were dyeing your hair?' said Mike. 'Just think, you could have dyed your legs and shaved your head by mistake. What a thought.'

'How can you be so sarcastic at ten o'clock on a Sunday morning?' demanded Izzy grumpily. Realizing that she was hungry, she wondered whether Kat would be amenable to the idea of cooking a gigantic breakfast.

'It comes naturally.'

'It isn't fair.'

'Life isn't fair.' Mike hauled himself into a sitting position, since natural sleep was clearly going to be denied him. 'The fact that I only see you two nights a week isn't fair. Izzy, if we're going to have a proper relationship we should organise ourselves more effectively.'

That was the trouble with Mike, thought Izzy, smiling beneath the bedclothes. It was also part of his charm; only Mike could expect her to 'organise herself more effectively'. As far as she was concerned, their relationship was perfect. Each week she spent two nights with Mike, two with Ralph and two nights working. Wednesdays were for rest and relaxation. And if that wasn't perfect planning, she didn't know what was.

'You're busy, I'm busy . . .' she murmured vaguely, cuddling up to him once more. 'Besides, you'd get bored. I lead a pretty mundane life, after all. You'd soon go off me if you had to sit and watch me scrubbing the kitchen floor and hoovering the hallway.'

Nothing Izzy ever did was mundane, thought Mike. He also seriously doubted that she even knew what a Hoover looked like, but sensed nevertheless that arguing the point would be futile. 'OK,' he said, gathering her into his arms and breathing in the faint, unmistakably Izzyish scent of her body. 'I give in. I'll expand my business empire and you can hoover to your heart's content. Just so long as *you* don't get bored and find yourself another man.'

'With a daughter like mine to give the game away?' said Izzy smiling up at him. 'Some chance.'

Chapter 2

'I don't understand,' said Gina hesitantly, her mind blotting out the words she knew she must have heard incorrectly. 'You aren't making sense. Let me get you a drink . . . there's roast lamb for dinner and it won't be ready for another thirty minutes.'

Moving jerkily towards the drinks cabinet in the corner of the sitting room, she became hideously aware of the fact that she no longer knew what to do with her hands. They seemed huge and ungainly, flapping at her sides as she walked. It was with relief that she picked up the bottle of Gordon's and poured Andrew his drink – half an inch of gin, three inches of tonic, just as he always liked it when he returned home from work.

But now she was faced with the new problem of where to look. Andrew, she knew, was watching her and although he couldn't possibly have meant what he'd just said, she found herself incapable of meeting his gaze. Her co-ordination had gone. She didn't know whether to stand up or to sit down. And how could something so *silly* be happening to her body when it was only a simple misunderstanding anyway? In less than a minute, no doubt, they would be laughing at her ridiculous mistake and her hands and eyes would behave normally once more.

But Andrew wasn't laughing. He shook his head when

she finally held the drink towards him, gesturing instead to a nearby armchair.

'Sit down. You'd better have that drink. God, I'm sorry, Gina – you must think I'm a real bastard, but I truly didn't expect anything like this to happen. I didn't want to hurt you . . .'

Gina tensed, unable to do anything but wait. Any minute now he'd break into a grin and say, 'I'm joking, of course,' and she would be able to relax and get on with the dinner. The parsnips needed to go into the roasting tin and the onion sauce, simmering on the stove, could probably do with a stir.

'I would have thought you'd be throwing things by now,' Andrew went on, hating himself for what he was doing but needing to provoke some kind of reaction. When Gina finally looked up at him he saw fear and confusion in her eyes.

'Are you joking?' she whispered at last, and the flicker of hope in her voice was almost too much to bear. Steeling himself against it, taking a deep breath, Andrew prepared to repeat the words which he had hoped to have to say only once.

'Gina, this isn't a joke,' he said, more brusquely than he had intended. 'I'm moving out of the house and I want a divorce. I've met someone else – I've been seeing her for almost six months now – and my staying here isn't being fair to either of you. I've rented a flat in the Barbican and I'll be going there tonight. I'm sorry,' he repeated helplessly. 'I really *didn't* want to hurt you, but sometimes these things just happen . . .'

'But you're my husband,' whispered Gina. Her knees

were beginning to tremble uncontrollably – he'd always said how much he liked her knees – and she was finding it hard to swallow. Placing the tumbler of gin and tonic carefully on the table beside her before she spilled it, she rose to her feet, then abruptly sank back down. 'We're married,' she said incredulously. 'We're *happily* married! Everyone's always saying how happy we are.'

Sympathy mingled with exasperation. Why couldn't she hurl something at him, for God's sake? Why wasn't she screaming, shouting, swearing and generally raising hell? It would, he thought grimly, make telling her the rest of it easier.

'I was happy,' he told her, willing her to react. 'But now I've fallen in love with someone else.'

'You said you didn't want to hurt me!' Gina's knuckles whitened as she pressed clenched fists into her lap. With a huge effort, she burst out, 'I could forgive you for having an affair. We don't have to be divorced . . . if you don't want to hurt me you can tell her it's all over and we'll carry on as if it never happened. It's only a fling,' she concluded breathlessly, choking on the words as hot tears – at last – began to fall. 'It doesn't mean anything, really it doesn't. Lots of men go through this kind of thing . . . it doesn't mean we have to get a divorce . . .'

'I want to marry her,' said Andrew tonelessly.

Gina stared at him, uncomprehending. Wasn't she giving him every opportunity? Wasn't she being as understanding as any woman could possibly be? 'But why?'

He reached for the tumbler of gin and tonic and drained it in one go. 'Because,' he replied slowly, 'she's pregnant.'

* * *

Brandishing her mascara wand and treating her lashes to a second coat, Izzy belted out the second verse of 'New York, New York!'. 'Kat, do you want a lift to the library, because I'm leaving in five minutes.'

The next moment Katerina appeared behind her, in the mirror. Izzy, overcome with love for her precious, clever daughter, spun round and gave her a hug.

'What would I do without you, hmm?'

'Get yourself into a muddle,' replied Katerina, ever practical. 'Now, are either of them likely to phone tonight?'

'Ralph might. He wants me to have dinner with him tomorrow . . . tell him I'll meet him at Vampires at eight-thirty. Mike shouldn't be phoning but if he does, just say that—'

'You're going for an audition,' supplied her daughter. 'Don't worry, I won't forget.'

'You're an angel.' Izzy hugged her again, then stepped back and regarded her with mock-solemn dark eyes. 'Am I really a disgrace?'

Katerina, at seventeen, knew nothing if not her own mind. Izzy had her faults – and her chronic untidiness could be particularly irritating at times – but as a mother she was one of the best. And who could ever describe such a warm, generous, optimistic and loving person as a disgrace?

'You've been seeing Mike for over a year,' she replied calmly. 'And how long has Ralph been around, nearly two years? You're faithful to them. You haven't promised to marry either of them. Everybody's happy . . . what can possibly be so wrong with that? When I grow up,' she added airily, 'I fully intend to go for multiple, part-time lovers myself.'

'And long may they drool,' said Izzy, who never failed to be amazed by the extent of her daughter's irrefutable logic. She glanced at her watch. 'Help, I really am going to be late. Do you want that lift or not?'

Katerina shook her head. 'Too cold outside. I can pop in on my way to school tomorrow morning. I've got an essay to be getting on with tonight, anyway.'

'OK.' In the chilly hallway, Izzy wrapped herself up in her brown leather flying jacket and flung a white woollen scarf around her neck. Grabbing her keys and helmet, she gave her daughter a final kiss. 'I'll be back by one-thirty, fans willing!'

'You'll be back a lot sooner than that,' said Katerina drily, holding up the carrier bag which Izzy had forgotten, 'if you don't take your clothes.'

Izzy hummed beneath her breath. Her teeth were chattering too violently to risk singing the words aloud; she'd end up with a shredded tongue. Her beloved motor bike, a sleek, black Suzuki 250, was a joy to ride during the summer months, and it was certainly economical to run, but travelling to and from work in sub-zero temperatures was – she couldn't think of a better way of describing it – a real bitch.

Still, at least the roads weren't too icy tonight. Maniacs notwithstanding, she'd be at the club in less than twenty minutes. And who knew, tonight might just be the night to change her life . . .

* * *

Having cleared away the debris of their early evening meal, changed out of her school uniform into black sweatshirt and leggings and emptied a packet of Liquorice Allsorts into a pudding bowl for easy access, Katerina settled herself in front of the fire and wondered what it must be like for people who hated solitude.

Katerina adored it, as much as she adored their small but cosy flat, situated over an ironmonger's shop in a quiet road just off Clapham High Street. It was only rented, of course, but Izzy had thrown herself into redecorating with her usual enthusiasm and flair for the dramatic the moment they'd moved in eighteen months earlier. And although she might not have been able to afford the luxury of wallpaper she had more than made up for it with richly shaded paints, striking borders and her own dazzling sense of style. Many hours of multi-coloured stencilling and artful picture-hanging later, the effect had been as spectacular as Katerina had known it would be and within the space of four days the flat had become a home.

It was one of Izzy's more unexpected talents and if Katerina had been less loyal, she might have wished that her mother would consider a career in interior design, or even good old painting and decorating. Admittedly, it wasn't likely to bring her fame and fortune beyond her wildest dreams, but it was decent, gainful employment and was even rumoured to bring with it a reasonably regular wage . . .

Katerina simply couldn't imagine what it might have been like, growing up with a mother who didn't sing. As far back as she was able to remember, Izzy had always been there, careering from one financial crisis to the next and at the same time eternally optimistic that the inevitable big break was just around the corner. When she was very small Katerina had perched on beer crates in dingy, smoke-filled pubs and working men's clubs, sipping Coke and listening to her mother sing while all around her the audience got on with the serious business of getting Saturday-night drunk. Sometimes there would be appreciative applause, which was what Izzy lived for. At other times, a fight would break out among the customers and Izzy's songs would be forgotten in the ensuing excitement. Periodically, the hecklers would turn out, either joining in with bawdy alternative lyrics or targeting Izzy directly and laughing inanely at their own imagined wit. Katerina's eyes would fill with tears whenever this happened and the longing to land a seven-year-old punch on the noses of the perpetrators would be so great that she had to grip the sides of the crate upon which she sat in order to prevent herself from doing so. In her eyes, her mother was Joan of Arc, a heroine hounded by ignorant peasants. Afterwards, Izzy would laugh and say it didn't matter because she'd earned £3.40, she would press the 40p into her daughter's small hand and give her a hug. It didn't matter, she would explain cheerfully, because everybody needed to start somewhere; that was a fact of life. And anyone who could survive an evening in a working men's club on the outskirts of Blackpool was going to find Las Vegas a doddle in comparison.

At school the next day, Katerina's teacher had found her poring over an atlas in search of that elusive town. In answer to the question, 'What's it like in Las Vegas?' Miss

Brent had replied with a disapproving sniff, 'It's a town where everybody gambles,' and Katerina had been reassured. Lambs gambolled in fields. In her imagination, Las Vegas became one big, emerald-green field, with all its inhabitants skipping and bouncing and smiling at each other. 'My mum's going to take me to Las Vegas,' she confided happily. 'When we get there, I'm going to gamble every day.'

Las Vegas, needless to say, hadn't happened. Izzy's big break had stubbornly failed to materialise and life had continued its haphazard, impecunious course, although at least working men's clubs were now a thing of the past. Platform One, where Izzy had worked for the past eighteen months, might not be Ronnie Scott's, but it was situated in Soho and the clientele, on the whole, were appreciative. Here, in London, as Izzy always maintained, there was always that *chance* of a chance . . . one never knew who might walk through the door one night, hear her singing and realise that *she* was the one they needed to take the leading role in the show they were currently producing . . .

This didn't happen, of course, but Izzy had never tired of the fantasy. Singing was her passion, what she was best at. She was doing what she *had* to do and Katerina didn't begrudge her a single impoverished moment of it. Who, after all, could possibly begrudge a mother who would cheerfully splurge on a primrose-yellow mohair sweater for her daughter and survive on peanut-butter sandwiches for the next week in order to redress the precarious financial balance? And if her impulsive generosity never failed to alarm Mike, who was one of those people who got twitchy if their electricity bills weren't paid by return of post, Katerina adored her mother's blissful disregard for such mundane matters as financial security. If the bomb was dropped tomorrow she'd much rather have a deliciously soft, mohair sweater to keep her warm, than wander the rubble-strewn streets wondering how all this was going to affect her pension plan.

She was a third of the way through the Liquorice Allsorts and already on to the second page of her essay when the phone rang. It was two minutes past eight. Smiling to herself – for despite all his apparent sophistication Ralph could never bring himself to miss *Coronation Street* – Katerina picked up the receiver.

'I suppose your mother's out,' said the brusque voice of Lester Markham.

Katerina replied sweetly, 'I'm afraid she is. How are you, Mr Markham? And how is—'

'Never mind that,' he interrupted harshly. 'I'll be a damn sight better when I receive the last two months' rent your mother owes me. Tell her I'll be round at nine o'clock tomorrow morning for payment. In full.'

Katerina popped another Liquorice Allsort – a black-and-brown triple-decker, her particular favourite – into her mouth and gave the matter some thought. Lester Markham looked a lot like Jim Royle from *The Royle Family*, only maybe a bit grubbier. He didn't have as much of a sense of humour either.

'I thought we only owed one month,' she said carefully.

'Plus another month in advance,' snapped Lester Markham, 'which she used up in December and conveniently appears to have forgotten about.'

Oops, thought Katerina. So that was how Izzy had acquired the money for their splendid Christmas Eve dinner at Chez Nico.

'Of course,' she replied in conciliatory tones. 'I'll tell her as soon as she gets home, Mr Markham. Don't worry about a thing.'

'I'm not worried,' he said in grim tones. 'You're the one who should be worried. Just tell your mother that if I *don't* receive that money – and I mean *all* the money – tomorrow morning, you'll both be out of that flat by the end of the week.' He sniffed, then added quite unnecessarily, 'And I'm not joking, either.'

Chapter 3

Gina didn't know why she was doing this – she wasn't even sure any more where she was – but she did know that she couldn't go home. Anything was better than returning to that empty house and having to relive the nightmare of Andrew's departure.

Her fingers tightened convulsively, gripping the steering wheel of the Golf so hard that she wondered whether she'd ever be able to prise them free. And she was definitely lost now, but since she didn't have anywhere to go, it hardly seemed to matter.

Having packed a couple of suitcases with guilt-ridden haste, Andrew had left their Kensington home at ten minutes past six and Gina, not knowing what else to do, had switched off the oven and run herself a hot bath. Then, unable to face the thought of taking off her clothes – she felt vulnerable enough as it was – she had pulled out the bath plug, watched the foaming, lilac-scented water spiral away, and reached instead for her coat and car keys.

Driving around the Barbican for forty minutes had been both stupid and unproductive. Gina knew that, but knowing too that somewhere amid the multi-layered nests of purpose-built apartments was her husband, she had convinced herself that if only she could locate him, he would come back to her. She had even found herself peering up at lighted windows, willing him to appear at one of them. Looking down into the street he might recognise her car. Then, overwhelmed by remorse he would rush down, fling his arms around her and beg forgiveness . . .

But, of course, it hadn't happened, because there were simply too many apartments and because by this time his silver-grey BMW would be locked away in one of those expensive, security-conscious car-parks. Furthermore, her husband would undoubtedly have far more interesting things to do than gaze out of a window. He had a mistress, a pregnant mistress, who was probably with him at this minute, exulting in her victory and listening with quiet amusement as he relayed to her the events of the afternoon.

How To Discard An Unwanted Wife, thought Gina bleakly, a lump rising in her throat once more as she accelerated, pulling out to avoid a haphazardly parked car. Andrew and his mistress were probably talking about it right now, reassuring each other that since they were in love, nothing else mattered. What was a used wife among friends, after all? They were probably in bed, too, making passionate love and laughing at the same time because Andrew had been so clever and it had all been so wonderfully *easy* . . .

Blinded by tears, she didn't see the junction looming ahead until much too late. The next moment a sickening thud and the grating shriek of metal against metal shuddered through the car. Screaming, Gina slammed on the brakes and slewed to a halt as another dull thud echoed violently through her eardrums. Trembling so violently that she could barely get the seat belt undone, she fought rising nausea and wrenched open the car door. Fear and panic propelled her – somehow – towards the figure of a motor cyclist lying immobile in a pool of ice-blue light reflected from a nearby cocktail bar. My God, she thought, whimpering with terror, I've killed him . . . he's dead . . . oh please, God, don't let this be happening . . .

Izzy wasn't dead. Dazed, distantly amazed by the extent of the pain tearing through her legs – and by the astonishing fact that she wasn't kicking up more of a fuss about it – she lay in her crumpled position at the roadside and listened to the sound of an hysterical female yelling, 'I've killed him . . . someone help . . . I've killed him.'

Opening an experimental eye, Izzy found herself at grating level. Now *everything* was starting to hurt and to add insult to injury the icy wetness of the road was beginning to permeate her clothes. But at least she could see her bike which was oddly reassuring, even if the front wheel was badly buckled and the handlebars appeared to have twisted in all the wrong directions.

Then she saw the legs of the female who was making all the noise. Thin, pale-stockinged legs in high-heeled, mud-splashed shoes loomed before her.

'He's not dead!' screamed the voice that went with them, and Izzy began to lose patience. Attempting to raise her head in order to see the injured man for herself – how many people had been involved in this accident, for heaven's sake? – she couldn't understand why she wasn't able to do so. Embarrassed by her own weakness, she glared at the skinny, stupid legs in front of her. 'Make up your mind,' she said irritably. 'And will you *please* stop screaming? He's still going to need a bloody ambulance, whether he's dead or not.'

'She isn't quite herself, but you mustn't let it worry you,' explained the young male doctor reassuringly. He neglected to mention that Izzy – to the delight of the night nurses – had just informed him that he had a gorgeous body. 'It's the after-effects of shock combined with the sedatives we needed to give her,' he continued, his eyes kind. 'She didn't sustain any concussion.'

It was three-thirty in the morning and the rest of the ward was in darkness as the doctor showed Katerina into the side ward beyond the sister's office. Dry-mouthed with trepidation, Katerina stood at the end of the bed and gazed down at her mother, propped up against a mountain of pillows and apparently asleep. With her dark hair spilling over her shoulders and her make-up smudged around her closed eyes she looked so small and pale that Katerina found it hard to believe that all she had sustained were cuts, bruises and a broken leg.

Then, as if sensing that she had company, Izzy opened her eyes.

'Darling!' she exclaimed, holding out her arms. 'Come here and give your poor battered mother an enormous hug.'

'How are you feeling?' Katerina said, kissing Izzy's cheek and sending up a silent prayer of thanks for whoever had invented crash helmets.

'Well, absolutely delightful as a matter of fact, but that's because of the pills they've been shovelling down me. Tomorrow, no doubt, everything will hurt like hell. Did they tell you about the madwoman ploughing straight into me? Apparently I went flying through the air like a trapeze artist, then . . . splat!'

'At least you're alive,' said Katerina, tears pricking her eyelids as she gave Izzy another hug.

'And you're positively indecent,' replied Izzy sternly, doing up the unfastened top buttons of her daughter's white cotton shirt. 'Make yourself respectable, child, before that young Adonis behind you starts getting ideas.'

'Mum!' She stifled a smile, not daring to turn around.

'Don't laugh. I know what these doctors are like. Do you hear me, young man?' she went on, waving an admonishing finger in his general direction. 'This is my daughter, seventeen years old and as pure as she is beautiful, so I want you to control yourself.'

'Don't worry about me, Mrs Van Asch.' The doctor, busy filling in charts at the foot of the bed, sounded amused. 'I'm a married man.'

'They're the worst kind,' said Izzy darkly, her eyes narrowing even as Katerina attempted to cover her mouth. 'And you should be ashamed of yourself for cheating on your wife. Why, she's probably at home right now, thinking you're busy at work, while all this time you're here instead, you wicked man, drooling like a pervert over my innocent teenage—'

'*Mother!*' It came out as an agonised whisper. Long accustomed as she was to Izzy's outrageous talent for extracting blushes from people who'd never blushed before in their lives, this was too much. This was truly mortifying.

'It really is quite all right,' the doctor smilingly assured Kat, as the door to the side ward slid open once more. 'Ah, you appear to have another visitor. Just five minutes, I think, then Mrs Van Asch really must get some rest.'

Having flown into a panic after receiving the call from the hospital, not believing for a moment that Izzy had sustained only 'minor injuries', Katerina had phoned Ralph and luckily found him at home. It was Ralph who had brought her to the hospital, Ralph who'd been waiting in the dimly lit corridor outside the ward, and Ralph, blond and handsome, who now entered the room and moved towards Izzy's side with love and concern in his eyes.

'Sweetheart, we were so worried about you . . .'

'I'm fine,' said Izzy happily, lifting her face for a kiss. Then she pointed at the metal cage covering her legs and gave him a woeful look. 'Well, I'm fine but my leg isn't. We aren't going to be able to have sex for *weeks*. Oh Mike,' she concluded piteously, 'isn't it just the most depressing thing you ever heard?'

Chapter 4

In medical parlance it was known, enigmatically, as 'complications' and they took a desperate turn for the worse the following day. Having hastily explained to Ralph that Izzy was under the influence of mind-bending drugs, Katerina had only partially – minimally, even – succeeded in convincing him that it had all been a ridiculous slip of the tongue. And when Mike had telephoned the flat the next morning to speak to Izzy, and Katerina had told him about the accident, she reasoned that she could hardly have done anything else. The man was in love with her mother, after all. He had to *know* that she was in hospital.

Consequently, and quite naturally, Mike had rushed in to visit Izzy, and to deposit armfuls of exotic hothouse flowers around her bed. It was sheer bad timing, combined with Ralph's lurking suspicions, which brought about the unfortunate *tête-à-tête-à-tête* that had subsequently ensued.

Although not a coward, Katerina was glad she hadn't been there. The way Izzy told it afterwards, it had all been too farcical for words.

'. . . so there was Mike, sitting on the side of my bed unravelling miles of Cellophane and dumping all these incredible flowers into hideous tin vases, when all of a sudden Ralph wrenched open the door and *erupted* into the room, just like the Wicked Witch of the North.' Izzy shuddered as she recounted the scene. 'Then he just stood there in the doorway and said, "Don't tell me, this is Mike." And of course Mike said, "Yes, I'm Mike. Who are you?" and Ralph – my God, darling, never go out with an actor – made himself look as tall as possible and said . . . no, *proclaimed* . . . "I am Izzy's other lover." '

She knew she shouldn't be enthralled, but Katerina couldn't help herself.

'Go on,' she urged, silently willing Izzy to have pulled it off. If anyone was capable of handling such an odds-against situation it was her mother.

Izzy shrugged, reading her mind. 'I'm sorry, darling, but what could I do? The nurses told me afterwards that Ralph had been lurking in the corridor for hours; obviously he'd been waiting for Mike to turn up. And you know how proud and dramatic he is. He simply delivered his lines – "It's over, Izzy. You'll never see me again" – and swept out.'

Katerina had liked both Ralph and Mike, although Ralph had definitely been more fun. He had also, she felt, been more of a match for Izzy, whereas Mike was quieter, more serious and more inherently thoughtful.

'And Mike?' she asked hopefully, aware that she was clutching at straws. He might be thoughtful, but he wasn't completely stupid.

'And Mike,' echoed Izzy in thoughtful tones. 'Well, it was all rather sad, actually. He gave me one of his looks – the same kind of look he uses when I eat chicken legs with my fingers – and said, "I'm sorry, Izzy, but I thought I could trust you. It seems I can't." Then he took all of the flowers out of the vases, wrapped them back up in their bloody Cellophane packets and left.'

'Oh, Mum,' said Katerina brokenly. It was all so sad and so unnecessary. It had also – at least partly – been her fault.

Izzy patted her arm. 'What will be will be,' she said philosophically. 'I know it's a bummer but I suppose I can't really blame them. Besides,' she added with a shrug and a smile, 'there'll be other flowers.'

Her mother was being so determinedly brave that Katerina knew she had to be upset. Between them, Ralph and Mike had made Izzy's life happy and complete. Now, through no fault of her own, she had lost them both and the unfairness of it all hit Katerina like a hammer blow.

'It isn't fair,' she repeated aloud. Izzy didn't even know yet about their imminent eviction from the flat and the implications, job-wise, of a broken leg had clearly not yet dawned on her. 'And maybe it isn't their fault. But I know who *is* to blame . . .'

It was surprisingly easy to find the house, tucked away though it was at the end of Kingsley Grove, a cul-de-sac a couple of hundred yards away from Holland Park. Although tucked wasn't really the word to describe it: an imposing three-storey Victorian residence with pale stone walls beneath ornate russet roofs and its larger-than-average, frost-laden garden, it dominated the other houses in the road. The garden, although overcrowded, was well tended and fresh paintwork surrounded glistening, flawlessly polished windows hung with draped and swagged curtains. Katerina, pausing at the front gates, pursed her lips and wondered whether all this soulless perfection was maintained with the help of outside staff or if Death-on-legs, as Izzy had casually referred to the driver of the Golf GTi which had mown her down, did it all herself.

She was relieved, however, to see the offending car in the driveway. The fact that it was there – gleaming, white and polished to within an inch of its life – indicated that its owner was indeed at home, which meant that Katerina hadn't caught two tubes and had her bum pinched at Westminster for nothing.

Despite the morning sunlight, it was desperately cold outside. Stamping her feet in an attempt to restore feeling in her toes and pulling her crimson coat more tightly around her, Katerina pushed open the gate and made her way up to the front door.

She wasn't by nature a vindictive person and her intention in coming here wasn't to deliberately hurt or to upset the woman. She simply couldn't bear to think of her shrugging off the incident, dismissing it from her mind and carrying on with her life as if nothing of any importance had ever happened. She needed to make sure the woman realised – truly *understood* – the extent of her careless actions, and that while her own life might proceed unhindered she had certainly succeeded in casting a blight over another human being's existence.

When the front door finally opened she was genuinely taken aback. If she *had* wanted to upset this woman she would have felt cheated, because obviously nothing could possibly make her more upset than she already was. The expression on her face was pitiful, her grey eyes red-rimmed and swollen from crying. Her pale skin looked as fragile as tissue paper about to disintegrate.

Katerina hadn't imagined for a moment that the accident would have affected her this drastically – the woman was positively *distraught* – and for a moment she was overcome by guilt. How embarrassing. And how on earth could she justify her sudden appearance on the doorstep without causing the poor, guilt-ridden woman even further distress?

'Yes?' said Gina wearily, barely seeming to notice Katerina. Her gaze was fixed upon a trailing tendril of creeper which had come adrift from its moorings above the porch.

'I'm sorry,' said Katerina, her voice gentle, 'but I felt I should come and see you. My name's Katerina. I'm Isabel Van Asch's daughter.'

Gina very nearly said, 'Who?' but managed to stop herself just in time. The name was obviously supposed to mean something, though she couldn't imagine why the girl should be looking so sympathetic.

Then . . . Van Asch. Of course. This was the daughter of the woman she had driven into the other night, the motor cyclist she had thought was a man. Normally she wouldn't have been able to think of anything else, but the past few days hadn't been exactly normal. Gina knew she should feel ashamed of herself, but somehow she couldn't summon the energy to worry about other people . . . Andrew had wrecked her whole life and the turmoil of simultaneously loving and hating him was tearing her apart . . .

'Of course,' she said, running agitated fingers through her lank, blonde hair. 'You'd better come in.'

'Th-thanks,' said Katerina, through chattering teeth. She was glad now that she had skipped school and come here; at least she could put the poor woman's mind at rest, before she made herself really ill. Guilt was a terrible thing, she thought with a fresh surge of compassion. How idiotic of her not to have realised that Gina Lawrence would be blaming herself and in all probability feeling every bit as bad as Izzy.

'Would you like some coffee?' said Gina, glancing up at the clock as she led the way into the immaculate sitting room. Walls of palest green were hung with tasteful prints and the peach velvet three-piece suite exactly matched the curtains. Katerina prayed that her best trainers weren't treading mud into the flawless carpet.

'No thanks.' She shook her head, deciding to come straight to the point. 'Look, you really mustn't blame yourself for what happened, Mrs Lawrence. I know it must have been a terrible shock for you, but it *was* an accident . . . it could have happened to anyone. If I'd realised you were taking it so badly I would have come round sooner. But what's done is done and thank God it wasn't any worse. Mum's quite comfortable now and the doctors say she'll be out of hospital within the next week, which is brilliant news. So you see, you really mustn't take it too much to heart,' she concluded reassuringly. 'It was just one of those things . . .'

Eleven-fifteen, thought Gina, gazing blankly at the girl with the sherry-brown eyes, pink-with-cold nose and dreadful black trainers. Andrew would be in his office now, working at his desk and scribbling down notes with the Schaeffer pen she had given him last Christmas. She wondered whether he was wearing one of the ties she had bought for him and whether the framed photograph of her which had stood on his desk for the last ten years was still there. Or had it been hidden away, replaced by a picture of Marcy Carpenter, the woman with whom he had replaced her?

The thought was so terrible that tears welled up in her aching eyes once more and she brushed them away hastily, although the girl had already seen them.

'Oh God, I'm so sorry . . .' wept Gina, sinking into a chair. 'Forgive me, but I just can't help—'

'Of *course* we forgive you,' Katerina broke in, leaping to her feet and rushing over to her. The woman definitely needed professional help, but psychiatry was a branch of medicine in which she'd become particularly interested recently, and it wasn't every day you came face to face with a real life case of reactive depression. Besides, Gina Lawrence was beginning to make *her* feel guilty.

Putting her arms comfortingly around the woman's heaving shoulders, she said, 'Maybe I'll have that cup of coffee, after all. You stay here and I'll make us both some.'

When she returned several minutes later carrying a tray bearing cups and matching saucers and a plate of chocolate biscuits, the storm of tears had subsided.

'I must say you have a lovely home,' said Katerina, placing the tray on a slender-legged coffee table which scarcely looked capable of supporting it. But she sensed that Gina Lawrence wouldn't approve of tea trays being plonked on the floor. 'I've never seen such a big kitchen before. And everything's so . . . tidy!'

'I haven't been able to stop cleaning things,' sniffed

Gina, shaking her head as the girl offered her a biscuit. 'Ever since Monday night I just haven't been able to stop myself *doing* things. I can't sit still . . . I can't sleep . . . it's so *stupid* . . . I've been getting up in the middle of the night and before I even realise what I'm doing I've scrubbed the kitchen floor. Last night I spent five hours cleaning and polishing all the windows and they didn't even need cleaning but I just had to be *busy* . . .'

'I understand how you must feel,' said Katerina firmly, 'but you have to force yourself to come to terms with what happened before you make yourself ill. We don't blame you for Mum's accident, so you mustn't blame yourself.'

For a long moment, Gina stared at Katerina as if she was quite mad. Not having taken in before what she was saying, only now did she realise that their entire conversation had been conducted at cross purposes. And that the girl seriously thought she was going through this living-bloody-hell purely on account of a stupid, unavoidable accident.

'I'm afraid you've made a mistake,' said Gina, realizing that she was teetering on the edge of hysterical – and horribly inappropriate – laughter. Thankfully it didn't erupt. 'I'm not like this because of . . . your mother. I mean, I'm sorry, of course, but it *is* only a broken leg . . .' She floundered, knowing that she wasn't making herself plain and searching for the right words. Not having told anyone of Andrew's departure, she was dimly able to appreciate the irony of having to say it aloud for the first time to a total stranger. 'You see, on Monday . . . my husband left me. For another woman.'

Later, much later, Katerina would send up a prayer of thanks for the fact that she wasn't a practising psychiatrist. The urge to hit the woman was so strong that she actually had to clasp her hands together.

As it was, she simply stared into the woman's tear-streaked face and said, very slowly, 'You selfish bitch.'

It was almost a relief to have someone to rail against. Gina, tears momentarily forgotten, threw her a withering look.

'You can't be more than sixteen. How could you possibly understand?' she demanded. 'My husband has left me and my life is ruined. I can't think straight, I can hardly *see* straight and here you are, expecting me to feel sorry for your mother simply because she has a broken leg? The insurance company will take care of that,' she went on derisively. 'But my life is over and who's going to take care of *me?*'

Katerina had had enough. She wasn't a bloody psychiatrist, anyway. How this woman had the bare-faced cheek to dismiss Izzy – who was funny and brave and so optimistic that it could bring tears to your eyes – in order to wallow in self-pity, simply because she was too much of a wimp to stand on her own two feet, was beyond her.

'Now you just listen to me,' she said evenly, because screaming abuse – tempting though it was – wouldn't achieve her objective. Death-on-legs would only scream right back and she wanted what she had to say to be listened to, to really sink in. 'You were the one who caused that accident. Thanks to you, my mother has lost her job, her home and two long-term boyfriends. She has nothing left and by the end of the week we'll both be homeless, so don't you *dare* ask me who's going to take care of you – you should be *ashamed* of yourself!'

Then, because she hadn't meant to let herself get quite so carried away, she stood up abruptly, rattling the coffee cups as she did so. 'I'm sorry, I suppose I've been very rude. I'd better go.'

'Yes,' said Gina icily. 'I think you better had.'

Chapter 5

Being in hospital wasn't so bad, Izzy decided. James Milton Ward, for orthopaedic cases, was really rather pleasant because patients with broken bones weren't actually sick, and now that she had been moved out into the main ward she didn't even have time to be lonely. The ward was a mixed one, morale was high, the food was surprisingly good and the fractured femur in Bed Twelve was absolutely gorgeous, even if he was a dentist in real life.

She had also been taught to play a mean game of poker, which was far more entertaining than battling with a weave-it-yourself laundry basket or with the increasingly grey and frazzled piece of knitting that the occupational therapist had urged her to 'have a go at'.

But for the moment, peace reigned. Those in traction were either dozing or reading, and everyone else had disappeared into the television room at the far end of the ward; they were desperate to watch some vital half-hour of a soap of which Izzy had never heard, but which they evidently lived for. Izzy, taking advantage of the brief hiatus, was engrossed in painting her fingernails a particularly entrancing shade of fuchsia. She couldn't reach her toes; they would have to wait until Katerina arrived later.

Her attention was caught moments later by the

appearance in the double doorway of a visitor, chiefly because of the sound of her high heels tapping rhythmically against the polished wooden floor. Glancing up, Izzy saw a tall, slender woman with blonde hair fastened in a chignon and an extremely sophisticated ivory-and-black Chanel-style suit. Pausing uncertainly in the centre of the ward, she surveyed the beds lining each side of the ward and adjusted the bag slung over her padded shoulder with a nervous gesture.

'They're all in the TV room,' said Izzy, pointing towards it with her nail-polish brush. 'Shit!' she exclaimed, as a glossy blob of fuchsia landed in her lap, wrecking for ever her second-best white T-shirt. Then she grinned, because the visitor had assumed a determinedly unshockable expression and was approaching the foot of her bed.

'Sorry. These things are sent to try us. Who is it you're looking for?' Privately, she had already made her decision. This had to be either the dentist's wife or Wing Commander Burton's daughter. Nobody else on the ward could afford even to know someone who wore those kind of clothes.

'Actually,' said the woman, her gaze flickering to the name card fastened above Izzy's bed, 'I think I'm looking for you.'

Not having known what to expect, Gina was nevertheless taken aback by the sight of Isabel Van Asch. When she had been lying in the road, her face obscured by the visor of her motor-cycle helmet, she had at first mistaken her for a man. Then, following that decidedly unnerving visit from her daughter, Gina had mentally envisaged her to be a large, somewhat butch female in her mid-forties, with short hair and an aggressive manner.

But this person sitting before her now was small and undeniably feminine. With her expressive dark eyes, smiling mouth and riotous bluey-black hair framing a heart-shaped face, she wasn't at all what Gina had had in mind while she had been plucking up the courage to come here. She looked younger than Gina herself, she was wearing a white T-shirt and bright pink, lycra cycling shorts and she didn't look the least bit intimidating.

Gina, however, who had learned over the past difficult few days not to take anything or anyone at face value, was intimidated anyway. Doing herself up to the nines and finding first the right hospital and then the right ward had sapped her strength completely. On the verge of losing her nerve, she sat down on Izzy's empty visitor's chair with a thump.

'But I don't know you,' said Izzy, looking puzzled. Her dark eyebrows disappeared beneath her haphazard fringe. Her fingers, their nails still wet with pink polish, were splayed in the air before her. Then, with a trace of suspicion, she said, 'You aren't a social worker, are you?'

'I am not,' replied Gina, as shocked as if she had been suspected of prostitution. Did she look like a social worker, for heaven's sake?

But now that the moment had arrived, she was unable to find the words to introduce herself. And surely, she thought with a surge of resentment, that terrifying teenage daughter would have described her to her mother. Isabel Van Asch must know who she was; she was just extracting maximum pleasure from an awkward moment.

'Oh well,' said Izzy, remarkably unperturbed. 'It's nice

to have a visitor, anyway, even if it is an anonymous one.' Reaching with difficulty for a half-empty box of chocolates in her locker drawer, she offered them to Gina. 'Would you like a rum truffle?'

'I'm Gina Lawrence,' Gina blurted out, because someone had to say it and the woman clearly wasn't about to oblige.

The expressive eyebrows remained perplexed. Izzy shook her head and Gina caught a waft of expensive scent. Thorntons truffles and Diorella, she thought darkly; so much for the homeless, impoverished, six-feet-below-the-breadline sob story spun to her by the daughter.

'I was driving the car that collided with your motor bike,' she said, enunciating the words with care. Although the accident had undoubtedly been her fault, her solicitor had cautioned her most sternly against admitting anything at all.

'Oh, right!' exclaimed Izzy, through a mouthful of truffle. Then, to Gina's amazement, she stuck out her hand. 'Gosh, no wonder you were so twitchy when you came in. And how nice of you to come and see me. I'm sorry, I really should have recognised you, but I was in a bit of a state that night. Apart from your legs, I didn't take much in at all. God, sorry – I didn't realise my nails were still wet . . . look, are you quite sure you won't have a chocolate?'

Bemused, Gina shook her head. 'Your . . . daughter,' she said falteringly, 'came to see me yesterday morning.'

'She did?' Now it was Izzy's turn to look stunned. 'Why on earth should she have done that? She didn't even mention it last night.'

'Mrs Van Asch,' began Gina. 'She—'

'Miss. I'm not married. But please call me Izzy,' said Izzy, chucking the box of truffles back on to her locker. 'But how strange. What did she want, anyway?'

'My husband left me,' said Gina hurriedly. There, another hurdle cleared. If she said it fast enough, it didn't make her cry. 'And your daughter told me that I was a selfish bitch. She said that as a result of the accident you'd lost two . . . er . . . boyfriends. I don't really *know* why I'm here, but I suppose I thought I ought to come to see you and apologise. And something else I don't understand,' she added with a burst of honest to goodness curiosity, 'is how you can lose two boyfriends at the same time. What happened?'

'So, she made you feel guilty,' mused Izzy, a wry smile lifting the corners of her mouth. 'My God, that girl has a positive talent for digging at consciences. She does exactly the same to me when I haven't hung my clothes up for a week. Still,' she added sternly, 'she shouldn't have called you a selfish bitch. That's going too far. Don't worry, I'll have a word with her about that. And you really mustn't worry,' she added, leaning forward impulsively and resting her hand upon Gina's. 'She can be a bit self-righteous at times but she doesn't really mean it. You know what teenagers are like.'

Gina shook her head, sadly. 'No, I don't.'

'Well!' Izzy rolled her eyes. 'Let me tell you that they can be the living end! Kat's an absolute angel but sometimes I almost wish I could disown her – like now. She might have twelve GCSEs, but she can still make an idiot of herself when she wants to. I really am sorry she upset you, Mrs Lawrence. And when I see her tonight I promise you I'll give her a good slapping.'

'Oh, but you mustn't—' Gina broke off, realizing a couple of milliseconds too late that the other woman was joking. Colour rose in her pale cheeks. 'Please,' she amended hastily. 'My name's Gina.'

She hadn't fooled Izzy, however, and they both knew it.

'Tell me about the boyfriends,' said Gina, changing the subject, and Izzy pulled a face.

'It has its funny side, I suppose, although I was too out of it at the time to appreciate the humour, and when I did realise what I'd done I was pretty pissed off. Maybe it'll be funny in a few weeks' time.' She shrugged, pausing to admire her painted nails, then briefly outlined the details of the mix-up, culminating in the prompt departure of both Mike and Ralph from her life.

The unorthodox arrangement – not to mention Izzy's pragmatic attitude towards it – was something quite outside Gina's experience. She'd never met anyone like her in her life.

'Aren't you devastated?' she said finally.

Izzy looked thoughtful. 'I suppose so, but wailing and weeping isn't going to do me much good, is it? Besides, Kat says it would only give me wrinkles.'

'Mmm.' Gina, who had spent the majority of the past few days weeping and wailing, experienced a twinge of guilt. At this rate, she supposed she was lucky not to look a hundred and fifty years old. 'Your daughter also told me that you were about to be thrown out of your flat. What will you do when that happens?'

'Well,' said Izzy in a confidential whisper, as a nurse strode briskly past, 'since I'm between men, as they say, I thought I might as well seduce my landlord. See if I can't persuade him to change his mercenary old mind . . .'

'Are you joking?' asked Katerina, two days later. She didn't know whether to laugh and the expression on her mother's face was making her feel decidedly uneasy.

'Of course not,' Izzy replied with enthusiasm. 'Would I joke about something as serious as our imminent vagrancy? It's perfect, darling. The answer to a desperate mother's prayer.'

'But she's an old witch!'

'She is not.' Seeing the mutinous glitter in Katerina's eyes, Izzy knew she had to be firm. 'She's just going through a rough time at the moment. I thought it was amazingly kind of her to make the offer – and it isn't as if we have much of an alternative, anyway,' she reminded her daughter briskly. 'I was going to ask Rachel and Jake if we could stay with them for a while, but they really don't have the room, whereas Gina's rattling around on her own in that big house of hers and she needs some company at the moment . . .'

'What about money?' Katerina demanded. The idea of having to keep that woman company was positively chilling; she'd rather share a hot bath with Freddie Kruger.

'Rent free for the first month,' Izzy replied with an air of triumph. 'And then the same as we've been paying Markham. Now isn't that a great deal?' she exclaimed. 'Be honest, where would you prefer to live, Clapham or

Kensington? Or was a plastic bench on Tottenham Court Road tube station what you'd really set your heart on?'

Since there wasn't really any satisfactory answer to that, Kat said nothing.

'There you are then,' concluded Izzy, glad that it was sorted.

'I still don't like her.'

'We're renting a couple of rooms in her house, we don't have to *marry* her.' She flashed a flawless smile at the dentist as he zipped past in his wheelchair with his smashed-and-plastered leg stuck out at right angles before him. 'And since we don't have any choice, we may as well make the most of it. Sweetheart, who knows? It might even be fun!'

Chapter 6

Gina didn't know what she'd got herself into. She was suffering from a severe attack of doubt which erupted from time to time into near panic. Never one to act upon impulse, she couldn't understand why she should have done so now, when her entire life was in the process of being turned on its head anyway and the last thing she needed was more trauma. And although she had tried to shift the blame on to Andrew, she was uncomfortably aware that from now on she wasn't going to be able to do that. As from last week, she had become unwillingly responsible for her own life and already she was making a diabolical mess of it.

Visiting Isabel Van Asch in the hospital had succeeded in taking her mind off Andrew for an hour, which was miraculous in itself. She had gone in order to salve her vaguely pricking conscience, and had come away impressed. She'd never met anyone like Isabel – Izzy – before and the novelty of the woman had been a revelation. Imagining what it must be like to live so carelessly, to be so *unworried*, had occupied her thoughts for the rest of the afternoon. But since she wasn't Izzy, and because she was quite incapable of casting off her own worries, as darkness had fallen so she had sunk back into depression. Women like Izzy simply didn't understand what it was like, not being able to stop thinking about disaster, Gina had realised miserably, whereas she was constantly haunted by reminders of Andrew.

And then at eight-thirty that evening, quite unexpectedly, Andrew had arrived at the house and she didn't need to imagine him any more because he was there in the flesh, achingly familiar and even more achingly businesslike.

'We have to discuss the financial aspects of all this,' he told Gina, refusing with a shake of his head her offer of a drink and opening his briefcase with a brisk flick of his thumb. He wasn't quite meeting her eyes and a fresh spasm of grief caught in her chest. Handle this with a shrug and a smile, Izzy Van Asch, she thought savagely. It was no good, it couldn't be done. When it was the husband you loved in front of you it wasn't humanly possible.

'We don't have to,' she had wailed. 'You could come back. I *forgive* you . . .'

Even as the words were spilling out she had been despising herself for her weakness. And they hadn't worked anyway. Andrew had given her a pitying look and launched into a speech he had prepared earlier, the upshot being that Gina was going to have to realise that money didn't grow on trees. The house was hers, inherited from her parents, and he naturally had no intention of staking any kind of claim upon it, but the credit cards were no longer going to be fair game, always there to allow herself such little treats as new furniture, holidays in the sun and the latest designer outfits.

'I've spoken to my solicitor,' Andrew had explained, more gently now. 'And I'll be as fair as possible, but I have to warn you, Gina, I won't be able to give you much at all. That flat of mine is costing an arm and a leg just to rent. And my solicitor says that, basically, there's no reason why you shouldn't be able to get yourself a job—'

'A job!' shrieked Gina, horrified. 'But I don't work. My job is looking after my husband! Why should I have to suffer when I haven't done anything wrong?'

Andrew shrugged. 'The law is the law. You don't *need* me to support you. You have this house . . . Marvin suggested that you might like to take in lodgers.'

The prospect was more than terrifying, it was unthinkable. When Andrew had – with undisguised relief – left the house thirty minutes later, Gina had made every effort not to think about it. By midnight she had come to the unhappy conclusion that pretending it wasn't happening wasn't going to make it go away. Andrew's third suggestion, that she might sell the house, move into a small flat and live off the interest on the money saved, was out of the question. She had spent her entire life here and the future was going to be scary enough without having to uproot herself from the only home she had ever known.

A job . . . the mere thought of it sent a shiver of apprehension through her. Apart from two terrible years spent ricocheting from one office to another in search of a job that was even semi-bearable, she had never worked. Andrew had burst into her life and she had abandoned the tedium of nine to five, office politics and fifteen-minute tea breaks without so much as a backward glance. The relief had been immeasurable; looking after a husband

and a home was all she'd ever wanted to do, for ever and ever, amen . . .

The very idea of allowing strangers into her house – lodgers, tenants, paying guests, call them what you will – was equally alarming. Pausing finally to consider this unpalatable option, Gina actually poured herself a vodka and tonic. Who hadn't heard the horror stories, after all, of dubious, fraudulent, sinister and sometimes downright sex-crazed characters lulling their landladies into a false sense of security and then either making off with the entire contents of the house or finishing them off with machetes? Gina, only too easily able to envisage her remains bundled into the chest freezer alongside the sole *bonne femme*, took a hefty gulp of her drink. Then she realised that she *was* going to pieces. The tonic was flat.

'I still don't understand,' said Katerina in challenging tones, 'why you're doing this. Why *did* you go back to see my mother and ask her – us – to come and live with you?'

It was a shame, Gina thought, that the daughter hadn't inherited her mother's happy-go-lucky nature. She thanked God that her house was a large one.

'I didn't ask her to come and live with me,' she replied coolly. 'I offered her a place to stay, and she accepted.'

Katerina dumped the assortment of cases and bags on to the narrow bed and gave the rest of the room a cursory glance. Magnolia walls, beige-and-white curtains, beige carpet; not awfully inspiring but exceptionally clean.

'But why?'

Gina decided to play her at her own game. 'If you must know, it was sheer desperation. If you really have to know,' she continued, her tone even, 'I need the money.'

'Of course,' murmured Katerina, not even bothering to sound scathing. Moving across to the window, she looked out over leafless treetops at the roofs of the elegant houses lining the street, and at the gleaming, top-of-the-range cars parked outside them. Gina's claim to 'need the money' was so ridiculous it was almost laughable, but she wasn't in a position to laugh. And Izzy had insisted that she behave herself.

'Well thanks, anyway.'

'That's all right,' said Gina awkwardly. 'I hope you'll both be happy here.'

'We've always been happy,' Katerina replied simply. 'Wherever we've lived.'

Then, glancing out of the window once more, she spotted an ancient white van hiccuping down the road. 'Great, here comes Jake with the rest of our things. I'd better go down and guide him into the drive.'

'Into the drive,' echoed Gina, paling at the sight of the disreputable vehicle being driven by a man whose hair was longer than her own. Marjorie Hurlingham was cutting back her forsythia next door. She prayed that Jake and the van wouldn't stay long.

'I can't get over it, this is fabulous!' declared Izzy later that afternoon. Seeing her new home for the first time, and observing with some relief that relations between her daughter and their new landlady weren't as bad as she had feared, a smile spread over her face. Katerina had obviously decided to behave, the house was wonderful and there was real central heating that actually worked . . .

* * *

It was eight-thirty in the evening. Izzy, her plastered leg flung comfortably across Jake's lap, was still regaling everyone with tales of her stay in hospital. Rachel, Jake's wife, had opened another bottle of wine and was singing happily along to the music playing on the stereo – which appeared to be the only electrical appliance Izzy possessed. Katerina, lying on her side on the floor, was eating raisins and looking through an old photograph album, pausing from time to time to show off the more embarrassing snaps of Izzy during her flower-power days.

Gina perched unhappily on the edge of a chair. She felt rather like a hostess no longer in control of her own party. Not having had time to think about Andrew – and the ritual of brooding over her past life with him had become comforting, even necessary – she was also feeling somewhat dispossessed. And Izzy, Katerina and their friends were so utterly relaxed in each other's company, laughing and teasing and giving the impression of being entirely at home in Izzy's bedroom, that she felt even more of an outsider than ever. This was her *own* home, she reminded herself, yet already her immaculate guest room was unrecognizable.

Despite his long hair and gold earring, Jake had seemed remarkably normal; nevertheless, Gina was glad when he and Rachel finally made a move. He might be a lecturer in history at one of London's largest polytechnics, but she couldn't help wondering what the neighbours would be saying about his terrible van. And now that they were leaving, she could do likewise and retire to the sanctuary of her own room. To sit in peace and think about what

Andrew might be doing, thinking and saying at this moment . . .

'Don't go,' Izzy urged, rolling on to her side and stretching out for the half-empty bottle of wine. 'Sod it, can't reach. Kat, do the honours will you, darling? Fill Gina's glass to the brim. Gina, don't look so nervous! Come on now, relax.'

Relaxing didn't come easily to Gina, particularly when she was instructed to do so. Her legs were knotted together and she didn't know what to do with her hands. Glancing at her watch, she said, 'I really should be—'

'No, you shouldn't,' said Katerina unexpectedly. Handing Gina her drink, she added, 'You're looking a lot better than you were when I last saw you, but you're still twitchy. Why don't you tell Mum what's been happening with your ex-husband? She's awfully good at cheering people up.'

Katerina still hadn't forgiven Gina for her selfishness the previous week, but she was also slightly ashamed of her own behaviour that day. This was her way of making amends.

'Of course I am, I'm brilliant,' said Izzy, her dark eyes shining. 'Tell me all about it, every detail. It's so unfair, isn't it, that men should be such pigs. Why on earth do we still fall in love with them?'

'. . . he was my whole world,' Gina whispered fifteen minutes later. Her wineglass, unaccountably, was empty. Her feet were tucked up beneath her. 'When we were first married I thought we'd have a family, but Andrew told me that we didn't need children to be happy because we had each other. After that, every time I mentioned it he just said he didn't want children . . . they were too expensive or too time-consuming or he needed to be able to concentrate on his career . . . and if I got upset he'd buy me a nice necklace or take me away on holiday . . . I wanted a baby *so much*, but he always managed to convince me he was right. And now,' she concluded hopelessly, 'he's got some woman pregnant and he's changed his mind. So I'm left on my own without a husband or a family and it's too late for me to do anything about it. I'm too old to have children now . . . I haven't got anything . . . it's all been *wasted* . . .'

Izzy, who had been listening intently, now looked perplexed. 'I'm sorry,' she said, eyebrows furrowed, 'but I'm not with you. He's been a bit of a shit, I'll grant you that, but why exactly has your marriage been a waste?'

'Because now I don't have a husband or a child,' sniffed Gina with a trace of irritation. 'If he'd told me ten years ago that he was going to leave me eventually, I could have cut my losses and married someone else who *did* want a family.'

Izzy's frown deepened. 'But you're only thirty-six.'

'Exactly! How long is it going to be before I even *feel* like looking for another man? How long is it going to be before I find someone I want to marry? It's just not fair,' Gina sniffed, tears glittering in her eyes. 'By then it'll be too late, I'll be too old.'

'This is crazy,' Izzy burst out, jack-knifing into a sitting position and spilling half her wine into her lap. 'If you want a baby that badly, you can have one. Nobody's going to stop you!'

Gina wondered for a moment what it must be like to be Izzy, to live so carelessly and with such total disregard for the conventions which had dominated her own life.

But it was too great a leap, even after three unaccustomed glasses of wine.

'*You* don't understand,' she said defensively, hanging her head. 'I couldn't do that. It isn't the kind of thing I could cope with on my own.'

'But you don't know that,' argued Izzy, struggling to curb her natural impatience. 'You just *think* you wouldn't be able to cope . . . I'll bet you any money you like that once it all started happening you'd sail through it. Well,' she amended with a grin, 'I would if I had any money to bet with.'

'It's no good, I'm not that kind of person,' Gina replied, defiant now but still close to tears. It *wasn't* any good; she had hoped that some of Izzy's optimism might rub off on her, but all she felt was intimidated. Their personalities, their attitudes to life were just too different. Rising somewhat unsteadily to her feet, she said, 'I'm going to bed.'

Izzy, equally frustrated by Gina's inability to realise that what she had been trying to say made absolute sense, glanced at her watch. 'It's only ten o'clock. Stay and have another drink, *please* . . .'

'I'm going to my room,' put in Katerina helpfully. 'I've got two essays to finish.'

'No, no,' said Gina, wondering what she had let herself in for. Her guest room looked and felt different – it even smelled different, thanks to Izzy's scented candles – and now she was beginning to feel like a hostage here. It had all been a terrible, impetuous mistake, which only served to underline the vastness of the gulf between them. She simply wasn't cut out to be impulsive and she was damned if she'd ever do it again. 'I'm tired,' she concluded, not daring to even glance up at the cuckoos who had invaded her own private nest at her own stupid instigation.

'OK,' said Izzy, conceding defeat. Then she brightened, because it was only a temporary defeat. 'There's no hurry, after all. We'll talk about it again tomorrow.'

Chapter 7

'So, how's it going at home?' asked Simon as Katerina cleared a pile of text books from the chair next to his and collapsed into it with a sigh. It was lunchtime and the sixth-form common room, buzzing with gossip, sounded more like a cocktail party in full swing. Handing her his half-empty can of Coke, he admired afresh Katerina's clever, slender fingers and her ability to look so amazingly good, even after three rigorous hours in the physics exam. Having quietly idolised Katerina Van Asch throughout their years together at King's Park Comprehensive, actually getting to know her and eventually becoming her best friend meant more to him than anything else in the world. If it hadn't been for Kat, he would have left school a year and a half ago; she was the one who had persuaded him to stay on and study for A levels and for that he would be everlastingly grateful. He had a sneaking suspicion that abandoning further education in favour of bumming around the country as a bass guitarist in a rock band might not, after all, have been as much fun as he had first imagined.

He was, nevertheless, fascinated by Katerina's bizarre lifestyle, wonderfully Bohemian in his eyes and as far removed as possible from his own sedate upbringing. Living in a semi-detached in Wimbledon with a bank manager father, housewife mother and two pain-in-the-neck younger sisters wasn't exactly wild.

Katerina, whose mother didn't nag her to keep her feet off the furniture as his own mother was forever doing, flung her long legs across the arm of the chair and tore open a packet of crisps.

'How's it going at home?' she repeated thoughtfully. 'Well, not great. Dreary Gina can't seem to talk about anything but her husband, Mum's hell-bent on cheering her up and I keep out of the way as much as I can. The really bad news is that our four weeks of living rent free are up and Mum's leg is still in plaster. When I left her this morning she was poring over *The Stage*, but how can she possibly get work in her state?'

'Elizabeth Taylor did *The Little Foxes* in a wheel-chair . . .' began Simon excitedly, but Katerina quelled him with a look that would have stripped the eyebrows of a lesser man.

'That was Elizabeth Taylor, this is the real world.'

'So, what are you going to *do*?' he persisted, enthralled by her casual acceptance of the situation.

She paused, considering his question for a moment, then shrugged and said, 'Find myself a job, I suppose. Something in the evenings that pays well and doesn't interfere too much with my homework. Failing that, I could always find my mother a new and dazzlingly wealthy man.'

She grinned suddenly and lobbed her empty crisp packet into the bin. 'Now that *would* be a smart idea. I could be the devoted stepdaughter. I'd make a great stepdaughter, don't you think? And the more money he had, the more devoted I'd be . . .'

Worried, Simon said, 'You're joking.'

'Of course I'm joking.' With a howl of despair, she pretended to hurl the Coke can at his head. 'Who needs men, for heaven's sake? Now stop agony-aunting and tell me everything you know about the medulla oblongata. It's human biology this afternoon, and I've got an essay to finish.'

Simon broke into a grin. 'I thought you didn't need men.'

'I don't,' Katerina replied crisply. 'I just need information. Besides, you aren't a man. You're a boy.'

Damn, thought Sam Sheridan, finally hanging up the phone at Heathrow and realizing that he and his suitcases had a couple of hours to kill before they could make their collective way to Kingsley Grove. Andrew was out of the office, there was no reply from the house and jet lag was already threatening to set in, which possibly served him right but didn't necessarily make it any easier to bear. If he had slept on the plane instead of falling into conversation with a rather intense but decidedly attractive female solicitor, he wouldn't be feeling quite so tired now.

But Gina was a creature of habit, he reassured himself, glancing at the watch he'd adjusted as the plane had neared the end of its transatlantic journey. Almost four o'clock, and it was a sure bet that she would be back home soon in order to prepare dinner. If he caught a cab he could be there by five, in time to stop her doing so. Then, when he'd grabbed himself a couple of hours' sleep he could take them both out to dinner to celebrate his return. It would be great to see Andrew again, after nearly six months away. And as for Gina . . . well, teasing and shocking dear, uptight, ever-shockable Gina had always been one of his very favourite pastimes . . .

Damn, thought Izzy, hopping helplessly into the sitting room and glaring at the now silent phone. Didn't people realise how much longer it took a broken-legged person to even reach the room the phone was in, much less get a chance to actually pick up the receiver? And was there anything in the world more frustrating than not getting that chance to find out who had been on the other end of the line?

Chucking a cushion at the offending machine – and missing it by three feet – she allowed her imagination to run wild for a few seconds. A single telephone call, after all, was potentially capable of changing entire lives.

Why, it might have been Andrew Lloyd Webber, begging her to accept the lead in his latest and greatest musical. It could have been Doug Steadman, her agent, phoning to tell her that an American producer wanted her – and only her – to replace Shirley MacLaine in a Broadway show. It might have been – it just *might* have been . . . a salesman ringing to make her a fabulous offer on double glazing . . .

'Damn,' repeated Izzy, aloud this time. Wheeling around, she headed into the hall, picking up her jacket and bag *en route.* Now that she was downstairs she might as well exercise her good leg and take a trip out to the shops before they closed. Having rashly promised to cook dinner for Kat and Gina tonight, it might be an idea to buy something edible. She had a feeling Gina might be expecting something a bit more substantial than tinned tomatoes on toast.

Through the side window of the cab Sam observed with fleeting interest the dark-haired girl in the short yellow skirt who was swinging her way along the pavement on crutches. Her legs, one encased in plaster and the other shapely and black-stockinged, were what had immediately captured his attention. But now, as the cab reached the end of Kingsley Grove and slowed to a halt, he glimpsed the girl's face in the orange light of the street lamp and was further impressed. For a brief second, as she paused to search in her jacket pocket for her keys, their eyes met. Dark eyes, wide mouth, crazy corkscrewing hair and an indefinable air about her . . . of vitality and humour and . . . daring . . . caused something, somewhere inside him, to click. Jet lag miraculously forgotten, Sam smiled at her without even realizing he was doing so, but it was too late. The girl had turned away.

Then, even as he watched, she moved – peg-leggedly but very definitely – towards Andrew's and Gina's house.

Better and better, he thought, hauling his cases out of the cab and pressing notes into the driver's hand. Within seconds, he had caught up with her on the front doorstep. 'Hi,' said Sam, flashing her a brilliant smile, one that this time she couldn't possibly miss. 'Well, I don't know who you are, but your timing's perfect. I thought Gina would be home by now.' He gestured towards the darkened windows. 'But she obviously isn't. And I'm afraid I've lost my front-door key.'

The girl, returning his gaze but not his smile, said

nothing. Realizing his mistake – he must be more jet lagged than he appreciated – Sam said, 'I'm sorry, how rude of me. I haven't even introduced myself. I'm—'

'I know exactly who you are,' Izzy interjected rapidly, at the same time wondering at the colossal nerve of the man. Glancing briefly down at the suitcases littering the doorstep she said, 'Gina didn't say anything about this to me. Have you spoken to her? Is she *expecting* you?'

Taken aback by the unpromising abruptness of her manner, Sam shrugged and said, 'Well . . . no, not exactly. As I said before, she was out when I phoned. But she won't mind, if that's what you're worried about. After fifteen years she's perfectly used to my—'

'I'm sure she is,' Izzy retorted, interrupting him for the second time and deciding it was high time somebody told Andrew Lawrence precisely what they thought of him and his diabolical behaviour. Not having seen any photographs, she had envisaged a slightly older, altogether less casual man, the type who favoured pin-stripe suits rather than scuffed-leather flying jackets and ancient Levi's, but even in the semi-darkness she could see that he undoubtedly possessed more than his fair share of good looks and charm. Only men with that particular, lazy, *uncultivated* degree of charm could do as he had done and expect to get away with it. And only a man with a total lack of humility, she thought darkly, could expect to roll back home and be forgiven, just like that.

'Oh yes, I'm sure she is,' repeated Izzy, leaning against the cold stone wall of the porch and with great deliberation dropping the front-door key back into her pocket. 'But that doesn't mean she has to keep on putting up with it. She may be too scared of offending you to tell you what a neat job you've done of wrecking her life, but I'm not. Look,' she snapped, realizing that Gina's husband didn't have the slightest intention of showing remorse, 'hasn't it occurred to you for even a single second that Gina might *not* welcome you with open arms when you turn up on her doorstep?'

'To be frank,' said Sam, wondering what the hell was going on, 'no.'

'Well, it bloody wouldn't, would it? You really are *incredible* . . .'

'I really am very tired.' He was beginning to lose patience now. 'Look, why don't you just tell me exactly what it is I'm supposed to have done wrong. Then, when you've got that off your chest, maybe you could introduce yourself. No, strike that. Tell me first who *you* are and let me decide whether or not I should even bother to listen to you. And where the hell are Gina and Andrew anyway? If they aren't coming back here tonight I'll save you the trouble and find myself an hotel.'

'Oh shit.' Izzy stared at him, appalled, then sagged slowly back against the rough stone wall behind her. Would there ever come a time in her life, she wondered, when she wouldn't go around saying *exactly* the wrong thing to *exactly* the wrong person, in the very worst way possible?

'Look, I'm going,' said Sam irritably. Turning to leave, he added, 'If it isn't too much trouble, maybe you could tell them I called.'

Grabbing his arm so quickly that she almost lost her balance and toppled over, Izzy said, 'Please, I'm sorry. I've made a hideous mistake. You must come in.'

By this time Sam was almost certain he was the one who'd made the hideous mistake. That initial, almost instantaneous attraction had taken a smart step backwards. This woman wasn't just rude, he thought, glancing down at her cold fingers around his wrist, she was downright weird.

'*Please*,' begged Izzy, reading his mind and fitting the key hastily into the lock. 'I'm really not mad, but until I explain everything you can't possibly understand. Look, let me take your jacket. What would you like to drink?'

'Sit,' commanded Sam firmly, steering her into the sitting room, switching on lights as he went and flinging his jacket over the back of Gina's immaculate sofa. Pouring hefty measures of Scotch into two tumblers, he handed one to the obediently seated madwoman and settled himself in the armchair opposite.

'Now, maybe we should start again. Properly, this time, and without resorting to a slanging match. How very pleasant to meet you, Miss . . .'

'Van Asch,' murmured Izzy, thankful that he had taken charge, and that he didn't appear to have taken her insults too much to heart. 'Izzy.'

'Yes.' He nodded, a smile hovering on his lips. 'You look like an Izzy. And my name is Sam Sheridan.'

'Hallo, Sam Sheridan.'

'And who exactly did you think I was?'

'Gina's husband,' she confessed, her brown eyes huge as she searched his face for a reaction. Then, hurriedly, she added, 'As soon as you said it, I knew you didn't know. They've split up. Andrew moved out a few weeks ago and Gina's absolutely distraught.'

'What happened?' said Sam, no longer smiling. He could imagine the effect Andrew's departure must be having upon Gina. Her entire life had revolved around him.

'He met someone else,' Izzy explained. 'And she's pregnant. They're living together in the Barbican.' Then she paused, eyebrows furrowing, and said, 'Are you a friend or a relative?'

Sam sipped his drink. 'Friend. Old friend.'

'Of Andrew's?'

'Yes.' He shrugged. 'Of both of them really. I was the best man at their wedding. When I moved over to the States six years ago they gave me a key to the house. Whenever I come back I stay here. Jesus,' he shook his head in disbelief, 'Gina must be going through hell.'

'Andrew should have warned you,' said Izzy. While he was otherwise occupied she seized the opportunity to observe this startlingly attractive 'friend of the family' about whom she had hitherto heard nothing at all. The tan, for a start, coupled with those mesmerizing grey-green eyes, would alone have been enough to seriously impress. But Sam Sheridan didn't stop there; his hair, streaky and sun-bleached, was just long enough to be interesting while the eyebrows were contrastingly dark and wonderfully expressive. His mouth was perfect. And as for the rest of the body . . . Having found herself in something of a sexual limbo recently, it made a nice change to be able to sit and admire such spectacular good looks. They might have got off to an unpromising start, she thought cheerfully, but who knew what might happen if Sam Sheridan were to move into what Kat had taken to calling 'The Nunnery'?

'I've been in Hawaii for the past month,' he said. 'Maybe he tried to contact me, and couldn't.' Then he glanced once more at Izzy and said, 'But I still don't know who *you* are.'

This was more like it, decided Izzy, running the fingers of her free hand through her rumpled curls in a casual manner. She grinned, suddenly.

'I live here. We're Gina's new lodgers.'

'We?'

'My daughter, Katerina. But we're almost completely housetrained,' she added, catching his look of alarm. 'And there's no need to panic, I'm sure this house is big enough to cope with one more.'

She was older than he'd first thought, a woman rather than a girl. Sam, guessing her to be around thirty, nevertheless found it extraordinarily difficult to imagine her as a mother. She didn't *look* like one. Furthermore, much as he liked children – in measured doses – he wasn't at all sure he wanted to share a house with some screaming toddler who doubtless would be up at unearthly hours of the morning just when he most needed to be asleep.

'I don't know,' he said, glancing at his watch. 'Now that the situation's changed I really think it might be better if I book into an hotel.'

At that moment they heard the front door open and close and Gina's high heels clicking across the hall.

'You talk to her,' said Izzy, martialling her crutches and manoeuvring herself to her feet. 'I'm sure she'd want you to stay. If you want me,' she added with a provocative smile over her shoulder, 'I'll be in the kitchen. You aren't a vegetarian, are you?'

'No.' She *was* weird, decided Sam. Beautiful, but definitely weird. 'Why?'

'I'm making a Stroganoff,' explained Izzy patiently. 'And since it's your fault that it's going to be late, the very least you can do is shoulder the blame and stay for dinner.'

Chapter 8

'Oh Sam, how could he have done it to me?' sniffed Gina over an hour later, dabbing at her mascara-smudged eyes with a sodden handkerchief, but knowing that the worst of the tears were over. Embarrassed at having broken down in front of him, but at the same time immensely comforted by his presence, she realised afresh what a good friend he had been to them both over the years. She'd always enjoyed his visits but this time his arrival was just what she needed. Sam, who could cheer anyone up more effectively than anybody else she knew, was on her side. And that knowledge strengthened her more than she'd imagined possible.

'Men,' said Sam, getting to his feet, 'are notorious for not knowing what's best for them. Sweetheart, I'm just going to see how Izzy's getting on. That Stroganoff smells great and I'm starving.'

'Don't get your hopes up,' said Gina waspishly. 'Izzy's cooking isn't her strong point. The most ambitious meal she's conjured up so far is fish-finger sandwiches.'

'You aren't Izzy,' said Sam, entering the steam-filled kitchen and beginning to feel somewhat surreal. A tall girl with swinging, shoulder-length, sherry-brown hair was standing at the table, carefully tipping sautéd potatoes from a frying pan into a shallow blue dish. She looked up, unsurprised by the intrusion.

'I'm Kat. Mum's upstairs trying to have a bath. Dinner will be ready in five minutes.' She paused, then added kindly, 'You look confused.'

'I am confused,' said Sam, running a hand through his hair, then shaking his head. 'I was expecting you to be about five years old. At the very most.'

She smiled, covered the dish of sautéd potatoes and put them into the oven. 'I'm mature for my age. How's Gina?'

'Damp, but she'll live. Did you make all this?' Deeply appreciative of good home cooking, he leaned forward to take a closer look at the Stroganoff into which she was now stirring double cream.

'It isn't difficult,' said Katerina. Then she added wryly, 'Unless you're my mother.'

'Well, I'm impressed. I'd planned on taking Gina out to dinner this evening, but I'm glad now that I didn't. What are you, a professional chef?'

'She's a professional schoolgirl,' said Izzy, who had been watching them from the doorway. Pink-cheeked from her bath and now wearing a white tracksuit, her glossy dark hair cascaded past her shoulders. Apart from the fact that the tracksuit top was unzipped to display a distinctly adult amount of cleavage, she looked absurdly young. 'So, what's the verdict?' she continued, her tone light but her eyes bright with challenge. 'Are you going to stay or is the thought of sharing a house with three neurotic females too much to cope with?'

'Objection,' put in Katerina calmly. 'Two neurotic females and an extremely staid schoolgirl.'

'All this,' murmured Sam, running his fingers through his hair once more, 'and jet lag too.'

Sam Sheridan hadn't got where he was by ignoring or underestimating women. Having grown up quietly observing his brother Marcus – a useful four years older than himself – plough through school and university, causing havoc with his flashing smile and superlative seduction techniques and provoking equally dramatic showdowns whenever he tired of his girlfriends and unceremoniously dumped them, Sam had gradually come to realise that his brother didn't even like the opposite sex all that much. Girls were for sleeping with. They were what one talked about rather than to. They were, as far as Marcus was concerned, nothing more than appendages. And, like cigarettes, when he'd finished with them he stubbed them out. Sam, on the other hand, had never found girls a bother, and as he grew older he found his brother's attitude towards them even harder to understand. He genuinely enjoyed their company and found them every bit as interesting to talk to as males. Then, of course, there was also the added attraction of sexual chemistry . . .

But Sam miraculously never encountered the problems which had so complicated Marcus's own life. For although there were many girls who were friends as opposed to actual girlfriends, such was his easygoing charm and immense popularity during those growing-up years that the amount of kudos attached to being one of Sam's girls-who-were-friends had almost outranked the other kind, simply because girlfriends were par for the course, whereas friendship without sex indicated that you had a personality really worth getting to know.

And since Sam had always made a point of remaining on good terms with his ex-girlfriends, he engendered virtually no bitterness. He enjoyed instead a riotously happy three years at university, ending up with a better-than-expected 2:1 in economics and a vast circle of friends of both sexes, none of whom could for the life of them envisage Sam Sheridan holding down a job in any kind of financial institution where his degree might be of any practical use at all.

But Sam, despite his easygoing nature, had – unbeknown to his peers – already hit on the answer to his needs, which were access to a good standard of living coupled with the indescribable pleasure of non-stop socializing. The weekend parties he had thrown in the crumbling Victorian house he had rented with three other students had been legendary. Naturally a night person, Sam revelled in them; they made weekdays bearable and the thrill of never knowing who might turn up at the next party – the Swiss penfriend of somebody's sister or the actress aunt of somebody else's flatmate – never ceased to send the adrenalin pumping through his veins. In three years he'd never held an unsuccessful party. In three years he'd become renowned for throwing *great* parties where people met, argued, debated, laughed and fell in love with each other. Some had even gone completely over the top and subsequently married each other.

But it was the art of creating the perfect atmosphere in which any or all of these events could be achieved that had really captured Sam's imagination. People enjoyed themselves and he was the one who had made it happen.

And he couldn't help wondering whether there was possibly a nicer way of spending the rest of his so far happy and ridiculously charmed life.

It had not, however, been easy. Persuading the banks to lend him money had required far more intellectual agility than finals; some of his financial arrangements had been frankly dubious and, when he had taken over the lease on the first less-than-desirable premises in Manchester, weekly juggling acts had ensued between the demands of the finance companies and his own staff. Then, as news of the latest night-club began to spread, sustaining the necessary balance between a desirable clientele and money-waving non-desirables occasionally taxed even Sam's determined mind. But, above all else, he knew that his very own club must maintain an impeccable image from the outset. It wasn't necessary for his clientele to be mind-bogglingly wealthy; it was simply imperative that they be the *right* kind of people, people who would contribute to the very particular ambience he needed in order to ensure that The Steps became and *remained* the ultimately desirable place to go and to be seen having fun in.

And – although not without a serious struggle at first – it did. Sam's reputation grew and within two years he had bought the premises. Eighteen months after that, he had sold it at a staggering profit, moved to London, and found to his relief that if the streets weren't paved with gold, they nevertheless held more than enough people desperate for his particular brand of night-club to make The Chelsea Steps more successful than even he had imagined possible.

His circle of friends had widened. The number of women in love with him – secretly or otherwise – increased. Men, aware of Sam Sheridan's reputation, prepared to dislike him and, having met him, promptly failed to do so. Sam was genial, charming, easygoing, able to talk about any subject under the sun with enthusiasm, and he never pursued other men's wives or girlfriends.

This in particular reassured the men immensely. It cheered the single girls even more. And the irresistible challenge he presented to the women who were attached – and with whom Sam steadfastly refused to become involved – was indescribably exhilarating and only made them want him even more.

The formula had been a winning one and Sam had wisely stuck to it. When, six years ago now, he had announced his plans to set up a new club in New York, his friends had been horrified. Everyone had warned him of the financial riskiness of such a venture, but he had done it anyway, handing over the reins of The Chelsea Steps to his under-manager, Toby Madison, and allowing himself a year in which to either make or break his long-cherished American dream.

And, being Sam, he had succeeded where everyone had feared he would fail. The New York Steps, founded at precisely the right time and in exactly the right location, had worked from the start. Sam's international circle of friends expanded still further and his success, seemingly effortlessly achieved, followed suit. No one knew quite how Sam Sheridan did it, but it worked. And Sam himself, treating the whole thing as a huge private joke, lived life to the full, never seemed to sleep and made sure he extracted as much fun as possible from his extended American holiday.

But although New York was magical, over-the-top and indeed his kind of town, it wasn't home. For the past couple of years his trips back to England had become not long enough, had gradually increased in importance. When he had begun to dream – seriously dream – about English rain and girls without shoulder pads, Marmite on toast and people who'd never been psychoanalyzed in their life, he knew that the time had come to return home.

Meanwhile, back in Gina's dining room, Izzy's steadily increasing interest in Sam was being monitored by Gina with anxiety bordering on dismay. Dinner wasn't even over yet and already they had achieved an easy, mutual rapport.

Sipping her wine, she gazed across the candlelit table at Izzy, who was so obviously enjoying herself. And she made it look so effortless too, thought Gina with resentment. Why, she was positively *glowing*. It would have taken years for her to get to know someone well enough to ask them the kind of questions Izzy was asking after just a couple of hours.

'But how can you possibly have spent six years in New York and not got married?' Izzy was demanding now, pushing up her sleeves and resting her brown arms on the table. Idly, she picked a slice of courgette from the vegetable dish and paused to admire it before popping it into her mouth. 'Everyone gets married in New York.'

'Maybe I'm gay.' Sam's dark eyebrows arched with amusement.

'But you aren't.'

'Mum,' said Kat warningly. 'You don't know that. Stop being embarrassing.'

'Of course he isn't gay,' said Izzy with an impatient gesture. 'So, come on, Sam, tell us everything. Did you leave New York because of a woman? Was it true love? Was it sordid? Was she too rich or too poor? Was she—'

About to say married, she stopped herself just in time, out of deference to Gina's feelings. Sam, second-guessing her and stepping effortlessly into the breach, said, 'She was certainly persistent. Every fisherman's dream, in fact. The one who wouldn't go away.'

'Pushy,' observed Izzy, helping herself to another slice of courgette. Then she grinned. 'I couldn't be like it myself.'

'My mother,' sighed Katerina. 'The original pre-shrunk violet.'

'I don't want this to sound funny,' Gina began, lacing her fingers together and looking decidedly ill at ease.

'In that case,' replied Izzy, deadpan, 'I won't laugh.'

Having known Sam for as long as she had, Gina was only too well aware of his reputation where women were concerned. In his apparently irresistible presence they simply forgot how to say no. And now she could see it about to start happening all over again, right here in her very own home.

But inveigling Izzy into the kitchen in order to talk to her alone had been the easy part. Finding the right words for what she knew she had to say wasn't easy at all.

'Look, this might not sound very fair,' she began, then

paused and took a deep breath. Her fingers, of their own accord, were reducing a paper serviette to shreds.

'It's certainly frustrating,' observed Izzy good-humouredly, 'waiting to hear what "this" is all about.'

'Sam's a very attractive man,' Gina blurted out, and Izzy's eyebrows shot up.

'My God, I don't believe it,' she laughed. 'You're secretly crazy about him and you want me to put in a few words on your behalf. Well, say no more . . . I shall be the soul of discretion and before you know it you'll be—'

'No!'

Izzy was still smiling. Gina was so easily shocked. 'Well,' she said, 'if it isn't that, what *is* it?'

'I've seen the way you've been looking at him and the way he looks at you.' In her distress, the words fell out in a rush. 'And I couldn't bear it if you and Sam were to—'

'Were to *what?*'

'Have an affair,' said Gina unhappily. 'In my house. My husband's left me for another woman, I've never been so miserable in my life and I absolutely couldn't cope with it.' She paused once more, then went on in a low voice. 'I'm sorry, I can't help it. I did warn you that what I had to say wasn't fair.'

Izzy tried and failed to conceal her dismay. Fixing her gaze upon the little pots of chocolate mousse lined up on the kitchen table and realizing that she was no longer hungry, she said, 'You want Kat and myself to leave.'

'I didn't mean that.' Gina, more embarrassed than ever, shook her head. 'And no, of course I don't want you to leave. I just don't want you and Sam to . . . start something. I don't want to feel like a gooseberry in my own home.'

'And if I promise to leave him alone you'll be happy?' This time Izzy had to hide her smile. Did Gina think she was a complete nymphomaniac?

'I've forgotten how to be happy,' said Gina, immeasurably relieved. Since Izzy's amusement hadn't escaped her she shrugged and managed a small smile of her own. 'Let's just say I'll be bearable.'

Chapter 9

'What a cheek,' Katerina protested the following morning. Polishing off the last of the chocolate mousse, she scraped the dish with vigour. 'That's emotional blackmail.'

'Financial blackmail,' corrected Izzy, who had unearthed a tube of glitter and was sprinkling it liberally over her hair and shoulders. 'She knows we can't afford to move out.'

Katerina gave her an old-fashioned look. 'He is rather gorgeous, though. Has this blighted your plans? Are you going to sink into a Victorian decline?'

'Not at all. It's rather exciting.'

'Hmm.' Katerina wasn't convinced. 'Doesn't sound very exciting to me.'

'You're too young to understand,' Izzy informed her cheerfully. 'Men like Sam aren't used to not getting what they want. I shall dazzle and intrigue him, and the longer he has to wait the more tantalized he shall be. It's going to be the most enormous fun.'

'How would you know?' Katerina gave her spoon a final, appreciative lick. 'You've never played hard to get before.'

Izzy looked serene. 'Don't worry, it always works. I read it in a Mills and Boon.'

Sam could easily have slept right through the day but he

knew from experience that the only way to beat jet lag was to ignore it. Besides, he had a lot to do.

'Oh, are you going out?' said Gina fearfully when he arrived downstairs at midday wearing a crumpled white shirt and Levi's, and with his hair still wet from the shower. With his deep Hawaiian tan and sun-bleached hair he looked even more startlingly exotic than usual and Gina wondered unhappily how on earth she could seriously expect Izzy to remain immune to his charms.

Edgy because she knew that sooner or later he would be seeing Andrew, she averted her gaze and busied herself with the coffee maker. 'Black or white? If you're hungry I could make you a bacon sandwich . . .'

'I don't want you to wait on me,' said Sam, who knew exactly what was bothering her. Removing the packet of ground coffee from her grasp, he pushed her gently towards a chair, realizing as he did so just how much weight she had lost. 'And if anyone needs a bacon sandwich, you do.'

'I haven't got much of an appetite at the moment,' muttered Gina. Then, defensively, she added, 'Don't worry, I'm not anorexic.'

Sam nodded. 'OK. It's allowed, I suppose, under the circumstances.'

Gina, however, wasn't going to be side-tracked. Abruptly, she said, 'You still haven't told me where you're going. Have you spoken to Andrew yet?'

'No.' Sam, who intended phoning him that afternoon, was able to reply honestly. 'I'm going to the club. And I have to sort out some transport – I'll rent something for now – then I thought I'd take a look at some properties.

Who knows,' he added teasingly, 'I may end up living next door. Isn't that the most terrifying thought ever?'

'It's not a terrifying thought,' said Gina, realizing that he was attempting to cheer her up. Giving him a quick, awkward kiss on the cheek, she said, 'And you don't have to rush out and buy the first thing you see. It's lovely having you here.'

Her utter inability to lie was one of her most endearing traits. Ruffling her smooth, blonde hair, Sam said, 'Thank you, sweetheart.' Then he grinned and added, 'But a word of advice. If you were thinking of going into politics . . . don't.'

Old friendships died hard and Sam had no intention of criticizing Andrew's actions. These things happened, long-standing marriages bit the dust every day and Sam wasn't about to apportion blame. In the long run it could well turn out to be the best thing that could have happened to both Gina and Andrew.

As long as Andrew, he reflected drily as he drove towards the Barbican in his extremely clean, newly rented car, hadn't made the biggest, most Godawful mistake of his life.

The tapas bar was crowded with after-work commuters having a drink before bracing themselves for the journey home. Although there were a couple of free tables outside – it was a mild, sunny afternoon that had seen the seasonal re-emergence of the Ray-Bans – Andrew evidently preferred the gloom of the bar's interior. As he paid for a bottle of Rioja and a bowl of tapas, Sam observed that he, too, had lost weight; his charcoal-grey suit was too big for him and the collar of his shirt was loose. It was six months since he'd last seen him and he looked five years older.

'So, are you happy?'

Andrew filled their glasses and grimaced. 'I've done it, haven't I? Too late to change my mind now.'

Sam said nothing, waiting for him to continue. Listening to other people was what he was good at.

'You'll meet her,' Andrew continued, glancing at his watch. 'She's joining us at six-thirty. God . . . I don't know . . . I thought I was in love with her, but it isn't easy. If opposites really do attract, she and Gina should get on like a house on fire. Do you know, she hasn't cooked a single meal since we've been in that flat?'

'Does she work?' asked Sam mildly, trying not to smile.

'Handed in her notice the day I left Gina. She doesn't do any housework . . . she doesn't do *anything*.' Andrew spilled his wine in his agitation. 'Hell, we'd have a nice view if we could only see out of the windows. So we go out instead; I spend a fortune I can't afford in Italian restaurants because she's developed a craving for spaghetti *alle vongole*, and we spend every evening telling each other how lucky we are to have found each other. Then we go back to the flat and screw ourselves stupid. After that,' he concluded lamely, 'Marcy falls asleep and I iron a shirt for the following day.'

'Is *she* happy, do you think?' said Sam, by this time seriously struggling to keep a straight face.

'Is the Pope Catholic?' Andrew riposted. 'Of course she's happy – she doesn't do a single thing she doesn't want to do, she has everything she's ever wanted . . .'

'So, what are you going to do?'

Andrew spread his hands in despair. 'Haven't I done enough? She's having my child – because she couldn't even be bothered to remember to take the bloody Pill – and I've left my wife. There's nothing I *can* do now, except live with it.' He shook his head, then drained his glass, pushing the bowl of tapas away untouched. 'Lust isn't love, Sam. Take a tip from an expert and don't ever let it fool you into thinking it is.'

Marcy arrived late, swaying into the darkened bar at ten to seven. Sam's first thought was that Andrew hadn't been kidding when he had told him Gina and Marcy were complete opposites. Not yet enormously pregnant, she was nevertheless decidedly plump; her legs, in pale grey tights, reminded him of those stone-carved cherubs that cavorted around fountains and her pink lambswool dress strained across an impressive bust. Although she had an undeniably pretty face – pink cheeks, big grey eyes and a small, rosebud mouth – her shoulder-length auburn hair looked distinctly uncombed and the only make-up she appeared to be wearing was the remains of yesterday's mascara smudged beneath her eyes.

She wasn't what he'd been expecting at all, and for once in his life Sam found himself caught completely off-balance by the enormity of the gulf between expectation and reality. Marcy's laid-back, extremely elocuted voice, her languorous gestures and the almost monotonous slowness with which she proceeded to plough through four bowls of fresh tapas, all combined to give the impression that her batteries were on the verge of giving out. Not that she said anything wrong; she seemed perfectly friendly and even smiled whenever necessary. It was just that Sam couldn't for the life of him imagine her being capable of summoning the energy to actually laugh.

'So, you're staying with Gina for the time being,' she observed, when she'd soaked up the last of the salad dressing with a chunk of crusty bread. 'How does she seem to you? Poor Gina, we're so concerned about her. Is she coping well?'

Sam envisaged Gina's reaction, should she ever find out that she had Marcy's sympathy. Spontaneous combustion, he decided, at the very least.

'As a matter of fact,' he replied easily, 'she's coping extremely well.'

'It must be awful for her,' Marcy continued, pushing her hair away from her face and taking a sip of Perrier. 'I hope you can understand our situation. We didn't mean this to happen, it just . . . did. The last thing I ever wanted was to hurt someone else, but when two people fall in love they can't help themselves, Sam.' She paused, then smiled across at Andrew. 'They really can't.'

'Oh Kat, you *must* come to the club,' pleaded Izzy. 'Sam's invited us. It'll be wonderful.'

'Simon and I have a lot of work to do,' Katerina replied calmly. Unwinding a long, navy-blue cotton scarf from around her neck, she dumped a pile of books on the kitchen table and motioned Simon to sit down.

Simon, enthralled by the invitation and as overwhelmed as ever by Izzy, said, 'Well, maybe we could just . . .'

'No, we could not . . .' Katerina quelled him with a look. 'A night at The Chelsea Steps isn't going to enhance my life half as much as a physics A level will. And there's no need to look at me like that, Simon – I'm just being practical.'

There were times, thought Simon darkly, when Kat was a damn sight too practical. Glancing across at Izzy for support, he was further cast down when all she did was shrug and say flatly, 'She is not my daughter. I took the wrong baby home from the hospital, I know I did. Somewhere out in the big wide world my real daughter is out having *fun*.' Then, making up for it slightly, she blew a kiss which encompassed them both. 'Darlings, I hope you have an exhilarating evening. Meanwhile, we old fogies will totter off and try to enjoy ourselves. Now, where did I put my bus pass . . . ?'

Chapter 10

By ten-thirty The Chelsea Steps was almost completely full. Sam, having concluded his brief business meeting with Toby Madison and reassured himself that all had been running smoothly in his absence, was reacquainting himself with old friends. Izzy, in her element, was engrossed in flamboyant conversation with a racing driver whose right arm was in plaster. Gina, finding herself briefly alone at the bar, wondered if she'd ever felt more uncomfortable in her life.

It wasn't fair, she thought miserably. Everyone else appeared to be able to switch with perfect ease into night-club mode; was she the only one genuinely incapable of doing the same? As Andrew's wife she had been an adequate conversationalist, if not a sparkling one, yet here . . . now . . . she couldn't even begin to imagine how it was done. This kind of socializing was what single people did – it was what single people like Sam and Izzy evidently excelled at – but she had been married too long even to remember what being single was like. She couldn't do it. All she wanted now was to be able to go home, crawl into bed and pretend that the events of the last few weeks had never happened.

Moments later, Sam materialised at her side.

'That bad, hmm?'

'It . . . it's a lovely club,' stammered Gina, not wanting

him to think her a complete wimp. Gesturing around her at the midnight-blue-and-bronze décor, she said, 'And it's obviously going well. Everyone's enjoying themselves . . . having fun . . . I'm always reading about it in the papers . . .'

'You don't have to feel guilty just because you aren't enjoying yourself,' he told gently. 'I'm sorry, I shouldn't have persuaded you to come.'

'I don't think I'm a terribly clubby person,' said Gina, her expression despondent. 'Izzy's having a marvellous time and she makes it all seem so easy.'

'She's had plenty of practice,' replied Sam drily, his gaze fixing upon Izzy. Shedding glitter at a rate of knots, she and the racing driver were now making their precarious way towards the bar in search of yet another bottle of champagne. As strong as his initial attraction had been towards her, Sam wasn't blind to her faults and keeping Gina company was the least she could have done, under the circumstances. Taking Gina's arm, he said, 'Come on, let's go home.'

She looked alarmed. 'We can't leave Izzy.'

'Why not?' said Sam evenly. 'She left you.'

The thought of Sam and Izzy having an affair had filled Gina with horror, but the prospect of friction between them was even more unnerving. Leaping to Izzy's defence, she said, 'Only for a couple of minutes, truly.'

He grinned. 'Don't panic, I'm not suggesting you kick her out into the streets. I'm just saying that she can be a bit thoughtless now and again. Loyal,' he conceded, the memory of her verbal attack on him last night still fresh in his mind, 'but still thoughtless, nevertheless.'

'But we *can't* abandon her,' Gina protested miserably. 'And you don't want to leave either. Why don't I just get a cab? I'll be fine, really I will.'

'Oh shut up,' said Sam, his tone affectionate. 'Come on, we'll tell Izzy we're going. She's a big girl, I'm sure she can find her own way home.'

Only Katerina Van Asch, thought Simon with rising frustration, could spend three solid hours discussing – in dizzying detail – the human reproductive process and not even spare a thought for the effect it might be having on her partner-in-revision.

'So,' she was saying now, as she stretched across the velvety carpet for the saucer of Liquorice Allsorts, 'let's just run through it again. I'm still not quite happy about testosterone levels.'

Simon wasn't happy about his own testosterone levels, which were skyrocketing; he was sure it couldn't be good for his health. Hauling himself into a sitting position he cast her a reproachful look.

'What?' said Katerina, twisting on to her side and meeting his gaze. Even in her frayed orange sweatshirt, khaki combats and holey green socks she looked irresistible. 'Simon, whatever's the matter with you tonight? You really aren't concentrating at all.'

Plucking up as much courage as he possessed, Simon pushed back his straight blond hair and said, 'Do you think it would be sensible to take an important maths exam without ever having worked out a single mathematical equation?'

He really was in an odd mood tonight, decided

Katerina. Humoring him, she replied obediently, 'No, of course it wouldn't.'

'Or . . . a chemistry exam, when you've never conducted an actual chemical experiment yourself?'

'No.'

'Yet you expect to pass biology purely on the strength of what you've learned from books,' he persisted, flushing slightly. 'Doesn't that seem . . . illogical?'

Having considered his argument for a few seconds, Katerina broke into a broad smile. 'You mean I should murder you, then dissect your body with Gina's best carving knife and eyebrow tweezers? Simon, it's a generous offer, but—'

The next moment his arms were around her, his mouth fastening upon hers and his frantically racing heart pounding against her chest. Astonished, Katerina almost laughed out loud but sensed it wouldn't be the diplomatic thing to do. She might be lacking in experience but even she knew that kissing and laughter didn't mix. 'I love you, Kat,' mumbled Simon, scarcely able to believe that his dreams were at last coming true. 'You must know how much I love you, it's been driving me crazy . . .'

'And you think we'd stand a chance of improving our grades if we got a little practical experience on the subject,' she said, pulling gently away from him. If this was what sexual passion was all about, well . . . on the whole she preferred Liquorice Allsorts. 'Simon, it's lovely of you to offer, but I really can't. It wouldn't be . . . right, somehow.'

'Oh damn,' Simon muttered unhappily. Realizing that he'd well and truly blown his chances – maybe his only chance – with Katerina, he slumped back on one elbow and gazed morosely at the pile of books lying open in front of the fireplace. 'I suppose you won't want to see me again, now.'

'Don't be daft,' she replied, smiling and passing him his half-empty can of lager. 'You're my best friend, aren't you?'

His expression still truculent, he said, 'I'd rather be your boyfriend.'

'No, you wouldn't.' She squeezed his hand. 'I'm a seventeen-year-old virgin and probably frigid to boot. There's nothing I can do about it; maybe subconsciously I'm rebelling against my upbringing. But it isn't your fault, OK?' she persisted, more forcefully this time. 'It's mine.'

'One day,' said Simon with resignation, 'some man will come along and sweep you off your feet and you won't know what's hit you.'

'He won't know what's hit him,' Katerina replied briskly. 'But it'll probably be my physics textbook. I've told you, Simon, I'm really not cut out for all that love-and-sex business. It just isn't *me*.'

There was nothing like a bit of good, old-fashioned sexual attraction to put a spring in one's step, thought Izzy, gazing down at her decidedly unspringy left leg the following morning. But although the sexual attraction was still there – on her part, at least – last night's plan appeared to have misfired in somewhat spectacular fashion. By chatting to Nicky Holmes-Pierce, cavalier racing driver and ex-husband of one of her oldest friends, she had hoped to prove to Sam that she wasn't overkeen on him and at the same time pique his interest. Instead, however, he had simply left the club with Gina and so far this morning had seemed totally unpiqued. And she'd put make-up on, too.

Now, with the sun streaming through the kitchen windows, he was ignoring her totally, poring instead over a pile of estate agents' details spread across the kitchen table. With Gina out shopping and Katerina at school, their previous easy camaraderie appeared to be in genuine danger of evaporating completely. Izzy was in danger of losing all faith in Mills and Boon.

'I could help you look for a flat, if you like,' she offered, swinging her good leg against her stool and making an effort to redress the balance.

Without even glancing up at her, Sam said, 'I'd have thought you'd be too busy, looking for some kind of job.'

Charming, thought Izzy. Aloud, she said idly, 'Why, is Gina worried about her rent?'

'She hasn't said anything,' Sam replied in even tones. 'She's too well mannered. Maybe that's why I thought I should mention it.'

Flicking her hair away from her face, she said crossly, 'I did *have* a job, right up until the moment when this terribly well mannered madwoman hurtled into my life. The accident wasn't my fault, you know.'

'I know.' Sam smiled slightly, because she looked so indignant. But he wasn't to be deflected. 'And I'm sure you wouldn't take advantage of her generosity,' he continued, more gently now. 'But I'm very fond of Gina and she's had a rough time of it recently. She needs as much support as she can get.'

'I'm not an underwired bra,' Izzy retorted, her dark eyes flashing.

You aren't wearing one either, thought Sam, admiring the faint outline of her breasts beneath the khaki army surplus shirt. Picking up the list of addresses, he rose to his feet. 'OK, don't sulk. Do you want to come with me or not?'

'Are you going to be beastly to me?' Izzy regarded him with suspicion.

'Only if it's what you really want.'

The tension had melted. She grinned, suddenly. 'I'd prefer outrageous flattery, if you could manage it.'

'Outrageous flattery,' mused Sam, his expression deadpan as he held the door open and waved her through. 'In that case I shall tell you that I heard you singing in the bathroom this morning, and I have to confess that I was impressed. Most impressed. You have an exceptional voice, Miss Van Asch, in fact a truly spectacular—'

'Bullshit.' Izzy burst out laughing. 'That was Liza Minnelli on the radio.'

Chapter 11

Within two hours of setting out on a whistle-stop tour of select properties in highly desirable areas of London, during which time he glanced at and summarily rejected apartments which Izzy would have given her eye-teeth to live in, Sam found what he'd been looking for. Situated on the top floor of a chic but unflashy low-rise apartment block in Holland Park, it was light, extremely spacious and commanded spectacular views over the park itself.

'Yes, this one,' he said simply, returning from his inspection of the bedrooms and standing in the centre of the vast sitting room. Pushing his hands into the back pockets of his Levi's, he gazed out of the floor-length windows at the park and nodded once more for emphasis. Then, turning to the dumbstruck estate agent, he said, 'I'll take it.'

Watching Sam choose a home had been an edifying experience. Izzy, thrilled by the ease with which he'd done it, said admiringly, 'I've known men take longer to decide on a new shirt.'

'Ah, but I know what I want,' said Sam, his eyes glittering with amusement. 'And I know what I like. So why waste time?'

With an involuntary shiver Izzy wondered whether – beneath that super-cool exterior – he wanted her. The thought was extraordinarily enthralling. Damn, she thought, she would have given anything right now to be out of this plaster cast . . .

Since it was lunchtime, they retired to a nearby winebar to celebrate. Sam raised his eyebrows when Izzy ordered a bottle of very expensive wine.

'Don't panic,' she said mockingly, unearthing her purse from her bag and waving it at him. 'We have the technology, we have the means to repay them. And it isn't as if I could even begin to do a runner.'

Aware that she was making the gesture to prove a point, Sam waved acceptance and sat back in his chair. 'OK, if you're sure.'

'I'm sure,' said Izzy, greedily perusing the menu. 'You aren't the only one around here who knows what he wants . . . and what I want is lobster salad. Come on now, choose something wonderful. It's on me.'

Sam raised an eyebrow. 'Have you been stealing credit cards?'

'Mr Sheridan, what a nasty, suspicious mind you have.' She gave him an admonishing look, then winked. 'Only little gold ones.'

'So, tell me,' she said five minutes later, 'how's Andrew? Did you meet the bimbo? Is it really the greatest love affair of all time?'

'How did you know I'd seen him?' countered Sam with genuine surprise.

Izzy shrugged. 'It stands to reason, doesn't it? He's your friend and you have a habit of not wasting time. You were bound to see him.'

'I suppose so.' He smiled, conceding the point. He

liked women who were on the ball. 'Well, it isn't going brilliantly. If Marcy wasn't pregnant he'd be back with Gina like a shot.'

Izzy, idly stirring her wine with a finger, said, 'Then it's lucky for Gina that Marcy is pregnant. Otherwise she just might be stupid enough to take him.'

'And you and Katerina would have to find somewhere else to live,' observed Sam drily.

Izzy bristled. 'That's a cheap shot. I don't happen to have a very high opinion of men like Andrew Lawrence; he's a shit of the first order.'

'Did your husband leave you for another woman?'

'Me?' She looked surprised, then shrugged dismissively. 'Kat's father did offer to marry me, if that's who you are thinking about, but I turned him down – very politely – and got out while the going was good.'

'Why?' asked Sam, interested.

'Because sooner or later I would have ended up like Gina.' Pausing, taking a sip of her drink, she added, 'And because he was already married when I met him.'

'Hmm.'

'I didn't know that, then. I was eighteen and gullible, and by the time I found out he had a wife it was too late; I was already pregnant. End of sordid story,' declared Izzy, as the waiter approached with their food. 'And don't look at me like that, because it wasn't tragic and it didn't ruin my life. I have a better daughter than any mother has a right to expect and the experience taught me everything I needed to know about men. I only told you about it so you'd understand why I feel as strongly as I do about Gina and Andrew. And you still haven't said anything about Marcy,' she complained, steering him neatly back to the subject in hand. Picking up a lobster claw and tilting her head to one side, she said, 'You met her, didn't you? So, what is she, a complete dog?'

'Oh, it's a hard life,' said Katerina mockingly as she washed up after dinner that evening. Izzy, who had propped herself against the draining board in order to dry the dishes, was regaling her with details of her day.

'It's such a beautiful flat,' she said with enthusiasm. 'They were *all* beautiful flats . . . and just think, darling, one day when we're rich beyond our wildest dreams, we'll live in a penthouse apartment every bit as fabulous as Sam's. Won't that be great?'

'Do excuse my mother, she's an incurable fantasist.' Katerina grinned at Sam, who had just walked into the kitchen. Then, her attention returning to Izzy, her expression changed to one of alarm.

'Mum, your gold chain – you aren't wearing it!'

Izzy's hand went automatically to the V of her open shirt. Then she shrugged. 'I must have left it upstairs.'

'But you never take it off,' began Katerina. 'You *always*—'

'It's upstairs,' Izzy repeated firmly, before she could say any more. 'Now give me that dish before you wash the pattern off it. When I'm rich beyond my wildest dreams I'm going to get myself a new daughter,' she continued smoothly, addressing Sam and silently defying him to comment on the fact that her cheeks were ablaze with colour. 'One who doesn't nag her poor old mother to death.'

* * *

When Sam returned to the living room he found Gina curled up on the sofa working out sums on the back of an electricity bill. Despite the fact that he had written her out a sizeable cheque that morning, her narrow blonde eyebrows were still furrowed with concern.

'Everything OK?' he said, touching her shoulder and making her jump.

'As well as can be expected.' Gina managed a wan smile. 'I hate to sound like a helpless housewife, but I simply hadn't realised how much it costs just to live.'

Experiencing a fresh surge of irritation as he recalled Izzy Van Asch's own cavalier attitudes towards such mundanities as household budgeting, he said brusquely, 'Particularly when you have freeloading lodgers to support. Sweetheart, you're too easygoing . . . if Izzy doesn't cough up soon, you'll have to ask her to leave.'

Gina looked up, surprised. Then, with a vigorous shake of her head, she said, 'Oh, I didn't get a chance to tell you. She's paid me two months' rent.'

It was now Sam's turn to look surprised. 'Good,' he replied, somewhat mollified. 'And about bloody time too.' She must have sold the necklace while he was signing forms in the estate agent's offices, he decided. At least it proved she had a conscience of sorts.

Pleased with himself . . . and, to be fair, with Izzy . . . he said, 'My little chat with her this morning must have sunk in after all.'

'I don't know, maybe it did.' Gina had turned her attention back to her sums. Then, absently, she added, 'But Izzy gave me the money yesterday.'

* * *

Having the plaster cast removed from her leg the following Friday was sheer bliss. Another advantage, Izzy discovered upon returning home several hours later, was that she could move silently once more, without her arrival everywhere being heralded by the noisy, give-away clunking of crutches.

'I'm back!' she announced delightedly, flinging open the door of Katerina's room.

Katerina, who was lying on top of her bed, jumped a mile and hastily shoved the book she'd been reading under the pillows. 'Mother! You're supposed to knock.'

'I wanted to surprise you,' said Izzy serenely. Advancing towards the bed, she added with a lascivious grin, 'And it rather looks as if I have. What's that you're hiding?'

'Homework,' Katerina protested, turning pink and wondering why she had to have the nosiest mother in the entire world.

But it was hopeless; no longer hampered by her plaster cast, Izzy was upon her in a flash, tickling her ribs unmercifully with one hand and tearing the book out from its hiding place with the other. Then, retreating triumphantly to the safety of the doorway, she held it aloft.

'*The Joy of Sex!* Honestly darling, what a waste of money. I could have told you how nice it is, for nothing.'

'Give it back,' wailed Katerina, mortified. When Izzy was in this kind of mood there was no stopping her, and no knowing what she'd do to extract maximum pleasure from Kat's embarrassment.

'But sweetheart, I thought you weren't interested in

boys,' continued Izzy gleefully. 'And even if you were, these pictures would be enough to put *anyone* off them for life. Will you look at that chap's haircut? And as for his beard . . . yuk!'

Katerina wasn't interested in boys, but Simon's unexpected and clumsy seduction attempt the previous week had had a more profound effect on her than she'd first realised. Just for a fraction of a second, she was able to admit to herself later, she had been tempted to go through with it just to see what 'it' was like, and only getting the giggles had saved her.

But had she really been saved? Sex might be a mystery to her, but everyone else seemed to enjoy it and if it were really that marvellous, then maybe she was missing out. Having given the matter a great deal of serious thought, Katerina had decided not to initiate a return match with Simon – great friend though he was, she felt instinctively that there should be more *emotional* involvement between lovers – but to pay at least a little attention to the more technical aspects of the procedure. It was only sensible, after all, to be prepared. Then, when the right person did come along, at least she wouldn't run the risk of making a complete idiot of herself by getting it hopelessly wrong. That, she thought with a shudder, would be even more humiliating than coming last in a chemistry exam.

But now, faced with her mother's helpless laughter and realizing that only the truth would do, she said firmly, 'It's research, that's all. Don't make a big thing of it, Mum.'

'A big thing . . .' murmured Izzy, catching sight of one of the more detailed illustrations in the book and wiping tears from her eyes with the back of her hand. 'Oh Kat, don't look at me like that . . . it's just so *funny* . . .'

'I could always break your other leg,' Katerina offered, moving towards her. 'Look Mum, why don't you calm down and just give me back the—'

She lunged forwards, but it was too late. Darting back through the doorway and out on to the landing, Izzy hurled the book down the stairs.

At precisely that moment, they both heard the front door open.

Katerina held her breath. Izzy, still shaking with laughter, sidled barefoot along the landing and peered over the carved wooden banister rail at Sam, who was standing at the bottom of the staircase with the book in his hand.

'Please mister,' said Izzy, adopting an expression of wide-eyed innocence, 'can we have our book back please?'

Observing the fact that the long-awaited removal of the plaster cast had taken place, Sam glanced at the cover of the book, then – without a flicker – returned his gaze to Izzy.

'Have I interrupted something,' he said drily, 'or is this an invitation?'

Stifling a giggle, Izzy said solemnly, 'Revision. Now that I've got my leg back, I thought I'd better refresh my memory. It's been so long, I may have forgotten how it goes.'

Chapter 12

Bored to the back teeth with inactivity, Izzy celebrated her return to the two-legged world by going out and getting herself re-employed.

Job prospects on the singing front being as dire as ever, it took two hours of cajoling and an extremely short skirt to persuade Bernie Cooper to take her back on at Platform One, the none-too-ritzy club in Soho at which she had been working up until her accident.

But in the mean time, she had been replaced by an enormously well-endowed blues singer called Arlette and Bernie was only able to offer her one evening a week, which meant she was forced to take a pub job as well.

The work at Brennan's Bar – in nearby Covent Garden – was hard, the atmosphere frantic and the pay ridiculously low, but at least it left her with most days free so she was able to attend auditions.

Gina's nights, meanwhile, were becoming increasingly prolonged and unbearable. The days she could just about cope with, because then at least the shops were open, but the evenings alone – when both Izzy and Sam had disappeared to their respective places of work and Katerina had retired to her room to study – were miserable and endless. Worse still, and because she was such a light sleeper, she invariably was woken at around three in the morning by the sound of Izzy and Sam returning home, laughing and joking together as they shared a late-night snack and watched a video before finally retiring to their beds an hour or two later.

One night, having told herself firmly that of course they weren't discussing her, Gina slid out of bed and pulled on a thin dressing gown. They sounded as if they were having so much fun downstairs . . . and she was so *lonely* . . .

But the laughter had subsided by the time she'd crept across the hall and when she paused by the sitting-room door she was able to hear their lowered voices quite clearly.

'. . . it's so crazy,' Izzy was saying with characteristic impatience. 'I've tried to make her realise that she's wasting her life, but she simply refuses to do anything about it. It's almost as if she enjoys being unhappy.'

Gina shivered, clutching the wall for support.

'Of course she doesn't,' she heard Sam reply in more reasonable terms. 'She just isn't able to help herself at the moment. I know it's frustrating—'

'Damn right it's frustrating,' said Izzy hotly. 'She spends more money on clothes than all the Royals put together, then panics because she can't pay the gas bill.'

'According to your daughter, that's exactly what you do.'

'But I don't panic, I enjoy it!' Izzy retaliated. 'What's really frustrating is the fact that Gina does it and she's *still* miserable.'

'She needs something to occupy her mind,' said Sam, above the clinking of glasses. 'Some kind of job, although when I mentioned it to her the other day you'd have thought I'd suggested prostitution.'

'She could take over my job.' Izzy was laughing now. 'And I'll take control of her cheque book. Poor old Gina, I do feel sorry for her, but there are times when I wish I could just shake some sense into that head of hers. For God's sake, how many weeks is it since she even *smiled?*'

'She's unhappy,' chided Sam. 'Haven't you ever been unhappy?'

The next moment, Izzy shrieked. 'Damn right I have! In fact, I'm unhappy at this very moment. Sam, how *could* you?' she protested, her voice rising in anguish. 'That last slice of pizza was mine!'

'Right, we're going to get you sorted out,' Izzy announced a couple of days later, steering Gina out on to the patio for what, hopefully, would be a productive woman-to-woman talk and waving a bottle of Chardonnay for emphasis.

'It's only eleven-thirty,' Gina protested, gazing in horror at the wine.

'Ah, but the clocks go forward tonight.' Izzy winked, then continued with great firmness. 'Besides, it's necessary. I want you to be totally honest and I want you to *relax*. If this fails,' she added cheerfully, 'we resort to Pentothal.'

'I know what you're going to tell me,' said Gina with a trace of defiance. This was like being fifteen all over again.

'I'm not going to tell you anything,' Izzy replied, pouring the wine, then kicking off her shoes and making herself comfortable on the wooden bench. 'For one thing, I'm hardly in a position to lecture. For another, your problems aren't – strictly speaking – any of my business.'

'Then why have you dragged me out here?' Gina demanded.

'Drink your wine before it evaporates,' replied Izzy sternly, knowing from experience that Gina was capable of nursing the same glass for hours. 'The thing is, I'd like to help, so I wondered if there was anything I *could* do?'

Feeling awkward and thinking that if she hadn't overheard Izzy's conversation with Sam she would have been touched by her concern, Gina shrugged and said, 'I don't think so.'

It was like pulling teeth. Waiting until Gina had taken a decent slug of wine, Izzy tried again. 'Look, I really do want to help. What would you like most in the world?'

Startled by the abruptness of the question, Gina's eyes filled with tears. 'I'd like the last two months to have never happened.'

'But they have,' said Izzy relentlessly. 'So, taking that into consideration, what *else* would you like most in the world?'

This wasn't fair. Gina, fumbling for a handkerchief, mumbled, 'I don't know.'

'Well, would it be nice to feel a bit more confident and start getting out and making some new friends?'

'Don't tell me.' Gina's mouth narrowed. 'I should get myself a job.'

'I'm not telling you to do anything,' Izzy reminded her, although it was a struggle not to. Then, struck by an idea, she said, 'Shall I tell you what *I'd* do, if I were you?'

Anything was better than enduring this inquisition. Gina nodded.

'I'd want to make sure my husband had really left me for good,' said Izzy, sitting back and improvising rapidly. 'I'd want to see him with his new girlfriend, so that at least I could stop *wondering* about her. It wouldn't be easy, but it would be worth it, because then I'd know it was over and I could get on with the rest of my life. And yes, I would get myself a job of some kind, even though I'd be scared to death because I hadn't been out to work for so many years that I'd think I'd make an idiot of myself . . . oh, please –' She broke off, realizing that Gina was crying harder than ever. 'I'm sorry, I've gone too far. Look, I'll stop. I won't say another word, but please don't cry any more.'

'No, no,' wailed Gina, her handkerchief by this time soaked through. 'You're absolutely right,' she sniffed. 'That's exactly what I *do* want to do!'

'We should have phoned,' Gina said fearfully as Izzy reversed the Golf into a parking space beneath Andrew's apartment building. Her courage was failing her now that they were actually here.

'No way,' said Izzy briskly, switching off the ignition and cutting Cliff Richard off in mid-flow. 'This time, you're going to have the upper hand. Here you are, dressed up to the nines.' She gestured with approval at Gina's svelte silk dress, the silver jewellery and the perfectly made-up face. 'And there *they* will be, all unsuspecting and unprepared. It's going to be the most brilliant fun,' she concluded with determination, praying that she wasn't making a hideous mistake.

* * *

Marcy, when she opened the door, was certainly unsuspecting. Her own auburn hair was tangled, her unflattering baggy sweater and tracksuit bottoms looked as if they'd been slept in and her face was pale.

'Yes?' she said, hanging on to the door handle and regarding the two women with disinterest. Behind her, a television blared.

Whatever Gina had imagined during those endless tortured nights, it wasn't this.

'We've come to see Andrew,' said Izzy helpfully, when it became apparent that Gina was too stunned to say anything at all.

'Oh, he isn't in.' The woman, who had a sleepy, cultured voice, sounded relieved, as if his absence solved the problem.

'Are you expecting him back' – Izzy allowed herself a tiny pause – 'shortly?'

'He's just popped out to the supermarket.' Unexpectedly, Marcy smiled. 'He shouldn't be long.'

In all the years she had been married to him, Andrew hadn't so much as registered the existence of such objects. Astounded by the thought that he was at this moment actually in one, and almost laughing out loud at the absurdity of the idea, Gina recovered her nerve.

'In that case,' she said, so smoothly that even Izzy gazed at her in admiration, 'perhaps we could come in and wait. I'm Gina Lawrence, Andrew's wife. And this is my friend, Izzy Van Asch.'

The flat was an absolute tip. Small and low-ceilinged to begin with, the suffocating central heating and incredible amount of clutter strewn around the room rendered it positively claustrophobic. Gina was cheered still further by the terrible sight. Marcy's lack of response to her introduction had been disappointing – she had geared herself up for high drama and received only a mildly surprised 'Oh, well then, of course you must come in,' in return – but other than that she could have hugged Izzy for bringing her here. This was all so much less terrifying than she had imagined, and meeting Marcy had filled her with such sudden, wild optimism, that she knew she couldn't fail. Baby or no baby, Andrew was bound to come back to her sooner or later. This plump, slow-moving, slovenly creature was no threat to her marriage after all . . .

'Tea,' announced Marcy, returning from the kitchen with two unmatched mugs, a soup spoon with which to fish out the teabags and a king-size bag of prawn-cocktail-flavoured crisps. 'Well, I must say this is all very civilised.' With a sigh of relief, she collapsed into a chair. Then, her grey eyes swivelling between her two guests, she gestured vaguely at the mugs of tea and smiled once more. 'I'm so glad you felt able to visit us. Problems with exes and in-laws are so unnecessary, I've always thought . . . please Gina, do help yourself to the crisps . . .'

Andrew's reaction, when he arrived back at the flat fifteen minutes later, was far more gratifying. Grinding to a halt in the doorway, bulging carrier bags dangling from both hands, he stared at his estranged wife and said, 'Jesus.'

Izzy opened her mouth, ready to leap into the breach once more, but Gina was too fast for her.

'Andrew,' she acknowledged gracefully, crossing one slim leg over the other and smoothing the silk dress over her knees with a composed, almost regal gesture. 'How pleasant to see *you* again, after all this time. I'm afraid we've called unannounced, but I didn't feel such an important matter could be properly discussed over the telephone. I hope you don't mind us coming here to your . . .' The word 'love-nest' hung unspoken in the air between them. Izzy held her breath. '. . . home,' continued Gina, the merest hint of a smile lifting the corners of her mouth. 'But we really do need to discuss the details of our divorce.'

'That was terrific!' exclaimed Izzy as they made their way back to the car. Bursting with pride, she said, '*You* were terrific. Really, I'm so impressed. And did you see the look on his face when you started talking about the divorce . . . !'

'Yes,' said Gina, so wrapped up in her own thoughts that she could barely concentrate on what Izzy was saying.

'And how about that female he's landed himself with. What a ditz. I thought he'd at least have gone for something with a bit of go about her . . . but you were so *brilliant* . . .' Lost in admiration, she shook her dark head, then broke into a grin. 'Don't you feel a million times better now that you've faced them?'

'Better than I've felt for months,' agreed Gina happily. Stopping at the edge of the pavement and glancing up at Andrew's rented apartment, she realised that now, at last, she was feeling alive again. Unable to stop herself, she reached out and clutched Izzy's arm. 'Better than I've ever felt in my life! Oh Izzy, I thought I'd lost him . . . it didn't even occur to me that I could get him back. And it's all thanks to you for making me come here . . .'

Izzy ground to a halt. Her heart plummeted. Somehow, somewhere along the line, she and Gina appeared to have got their wires very crossed indeed. 'But you don't want him back!' she countered strongly. 'He's a liar and a cheat and you're better off without him. You came here to prove all that to yourself . . . to lay the ghost . . .'

'But now I've found out that I don't need to,' replied Gina, her eyes alight with joy. 'And I can stop worrying, because it's all going to be all right. He doesn't love her, don't you see? He *will* come back.'

'Oh God,' said Izzy with a groan. But Gina didn't even notice; she was miles away.

'He will come back,' she repeated with dreamy conviction. 'To me.'

Chapter 13

'It's all my fault,' Izzy admitted gloomily as Sam gave her a lift to work that evening on his way to The Chelsea Steps. Peering into her hand mirror and putting the finishing touches to her lipstick, she said, 'I've made an absolute pig's ear of the whole thing. And all I was doing,' she added with an impatient gesture, 'was trying to help.'

'I wondered why she was so much more cheerful,' remarked Sam drily. Then, swinging the car into the outside lane to avoid a braking cab, he said, 'But is that really so terrible?'

They had reached Trafalgar Square. Reminded by the sight of Nelson's Column that she had a Cadbury's Flake in her bag and immeasurably cheered by the thought, Izzy rummaged until she found it, then offered half to Sam. Even more happily, he shook his head, which meant a whole Flake to herself. 'Gina's like an addict with a fix after six weeks of cold turkey,' she informed him, between mouthfuls. 'It's completely disastrous! Just think what she'll be like when it wears off.'

Amused by her agony-auntish attitude, as well as by her ability to eat chocolate and apply mascara at the same time, he said, 'Don't you ever make mistakes?'

'Oh zillions.' Make-up completed, Izzy dropped the mascara back into her capacious bag and polished off the last of the Flake, licking her fingers with panache. 'But that only makes me more of an expert at seeing where everyone else is going wrong. And the one thing I'd never do,' she added as a careless afterthought, 'would be to lust after a man who didn't lust back. Now that *is* asking to be kicked in the teeth. That's just *stupid*.'

Brennan's Bar was still relatively empty when Ralph walked in. Izzy's stomach did a quick backward somersault and for a millisecond she considered diving down behind the bar. Since she was in the process of giving a fat businessman his change, however, it wasn't entirely practical.

Ralph, on the other hand, didn't even flinch when he saw her. 'Hallo, Izzy,' he said evenly. A faint smile lifted the corners of his mouth. 'Well, well. Of all the bars in all the world you had to be working in this one.'

He might be an actor, but the casual line didn't fool her for a moment. With a grin, she said, 'You knew I was here.'

'Word gets around.' Leaning against the bar, tanned and narrow-eyed, looking only slightly over the top in a beige trenchcoat worn open over a T-shirt and white jeans, Ralph surveyed her with practised thoroughness. Then he lit a Gauloise and Izzy realised that he was doing his Alain Delon bit, which meant that beneath the cool façade he must be nervous. 'So, how are you?'

At least he wasn't using a French accent. Stepping back and showing him her legs – and glad now that she'd worn her short, charcoal-grey lycra dress – she said simply, 'Mended.'

He nodded. 'And how's Kat?'

Ralph and Katerina had always got on so well together. An unlikely father figure, he had nevertheless formed a close and genuinely affectionate relationship with Kat, and their good-natured verbal sparring had been capable of keeping them happily occupied for hours. Experiencing a rush of belated gratitude, Izzy seized a bottle of Lanson and said, 'Come on, my treat. It really is lovely to see you again.'

Happily, the bar remained quiet and she was able to catch up on all the gossip concerning their old friends.

'And what about you?' she asked finally. Knowing Ralph as she did; she was perfectly well aware that he was holding out on her.

He half-smiled, trying not to look too pleased with himself. 'Oh, not too bad. This and that, you know.'

'How can I know unless you tell me?' she persisted, beginning to enjoy herself. Sam was still off-limits, after all, and if Ralph had finally decided to forgive her . . . well, she reasoned, he did have the most gorgeous eyes, and he could always make her laugh. Besides, when Sam had caught her with Kat's sex manual, there had been more than a modicum of truth in her riposte that she was badly out of practice . . .

'Well, as a matter of fact my agent rang me this afternoon,' he admitted, breaking into a grin at last. 'To tell me that I've landed the lead in a new TV drama series.'

Izzy's shriek of delight startled even the seen-it-all-before stockbrokers sitting at a nearby table. 'Ralph, that's fantastic! My God, you must be so thrilled . . . tell me everything, every *detail* . . . quick, have another glass of champagne . . . you should be out celebrating!' Leaning across the polished bar, she took his face in her hands and gave him a kiss. To her further delight, he didn't show the least sign of resisting.

'Maybe I wanted to celebrate with someone who'd really understand.' Then, his eyes narrowing once more, he said, 'Are you still seeing that other guy?'

'Of course not!'

'Anyone else?'

Not yet, thought Izzy, crossing her fingers beneath the bar. 'Whoever in the world would want anything to do with a hopeless case like me?' she said lightly. Then, since he continued to glare at her, she smiled and shook her head. 'No. Nobody else.'

Ralph relaxed at last. 'In that case, what time can you get away?'

'Ah, there you are,' said Sam, crossing to the bar and observing with amused interest the way Izzy jumped at the sound of his voice. Even more intriguing was the sudden rush of colour suffusing her cheeks, since as long as he'd known her she'd never blushed.

'Sam . . . what on earth are you doing here?' she demanded, far too quickly.

'Such gratitude!' He tut-tutted with mock reproval, then winked and pulled her purse from his jacket pocket. 'I found it on the floor of the car. It must have fallen out of that disgraceful bag of yours while you were doing your make-up. Oh, and I phoned Kat in case you were panicking about it,' he continued easily, apparently quite unaware of Ralph's glowering presence beside him. 'She said that if we were thinking of stopping off at the Chinese on our way home, could she please have lemon chicken with egg fried rice and double pineapple fritters.'

'What did I say?' protested Sam, as they made their way back to the house several hours later.

Izzy, with six boxes of Chinese food balanced precariously on her lap, threw him a suspicious sideways glance, but his immaculate profile was giving nothing away.

'You know exactly what you said,' she told him, still undecided whether to laugh or empty the carton of prawn crackers over his head.

'OK.' He nodded, keeping his own amusement to himself. 'But what did I say that was so wrong? That guy stormed out so fast I didn't even get a chance to admire the medallions around his neck.'

'He doesn't wear medallions.' Despite herself, Izzy smiled into the darkness. It had been she, two years ago, who had had to break the news to Ralph that real men didn't wear necklaces. 'And before you say anything else,' she continued in severe tones, 'you're talking about the man I loved.'

But Sam was already acquainted with the saga of Izzy's recent entanglements. 'Don't you mean one of the men you loved?' he remarked, deadpan.

'It isn't funny,' she said, with a touch of irritation. 'And you deliberately said those things to give him the wrong impression. You might find it amusing, but I spent my entire evening's wages on that bottle of champagne.'

'And now I've spoiled your hopes of a romantic reconciliation,' he mused cheerfully. 'Really, Isabel. I thought you didn't lust after men who didn't lust after you. If he can't even cope with tonight's little misunderstanding, he can't be that smitten.'

Enraged, she shouted, 'You've wrecked my non-existent love life and it has nothing whatsoever to do with you! How would you like it if I stuck my oar in, just as you were about to make *your* move with some bimbo at The Steps?'

How indeed? Having known Izzy Van Asch for some weeks, Sam's feelings towards her were still decidedly mixed. That initial jolting attraction had knocked him sideways, but there was so much more to Izzy than simply the physical appeal of big brown eyes, riotous hair, a curvy body and stupendous – now that they were both visible – legs. She exuded fun, laughed more than anyone he'd ever known and her optimism was irrepressible.

Yet at the same time, she could be thoughtless, illogical and infuriatingly cavalier in her attitudes and lifestyle. Wildly generous one day, she would be shamelessly cadging a fiver from her daughter the next, and although she was undoubtedly capable of hard work when it suited her, she was also better at whiling away an afternoon in sybaritic indolence than almost any other woman he knew. She was so exasperating, loving, sometimes downright astounding – and he was never entirely sure whether the things she said and did were deliberately calculated to shock – that Sam couldn't decide what he wanted to do more; shake a bit of much-needed sense into her dizzy head or tumble her into bed.

And there, he reflected ruefully, lay the other half of his dilemma. Attracting women was not something he'd ever had to think about before. It just happened, and gently rebuffing the ones who didn't attract him in return had been the only mildly tricky part. But surely, no other woman on this planet had ever sent out signals as conflicting as those signalled by Izzy. Time and time again, just as he'd thought he had her sussed, she would move smartly into reverse and he would be left wondering . . . once again . . . whether he even knew her at all.

Until now he'd been both amused and intrigued by her behaviour. Tonight, however, something had changed. And maybe tonight, Sam mused as he drew up outside the house and switched off the car's engine, he should do something about it.

'You still haven't answered my question.' Izzy spoke with an air of truculence. She hadn't forgiven him yet.

'Ah yes, the bimbo.' Sam nodded, giving the question some thought. Then, taking the cumbersome pile of boxes from her lap, he gave her a brief smile. 'I suppose it would rather depend,' he said finally, 'on what she was like.'

It wasn't the most romantic of situations, thought Izzy, but at least it was finally happening . . .

She had been dumping the dirty dishes into the sink when Sam had moved up behind her, resting his hands on the edge of the draining board on either side of her so that she was effectively pinned in. There was no physical contact, but she could feel his warm breath stirring her hair and smell the faint scent of his aftershave.

Hoping that he, in turn, couldn't see the tiny hairs prickling at the nape of her neck, Izzy turned on the hot tap and squirted far too much Fairy Liquid into the bowl.

She hadn't planned on actually doing the washing-up, but it looked good, and such a show of domesticity was bound to impress. Sam was always making pointed remarks about her appalling lack of it.

'Come on now, be honest,' he murmured, as she watched the foam cascade over the edges of the bowl like champagne. 'Ralph really wasn't your type anyway.'

'He was my type for two years,' Izzy replied with outward calm. Her hands, however, were shaking so she seized Gina's beloved rubber gloves, pulling them on in a hurry and plunging them into the washing-up. Then, nodding towards the tea towel, she said, 'And if you really want to be useful, you can dry.'

Taking half a step backwards, Sam admired the deep V of tanned flesh revealed by her dress, which was virtually backless. Resisting the urge to run a finger down her spine, he said mildly, 'You're changing the subject.'

'I don't know what the subject is.' She took a deep, steadying breath and sloshed fresh water over a haphazardly scrubbed bowl. 'I just know that Gina does her nut if the dishes aren't put away.'

'Izzy,' he said gently. 'You may be many things, but you aren't stupid.'

Unable to think of a suitable reply to this statement, she played safe and said nothing. A moment later, Sam's mouth brushed the nape of her neck and Izzy, who had been bracing herself for something like this, was quite unable to prevent the shudder of longing which ricocheted up from her stomach. When his warm hands came to rest at her waist and his lips travelled to her bare shoulder, she almost gave in.

But this was Gina's house and she had made her a promise. Besides, Sam was due to move out in less than a fortnight . . . and a little waiting had never harmed anyone. Least of all, she reminded herself firmly, a man like Sam Sheridan, who had probably never been kept waiting before in his life.

But his tongue was idling along the line of her collar bone now, a manoeuvre to which Izzy had always been particularly susceptible, and that wasn't fair at all. Squirming with suppressed desire, she had to employ every last ounce of will-power in order not to turn around. Instead, concentrating fiercely on the washing-up, she managed – somehow – to clean another plate. Then, when she finally judged herself able to speak in something approaching normal tones, she said with deliberate flippancy, 'Did they slip something extra into your sesame king prawns, Sam, or do you just have a bit of a thing for Marigold gloves?'

With a shrug, he dropped a light kiss on the top of her head and stepped back. 'I'm just curious.'

'About me?' said Izzy, torn between relief that he had stopped and irritation that he couldn't have tried a little harder. There was such a thing as giving up too easily, after all. 'You thought I'd be a pushover,' she continued, her eyes bright with challenge. 'Is that it?'

'Not at all.' Moving across to the dresser, he uncapped a bottle of Scotch and poured hefty measures into two glasses. 'I was simply curious, as I said. I don't want to shock you,' he added with a glimmer of a smile, 'but when two people find each other attractive, when they're both unattached and over the age of consent . . . well, sometimes they . . .'

'I know about all that,' replied Izzy swiftly. Not wanting to annoy him, she smiled back. 'Kat told me all about the birds and the bees when she was twelve. But . . .'

'But?' Sam echoed with a trace of irony.

Uncomfortably aware that she hadn't really thought this through, Izzy wiped a tendril of hair from her forehead with the back of a foamy hand and said as cheerfully as she could, 'Well, it might spoil things. We get on well, now. We're friends, aren't we?'

Sam nodded, not believing her for a moment but intrigued nevertheless to hear what she was going to come up with.

'So, it might spoil our friendship,' she continued hurriedly, 'and that would be awful.'

'It might not, and then it wouldn't be awful at all.'

This time she drew a deep breath. 'It still isn't a good idea.'

'OK.' He held up his hands. 'If that's what you really feel. And there's no need to get into a flap about it, anyway. It was just a thought.'

'Well, it was nice of you to think of me,' said Izzy lamely, miffed by his refusal to make any kind of serious attempt to seduce her. If this was the extent of his persistence, she wasn't surprised he'd never been married.

'That's OK,' said Sam, by this time openly amused. 'My mistake. I should have realised that you weren't that sort of girl.'

'No hard feelings?'

He gave her a rueful smile. 'Hardly any at all now, thanks.'

'Good.' She was pushing her luck, she knew, but victory over someone as desirable as Sam was infinitely sweet. And next time . . . in about two weeks' time to be precise . . . she would achieve an even greater one. Chucking the washing-up cloth into the sink and crossing the dimly lit kitchen, she stood on tiptoe and planted a careful, sisterly kiss on his cheek. 'Good friends are more important than lovers,' she murmured. 'Every time.'

'Depends how good they are,' said Sam, keeping himself firmly under control. The bitch, he thought. Now he knew she was playing games.

'Good night, Sam,' said Izzy serenely.

'Good night, John-boy.'

Chapter 14

Galvanised into action by the realization that she could get Andrew back, Gina had embarked upon a whirlwind plan of campaign in order to do so and stubbornly refused to listen to Izzy's protests that this wasn't what she'd meant at all. The terrible apathy which had dogged her for the past months was stripped away like Clark Kent's office suit, to be replaced by a positive tidal wave of enthusiasm. Having lost almost a stone in weight – which didn't particularly suit her – she regained her appetite and began eating again, had her hair rebobbed and her legs eye-smartingly waxed. Oblivious to the bank manager's unamused letters she launched into a fresh orgy of spending, but this time it was carried out joyfully and with real purpose because nothing was too good for Andrew and whoever would dream of wearing underwear which didn't match their clothes and clothes which didn't match their Kurt Geiger shoes anyway?

And since nothing seemed impossible any more, gaining new-found independence in the form of a job no longer struck terror into Gina's soul. Her determination to prove herself different in every way from that slothful, unkempt creature with whom Andrew had so stupidly – and *temporarily* – gone to live was a far more effective incentive than Izzy's airy exhortations to 'get out and do something' had ever been.

'Where are you going?' Izzy demanded with suspicion a couple of days later when Gina presented herself downstairs made up and scented and wearing a new, navy-blue Chanel-style suit which looked suspiciously like the genuine article and which would no doubt reduce the bank manager to new depths of depression. At this rate, Izzy could almost feel sorry for him.

Gina, who had been practising a new, slightly deeper and hopefully more authoritative voice in the privacy of her bedroom, said, 'I've got a job interview.' But Izzy only looked more alarmed.

'Are you going down with something infectious?'

'No, I am not.' Disappointed, Gina reverted to her normal tones. 'And you're supposed to be encouraging me.'

'I tried doing that,' Izzy reminded her. 'And it went horribly wrong.' Then she pulled herself together. 'But I'm glad you're looking for work; it'll do you the world of good. What kind of job is it?'

It was indeed going to do her a world of good, thought Gina, scarcely able to control her smile. She had run through the plan a hundred times, yet the thought of it still sent the adrenalin racing through her body. The interview, set for eleven o'clock, was bound to be over by midday. Then, having secured the job she would arrive at Andrew's office just before twelve-thirty and insist . . . *insist* that he join her for lunch in order to celebrate. From there on the details grew a little hazy; all she knew was that Andrew would be seeing her at her new and absolute best, she would be seeing him without that awful Marcy in tow and it would be the happiest afternoon of her life . . .

'Are you *sure* you're OK?' Izzy waved a hand in front of her face, bringing her back to earth.

'Of course I am. It's a sales job,' said Gina with renewed pride, 'at Therese Verdun, just off Bond Street.'

Therese Verdun was one of the most exclusive dress shops in London.

Of course, thought Izzy wryly, silly me for asking.

'Yes?' snapped Andrew, when his secretary buzzed through to his office at midday.

'Er, Mr Lawrence, your wife is here to see you,' said Pam, struggling to contain her excitement. Having stayed up late the previous night to watch *Fatal Attraction*, she had high hopes for this real-life confrontation. Gina didn't look as if she was carrying a gun, but you never knew. And Andrew Lawrence had been in such a lousy mood for the last couple of weeks that whatever he had coming to him now, Pam condoned absolutely.

'Send her in,' commanded the tinny voice over the intercom. Gina smiled at Pam. Pam, deciding that maybe she wouldn't take her lunch hour just yet after all, smiled back. Andrew, ensconced in his office, didn't smile at all.

'Darling!' said Gina, when the door was safely shut behind her. Swooping down on him like a thin, elegant bird and enveloping him in a cloud of freshly applied Shalimar, she kissed his cheek. 'Isn't this a surprise? I should have phoned, but I was so excited I simply had to come and tell you . . . I've just found myself the most marvellous job and I wanted you to be the first to know!'

'That's—' began Andrew, caught totally off-guard by

her arrival, but Gina had rehearsed her lines too often to allow him to interrupt.

'And it's all thanks to you, because if you hadn't left I would never have even thought of going out to work!' she gabbled joyfully. 'So I insist, absolutely, upon taking you for lunch.'

'Ah, well . . .'

'No excuses,' she continued with mock severity. 'I checked with Pam to make sure you didn't have any other appointments, and besides . . . what on earth is the point of having a civilised divorce if one can't treat one's husband to a superb lunch at Emile's once in a while?'

It was all going disastrously wrong, she thought numbly an hour later. Here she was, doing and saying everything according to plan, here they were in Andrew's favourite – and ruinously expensive – restaurant, and here was Andrew refusing to co-operate with all the quiet stubbornness of a small boy who doesn't want to return to boarding school.

'Another bottle of wine?' she asked in desperation, but he simply shook his head and glanced yet again at his watch. Gazing helplessly around at the other tables, Gina saw only couples enjoying themselves. She was running out of bright conversation at a rate of knots now. Her new job had become more and more grand . . . she was practically running the entire company . . . and Andrew still wasn't as impressed as he was supposed to be. He also took little apparent interest in her wildly exaggerated stories of what sharing a house with Izzy and Sam was like. Unless he pulled himself together and started making an effort very soon, thought Gina as the first signs of real panic began to gnaw at her stomach, she didn't know what she might do.

'I hope Marcy isn't cooking you a huge dinner,' she said, although he hadn't really eaten much at all.

Andrew shook his head. If he looked at his watch one more time, thought Gina, she would tear it off his wrist and hurl it across the room.

'And the baby?' she continued, too brightly. 'Is everything going smoothly there? I expect Marcy's up to her ears in ante-natal classes at the moment . . .'

'Gina, don't,' he said abruptly. 'Look, thanks for the lunch and I'm really very pleased for you about the job, but I have got to get back to the office. There's no need for you to drive me back, I can take a cab.'

The fantasy hadn't materialised; the charade was over. Unable to bear it, Gina's eyes filled with tears and she rose jerkily to her feet, knocking the fork from her plate and splattering the front of her skirt with Madeira sauce. 'Andrew, please, you can't just leave like this. You don't understand—'

'I do understand.' He didn't know whom to feel most sorry for, Gina or himself. He was merely unhappy, whereas she was chronically insecure. 'You've landed yourself a wonderful job, you're making a new life for yourself and I'm *glad* about that.'

The tears were in full flood now, streaking her make-up and attracting the attention of other diners. 'But I don't *have* a new life,' she sobbed, scrubbing hopelessly at the burgundy stain on her skirt with a snowy napkin. 'And I don't have a wonderful job, either. I don't have any kind of job because they turned me down. They told me I needed experience,' she wailed accusingly, 'and I didn't have any because all I'd ever been was a wife!'

Somehow he managed to get her out of the restaurant. A handful of tenners he could ill-afford to lose only just covered the bill. By the time they reached the car, Gina was shivering violently and barely able to stand. The fact that she was oblivious to the stares of passers-by convinced him that her grief was genuine.

'I can't drive, d-don't make me d-drive,' she begged, through chattering teeth. 'The last time I was like this I nearly k-k-killed someone.'

'All right, don't worry,' he said rapidly, praying he wasn't over the limit. 'I'll take you home.'

'I'm so ashamed.'

'Blimey,' said a man unloading a van. 'What's she got, syphilis?'

'Get in the car,' ordered Andrew, torn between irritation and sympathy. Once again the crushing weight of responsibility was bearing down on him. While he accepted that he was to blame for this entire sorry mess, he couldn't help wondering why he should be the one with the wife who couldn't handle it while other men seemed to escape scot-free.

'Blimey.' Katerina, spending the afternoon studying at home, unknowingly echoed the van driver when she answered the front door and saw Gina's swollen, ravaged face.

'I'm sorry.' Andrew waved apologetically in the direction of the doorbell. 'Gina couldn't find her key.'

Katerina regarded him with interest. Gina in tears was nothing new – although she did look quite spectacularly dreadful – but as far as Katerina was aware she had left the house this morning in unusually high spirits, looking forward to her interview. From the look of her now, she could only assume that Gina hadn't been offered the job. 'That's OK,' she replied easily, wondering if this man was the owner of the dress shop. 'But I'm intrigued. Who are you?'

It was a bizarre situation; for the moment Gina was quite forgotten. Having already deduced who Katerina was, Andrew could only return her unflinching gaze. She was wearing a faded honey-coloured sweatshirt and knee-length white leggings and her glossy brown hair hung straight to her shoulders. Her eyes were huge and light brown, her teeth very white. In her right hand she held a pen; in her left a marmalade sandwich.

'Andrew Lawrence,' he said and waited for her expression to change to one of disdain. Izzy's dislike of him had been only too evident during their brief meeting the previous week.

Katerina, however, broke into a smile and gave him a look of such complicity that he knew at once she was on his side. The relief was overwhelming.

'Right, of course you are.' She stepped aside, enabling him to lead Gina towards the sitting room. Andrew found himself unable to tear his eyes from her rear view; those slim hips and long legs were almost hypnotizing in their simple elegance. She couldn't possibly be more than eighteen.

'Well, I'd better leave you to it.' In the sitting room,

text books littered the carpet. Within seconds Katerina had retrieved them and was standing in the doorway. When she had watched Andrew deposit his wife in one of the peach upholstered armchairs she said calmly, 'Do you know who *I* am?'

He straightened, adjusting his tie and dropping Gina's car keys on to the coffee table. He might not have contributed much towards the conversation in the restaurant, but he had at least listened. 'You're the clever one,' he told her, his voice even, 'who does the washing-up.'

'Right.' This time Katerina laughed. 'Of course I am. And how clever of *you* to have guessed.'

Having planned to drop off Gina and leave immediately, he found himself phoning the office instead and telling them he wouldn't be back that afternoon, which would fuel office gossip no end. And after thirty minutes of half-heartedly attempting to console his inconsolable wife, he was rewarded by the sound of footsteps descending the staircase. Snatching Gina's teacup from her hands and murmuring something about a refill, he shot out of the room and slap into Katerina.

She was wearing a denim jacket and carried a vast canvas bag stuffed with books.

'How's it going?'

Andrew pulled a face. 'Same as ever. Look, it's about time I was leaving, but I'd like to talk to you . . . about Gina. Can I offer you a lift to wherever you're going?'

She gave him another of those solemn mesmerizing looks. 'I'm afraid not.'

'Oh.'

'It isn't that I don't appreciate the offer,' she explained, breaking into a slow smile. He looked so dismayed, it was almost heartbreaking. She leaned closer and said in a stage whisper, 'But you don't have transport.'

'Damn.' At the same time, Andrew experienced a surge of relief, because the rejection wasn't personal. Putting the memory of the lunch he couldn't afford behind him, he said, 'I'll phone for a cab.'

Katerina's smile widened as she hauled her heavy bag over her shoulder. 'Why don't we just walk to the tube station? Then we can talk on the way.'

I'm in the Victoria and Albert Museum and something very strange is happening to me, thought Katerina carefully, an hour later. She didn't know how or why it was happening; it just was. And there was nothing, absolutely nothing on earth she could do to either stop or control it.

She didn't even know what they were doing in the museum, for heaven's sake; there had simply been too much to say and not enough time in which to say it, until Andrew had suggested they stop *en route* for a coffee and *en route* had somehow become the dear old V & A. Now, as they sat side by side in the ground-floor restaurant, surrounded on all sides by noisy, overweight Americans and tiny, chattering Japanese tourists, Katerina was aware only of the momentousness of a situation she didn't even fully comprehend. On the outside she was still herself, twirling a strand of hair between two fingers as she discussed – in purely practical terms – Gina's lack of confidence and what they could possibly do about it.

But on the inside she wasn't herself at all. While her mouth was doing the talking, her stomach had tied itself up in a gigantic knot and the inside of her wrist, where Andrew had accidentally brushed against her, was still tingling, really *tingling*, as a result of that momentary physical contact.

As long as she continued to talk, however – and discussing his marital problems in a detached, adult manner was astonishingly easy – she was able to study Andrew Lawrence in detail. And while he wasn't as startlingly good-looking as some men . . . Sam, for example . . . there was something about his shadowed grey eyes, thin cheeks and floppy, light brown hair that was somehow infinitely more attractive. He looked careworn, exuding an air of fighting against the odds to make the best of what he had to put up with, and when he actually smiled his features were transformed; his whole face lit up and the years melted away.

'I shouldn't really be telling you all this,' he said eventually, stirring milky coffee which had long since gone cold. 'It isn't your problem, after all.'

'But it's so awful!' exclaimed Katerina, her eyes on the verge of filling with uncharacteristic tears. 'And so unfair . . . God, we have no idea! Mum did say that—'

'Yes?' Andrew prompted gently. 'What did Mum say?'

Incapable of lying to him, fixing him with those huge brown eyes, she murmured, 'Well, she mentioned in passing that Marcy was a bit of a ditz.'

He acknowledged the words with a thoughtful nod, then smiled because at least he was here, with Katerina Van Asch. Life, it seemed, had its compensations. He just wondered how he was going to cope with the particular compensation facing him at this minute. The urge to touch her once more . . . accidentally, of course . . . was almost overwhelming.

'It's all my fault; I've been a complete idiot,' he admitted. 'I was married, I thought I'd fallen in love with another woman . . . and by the time I realised I hadn't, it was too late.'

'You shouldn't blame yourself,' said Katerina indignantly. 'Getting pregnant was her own stupid fault. Plenty of other men would have just dumped her.'

The restaurant was rapidly emptying; it was almost six o'clock and cleaners were pushing mops around. Aware of their baleful stares, and of the fact that time was running out, Andrew was unable to stop himself. Taking Katerina's hand and giving it a brief squeeze, he smiled. 'Thank you. I wish I'd met you six months ago.' Even better, he thought, he wished he were twenty years younger and still single.

But Katerina, knowing only that Andrew Lawrence had already changed her life and throwing seventeen years of caution to the wind, reached for the hand he had withdrawn and held it between her own. She was trembling slightly, her stomach had long since disappeared and she had never been happier in her life.

'It doesn't matter,' she heard herself saying, as if from a great distance. 'You've met me now.'

Chapter 15

Determined not to be too obvious or too eager, but at the same time nerve-wrackingly aware that single men like Sam were in constant danger of being snapped up by less patient women than herself, Izzy maintained a decorous distance when he eventually moved out of the house and into his new apartment and, in a state of intense and delicious anticipation, managed to hold out for almost an entire week.

Waking up the following Saturday afternoon, however, and realizing that now was the perfect time to see Sam and put her brilliant plan into long-awaited action, the anticipation became at once almost unbearable. It was sunny. It was warm. She was – boasting apart – looking great. And best of all, Izzy discovered when she eventually got up and moseyed into her daughter's empty bedroom, Katerina had decided against wearing her new pink denim skirt. If that wasn't fate, she thought happily as she slung it over one arm and headed towards the bathroom, she didn't know what was.

Gina was downstairs, disconsolately watching an old black-and-white film on the television.

'Going somewhere nice?' she asked, when Izzy appeared in a pale pink denim skirt worn with a minuscule white vest and clinched at the waist with a twisted charcoal-and-pink fringed scarf. Navy-blue eyeshadow and more mascara than usual conspired to make her eyes look enormous and she was even wearing pink lipstick. Stupid question, thought Gina miserably. Of course she was going somewhere nice.

Recognizing the note of desperation in her voice and realizing that Gina was likely to ask if she could come along too, Izzy replied briskly, 'Audition,' then smiled to herself, deciding that in a way, that was exactly what it was. And a mutual one at that.

'Oh.' Losing interest, Gina returned her attention to the film which was bound to make her cry. 'Kat asked me to tell you that she's gone over to Simon's house, by the way. She won't be back until late.'

Snap, thought Izzy cheerfully, scooping Katerina's alligator earrings out of the bowl on the mantelpiece and fastening them into her ears. Aloud, she said, 'Hooray for A levels,' because Katerina hated it when she borrowed her earrings. Then, tipping her head to one side as she examined her reflection in the mirror, she added, 'Although if you ask me, there's more to these disappearing acts of hers than meets the eye.'

'What on earth do you mean?' Gina, who had watched a nightmarish programme about teenage junkies the night before, thought immediately of drugs. God, that was all she needed . . .

'Kat and Simon,' explained Izzy patiently. 'They can't possibly spend this much time together simply revising. Haven't you noticed how different she's been these past few weeks? Physics and chemistry haven't done *that* to her,' she concluded with satisfaction, fluffing up her hair and adjusting the straps of her top to reveal a fraction more cleavage. 'I know, I can hardly believe it myself, but it seems that my brilliant, backward daughter has finally discovered what little boys are made of. Bless her little heart, she's in *lurve*!'

'There are crocodiles in your ears,' observed Sam, who had been in the shower when the doorbell rang. The fact that he was wearing only an olive-green towel slung around his hips made Izzy unaccountably nervous, which was ridiculous. If she got her way later on this evening, she reminded herself, he would be wearing rather less than a bath towel, after all.

'There are hares on your chest,' she countered; a feeble joke even by her own terrible standards.

He winked. 'Ah, but I didn't borrow them from Katerina without asking her first.'

'How do you know I didn't ask her?'

'If you had,' he said with a grin, 'she would have said no.'

Izzy almost bit her lower lip but all that would achieve was unattractive lipstick-stained teeth, so she settled instead for an expression of penitence. 'Are you going to call the police?'

'Not if you've brought champagne,' he said, glancing at the bulky carrier bag clasped to her chest.

'Single men are famous for keeping their fridges stocked with champagne,' she replied, making her way through to the kitchen. 'And very little else. I've brought something much more useful. Food.'

'You mean you're going to cook something?' Sam looked alarmed. 'To eat?'

'Don't panic, I went to the Italian delicatessen,' she said soothingly. 'All we have to do is unwrap it.'

He couldn't quite put his finger on it, but there was definitely something different about Izzy. Over a leisurely late lunch of smoked salmon, marinated mushrooms, salads, French bread and Camembert, the effortless conversation continued as ever . . . business at The Chelsea Steps, Katerina's budding love life, Gina's third unsuccessful interview . . . but there was something else, too. Two small glasses of champagne hadn't had this much of an effect on her; Izzy was definitely hiding something.

'Never mind Katerina and Simon,' he said at last, eyeing her with suspicion. 'What's been happening with you? Are you in love?'

Izzy popped a black grape into her mouth and smiled. 'Me? Whoever would I be in love with?'

'I don't know. Somebody wildly unsuitable, no doubt.' Recalling the medallion man he had met at the pub the other week, Sam experienced a twinge of irritation. He was surprised to find how much he minded. 'You have terrible taste in men, you know.'

She shook her head vigorously. 'I don't.'

'Yes, you do.'

How sweet, thought Izzy, in raptures. And how ironic. Twirling a tendril of hair between her fingers, she fixed Sam with an innocent gaze. 'Are we having our first quarrel?'

'Possibly.' God, she was infuriating. 'Why, is that the reason you came over here?'

'Not at all. It's just that I'm right and you're wrong and I love it when that happens.'

As far as Sam was aware, it never *had* happened. Izzy had a positive talent for mistakes, she got *everything* wrong. 'So, who is he?' he said, attempting to sound as if it didn't matter to him anyway.

Izzy, enjoying herself enormously, began to dismantle the last bunch of grapes. 'Well, I don't know whether I'm actually in love, but there's definitely a bit of lust involved. He's wildly attractive.'

'Oh, top-priority stuff,' Sam retaliated. 'Don't tell me, he wears white, patent-leather shoes, too.'

'There's no need to make fun of me,' she said, deadpan. 'Looks *are* important. Would you go out with a dog?'

Realizing that he was in danger of losing this particular argument, he said, 'So, is it fairly serious between you and this . . . man?'

The bait had been well and truly taken, Izzy appreciated happily. Her mission accomplished – for now, at least – she drained her glass and pushed back her chair. With a careless shrug, she said, 'Who knows what will happen? It may turn out like that. Whichever, it'll certainly be fun finding out.'

As she reached for her bag, Sam said, 'Are you working tonight?'

Izzy pulled a face. 'Yes. And you?'

He nodded.

'Right. Well, I'm off.' Tossing her bag over her shoulder, she gave him a dazzling smile. 'Have a nice night then, Sam. And enjoy yourself. I'm certainly going to!'

* * *

It was just after midnight when Sam caught a glimpse of Izzy through the crowd at the edge of the dance floor. She had her back to him and he was unable to see who she was with, and for a few seconds he hesitated at the bar, unsure whether he actually wanted to meet this new man of hers. Having felt uncharacteristically edgy all evening he didn't altogether trust himself not to say something he shouldn't.

But Izzy, at that moment turning and spotting him, smiled and waved and made her way over. Looking dazzling in an iridescent petrol-blue dress he hadn't seen before and with her hair piled up in a glossy, disorganised topknot, she gave him a quick kiss.

'Sam, I love this place! I've just bumped into Robbie Williams . . . !'

'As long as you didn't sing to him,' replied Sam evenly. If it meant furthering her career, Izzy wouldn't think twice about pulling such a stunt. Glancing over her shoulder, he said, 'So where's Mr Universe?'

'Who?'

'The white-shoed wonder. You didn't bring him along, or has he collapsed under the weight of his jewellery?'

Izzy smiled and leaned against the bar. 'Ah, maybe he's here. Maybe I'm just playing it cool like they tell you to in all the magazines.'

'You mean he isn't here,' said Sam with some relief. 'Come on, I'll buy you a drink.'

'I don't want a drink.' She shook her head at the approaching barman, paused for a second, then said slowly, 'I want to dance. With you.'

It was like dancing with a cyberman. 'I'm sorry,' said

Sam in her ear. 'I can't do this. I just don't dance with my customers.'

'I can see why,' Izzy replied, disappointed by the temporary setback. She was doing her best, the slow, sensual music was – God knows – doing *its* best, but Sam remained as unrelaxed as it was possible for a cyberman to be. 'And I'm not even a real customer,' she chided, 'so I shouldn't count.'

'I know, I know. But people are watching.' Sam wondered if Izzy had any idea how uncomfortable she was making him feel. Furthermore, how was it possible that she was able to dance with such apparent decorum – their bodies were barely touching, for heaven's sake – while at the same time managing to give him the distinct impression that this was more of a seduction than a dance?

'Your reputation will be in tatters,' she murmured, moving fractionally closer so that he could breathe in her scent. 'You know what women assume about men who can't dance.'

'I can dance,' replied Sam through gritted teeth. 'I just can't do it here.'

'Oh.' Izzy smiled. 'So, where exactly *can* you do it?'

'What?'

'Go on, prove it.'

Something was definitely going on. There was a deceptive innocence about her eyes, yet at the same time she looked as if she was bursting with the most marvellous secret. As the music ended, Sam reached for her hand and led her off the dance floor, resolutely ignoring the looks of intrigue he was receiving from regular customers.

When they reached his office on the first floor he

steered Izzy inside and closed the door firmly behind him.

'Right. What's this all about?'

'Alfieee,' sang Izzy under her breath. But, encouraged by the fact that he still hadn't let go of her arm, she said, 'I just want to know if you really can dance.'

'Very funny.'

'Gosh, Sam.' She fluttered long eyelashes. 'You're awfully attractive when you're angry.'

'Izzy, the club is packed, Ewan McGregor will be arriving shortly and the Press are milling around outside like meerkats on heat. I have better things to *do* than stand here and—'

'Why don't you shut up,' said Izzy fondly, 'and give me a kiss?'

Chapter 16

Two minutes later she took an unsteady step backwards and slowly exhaled.

'Gosh, Izzy. You're awfully attractive when you're ruffled,' mimicked Sam.

She shook her head, putting up a hand to smooth her hair. 'I didn't expect you to . . . well, do that.'

'You asked.' He shrugged, a faint smile tugging at his lips. 'You got.'

'Oh I got, all right.' Izzy wondered whether a repeat performance might be on the cards. 'I'm just surprised.'

'Because you wanted to shock me and you didn't? Really, Izzy, I'm not that naïve . . . and you aren't that subtle, if you don't mind me saying so, although I still don't understand why you should have changed your mind about me. A couple of weeks ago,' he reminded her pointedly, 'you didn't think I was such a great idea.'

Having planned on being the seducer, Izzy was now caught on the hop. She certainly hadn't expected Sam to be this masterful, so totally in control. 'A couple of weeks ago,' she murmured, colouring slightly at the lie she was about to tell, 'you were still living in Gina's house. I didn't think it would be kind to her, if anything should . . . happen . . . between us. She's feeling lonely enough as it is.'

'Really,' drawled Sam. 'How incredibly thoughtful of you.'

Izzy shrugged and maintained a modest silence.

'And there I was,' he continued softly, 'thinking it might have had something to do with the fact that Gina had actually asked you not to get involved with me while we were both living under her roof.'

She burst out laughing. 'You cheat! What have you been doing, crossing off the days on the calendar and laying bets with yourself on how long it would be before I hurled myself shamelessly into your arms like the brazen hussy I am?'

'Laying bets with my entire staff, actually.' He managed to keep a straight face, but Izzy's ability to laugh at herself was one of the things he found most irresistible about her. Far too many women, desperate to make a good impression, lost their sense of humour completely whenever they themselves were the butt of the joke.

Izzy, however, was still smiling, quite unabashed. 'And did you win?'

As he drew her towards him once more, breathing in the scent of Diorella and feeling her body quiver helplessly beneath his touch, Sam recognised that her state of arousal was equal to his own. 'I think,' he murmured in her ear, 'I'm just about to find out.'

The shrill of the phone on his desk moments later provided a rude interruption. Izzy, who was practically sitting on it at the time, jumped a mile.

'That'll be Wendy, ringing from the front desk to let me know that Ewan McGregor's arrived,' said Sam with some reluctance.

Izzy pulled a face. 'Tell him he's just lost himself a fan.'

But when Sam picked up the receiver and began to listen, she knew at once that something was wrong. 'Tell her I'm not here,' he said tersely, and Izzy's heart sank. Then, eventually, he snapped, 'OK, OK, I'm coming down,' and slammed down the phone.

'Shit,' said Sam with feeling.

'Seconded,' she murmured, bracing herself for the worst. 'Who is it?'

Glancing at his watch, then back at Izzy's disappointed face, he heaved a sigh and said, 'Her name's Vivienne Bresnick; I met her just over a year ago in New York and we had one of those on-off relationships . . . it was doomed to failure from the start, but Vivienne is one of those women who are hard to shake off. She wouldn't give up. She wasn't the reason I left New York,' he said evenly, 'but she was certainly an added incentive.'

'So, you aren't madly in love with her?' Izzy brightened at the thought that all was not lost.

'I am not,' he replied, his tone firm and a glimmer of amusement lifting the corners of his mouth. 'But she's turned up here in the middle of the night and she isn't likely to leave quietly on the next flight back to the States.' Running an affectionate finger along the curve of her cheek, he added with a regretful smile, 'I'm sorry about this.'

Talk about *coitus interruptus*, thought Izzy. Apart from anything else, she had shaved her legs for nothing. 'Not half as sorry,' she said ruefully, 'as I am.'

Having laid a private bet with herself that Vivienne

Bresnick would be tall, tanned and dangerously blonde, Izzy would have recognised her immediately, even if she hadn't been surrounded by suitcases – matching Louis Vuitton suitcases at that.

'Sam!' exclaimed Vivienne, tossing back her practically waist-length hair and flying into his arms the moment he reached the bottom of the staircase. 'I know I should have phoned, but I wanted to be a surprise!'

'There but for the grace of Vivienne go I,' muttered Izzy under her breath as she slipped, unnoticed, along the dimly lit oak-panelled hallway and out of the club. Maybe she'd stop off at the Chinese on the way home and pick up pork su mai and prawns with pineapple as a treat for Katerina.

But when she let herself into the house forty minutes later, her daughter wasn't there.

How was it possible to be this happy? wondered Katerina, still unable to believe that such a state – and such an all-engulfing state of *rightness* – could truly exist. As they turned into the road which would lead them back to Kingsley Grove, however, some of the pleasure began to dissipate. She leaned closer into the curve of Andrew's arm around her waist, praying that the evening could stretch on into infinity . . .

'I wish there could be more,' said Andrew, seemingly able to read her thoughts.

In reply, Katerina squeezed his arm. 'I don't care, this is enough. At least we have each other.'

'But I *want* more.' Gazing moodily at the rooftops of the opulent Georgian terrace silhouetted against an orange-tinted sky, he considered the irony of so many houses and nowhere to go – nowhere to spend an entire night with Kat.

Now, drawing her slowly into the shadows and leaning back against a high stone wall, he kissed her and said, 'It's not fair on you.' Then, as she opened her mouth to protest, he covered it with his fingers. 'It isn't fair on either of us, but particularly you. This isn't how a beautiful seventeen-year-old girl should be spending her evenings.'

'You don't know what my evenings used to be like. All I ever did was study. You wouldn't believe how *important* I thought it was! I just didn't realise there were other things in life that could be more important . . .'

'And you don't realise how important you are to me,' murmured Andrew, 'but this still isn't what you deserve. I'm too old for you, I'm going through a divorce and I'm trapped in a hopeless relationship with a woman who—'

'But that isn't your fault,' Katerina interrupted, before he could mention the baby. She hated to even think of it; in her fantasies Marcy broke down in tears, confessed that Andrew was not, after all, the father, and promptly emigrated to New Zealand.

'What difference does it make?' Andrew frowned into the darkness. 'I'm screwed, financially. All I want to do is whisk you away to an hotel and at the moment I can't even afford to do that.'

Katerina was privately relieved. Despite everything she felt for Andrew, her conscience still troubled her; as long as they weren't sleeping together, she was able to tell herself that she wasn't doing anything *too* terribly wrong.

And although she knew she was being silly, she was

also afraid of taking that final step. Being with Andrew . . . kissing him, spending hours in his arms and acknowledging their mutual desire . . . was one thing, but actually *doing* it was quite another, and an altogether more alarming prospect. She wouldn't know what to do. She could get it all embarrassingly wrong and Andrew might lose interest in her. The idea was too terrifying even to contemplate.

'It doesn't matter,' she repeated, smoothing Andrew's hair away from his forehead and watching his frown lines magically disappear. If only she could solve their other problems as easily.

'I love you,' said Andrew, and she shivered. How could those small words make her *shiver* like this?

'I know,' she said simply, moving back into his arms and resolutely refusing to think of Gina, Marcy . . . the unborn child . . . 'I love you, too.'

'But I *love* you,' repeated Vivienne, frustrated beyond belief by Sam's uncompromising attitude. Flinging herself down on to the sofa and tossing back her hair, she deliberately didn't bother to adjust the rising hem of her skirt. She was wearing a pale grey jersey top which emphasised the unEnglishness of her tan; only faint shadows beneath her spectacular eyes betrayed the fact that she had gone far too long without sleep. 'And there's no need to look at your watch, either,' she said in despairing tones. 'Jeez, Sam, you sure know how to make a girl feel welcome.'

It was five o'clock in the morning and he had been wondering whether Izzy was asleep. If Vivienne hadn't turned up with her usual miraculous sense of timing . . .

'You should have let me know you were coming over.' Not wanting to sit down, he was pacing the sitting room, drinking black coffee and watching the sun rise over the park.

'You would only have gotten crazy.' Vivienne pouted, wriggling still further down in her seat, and Sam realised how quickly he had readjusted to the English accent; her lazily elongated vowels sounded incredibly put-on. In addition, she had always adored a bit of drama.

'I would have told you that it was a wasted journey.' A full-scale row wasn't what he needed right now; he had a business meeting at nine o'clock and a couple of hours' sleep beforehand would have helped.

'Oh, Sam!' Kicking off her shoes, she drew her feet up beneath her. 'So, what are you going to do, kick me out on to the streets?'

That was really likely. The reason Vivienne found it so hard to believe he was no longer interested in her wasn't a million miles removed from her bank balance. The only daughter of Gerald Bresnick, a genuine Texan oil baron, she could in all probability – if she really wanted to – rent every suite in the Savoy and have change left over for the doorman.

'I'm going to bed,' said Sam quietly. He didn't have time for arguments. 'You can sleep in the spare room, if you're staying.'

'That takes me back,' mused Vivienne, her tone playful. 'You're beginning to sound like my ex-husband.'

Sam, moving towards the door, didn't reply.

'And there I was,' she continued softly, 'thinking that you might be my next husband.'

He turned back to face her. 'Vivienne, it's over. You really shouldn't have come here.'

'Maybe I shouldn't.' She shrugged, apparently unperturbed, then gave him a slow, languorous smile. 'But, on the other hand, maybe I should. My mom always taught me that if a man was worth chasing, he was worth chasing all around the world, so flying over from the States wasn't even that far to come. Besides,' she added with a careless gesture, 'what the hell did I have to lose?'

For the second time, Sam kept his mouth very firmly shut. A mental image of Izzy flashed through his mind . . . notoriously impatient, unreliable, why-stop-at-one-man-when-you-can-have-two Izzy Van Asch, with whom he would so much rather have spent the night. Vivienne might not have had anything to lose, he thought drily, but if her intention had been to come over here and put paid to any romantic attachments he might be in danger of forming, she had certainly won the first round, hands down.

Chapter 17

It was so hard, struggling to appear cheerful when all you wanted to do was crawl into bed and let the rest of the world carry on without you. And it was harder still, Gina decided sourly, when she had to put up with Izzy indulging in one of her favourite pastimes – getting ready to go out.

Now, as Izzy burst into the sitting room for the third time in fifteen minutes and did an extravagant twirl to show off her red velvet dress – with the red shoes, this time – Gina gave up trying.

'Well?' said Izzy, glossy-mouthed and seeking approval. 'Which looks better, red or black? And are the stockings too much . . .?'

The stockings had red hearts stencilled up the back of them. Izzy, who was booked to sing at a charity ball in Henley, looked like a saloon girl. She also looked, thought Gina, exactly like . . . Izzy.

Irritation, which had been welling up, now spilled over 'Since you ask,' she retorted, 'they're perfectly hideous. But I'm sure you'll wear them anyway.'

Izzy halted in mid-twirl. 'What?'

'You wanted my opinion, I gave it to you.' It was surprisingly satisfying, watching the expression on Izzy's face change and the wide smile fall away. Why did she always have to be so bloody cheerful anyway? 'Although I don't know why you bother, because you never take a blind bit of notice of anything I say,' Gina continued, inwardly amazed at her own daring but at the same time almost exhilarated by it. 'You simply carry on regardless, thinking everything's great and not even stopping to wonder what other people might think of *you*.'

Accustomed as she was to dealing with the occasional heckler when she was working, Izzy was so stunned by this full-frontal attack on her personality that for a moment she couldn't even speak.

'I see,' she said finally, wondering whether Gina might be in the throes of some kind of nervous breakdown. Apart from hogging the bathroom for an hour earlier she couldn't imagine what might have annoyed her enough to trigger such an outburst. 'And what exactly *do* other people think of me?'

'I don't know,' said Gina, her expression truculent. The adrenalin-rush was ebbing away; she had wanted to hurt Izzy and she'd succeeded. Now she felt slightly ashamed of herself.

'No, go on. Tell me.' Izzy's eyes were beginning to glitter. 'I'm interested.'

'You're nearly forty,' Gina said defensively. 'You shouldn't be wearing stuff like that.'

'And?'

Gina shifted uncomfortably in her chair. 'OK. If you must know, I find it embarrassing when my friends ask me what you do for a living and I have to tell them you're a barmaid.'

There, she'd said it. And it was true; apart from anything else, Izzy was too *old* to be a barmaid.

'I see,' said Izzy again. Shock was giving way to anger

now; how *dare* Gina look down her nose at the way she earned enough to pay their rent? Tilting her head to one side, she enquired softly, 'And are you embarrassed when they ask you what you do for a living?'

Bitch, thought Gina, turning red. Pushing back her hair with shaking fingers and beginning to feel outmanoeuvred, she said, 'At least I'm not reduced to working in a bar.'

'Of course you aren't. You're lucky,' Izzy retaliated. Then, out of sheer pride, she added, 'And that isn't my *career*, anyway. I'm a singer.'

'I know you're a singer. Everybody knows you're a *singer*,' blurted out Gina, without even thinking this time. 'You tell the whole bloody world about it and if you really want to know, that's what makes it all so laughable . . . As far as I can gather you've spent your entire life thinking that one day you'll be discovered and turned into some kind of *star* and you don't even realise that there are hundreds of thousands of other people out there who can sing just as well as you. Being able to sing is . . . nothing!'

All her frustration was spilling out now. The frustration of being unloved and always alone while the rest of the world had fun. The frustration of finally falling asleep at one o'clock in the morning, only to be woken again at two by Izzy's key in the front door and the sound of her footsteps on the stairs. The frustration of answering the phone for the past two and a half months and endlessly having to say, 'It's for you . . .'

'Well, thanks,' said Izzy finally. 'So, tell me, how does it feel to be perfect?'

* * *

Wearing her stencilled stockings with defiance, Izzy sang her heart out during her hour-long set at the Davenham Ball, although whether anyone truly appreciated it was another matter. Spirits were sky high and the general noise level incredible. She could have sung hymns and they would have carried on shrieking and dancing regardless.

It was also blisteringly hot and, by the time she left the stage to patchy applause, both her stockings and her pinned-up hair were beginning to droop.

But it wasn't until she saw Sam, waiting for her at the side of the stage, that she realised how thoroughly miserable she really was.

'Oh, hell, I never cry,' she mumbled against his chest, reluctant to move away because then he would see the mascara stains on his clean white shirt. 'I can't think what you're doing here, but I'm awfully glad to see you . . . it's been the most horrible night . . .'

Bread rolls, as is apparently their wont at such functions, were hurtling through the air. Sliding his arm around her waist, Sam guided Izzy through the maze of bottle-strewn tables and gyrating dancers and led her outside.

'I truly never cry,' she repeated in a subdued voice when they at last sat down on a stone bench. Blowing her nose in the handkerchief he'd passed to her, she shook her head and shivered. 'But honestly you wouldn't believe the go Gina had at me this evening . . . and now we'll have to move out and it's such rotten timing, what with Kat's A levels coming up . . .'

'Gina rang me. She told me what happened and asked me to come and find you.'

'What for?' Izzy sniffed. 'Did she think up another dozen or so reasons why I should be ashamed of myself?'

'She's sorry,' he told her firmly. 'She wants you to know that she didn't mean any of it, but she was afraid that if she came here herself you'd refuse to listen to her.'

'She was right.'

'And she was also afraid,' he went on, 'that you wouldn't go back to the house tonight.'

'You mean she was worried in case I crept in, packed my things and made off with her precious Royal Doulton dinner service,' Izzy retaliated, lifting her chin in defiance. 'According to Gina, I'm the laughing stock of London and the Home Counties, and about as socially acceptable as a bed bug.'

'Look, she really is sorry,' said Sam, relieved to see that the tears had stopped. 'And if you were to give her a hard time, nobody would blame you. But it isn't you she's really getting at . . . it's herself.'

'Really?' It was gratifying to know that Gina was consumed with guilt, but Izzy wasn't going to give up that easily. 'She certainly had me fooled.'

'And you aren't the kind of person to hold a grudge,' Sam continued, his voice low and encouraging. 'It isn't your style.'

'Nobody's ever spoken to me like that before,' she countered, 'so how would anyone know what my style is? She *hurt* me, Sam.'

'I know, I know, but she envies you.'

Izzy pulled a face. 'And there I was, just beginning to believe you. Now you've really blown it.'

'You're happy, she's not,' he said simply.

'I'm not happy. I'm a barmaid.'

He gave her a hug. 'You're a singer.'

'But an unsuccessful one, without any future.' Drawing away from him, she shook her head and looked miserable. 'That was what *really* hurt, Sam. Gina was right about that.'

For the first time, Katerina was seriously tempted to tell her mother about Andrew. The way everyone took care of Gina, sheltering her from real life and making endless allowances for her, made her sick. Sharing her wonderful secret with Izzy would make it all that much more bearable.

And although she hadn't planned on falling in love with Andrew Lawrence, in a peculiarly satisfying way it evened the score, which would surely cheer Izzy up . . .

Some sixth sense, however, prevented her from saying the words. Perching on the edge of Izzy's bed, Katerina handed her a mug of coffee instead and said, 'Look, you mustn't even *think* about my exams. She's a complete bitch and I don't care where we live or how soon we move.'

Considering that it was eight-thirty in the morning, Izzy was astonishingly alert. Rumpling her daughter's glossy hair, she grinned. 'We aren't going to move. Gina's apologised and it's all behind us now.'

Katerina pulled a face. 'I can't imagine Gina apologising for anything. What was it like?'

'Oh, very *Little Women*. She cried a bit, grovelled a bit, lied a bit . . . and I was terribly understanding; wounded and subdued, but prepared to forgive her because I'm such a wonderful human being.'

'Yuk. Sounds horrible.'

'It wasn't horrible.' Izzy assumed a saintly expression. 'It was quite spiritually uplifting, as a matter of fact. From now on, I'm sure we're all going to get along wonderfully.'

'Why?' Katerina shot her a suspicious look.

'Because forgiveness is a virtue, my darling.' Then Izzy winked and drained her coffee cup with a flourish. 'And because to make up for being such an old bitch, the old bitch has waived this month's rent!'

Chapter 18

Doug Steadman was on the phone when Izzy pushed open the door and waded through the piles of junk in his office. Other theatrical agents, she reminded herself with amusement, had plush suites, glittering windows and rows of filing cabinets lined up, military style, against the walls. They had computers, air-conditioning and alarmingly efficient staff capable of working both.

Only Doug, however, could operate out of such Dickensian chaos and manage – somehow – to make a living out of it.

He gave her an abstracted wave, straining the seams of his shirt as he did so, and said, 'Yeah, fine, I'll tell him when he next calls.' The moment he replaced the receiver, it rang again. Izzy, who was familiar with this pattern of events, removed a couple of bulging box files from the only other chair in the office and sat down.

Ten minutes later, Doug finally left the receiver off the hook, took a noisy slurp of Diet Coke from the can teetering on the edge of his desk and mopped his face with a massive handkerchief. Then he grinned and said, 'Hi.'

'I should have worn my dark glasses,' Izzy chided. 'Then you'd have thought I was Cher and unplugged the phone straight away.'

'I would have told you to come back this afternoon.'

He roared with laughter at the idea. 'Her appointment isn't until three-thirty.'

'Dream on, Doug.'

He shrugged, still enjoying his own joke. 'We all have our little fantasies . . . anyway, how did it go last night? Some twenty-first birthday bash in Wimbledon, wasn't it?'

His memory was about as efficient as his filing system. Much as she adored her agent, Izzy often wondered whether her once-in-a-lifetime big break might not have come and gone without her even hearing about it because Doug, overworked and under pressure, had allowed it to slip his mind.

'Davenham Hall,' she reminded him, slipping out of her jacket and pushing up the sleeves of her white shirt. The sun was beating through the dusty windows but if she risked opening them a single draught of air might send five million pieces of paper swirling and Doug's fragile filing system would be destroyed for ever. 'In Henley,' she added as she settled back into her chair. A germ of an idea had begun to unfold and in order to press her point further she gave him a look of gentle reproach.

'Whatever,' said Doug with an airy, unrepentant gesture. Then, glancing sideways at the disconnected phone, he remembered that time was money. Mopping his face once more, he said, 'So, what brings you here, my darling? Not that it isn't always a treat to see you, but . . .'

'A year or so ago you got me a fortnight at an hotel in Berkshire,' said Izzy, leaning forward and propping her elbows on his desk. 'Allerton Towers, I think it was called. And I shared the bill with another client of yours, a blond chap in his twenties who sang and played a guitar. He isn't with you now – he told me he was going back to teaching. Doug, can you remember his name?'

He frowned, thought hard for several seconds, then shook his head. 'Can't say I do, sweetie. Can you give me any more clues?'

Izzy hadn't seriously expected him to remember. Doug's memory banks were notoriously selective; when he no longer needed to remember something, he didn't. But by trekking into his Soho office she had hoped to bully him into ploughing through a few box files in search of an answer.

'No,' she said helplessly, 'but I really need to contact him. His name's Billy or Bobby . . . something like that . . . and he was living in Willesden at the time. You must have some kind of Cardex,' she went on. 'If you could give me a list of all your ex-clients I'm sure I'd recognise his name as soon as I saw it.'

She needed to find that name – it was why she had come here, after all – but the fact that Doug was shifting uncomfortably in his seat – if he possessed such a list he clearly had no idea where to lay his hands on it – seemed at this moment to be almost propitious.

'You don't have a list,' she declared flatly.

'I do, I do,' Doug protested. 'Somewhere . . .'

'You need a personal organiser.'

He frowned. 'You mean a Filofax? Izzy, spare me that!'

'I mean the walking-talking-filing-hardworking-*organising* kind of personal organiser,' announced Izzy triumphantly. 'And I know just the person for the job.'

By this time Doug was looking plainly horrified. '*You?*'

'Don't be silly,' she replied with tolerant amusement. 'I said organised, didn't I?'

The last thing in the world Gina wanted to do was work for Douglas Steadman, but after the events of the last couple of days she didn't have the courage to say no. She had behaved abominably and this was her penance, she told herself as she adjusted the shoulders of her neat navy-blue suit and checked the line of the skirt in her wardrobe mirror. Besides, it might not be too awful; all she had to do, according to Izzy, was pull a filing system into some sort of order, answer the telephone and set up appointments. She would be a clerk-cum-receptionist and at least it meant that while she was sitting at her desk she would be meeting new people and taking the first steps towards building a new life for herself . . .

Izzy was lying full-length across the sofa when Gina returned home less than two hours later. Stuffing the envelope upon which she had been scribbling into her shirt pocket, she sat up and said bleakly, 'You've walked out.'

'That place is a pigsty,' Gina retaliated, standing her ground and daring her to deny it. 'Why didn't you tell me?'

'You wouldn't have taken the job. And now you're giving up, simply because it isn't *Homes and Gardens* enough for you.' Then, with a trace of irritation, she added, 'And what on earth are you planning to do with that?'

Having dumped her bag on a chair, Gina was now painstakingly removing the price sticker from a large aerosol spray of anti-perspirant for men.

'Who says I'm giving up?' she countered, dropping the aerosol back into her bag and moving towards the door. 'I came home to change into something more suitable. That place needs a damn good clean.'

'With deodorant?' said Izzy faintly, and for the first time in weeks Gina broke into a real smile.

'That's for Douglas Steadman,' she replied, her tone brisk. 'You told me he was a nice man, and he is. But Izzy, somebody has to *do* something about him. He *smells*.'

Doug Steadman might not have known what had hit him – or his poor office – in the days that followed, but for Gina they were some of the most satisfying of her life. Much to her own amazement she was really enjoying herself and the sheer pleasure of transforming unkempt, dusty chaos into pristine order brought a glow to her cheeks that had been absent for months. She was achieving something, doing something worthwhile . . . and the fact that the task was such an enormous one only made tackling it that much more fun.

With the files stacked in tea chests and Doug – together with his precious phone – relegated to the broad corridor outside the office, Gina scrubbed and scraped at every last disgusting corner, threw out the ancient tattered rugs on the floor, polished the floorboards, cleaned the windows until they glittered and washed down the nicotine-stained walls. Then, just as he breathed a sigh of relief – it was over; he could move back in – she reappeared with three enormous cans of vinyl emulsion and proceeded to paint everything white.

Apart from the ceiling, which she had decided should be primrose yellow.

'My God,' Izzy gasped, when she saw it for the first time a week later. 'Where's the plaque?'

'What plaque?' said Gina, looking worried. If she'd thrown away some irreplaceable award . . .

'The one Princess Anne's going to unveil!' Izzy stuck her arm through Doug's – so much nicer to be near, nowadays – and gazed around the office, whistling approval. Shamed into action by Gina's untiring efforts, Doug had allowed himself to be trundled down to John Lewis and had miraculously forked out for yellow vertical blinds, brass spotlights and a charcoal-grey desk whose price had left him gasping but which Gina assured him was perfect. Even the theatrical posters were now neatly framed, Izzy noted, instead of being taped up, yellowing and curly-edged, on the walls.

And the office wasn't the only thing to have changed, she thought, pleased with herself for having engineered the situation so brilliantly. The transformation of Gina, if anything, was even more startling; whoever could have imagined that she would enjoy getting so dirty, and that she could *smile* like that . . .?

'It's nice, isn't it?' Gina was saying now, her eyes alight with pride and her hair still paint-streaked. 'It looks like a real office. Of course the filing system still needs to be organised, but if I start on it right away I should be able to get it sorted out by Friday.'

The files were still dumped in their tea chests, but the cabinets, dust free and gleaming, stood empty and at the ready. Having listened to Doug and got the gist of what would be necessary, she had already decided how the system should be run. And at least they were agreed on one thing: no computer. Indexes and cross-referencing she could handle, but programs and floppy discs were way out of both their leagues.

'It's great, really great,' said Izzy, gazing longingly at the tea chests. 'And as soon as this lot's organised you'll be able to tell me the name of that chap who played the guitar at Allerton Towers.'

Gina looked surprised. 'Allerton Towers? Andrew and I went there quite regularly last year . . . we had friends in Berkshire.' She frowned for a moment, concentrating hard, then her face cleared. 'You aren't by any chance talking about Benny Dunaway, are you?'

Chapter 19

It was egg-and-chicken time, Izzy decided a couple of days later. Gina was out at work, Kat was at school and she had the sun-drenched patio all to herself. In three hours' time she would be seeing Benny – still living in Willesden and now working as a maths teacher at a local comprehensive – and he would be able to tell her which came first, but overcome with shame at her own ignorance she was desperate to have something . . . anything . . . to show him, to prove that she was serious.

And all she had so far, she thought, were untidy, scribbled-on scraps of paper which looked more than anything else like a harassed housewife's shopping lists.

Gloomily surveying them now, she realised that if he were to mark her out of ten she'd be lucky to get one and a half. These were the motley sum of her ideas so far and they looked – even to her own eyes, let alone those of a mathematician – pathetic.

Deciding that she could at least make them *look* more impressive – Presentation is Important, as her old English teacher had been so fond of chanting, particularly when Izzy's work had been under scrutiny – she shuffled the scraps of paper together and jumped to her feet. Katerina, to whom perfect presentation came naturally, possessed A4 refill pads, rulers, felt-tipped pens and highlighters galore . . .

* * *

Not wanting to disrupt any work in progress, Izzy first helped herself to a selection of coloured pens, a ruler and a startlingly pink highlighter, then sifted carefully through the A4 pads in search of a decent-sized batch of unused paper. Most of the papers were filled with incomprehensible essays, neatly executed diagrams and equations. My clever daughter, she thought with renewed pride, turning over another page and catching a loose sheet of folded, unlined paper as it slid out into her lap.

Idly unfolding it, Izzy began to read.

Ten minutes later, having read the contents of the page three more times and given them a great deal of thought, she rose slowly to her feet, folded the single sheet of paper into quarters and slipped it into the pocket of her jeans.

'Izzy, it's great to see you!' Benny Dunaway, standing in the doorway of his Victorian terraced house, opened his arms wide and gave her a big kiss. Izzy, briefly ashamed of the fact that she hadn't even been able to remember the name of this genuinely nice man, hugged him in return and allowed him to lead her inside.

'That'll give the neighbours something to gossip about,' he told her cheerfully. 'Now that I'm a staid schoolmaster I don't get much opportunity to kiss gorgeous women . . . apart from my wife, of course,' he added with an unrepentant grin. 'Now, come into the kitchen and tell me what you've been up to. What would you like, tea, coffee or a beer? No, sit in this chair, that one's got a wonky leg . . .'

It was all very well for those who didn't mind taking

the risks, he explained over coffee, but when the baby had come along – ten months ago, at eight and a half pounds and with a shock of white-blonde hair that made her look like a dandelion puff – he had been forced to face up to his responsibilities. Teaching might not be as much fun as singing, but he was good at it, it paid the mortgage and the family wouldn't starve. Every now and again he was able to take his guitar down to the local pub and let off a little gentle steam, and in his spare time he still indulged in the odd bit of song-writing . . .

'And this, of course, is where you come in,' he said, refilling her coffee cup before settling back down in his chair and lighting a cigarette. 'So, come on, tell me exactly what kind of help it is you need.'

'You must think I have a terrible nerve,' said Izzy, 'contacting you out of the blue. I'm still singing but I'm not . . . getting anywhere. And I'm not rich,' she added with a brief smile. 'Benny, if I'm ever going to achieve anything, I have to learn how to *write* songs, and I haven't the least idea how to go about it. Is it something anyone can do? Which comes first, the melody or the lyrics? And is it possible to teach a complete nincompoop,' she concluded shamefacedly, 'who's totally . . . musically . . . illiterate?'

Benny threw back his head and roared with laughter. 'You aren't serious . . . you really can't read music?'

'Can't read it, can't write it, can't play any musical instruments,' confessed Izzy. 'I know, I'm nothing but a fraud with a great memory. And if there's any way you think you *can* teach me, I'd better warn you now that I wouldn't even be able to pay you because I'm so broke.' She paused, then gave him a hopeful, beguiling smile.

'But I could promise you years of free babysitting . . .'

Great teacher that he was, Benny enjoyed nothing more than a real, honest-to-goodness challenge. Izzy had a great voice and more enthusiasm than an entire classful of fifth formers . . . just sitting opposite him now she positively radiated energy and eagerness to learn.

'I can do songs in my head,' she continued anxiously, terribly afraid that he was on the verge of turning her down. 'I make them up all the time, but I just can't write them down . . . I even sang into a cassette recorder once, but it sounded so silly afterwards . . . I'm sure I *could* do it properly, though, if only I could get the songs *out* . . .'

'In that case, maybe we'd better give it a go. How could I ever forgive myself, after all,' he added drily as Izzy let out a shriek of delight, 'if I missed out on the opportunity of teaching the songwriter of the century?'

'Just call me McCartney.' Izzy, tossing back her tangled curls, gave him her breeziest smile.

'My pleasure,' said Benny, imitating the gesture and running his fingers through his thinning, short blond hair. 'Just call me Mr Twenty Per Cent of the Profits. What *is* twenty per cent of eighty-seven million pounds?'

'You're the maths teacher, I'm the genius songwriter,' Izzy scolded. '*You* work it out.'

If Vivienne Bresnick wasn't embarrassed to open the front door wearing only a small towel, Izzy wasn't going to let it put her off her stride either.

'Hi,' she said, removing her sunglasses and envying the girl her tan. 'Lucky I'm not the man who's come to read the meter.'

'Lucky for who?' countered Vivienne, appraising Izzy in turn. 'You might have been gorgeous.' Then she paused and burst out laughing. 'No offence intended. What I meant was, you might have been a gorgeous man, whereas in fact you're Izzy Van Asch. Am I right?'

'Brilliant.' Izzy was impressed, both by the accuracy of the guess and the fact that the girl appeared to have a sense of humour, which was something she hadn't expected. 'I know who you are too.'

'Great, so now we don't need to bother with all those boring introductions. Nice to meet you, anyway,' said Vivienne, stepping back and waving Izzy into the apartment. 'Sam isn't here, he had to go to some meeting, but he should be back soon. Can I get you a drink while you're waiting?'

'Just coffee, thanks.' Izzy's admiration increased further when she saw the state of the sitting room. Evidence of female occupation – in the form of stray shoes, a discarded négligé, scattered glossy magazines and a variety of earrings and cosmetics littering the mantelpiece beneath the mirror – abounded. The girl was untidy, and defiantly so. It must, she thought with the kind of comradely cheerfulness which could only come from a fellow sufferer, be driving Sam wild.

'I know, I know.' Vivienne, observing the look on her face, gave an unrepentant smile. 'The place is kind of a mess. I don't understand how it happens . . .'

'It's the same with me,' Izzy told her reassuringly. 'My daughter says I have a primaeval need to mark out my territory.' Then, in case Vivienne thought it was some kind of sly dig, said, 'So, how did you know I was me?'

The kettle was taking its time. Picking up the ivory satin négligé and pulling it on, Vivienne allowed the towel to slide to the floor and stepped away from it. Then, tilting her head to one side and considering Izzy for a thoughtful second, she replied, 'Sam told me. An up-front lady with crazy hair, he said . . . or words to that effect. You have a neat daughter, no money and a pretty good singing voice, right?'

'Right,' said Izzy with a grin. It seemed a fair enough resumé, after all. 'Except that I'd have preferred "great" for the voice. And my daughter,' she added as an afterthought, 'isn't just neat. She's brilliant.'

'I can't sing for toffee,' said Vivienne comfortably. 'Go on, it's your turn now. What did Sam say about me?'

'Rich. Blonde. And rich.' Izzy burst out laughing. Was this really her rival in love? 'I can't think what's wrong with him . . . I'd marry you tomorrow!'

Having finally remembered to make the coffee, Vivienne handed her one of the cups and dropped gracefully on to the sofa. 'Something he didn't tell me . . . excuse me if this is a rude question . . . were you and he having a fling when I turned up? Did I put a kind of spoke in the old wheel?'

'No,' Izzy replied truthfully, to the first part of the question.

Vivienne nodded. 'Well, good. That makes things less complicated, I guess.' Then she shrugged and grinned. 'It's just that something else Sam didn't mention was how pretty you are.'

A compliment for a compliment, thought Izzy. She sipped her coffee and said slowly, 'Well, I saw you on the night you turned up at The Steps. And I can't tell you how much I admired your . . . luggage.'

You couldn't help warming to the kind of girl, Izzy decided fifteen minutes later, who, when she heard Sam's key turning in the front door, appeared to notice for the first time the damp towel crumpled in a heap in the centre of the carpet and who, instead of picking it up, kicked it vaguely in the direction of the coffee table. Much to her own surprise she found herself liking Vivienne more and more. She was also mightily intrigued to see the two of them together. Whatever Sam might have said that night at The Steps, Izzy found it hard to believe that he could be sharing his apartment with Vivienne and not sleeping with her.

'Look, darling . . . Izzy's here,' announced Vivienne delightedly, and Izzy had to force herself not to fluff up her hair because the last time she'd seen him she'd been looking diabolical and she didn't want him to think she was turning into a frump. Quite suddenly, next to Vivienne, she felt small, dark and decidedly insignificant. How, after all, could jeans and a floppy black sweatshirt compare with ivory satin, miles of deeply tanned leg and a staggering amount of cleavage?

Sam's expression, however, gave absolutely nothing away. The habitual lazy grin, when it appeared a second later, was unchanged. Izzy wondered if he was ever really taken by surprise.

'We've been getting along just fine,' Vivienne continued, her Texan drawl deepening as she stretched like a cat and patted the seat next to her. Then, with a wink in Izzy's direction, she added, 'Talking all about you.'

'No, we weren't,' put in Izzy hastily. Beaming at Sam, who hadn't taken up Vivienne's unspoken offer – he was leaning against the window-sill instead – she said, 'As a matter of fact we were talking about someone far more interesting. Me.'

'Far more interesting, of course,' he agreed, attempting to keep a straight face.

'Of course,' she echoed, unperturbed. This was, after all, why she had come here. 'I was just telling Vivienne, I'm going to write songs. This brilliant friend of mine is going to help me . . . before you know it we'll be out-Garfunkeling Simon and Garfunkel . . .'

'The last time Izzy got this excited about something,' Sam informed Vivienne drily, 'it was peanut-butter ice-cream.'

'This time I'm serious,' she insisted with pride.

'But you said you can't read music.'

'Ah, but Benny can. I have all the ideas,' Izzy explained, tapping her forehead, 'and he has the know-how. It was what Gina said the other night that made me realise. I had to *do* something . . . and now it's going to happen!'

'And you never thought of doing this before?' enquired Vivienne looking genuinely puzzled.

'I didn't think it was physically possible,' Izzy confessed. 'What with me not being able to play any kind of musical instrument, I suppose I just thought it was one of those things which can't happen, like waking up in the morning and suddenly being able to speak Russian, or looking in the mirror and realizing that your eyes have turned green.'

Vivienne burst out laughing. 'Honey, all you had to do was ask. I would have lent you my tinted contacts.'

Chapter 20

It was certainly an odd situation to find oneself in, Izzy mused as she got herself ready for work that evening. Until this afternoon, Vivienne Bresnick had been nothing more than an untimely intrusion. Now, having met her, she found herself liking the girl immeasurably and almost wishing her and Sam well. They were such a striking couple . . . in many ways so perfectly matched . . . that it was impossible to imagine them not being happy together.

As far as Izzy herself was concerned, she didn't know whether it was sad or funny. And even more frustrating was the fact that she *still* didn't know whether or not Sam and Vivienne were once again sleeping together.

Putting the finishing touches to her mascara, then stepping back and idly wondering how she'd look with long, white-blonde hair and Bahama-blue eyes, Izzy said aloud for the second time in twenty minutes, 'She really is a nice person, you know.'

Gina, who was kneeling on the sitting-room floor sifting through a carton of tattered files, glanced up at Izzy's reflection in the mirror.

'Of course she is,' she replied evenly. 'She's Sam's girlfriend, isn't she? Whyever would he want to waste his time with some brainless bimbo?'

Izzy shrugged. 'Men have no taste; it's a common failing.' She considered holding up Andrew as a case in point, then decided against it. Since starting work at the agency, Gina had seemed so much happier. If the old wounds were beginning to heal, she wasn't going to be the one to reopen them.

'Not Sam,' replied Gina flatly, leaning back on her heels and flexing her aching shoulders. Really, she sometimes wondered whether Doug even knew the meaning of the words 'alphabetical order'. Given this box, a chimpanzee could have produced more organised chaos. 'But aren't you glad that *you* didn't get involved with him?' she continued in cheerful tones. 'You can see now that it would never have worked . . . you aren't Sam's type at all.'

Katerina was working in her room, attempting to concertina a week's homework into one evening and trying to banish all thoughts of Andrew from her mind while she concentrated instead on the less exciting prospect of her forthcoming exams. Love and essays didn't go together – she knew it, but she didn't care – and, although she was shamefully behind with her revision, she couldn't even summon up the energy to panic.

It was almost one o'clock in the morning when she heard Izzy letting herself into the house. Clipping her felt-tipped pen to the top of her writing pad, Katerina wriggled into a sitting position and hoped her mother would arrive bearing prawn crackers.

'Hi, sweetie.' Pushing open the door to her daughter's bedroom, Izzy wondered whether it was possible physically to burst with pride. How could a seventeen-year-old girl – the miraculous product of her own disorganised and undeserving body – be so beautiful, so brilliant . . . and so good?

Katerina, surrounded by books, grinned back at her. Izzy was indeed carrying a haversack-sized bag from the Chinese takeaway. 'How was work?'

'The pits, but what's new?' Collapsing on the bed and heaving an extravagant sigh, Izzy helped herself to a handful of Liquorice Allsorts. She enjoyed their night-time chats, when it seemed that the rest of the world was asleep. 'But I don't care. I know you think I'm doing my usual pie-in-the-sky thing, but I really do have a gut feeling about this song-writing business. And just think, if that took off . . .'

If seventeen years of being her mother's daughter had taught Katerina anything, it was never even to attempt to quash her eternal optimism. They had survived everything, and that in itself was an achievement of which to be proud. Leaning forwards, she gave Izzy an affectionate kiss. 'If anybody can do it, you can.'

'With Benny to help me,' Izzy admitted. 'Sam thinks I'm quite mad; he said it would be like instructing a blind man to paint a masterpiece.'

Katerina nodded; the observation was somewhat apt. 'But even if you can't write music,' she protested, 'you can do the lyrics. Look at Tom Rice . . . he's made an absolute fortune!'

Izzy laughed. 'Tim Rice, darling. But yes, lyrics are important.' Here was the perfect opening, she thought with some relief. 'As a matter of fact, I—'

'Mum, if that pub's so terrible, why don't you leave?' Katerina interrupted. She had been giving the matter some thought recently, and the solution was so obvious she couldn't understand why Izzy hadn't thought of it herself. 'Why don't you ask Sam if you can work at The Steps? The tips would be better, the pay couldn't possibly be any worse and at least it isn't a dive. It's the very opposite of a dive,' she added persuasively, recalling an item in last week's *Daily Mail*. 'And if it's good enough for royalty . . .'

Izzy shifted uncomfortably on the edge of the bed. Picking idly at the remains of the Liquorice Allsorts, she said, 'I've already asked him. He said he didn't have any vacancies.'

On behalf of her mother, Katerina was outraged. 'The pig! So what does that mean, translated into English?'

'He doesn't want me there.' It had bothered Izzy, which was why she hadn't mentioned it at the time, but she wasn't going to let Kat pry into the possible whys and wherefores. In her more optimistic moments she had managed to convince herself that company policy decreed no mixing of business with pleasure. And if it wasn't that, it meant he simply knew her too well, which didn't exactly boost a girl's confidence.

Besides, she had more important matters to discuss with her daughter. 'Kat,' she began. 'I've got something to—'

'The big shit!' Katerina exploded, her brown eyes flashing with indignation. 'Who *does* he think he is?'

'It doesn't matter,' said Izzy, more sharply than she had intended. 'Kat, working in a night-club – even The Steps – isn't my ultimate fantasy. Now stop interrupting, because I'm trying to tell you something.'

'Sorry,' said Katerina, immediately contrite. Folding her arms and leaning back against her plumped pillows, she assumed a listening expression.

'And this is important,' Izzy told her seriously, 'because you know I would never deliberately pry into your personal . . . things.'

If Katerina had been a thermometer, her mercury level would at that moment have plummeted. Quite simply, she froze.

'This morning,' her mother continued, apparently oblivious to the effect her words were having, 'I needed some writing paper and I knew you'd have some, up here.'

'Yes,' replied Katerina in guarded tones. So this was it. Unable – for obvious reasons – to send her letters through the post, Andrew had taken to handing them to her as they parted, so that when she returned to the house she could read them, over and over again, in the privacy of her own room, and know that his feelings for her were genuine.

And whereas every other mother in the world would react with shock and revulsion to the discovery of such letters, she realised with rising panic her own mother was about to behave with typically Izzyish non-conformity. She was going to be *understanding*, and indulge in one of those embarrassing woman-to-woman discussions of hers which no daughter should ever be asked to endure. Besides, she thought as resentment mingled with panic, those letters were addressed to her, and she had taken the utmost care to hide them among the pages of her physics homework, where no sane mother would ever think to look. They were *private*.

'I found this,' Izzy continued, reaching into her bag and pulling out a folded sheet of paper.

'Mum, it's none of your business,' said Katerina, prepared to fight.

'I know, of course I know that,' her mother replied, her tone unrepentant. 'But now that I've read it, it is.'

She was unfolding the letter now. Realizing that she was planning to read it aloud, Katerina experienced a rush of fear. First the humiliation, then the interrogation, she thought wildly. And there was absolutely no way of telling what else Izzy might do. She wouldn't put anything past her.

'This isn't fair,' she pleaded, unable to even contemplate the horrific possibilities. If Izzy were to tell Gina . . . 'It's private, and I don't want to discuss it, so why don't you just give me that' – jack-knifing forwards, she attempted to snatch the letter back, but Izzy whisked it out of reach – 'and forget you ever saw it.'

'Young love!' exclaimed Izzy, her dark eyes alight with amusement. 'Really, darling, I'm not so ancient that I can't remember how it feels . . . but this is nothing to be ashamed of.' Tapping the page with her forefinger, she continued triumphantly, 'It's brilliant! Better still, it *works*.'

'Works,' Katerina echoed, falling back against her pillows. That was it; she gave up. Closing her eyes for a second, then slowly reopening them, she said wearily, 'Mother, what on earth are you talking about?'

Izzy said, reading aloud:

'Never, never
Understood how
The rest of the world
Felt, until now.
Was I ever, ever
Alive before now?
You showed me how
It could be.
Lucky me, lucky world,
I'm a woman, not a girl.
You taught me how
To love. And now,
As long as I have you,
You'll always, always
Have me.'

Izzy stopped reading. Katerina, so geared up for the confrontation that she almost shouted, 'But that isn't what we were talking about,' had to exert actual physical control in order not to.

Her secret was safe, after all. She had been reprieved and as the realization sank in, she knew that it had indeed been a lucky escape because never in a million years would Izzy have taken the news of her involvement with Andrew as lightly as she had – for those few bizarre moments – imagined. Not even Izzy, thought Katerina wryly, was that liberal.

'It's a poem,' she said, sagging still further into her cocoon of pillows, but disguising her relief with truculence. 'And it's totally crappy. You shouldn't have read it.'

'It isn't totally crappy,' Izzy contradicted her. 'Admittedly, I don't think Wordsworth need lose too much sleep over it . . .' She paused, then squeezed her daughter's cold hand. 'But that's what I was trying to tell you, darling. When I read it, it *wasn't* a poem . . . it was a song! I heard the music . . . I knew exactly how it would sound . . . powerful and haunting, happy and sad at the same time . . . it's the kind of song people remember for the rest of their *lives*.'

Despite herself, Katerina smiled. 'Mother,' she said tolerantly, 'you're mad.'

'No, I'm not,' Izzy insisted. 'I'm right!'

'Quite mad.'

Izzy waved the sheet of paper. 'But will you let me give it a go? Can I at least *try*?'

In a few days, thought Katerina, her mother would have forgotten all about it. Her enthusiasms, wildly embraced, seldom lasted. This one would be lucky if it survived the week.

'Of course you can use it,' she conceded, 'if you really want to.'

'You're an angel,' declared Izzy, enveloping her in a hug. 'And just think,' she added with an air of triumph, 'this could really be the start of something big . . . fame, fortune and toyboys coming out of our ears . . .'

'I'm too old for toyboys,' protested Katerina.

'They're for me, silly.' Izzy gave her a pitying look, then broke into a grin. 'You don't need them – you've already found the love of *your* life. And speaking of love,' she continued, lowering her voice to a conspiratorial whisper, 'what did he say when he read the poem? What did Simon think of it?'

Reminding herself that at least she wasn't telling a lie, Katerina returned her mother's gaze with equanimity. 'Nothing,' she replied, her voice calm. 'I didn't give it to him.'

Chapter 21

The doctor had been quite definite, although Marcy still didn't understand how it possibly could be true. Now, back at the flat, she gazed at her naked reflection in the mirror, running a trembling, experimental hand over the rounded swell of her stomach. However could she *not* be pregnant, looking like this?

But . . . a phantom pregnancy, he had told her. A non-existent baby. God, nature was weird, thought Marcy, not knowing whether to laugh or to cry at the bizarre trick that her own body had played on her. And not only a bizarre trick; a particularly cruel one as well. Having longed for a baby so desperately that at times it seemed as if she were incapable of even *thinking* about anything else, the realization that she was finally pregnant had been one of the most wonderful discoveries of her life. She had felt complete . . . replete . . . and so happy it was positively sinful.

She had guessed, of course, that Andrew's own initial reaction had been less enthusiastic. The professed delight had been tempered with unease, maybe even a trace of alarm, but that was only to be expected under the circumstances. Consequently, she had put no immediate pressure upon him, merely revelling in her own private joy, allowing him to come to terms with the idea in his own time and only mentioning in passing that maybe this was the excuse he had been waiting for – the perfect opportunity – to leave his unhappy marriage.

And gradually, as she had known would happen, he *had* come to terms with the idea. The pull of impending fatherhood was strong; Andrew had realised that this, after all, was what was important, what was *needed* in order to complete their lives, and her own happiness had in turn become absolute. It was all so perfect . . .

And it had all been a lie, because there was no baby. Even the cravings for salt-and-vinegar crisps and spaghetti *alle vongole* had been nothing more than an inexplicable illusion.

Pulling on her dressing gown, covering her traitorous body, Marcy turned away from the mirror and experienced the first pangs of fear. It wasn't her fault. She hadn't done it on purpose. But would Andrew believe that?

Telling him that she was on the Pill had been only the first lie. The second, that the home pregnancy testing kit had proved positive, wasn't going to be so easy to explain away.

Yet she truly hadn't meant to deceive him. It had just seemed so unnecessary under the circumstances, and upon discovering that such silly little kits cost almost ten pounds she had reeled away from the chemist's counter in shock and spent the money instead on the latest Jackie Collins novel and a tub of Häagen Dazs chocolate ice-cream.

Now she fervently wished she hadn't, but the chilling question remained: what was Andrew going to say when he found out?

She didn't have long to wait. Unusually – and because, unknown to Marcy, Katerina had been unable to meet him straight from the office as she usually did – he was home by five-thirty. And this time she was painfully aware of his look of irritation when he glanced around and saw that, yet again, she hadn't tidied the small flat.

'Darling,' she said, going up to him and giving him a kiss. It would have landed on his mouth if he hadn't turned his head at the last moment, leaving her only his pale, aftershaved cheek. 'You're early.'

'Would it have made any difference?' he countered, gesturing towards the coffee table littered with magazines and teacups. He was early, hungry and tired, and still Marcy was incapable of making any effort. That, combined with the fact of not being able to be soothed by Katerina, fuelled his annoyance. In her panicky state, it also made Marcy only more hyper-aware of the precarious state of her own situation.

'I'll make us something to eat,' she said, at the same time wondering what on earth she might possibly conjure up. All she knew for sure was that there was enough maple-and-walnut-flavoured Angel Delight to feed an entire school, an awful lot of crisps and maybe some malt loaf that was only slightly mouldy. 'Sweetheart, you look worn out. Why don't you sit down and relax?'

'I have to go out again, later.' Andrew's gaze was fixed on the television screen as he spoke. Katerina had said she might be able to meet him at nine. 'A party of Dutch clients are staying overnight; they've invited me to join them at some restaurant in Belgravia.'

'In that case, you'd better not eat now,' said Marcy,

overcome with relief. It also meant she would be able to watch her favourite soap in peace.

Andrew nodded, his mind elsewhere. Then, as if remembering his duty, he said, 'So, what have you been doing today?'

The icy grip of fear churned in Marcy's stomach. Instinctively, she rested her hand upon the fraudulent bump. 'I went to see my doctor.'

Now she had Andrew's attention. He sat forward, his grey eyes searching her face. 'What did he say? Is anything wrong?'

She loved him. He had left his wife for her. And it wasn't her fault that nature should have chosen to play such a vile trick on her.

Crossing her fingers beneath the folds of her dressing gown, Marcy smiled and shook her head. Like Scarlett, she would think about it tomorrow. 'Nothing's wrong,' she said, her tone gently reassuring. 'I'm fine, darling. We're both *fine*.'

Recognizing the back view of the person ahead of him, Sam braked and slowed his car to a crawl, admiring as he did so the allure of such very good legs and such a perfect bottom. What this particular person was doing being carted along the pavement by a sandy-blond Great Dane he couldn't imagine, but they certainly made a striking pair . . .

'Hi,' he said, when he had pulled alongside her. The dog, tail wagging, immediately bounded up to the open window and sniffed with interest.

With a pointed glance at the heavy chain around its

neck, Sam shook the proffered paw and said solemnly, 'You must be Izzy's latest boyfriend.'

'Very witty,' said Izzy with a half-smile. 'Where were you when we needed you, anyway? Jericho didn't want to take the tube, which means we've had to walk *all* the way from Hampstead.'

Jericho, whose dark brown eyes were even larger than Izzy's, barked in happy agreement and attempted to lick Sam's face.

'And now you're almost home,' he remarked, pushing the dog away while he still had some aftershave left. 'Of course, I *would* offer you a lift, but . . .'

'You forgot to bring the juggernaut,' supplied Izzy, holding up her free hand. 'It's OK, we're getting used to it. The cab drivers we tried to flag down felt the same way.'

He laughed at the expression on her face. 'So, what's this all about? You've given up song-writing in favour of professional dog-walking? I don't know how to break this to you, sweetheart, but you're going to have to walk twice around the world before this new venture makes you rich.'

'He's ours,' Izzy replied proudly. 'Our new male lodger.' Then she broke into an irrepressible grin. 'But this time we've got ourselves one who's housetrained.'

Sam, whose new washing-machine had broken down, and who had driven round to Kingsley Grove in order to use theirs, had been quietly surprised by the news that Gina had acquired a dog. It wasn't until he saw the expression on her face when Jericho loped into the kitchen that he realised that Izzy had done it again.

'Aaagh!' said Gina, backing away into the corner next to the fridge.

'Woof,' replied Jericho, regarding her with polite interest.

Despite himself, Sam wished he had a camera.

'Whose dog is that?' Gina squeaked, pointing at the intruder with a shaking finger. Whereupon Jericho, ever hopeful of a biscuit, stepped forward and attempted to investigate the outstretched hand before it was snatched away. Disappointed, he snuffled around Gina's slim ankles instead.

'Isn't he gorgeous?' sighed Izzy, blithely unaware of the havoc she was causing. Then, thrusting the end of the chain in Gina's cowering direction, she announced, 'He's yours.'

'No, he isn't!'

'Of course he is; he's a present. A thank-you present,' she added happily, 'because if it hadn't been for you, I never would have realised that I had to be a song-writer if I was ever going to get anywhere. You've changed my life, Gina,' she concluded, her eyes alight with gratitude. 'And I'd been wondering for *days* what to get you . . .'

A husband, thought Gina numbly. And a peaceful, dog-free, Van Asch-less home.

'. . . then I saw this advert in the paper this afternoon and it all fell into place, so I rushed over to Hampstead and snapped him up!'

'He looks as if he wants to snap me up,' Gina said, her voice faint, but Izzy was already down on her knees, fondling the enormous dog's ears with affection and freeing him from his chain.

'He's just hungry, bless him. We both are. Oh look, he's shaking paws again . . . isn't he adorable? And just think,' she added triumphantly, 'of all the advantages of having a dog!'

'Burglars,' said Sam. Izzy was an utter disgrace, but her heart was unarguably in the right place. A dog lover himself, he was incapable of remaining as impartial as he should have been. As long as he had known Gina he had known how much she mistrusted dogs.

'Men!' exclaimed Izzy, so thrilled with her own reasoning that she was unable to keep the discovery to herself. 'You see, that's what's so brilliant! I was reading an article in the same paper about husband-hunting . . . about ways of meeting new men,' she amended rapidly. 'And taking your dog for a walk in the park was top of the list. It's sociable without being obvious, you start off by saying, "Hallo, how are you this morning?" and before you know where you are, the dentist with the golden retriever is inviting you out to dinner. It's a cinch!'

Sam had to admire her style. Helping himself to a can of lager from the fridge, he sat down to enjoy the ensuing argument.

'It's great exercise, as well,' Izzy added as an afterthought, since Gina didn't appear to be as thrilled with her present as she should have been. 'And of course Sam's absolutely right; he'll see off any burglars, not to mention carol singers, in a flash . . .'

'I'm scared of dogs.' Gina spoke through gritted teeth; at this very moment in time Jericho was eyeing her keenly, salivating and presumably anticipating the prospect of her ankles. If Izzy had to give her a dog, why couldn't it at least have been something small and manageable?

'But that's ridiculous,' Izzy declared passionately, still on one knee and with her arms open wide. 'Nobody on earth could possibly be afraid of Jericho! The only reason his previous owners had to let him go was because *he* was scared of their poodle. He needs love and understanding,' she went on, sensing weakness, 'to build up his confidence. And lots and lots of wonderful walks in the park . . .'

It said much for Izzy's powers of persuasion that within the space of two hours she had managed to dispatch Gina and Jericho, albeit with some reluctance, to the nearby park, with instructions to take a turn around the pond and enjoy the last of the sun.

Sam, however, was doubly impressed by Izzy's subsequent dash to the phone and her heartfelt pleas with not one but three dog-owning male friends. If they would just do her the biggest favour in the world, take their animals for a quick zip around the pond on the east side of Kensington Gardens and say something friendly in passing to the nervous blonde with the Great Dane, she would be for ever in their debt . . .

The real miracle, of course, was that they agreed to do so. But if Izzy possessed anything in abundance, Sam reminded himself, it was charm. Besides, she also had some extremely weird friends.

'Your washing's done,' she observed, as the machine finally subsided into exhausted silence forty minutes later.

'And you're trying to change the subject.' Clean shirts were only half the reason for his visit. Stranger even than Izzy's friends had been the urge . . . almost a physical *need*

. . . to see her again. He might still be saddled with his own unwanted house guest, but Sam hadn't forgotten that evening in his office, whereas as far as Izzy was concerned it might never have happened. They were back to square one, he thought, and her apparent amnesia for the event was becoming, as far as *he* was concerned, bloody irritating.

'I'm worried about that red shirt,' said Izzy, who hadn't forgotten at all. Before, biding her time and enjoying the interplay between them had been fun. Now, however, the situation had changed. Knowing and liking Vivienne had put a real dampener on things, and she had decided to keep her distance until the situation resolved itself. It wouldn't do any harm, she had told herself, and in the mean time she could concentrate her attention on her work.

Now, slightly flustered, she repeated, 'Your red shirt. It might have run.'

Sam simply looked at her and said nothing.

'Oh, shit,' said Izzy, with feeling. For something to do, she yanked open the door of the washing-machine and began pulling out damp clothes. 'Look, whether you wanted it to happen or not, the fact remains that Vivienne is living with you in your flat.'

'Staying,' he corrected her. 'Not living.'

'Whatever,' she sighed. It was easier to talk when she didn't have to look at him. Serious eye contact, under the circumstances, was decidedly unsettling. 'For once in my life I'm trying to do the honourable thing, so it really isn't fair of you to give me a hard time.'

'It isn't very fair on me, either,' Sam pointed out.

Drumming his fingers against his now empty lager can, he wondered just how much this had to do with the new man she'd told him about, the 'very attractive' man after whom she had lusted so vigorously. He frowned. 'Are you still seeing that guy?'

Izzy, who had forgotten all about her own private joke, assumed he was referring to Benny Dunaway. Still with her back to Sam, she said, 'Of course I am.'

'Of course,' he echoed with a trace of irony. Determined as she was not to come between Vivienne and himself, the question of her own monogamy never even occurred to her. In her eyes, it simply wasn't an issue.

A volley of barks interrupted his train of thought at that moment, which under the circumstances, Sam decided, was just as well. As long as Vivienne remained in his flat and Izzy continued to see her partner-in-lust, there was precious little to either say or do.

The next moment, Jericho clawed open the kitchen door and, recognizing Izzy crouched before the washing-machine, hurled himself at her in a frenzy of delight. Sam's red shirt went flying and landed in the bowl of water which had been set out for Jericho earlier.

'Well?' said Sam. Gina's face was flushed and she was out of breath.

'Well, what?'

'Did he behave himself?' said Izzy brightly, and Gina swung round, looking more startled than ever.

'Who?'

Izzy rolled her eyes in despair. 'Jericho! Are we keeping him or must he go back to face a life of miserable tyranny at the paws of a poodle named Pete?'

'Oh . . . he was very well behaved,' Gina replied, not altogether truthfully. With a quick glance in his direction – he was at this moment burying his nose up the sleeve of the hapless red shirt – she took a gulp of air and attempted to steady her breathing. 'I don't think it would be very fair, sending him back,' she continued with a brief, tentative smile. 'Not now that he's got to know us.'

'Of course it wouldn't.' Izzy smiled back, making a playful grab for the dog's ears. 'Ah, look at him . . . he's tired. But how about you, did *you* enjoy the walk?'

Gina sat down suddenly on one of the kitchen chairs, her eyes brighter than ever. 'As a matter of fact, I did. And I didn't believe you when you said it,' she added, torn between a mixture of embarrassment and pride, 'but you were certainly right about meeting other people walking their dogs. It just seems to . . . well, *happen*.'

'Heavens, how exciting!' Izzy sent up a silent prayer of thanks. She'd been pretty sure of Tom and Luke, but Alastair had said he might not be able to spare the time. 'So, how many men actually spoke to you?'

'Well,' said Gina, blushing prettily. 'As a matter of fact, five.'

Chapter 22

It wasn't easy, transmitting her definite ideas as to how 'Never, Never' should sound to someone who then had to battle with the logistics of such a scheme and make it workable. Frustration hadn't been the word for it; at times Izzy found herself with her fingers ravelled up in her hair and her voice hoarse with the effort of attempting to imitate the precise tone of a tenor saxophone, while Benny frowned and enquired for the tenth time whether she was absolutely *sure* it should precede the vocals by half a beat. Didn't she think it would be better to synchronise the notes and allow the piano to form the echo effect . . .

But slowly, with much concentration, a few tense moments and many hours of hard work, the miracle began to happen. The song was coming together in a recognisable form and if Izzy had broken a few of the very oldest rules in the book, Benny had demonstrated one of the talents possessed by every great teacher and allowed her to do so. Some of the mistakes had been horrendous. Astonishingly, others had worked, and it was the very unexpectedness of those departures from tradition which helped to create an indefinable sense of magic.

And Izzy, like a child finally mastering the art of riding a bike, didn't want to stop. Having adapted 'Never, Never' from Katerina's poem, she was now bursting with ideas of her own. Lyrics tumbled effortlessly on to the pages of her writing pad and as soon as she saw them she found herself able to hear the accompanying music. Benny had to struggle to keep up, roughing out her ideas before they slipped away. Biting his tongue whenever she made such remarks as, 'This bit's a duet for voice and clarinet,' he allowed Izzy's untutored imagination free rein. And there was indeed a lesson to be learned by musicians everywhere, he discovered later in the evenings when she had left to go to work and he went back over the annotated scores he had scribbled down according to her jumbled instructions. Some of her ideas were downright impossible, while others, though technically feasible, he knew would never work in practice. But some, he had to concede, were astonishingly good. Izzy hadn't been joking when she'd told him she knew she could do it. And a shiver snaked its way down Benny's spine as he realised for the first time that with expert help, the right backing and a lot of luck, she could maybe . . . just maybe . . . be great.

'Boy, am I glad I phoned you,' confided Vivienne, stirring her drink and offering Izzy a cigarette. 'It gets *sooo* boring here, what with Sam doing the rounds and me not knowing a soul. I'm sure the only reason he encourages me to come to The Steps is because he's hoping I'll meet some other guy and leave him in peace.'

'Do you think you will?' Izzy tried not to look too optimistic.

Vivienne laughed. 'Are you kidding? Izzy, we have what the columnists call "a tempestuous relationship" . . . it'll take a lot more than this little fall-out to send me running home to Daddy. I haven't given up on Sam yet, not by a long chalk.'

Oh sheeit, thought Izzy, because a Texan drawl is alarmingly infectious.

'But that isn't to say I can't have a little fun in the mean time,' Vivienne added, her eyes dancing. 'And who knows, once Sam sees me having fun with other people, he might get his act together.'

'I could do with meeting some new people myself,' Izzy mused, recalling the depressing conversation she'd had earlier that day with Benny. 'You wouldn't happen to know any rich record producers, I suppose?'

Vivienne stubbed out her barely smoked cigarette and pulled a face. 'I'm such a selfish bitch – I haven't even asked how you're getting on with this song-writing kick. How's it *going*?'

'Brilliantly,' said Izzy, then she shook her head. 'But writing the songs is the easy part. The next move is taking them into a recording studio and getting a demo tape made up.'

'Hey, that's great . . . so, when does it happen? Could I come and watch?'

Izzy smiled. 'It happens when we can afford to rent out a recording studio. Remember what Sam told you about me: crazy hair, great voice, no cash? Well, hiring a halfway decent studio for even a single day costs twelve hundred pounds, which is more than either Benny or I can raise . . .'

'Oh.' Vivienne looked bewildered; this was something outside her own experience. Then her face brightened. 'Borrow it,' she said promptly. 'From Sam! He'd lend you the money in a flash, and then as soon as you get rich you can pay him back.'

It was a solution which had occurred to Izzy. For a second she reconsidered the idea, then shook her head once more. 'I really can't.'

Vivienne looked perplexed. 'Why not?'

Wriggling uncomfortably in her seat, Izzy said, 'It's hard to explain, but I just know I've got to try and do this on my own. As far as Sam's concerned, I'm a walking disaster, financially. A spendthrift. And, of course, he's absolutely right,' she admitted with a brief smile, 'but I can't help it, it's just the way I am. If I asked him to lend me the money, I'd feel . . . uncomfortable.' It wasn't the word she'd been looking for, but it would do. Being in Sam's debt, she felt, would only confirm his opinion of her. And a girl had her pride, after all.

'You mean he'd lecture you?' asked Vivienne, still trying to understand. 'He'd keep asking you when he was going to get his money back? Jeeze, what a bastard! I never thought he was like that.'

'Oh, no,' Izzy said hastily. 'He isn't. He wouldn't say a word about it.' With a gesture of despair, she concluded, 'That's *exactly* what would make it so unbearable.'

'No, please don't,' said Vivienne a moment later, as Izzy reached for her purse and made a move to stand up. 'My treat. I dragged you down here, after all.'

Izzy burst out laughing. 'Don't tell me, I've spun my poor-little-match-girl-story and now you're having a guilt attack. Listen, the nice thing about spendthrifts is they can always afford to buy a round of drinks, so instead of looking at me like that, why don't you tell me what you'd like? Another tequila sunrise?'

But Vivienne, clasping her arm and pulling her back down into her seat, shook her head. 'Hey, Sam brought me here tonight, so the least he can do is keep us fed and watered. And the only reason I suggested him just now was because I thought you two were such great friends. What I'd really like,' she went on, catching the attention of the bar manager and mouthing her request, 'would be to lend you the money you need, myself.'

Izzy's mouth dropped open. Having just declared herself a bad risk it hadn't occurred to her for a moment that Vivienne would make such an offer. 'My God,' she said eventually. 'Do you really mean it?'

'Why wouldn't I mean it?' countered Vivienne cheerfully, as the bar manager materialised with a bottle of Moët and two glasses. 'It's not such a big deal. You can pay me back whenever you like.' She smiled and thanked the bar manager, then winked at Izzy. 'And Sam need never know.'

'This is fantastic,' said Izzy, overwhelmed with gratitude. 'I don't know how to thank you.'

'Hell, what are friends for?' Vivienne laughed and began to pour the champagne into their glasses. Izzy hastily covered hers with her hand.

'I wouldn't want Sam to accuse me of freeloading. I'll stick to orange juice. Really.'

'We're celebrating,' insisted Vivienne, removing her hand and sloshing Moët into the glass. 'Don't let Sam intimidate you, honey. It isn't your style.'

'Oh well, in that case,' said Izzy happily, 'cheers.'

Ten days later, she stood gazing out at the view from the

window of Doug Steadman's office and listened to the sound of her own voice echoing through the room. Behind her, Gina and Doug, Benny and Vivienne were sitting in silence, hearing the finished results of a single nineteen-hour day in the recording studio recommended to them by a friend of Benny's. The demo tape held four tracks and now they were nearing the end. Izzy's voice soared, echoing the haunting, plaintive notes of the tenor saxophone, then dropped to barely a whisper as the final bars of 'Never, Never' approached. A heartbeat of silence, then the rising crescendo heralded by a gently gathering drum roll . . . She had striven for the effect of Juliet's last impassioned words to the absent Romeo . . . the final, powerful line which this time rose high above the sax . . . and it was over.

Awaiting her audience's reaction was worse than any stand-up audition. Unable to turn around, she reached out instead and encountered Jericho's smooth head. His whiskers tickled her wrist. Her fingers were tingling and she felt dizzy . . .

The moment's silence, however, was broken by an ear-splitting whistle of approval rendered as only a true Texan knows how. Vivienne cried jubilantly, 'Izzy, you're a star!' and when Izzy finally turned to face them, it was Gina who led the round of applause. Jericho, realizing that his enforced silence was over, released a volley of joyful howls and sent a coffee cup flying from the desk with his tail. Benny was grinning broadly. Gina, still applauding, said, 'That was fantastic,' over and over again.

But Izzy was waiting for Doug, who had so far said nothing. She had taken the financial gamble and done her very best, but as her agent and as a professional she needed, above all, his approval. Regarding him with mounting nervousness she tried to say, 'Well?' but the word stuck in her throat and all that came out was a laryngitic croak.

But Doug, hauling himself out of his chair and mopping his face with a blue-and-white spotted handkerchief, had no intention of saying anything. Instead, crossing the small office, he came to a halt in front of Izzy and waited a full second before breaking into a smile. Then, reaching up and taking her head in his hands, he gave her a resounding kiss first on one cheek then the other.

Izzy's eyes promptly filled with tears.

'Do you really like them?' she whispered, as he stepped back and held her at arm's length.

'Do I like them?' Doug shook his head, experiencing a rush of almost paternal affection for the confident, wayward girl whom he had known for so many years. Her optimism and energy were boundless; she had never been afraid of anyone or anything in her life. Now, seeing her uncertainty and desperate need for approval, he only loved her all the more.

'You know me' he told her, with a reproving look. 'I *like* Roger Whittaker and Val Doonican. Your songs might not be my personal cup of tea, but even I can tell that they're good. Very good.' He paused, then admitted gruffly, 'I didn't expect them to be, but they are.'

Izzy's cheeks were wet and her mascara was dissolving fast. She sniffed and smiled. 'Don't you like them even a little bit?'

'Stop crying,' Doug ordered. 'Of course I do. When have I ever disliked anything that's going to make me rich?'

Chapter 23

With her light brown hair swept up in a glossy topknot, her neat little black dress and unaccustomed high heels, Andrew realised that Katerina had worked to make herself look older, and was touched by her efforts. She could easily pass for twenty-one now, which – under the circumstances – was less eyebrow-raising than seventeen. Not that the discrepancy in their ages bothered either of them any longer, but sly glances and unsubtle smirks weren't exactly calming.

Katerina, however, was less inhibited. Arching her own eyebrows in amazement when she heard Andrew give the pretty hotel receptionist their names, she promptly burst out laughing. Even the receptionist had to smile.

'What's the matter?' He looked round, puzzled.

'Mr and Mrs Lawrence,' giggled Katerina. 'You can't put that! We don't have to pretend to be *married*, do we?'

It was so sweet of him to want to observe the proprieties, she thought with a rush of affection. Then, seeing the expression on his face, she tucked her arm through his and gave it a squeeze. 'And there's no need to be embarrassed. People will only guess, anyway, when they see us talking non-stop through dinner. Real married couples don't do that – it's written into their contracts.'

Andrew gave the receptionist an abashed smile and handed Katerina his pen. She signed her name with a flourish. 'There! Who needs to travel incognito, anyway?'

I do, thought Andrew wryly. At least he would be settling the account in cash, even though he could barely afford it. Then again, he wasn't going to run the risk of letting Marcy discover a giveaway Visa slip in his suit pocket . . .

'Shall I ask the porter to take your luggage up to your room?' said the receptionist, grinning at Katerina and wishing that even half her guests could be as honest.

'That's OK.' Katerina winked. 'I wouldn't want him to hurt himself. It really is an incredibly heavy toothbrush, after all.'

She couldn't help wondering whether her hunger pangs were psychological. Did she really want to eat or was she simply playing for time, putting off the moment when there would be just the three of them alone together: Andrew, herself and that great big double bed?

But no, although the devil-may-care bravado might be a front, she was happy to discover as the first course arrived at their table that the hunger was genuine.

'So, where does your mother think you are tonight?' said Andrew, as she demolished the last langoustine with her fingers. Having no appetite himself, he had left his own plate virtually untouched; watching Katerina enjoy her food was pleasure enough.

'Staying with the love of my life.' She grinned with her mouth full. 'Simon, of course, although it's not terribly likely that she'll remember; apparently Mum played her demo tape to Doug this afternoon and he was impressed. By the time I got home from school there was an extremely noisy party going on, so I told them I couldn't possibly study for my exams with that kind of distraction, and that I was going over to Simon's house. They won't miss me,' she concluded airily. 'As I was leaving, Sam's girlfriend was teaching Gina to Charleston and Mum was doing her Bette Midler impression, using a courgette as a microphone. Benny and Jericho were playing the piano . . . rather badly, I must say . . . and Doug was pleading with them to do "Paddy McGinty's Goat" . . .'

It all seemed highly unlikely; Andrew simply couldn't envisage such goings-on in sedate Kingsley Grove. The Neighbourhood Watch must be bristling with disapproval.

'We don't have a piano,' he said finally.

Katerina licked her buttery fingers. '*You* didn't,' she corrected him. '*We* do.'

He couldn't imagine Gina dancing the Charleston, either, despite Katerina's repeated assurances that – slowly but surely – she was loosening up. 'Coming along nicely', was how she described it, and although they had initially struck sparks off each other, their relationship had evidently mellowed in recent weeks. Katerina approved of the fact that Gina had finally 'got off her bum' and started working, while Gina, in turn, appreciated Katerina's culinary abilities, as well as her aptitude for washing-up. Even more strangely, Katerina was quite open to discussion where Gina – his estranged wife – was concerned, whereas any mention of Marcy was met with instantaneous freezing out.

'When do your exams start?' he asked, more out of a desire to change the subject than anything else. As long as he had known Kat, she had been gearing herself up for

A levels, but now she rarely even mentioned them.

The waiter arrived at that moment with their main course, delectably pink lamb cutlets for him and *tournedos Rossini* for Katerina. She shrugged and smiled. 'Nine o'clock tomorrow morning.'

'You're joking!'

'Don't panic.' She seized his hand, just as she had done on that first day in the Victoria and Albert Museum. 'The only reason I didn't tell you was because I didn't want it to spoil our night. When you said you'd booked us into this hotel I was so *happy*. Nothing else matters, only us.'

For a split second, Andrew wondered whether knowing in advance would have been enough to make him cancel the night. Although he loved Katerina desperately, he was still achingly aware of the differences separating them, and he knew how important her exams were to her.

But no, he had to admit that he wouldn't have done so. Their precious time together was even more important to him. And this night of all nights was to be the culmination of such long-awaited yearning . . .

'We'll have to leave here by seven-thirty,' he warned her. The rush-hour traffic from rural Berkshire into central London was diabolical.

'In that case,' said Katerina, her eyes shining and her hand trembling slightly as she raised her glass to his, 'we'd better have a very early night.'

But had there ever been a more nerve-wracking exam than the one she was about to face? In the bedroom, Andrew waited for her. Katerina, gazing at her reflection in the bathroom mirror, reminded herself that as long as a couple truly loved one another, nothing else mattered. She didn't understand why she should be feeling this way. If making love was so natural and . . . wonderful, why did she feel as if she were about to be sick?

She was being stupid, she thought briskly, reaching for her toothbrush and running the cold tap full pelt. What a wimp; seventeen years old and behaving like a child. Since there was absolutely no need to be scared, she wouldn't be. *Nothing* was going to be allowed to spoil the most momentous night of her life . . .

Much later, when Andrew had fallen asleep, Katerina rolled on to her side and gazed at the luminous blue figures of the digital clock beside the bed. One-thirty in the morning, she had done it and it had been OK. Nothing like in the movies, she thought with a wry smile, but then what was? OK was OK, it was at least better than she had been expecting, and it really hadn't lasted long at all, which was an added bonus. She hadn't stuck her big toe in Andrew's ear, giggled at the wrong moment or got herself hopelessly entangled in one of those terrifying positions described in that book of which Izzy had made so much fun.

She hadn't made an idiot of herself, and for that she could only be grateful. Ecstasy might – and hopefully *would* – feature at a later date, but in the mean time it was something she could quite happily live without. At least she hadn't lost her pride.

'Darling,' murmured Andrew, his arm sliding around her slender waist. As he pulled Katerina towards him, he realised that he was becoming aroused once more. 'Are you too tired . . .?'

He was kissing her neck. Wriggling away, terrified he'd forget, she reached under the pillows and drew the small, flat box out from its hiding place.

'This is the last one,' she said, feeling ridiculously like her old schoolteacher doling out coloured felt pens.

'Wrong.' Andrew, who had set the alarm clock for six-thirty, smiled into the darkness. 'There are always three in a packet.'

'Wrong,' replied Katerina, secretly relieved. 'I filled one up with water earlier, and swung it about a bit. Just to make sure they really worked.'

Simon was hovering at the school gates when Andrew's car screeched to a halt at five past nine and Katerina, still wearing last night's little black dress, leapt barefoot out of the passenger door.

'Jesus, Kat! Are you out of your mind?' His voice betrayed his agitation and anger. How she could take such stupid risks was beyond him.

Unable to look at the driver of the car, he averted his eyes as Katerina leaned through the open window and gave Andrew a hasty goodbye kiss.

'No need to panic,' she said briskly, detaching his clammy hand from her arm as Andrew's car disappeared and Simon attempted to drag her through the gates. 'I'm here now, with seven minutes to spare. We've even got time for a quick coffee if we—'

'What!' Simon shouted, his blond hair practically standing on end. She broke into a grin.

'Just my little joke.'

'You're the joke.' He glared at her. 'I can't believe what's happened to you, Kat. Having an affair with a married man isn't clever, it isn't an *intelligent* thing to do . . . and you don't even seem to realise the kind of *risks* you're taking . . .'

Attempting to chivvy him out of his bad mood – which was something she'd never encountered before – Katerina smiled. 'I may not be intelligent, but even I've heard of safe sex,' she riposted. 'Condoms rule, OK?'

But Simon's eyebrows remained ferociously furrowed. 'I'm not talking about those kind of risks.'

'And you don't have the experience to lecture me on any other kind,' declared Katerina flatly as they climbed the steps leading to the main entrance of the school. 'So don't lecture *me*.'

Shaking his head, he said, 'You're making a fool of yourself.'

In reply, she gave him an icy stare. 'And you're becoming incredibly boring.'

Ahead of them at the end of the corridor was the examination room. Standing in the doorway, their physics teacher gestured frantically to them to hurry up and take their seats.

'I'm trying to be your friend,' said Simon in a low voice.

Katerina, feeling slightly ashamed of herself, squeezed his hand. 'I know you are,' she whispered back. 'You're just going about it the wrong way. Oh Simon, I haven't revised for a week. I'm scared. Give me a kiss for luck?'

'No,' he said grimly, recalling the incident at the school gates. 'You've had one of those already.'

Chapter 24

'There was no need for you to come all the way down here,' Gina protested, when Izzy arrived in the office. Breathless with the effort of hanging on to Jericho's lead as he belted across roads without looking, Izzy collapsed in a heap on to the window-seat and drained a can of Perrier in one go.

'I'm excited,' she said, wiping her mouth and kicking off her sandals. Jericho promptly grabbed one and buried himself beneath Gina's desk. 'Go on, tell me again what they said on the phone.'

'The people at MBT have listened to your tape,' repeated Gina patiently. 'They found it interesting. One of their A&R men will be coming to listen to you tonight at Platform One. His name is Joel McGill and he'll introduce himself after the show.'

Izzy liked the sound of Joel McGill. It was a good name, a good omen, and she had been singing it in her head all the way from Kensington to Soho. She had also been able to picture him in her mind quite clearly; he would be tall and dark with gypsyish eyes, a gorgeous smile and positively *no girlfriend*. And he, in turn, would be dazzled, absolutely *smitten*, by Izzy Van Asch . . .

'Gina,' she said, breaking out of her reverie, 'would you be an angel and lend me a hundred pounds?'

Gina looked startled. 'You're going to bribe him?'

'A new dress,' Izzy begged. 'Oh please, I need something special.'

'But Izzy, you possess an entire wardrobe of special somethings at home. There must be something among your collection you could wear.' Gina, who hadn't allowed herself a single new item of clothing for over a month, shuffled papers and looked disapproving. 'Can't Vivienne lend you the money?'

'I tried her first,' confessed Izzy with disarming honesty. 'She was out.'

Less than two minutes after Izzy, Jericho and Gina's one hundred pounds had collectively departed, the door swung open again. Gina sat up straight and gave the visitor her best receptionist's smile.

'Hi,' said the visitor, smiling back at her in such a way that she almost looked over her shoulder to see if someone more interesting was lurking behind her. 'You're new. And so is this office.' With only a slightly over-the-top double take, he paused to survey the pristine surroundings before returning his gaze to Gina. 'I came to see Doug. Am I in the wrong building?'

She felt the colour rising in her cheeks. Unfortunately, it had a distressing habit of collecting in blotches around her neck, too. Goodness, he was handsome.

'Right building,' she said, almost as breathless as Izzy had been earlier, 'but I'm afraid Doug's out at the moment. Perhaps I can help you?'

'I'm sure you can.' Dropping into the chair opposite her, he pushed his fingers through his hair and gave Gina the benefit of his attention once more, with such perfect thoroughness that her knees, beneath the desk, became boneless.

'I'm Gina Lawrence,' she said, in order to break the silence which didn't appear to bother her visitor in the least. 'I'm . . . I'm Doug's new assistant.'

He nodded, still smiling, then gestured around the office. 'And you did all this?'

This time it was Gina's turn to nod. Her neck, she realised, had gone completely numb.

'Then you are a miracle worker. I can't believe the difference you've made to the old place.'

Gina couldn't believe the difference he was making to *her*. Since Andrew's departure she had been physically incapable of reacting even faintly normally to the attentions of any man. Not that there had been a great deal of opportunity, but the odd friendly word or appreciative glance had left her icily unmoved. She was immune to the opposite sex.

But here, now, long-dormant hormones were unaccountably slithering back to life at a rate of knots . . .

'I'm sorry, how rude of me,' said the visitor, delving in his jacket pocket and pulling out a large, folded envelope. 'You're busy and I'm wasting your time. My name's Ralph Henson and I came here to return a contract. I've read it and signed in the appropriate places. All Doug has to do now is bury it . . . except that there doesn't appear to be anywhere left for him to bury anything.'

Gina, glad of something to do and relieved to discover that her legs still worked, turned back from the D to J filing cabinet with a bulky, charcoal-grey file. 'It all goes in here, from now on.'

Ralph grinned. 'Amazing. More than a miracle.'

'Gosh, ITV,' said Gina, gazing at the contract.

Nervy but attractive, thought Ralph, admiring the excellent cut of her sleek blonde bob as she bent her head to return the file to its rightful place in the cabinet. Better still, his name obviously didn't mean anything to her.

'I know,' he said with a modest shrug. 'The producer warned me that once the series goes out, my life will never be the same again. I don't really know whether to celebrate or panic.'

'But that's amazing.' Gina's eyes shone. 'You must celebrate.'

'OK.' Ralph, rising to his feet, rested his hands lightly on the edge of the desk. 'But only if you'll celebrate with me. Tonight.'

Gina could smell his aftershave. She knew she must have misheard him.

'What?'

'Dinner at Bouboulina's. Eight o'clock,' he said steadily. Touching her left hand with his index finger, he added, 'You aren't married; I checked first.'

'But . . . but I don't know you,' she stammered. Nothing like this had ever happened to her in her life before. One minute she was harmlessly fantasizing, the next it was becoming scarily true. 'And you don't know me.'

Ralph, who had thought he'd known Izzy Van Asch, simply shrugged. 'Sometimes that's the best way. All you have to do is say yes.'

'No,' said Gina, panic-stricken.

'Are you scared of me?'

'No!'

'Then say yes.'

She closed her eyes for a second. What would Izzy do now? Was going out to dinner with an attractive man such a huge ordeal, after all? And which would she most regret later: accepting the invitation or refusing it?

'OK,' said Gina, before she had the chance to start panicking all over again. 'OK, yes.'

'That's better.' Ralph, who had overheard Izzy cajoling Gina into lending her some money and had watched Izzy leave the building ten minutes earlier – she was being towed along the pavement by some massive dog and looking extremely pleased with herself – couldn't wait to see her face when he turned up at her house this evening. Pulling a battered Filofax from his other pocket, he picked up a pen. 'Just give me your address and I'll pick you up at eight sharp.'

For once, Andrew didn't even notice the state of the bedroom. Pushing aside a towelling robe and a box of tissues, he sat down on the edge of the bed and stared at the wall. Behind him, Marcy wiped her eyes and reached for his hand.

'Oh darling, I'm sorry.' The words came out jerkily, between sobs. To her relief the tears flowed on cue. 'It happened yesterday afternoon. I wasn't feeling terribly well all morning, then after lunch I started to get these terrible cramping p-pains. It all happened so . . . quickly.' Encouraged by the fact that Andrew was holding her hand, she allowed her eyes to fill up once more. 'By the time the doctor got here, it was all over. The b-baby was gone.'

Andrew took her in his arms and held her while she sobbed quietly against his chest. 'You should be in hospital,' he said, stunned by the news. 'You should have *phoned* me, for God's sake.'

'The doctor examined me, made sure I was OK,' whispered Marcy bravely. 'And I didn't want to disturb you . . . I knew how important your conference was. There wasn't anything you could do, and I wanted to be on my own to have time to come to terms with . . . what had happened.'

'You should have phoned,' repeated Andrew, stroking her hair and wondering how it was possible to feel this numb. Guilt warred with relief that she hadn't tried to contact him, but for the loss of the baby he was unable to summon up any emotion at all. A child wasn't something he'd ever wanted in the first place, and even knowing that Marcy was pregnant, he'd found it curiously difficult to envisage the end result.

Except that now, there would be no end result. Which meant that his fate – Marcy, marriage and fatherhood – was no longer sealed. Katerina . . .

'Poor darling,' he said absently, his mind racing on ahead. 'Can I get you anything? What would you like?'

Sex would have been nice. Marcy wondered how soon she could decently resume that side of their relationship. The prospect of weeks of enforced celibacy wasn't exactly cheering.

'I'm OK,' she said, her voice husky from crying. 'How did your conference go, anyway?'

'Hmm?' Andrew was still lost in thought. He had arranged to meet Kat later this evening; clearly he wouldn't be able to do so now. He could scarcely abandon Marcy, but dare he run the risk of phoning her at Gina's house to let her know of the change of circumstances?

'The conference,' Marcy repeated, nestling into the curve of his arms and thankful that he hadn't asked any further difficult questions. 'Was it a success?'

An image of Katerina, sitting up in bed sipping her morning coffee and smiling at him, flashed through Andrew's mind. Naked, happy and utterly desirable, she was everything he'd ever dreamed of.

'Oh yes,' he said, wondering whether the telephone cord would stretch as far as the bathroom. 'It went very well. Very well indeed.'

Chapter 25

Izzy hadn't decided whether to be amused or annoyed with Ralph for playing such a filthy trick. On the one hand, it was flattering to know that he still cared, yet on the other it was poor Gina who was being used, and who was going to be hurt, and Izzy herself who, in turn, would have to suffer the inevitable consequences.

The decision was made for her in a flash when she answered the door at a quarter to eight. Ralph, in all-too-familiar acting mode, did the faintest of double takes and said in astonished tones, 'I don't believe it! Izzy . . . ?'

'Oh, cut the crap, Ralph.' Grabbing his arm, she hauled him briskly inside. When they reached the sitting room she closed the door and leaned against it, taking in the sharp, charcoal-grey suit, pale pink shirt and . . . ugh . . . grey shoes. When he lifted his arm to push back a lock of hair she even glimpsed a flash of gold bracelet. Thank goodness Sam wasn't here.

'Now look,' she began, her voice low and her expression deadly serious. 'Gina will be down here any minute, and because she doesn't know what a bastard you are, she has spent four hours getting ready to go out with you. She hasn't so much as looked at another man since her husband left her. This is her first date in probably fifteen years. So I'm just warning you, if you hurt her, you're in big trouble.'

'But—' said Ralph, looking injured and inwardly cursing the failure of his plan. He had been relying on the element of surprise; it simply hadn't occurred to him that Gina would tell Izzy the name of the man who had invited her out to dinner.

'But nothing.' Izzy was listening to the sound of Gina's footsteps on the stairs. 'Just remember that if you hurt her, I shall personally kill you.'

'Did I hear the doorbell?' said Gina. Her nerves had miraculously vanished and she was feeling quite giddy with excitement. At that moment the phone rang.

'Ralph and I were just introducing ourselves,' Izzy explained. 'Don't worry, I'll answer it. You two go off and have a lovely time. And make sure he takes you somewhere expensive,' she added, giving Ralph the benefit of her most innocent smile. 'He looks as if he can afford to show a girl a good time . . .'

'Don't take any notice of Izzy,' she heard Gina saying as she left the room. 'She's only joking.'

Izzy picked up the phone in the kitchen and said, 'Hallo?'

Andrew hesitated. It wasn't Gina, but was it definitely Kat?

'Hallo,' repeated Izzy in neutral tones, still planning in her mind a suitably apt murder.

On the other end of the line, Andrew anxiously waited for her to say something else so that he might glean a clue as to the identity of the voice, and Izzy, who could hear him breathing, rapidly answered his prayer. In a voice rigid with disdain, she said, 'Piss off, pervert,' and hung up.

Definitely not Kat, thought Andrew.

* * *

If Joel McGill was as tall, dark and handsome as she had imagined, thought Izzy, then he must be hiding beneath one of the tables. For no man fitting that description – in even its loosest terms – was visible to the naked eye.

She was not, however, going to let that put her off. Since nobody in the audience was wearing a jacket emblazoned with the famous yellow-and-white MBT logo, nor even a discreet badge proclaiming, 'I am an A&R man,' she had simply sung her heart out and ensured that even the least interested and most unlikely looking customer had been singled out during the course of the set for special attention and a dazzling smile.

Now, for the penultimate song of the evening, she stepped down from the stage and moved towards the nearest tables, where a group of businessmen had been applauding with particular enthusiasm. Behind her, Terry the pianist struck up the bluesy opening chords of 'My Baby Just Cares For Me', and the audience, recognizing the song, broke into renewed applause. The regulars among them knew that this was one of her particular favourites. For her finale, Izzy would return to the stage and belt out 'Cabaret' and every spine in the house would tingle because the power and passion in her voice made it impossible not to.

The evening had gone well, the audience were appreciative and Izzy was enjoying herself as she swayed among the tables. When the song was almost over she began to make her way back towards the stage, smiling as she did so at one of the quieter-looking middle-aged businessmen. She was mid-verse when she let out a scream. 'OUCH!'

The quiet, middle-aged businessman's hand, which had shot up the back of her skirt and pinched her thigh, was gone again in a flash. Izzy swung around, stared at him, saw his leery smile. She continued singing, as if the hesitation had been deliberate, and coolly ignored the nudges of his companions.

'Last song, now,' she murmured into the microphone, and nodded to Terry to indicate that she was staying where she was. The audience applauded once more as Terry moved smoothly into 'Cabaret', and Izzy, giving the quiet businessman an encouraging smile, prayed harder than she'd ever prayed before in her life that he wasn't the man from MBT.

As she sang her way through the opening verse, she moved closer to him, swaying her hips like Liza Minelli and reaching out until her fingers were only inches from his shoulder. He was grinning up at her now, his yellowed teeth revealed and his face glistening with sweat.

It was like ripping off an Elastoplast, all over in a flash. Izzy, dancing away, was up on the stage almost before he realised what had happened.

'. . . *Life is a grey toupee, old son, come to the grey toupee* . .' she sang joyously, waving the trophy above her own head like a big hairy handkerchief, and the audience, many of whom had witnessed the businessman's initial crude assault, rocked with laughter. The ensuing cheers almost brought the house down. Izzy bowed and tossed the toupee back to its apoplectic owner, whose friends were laughing more loudly than anyone else.

'Since I doubt very much whether I still work here,' Izzy announced cradling the microphone in both hands,

'I shall just say that I hope you enjoyed the show. You've been a wonderful audience. Thank you, and good night.'

Joel McGill was still crying with laughter when he entered the tiny cubbyhole which Izzy called her dressing room. She had to sit him down on the only chair, hand him a box of Kleenex and pour him a drink before he could even speak.

'I thought it was part of the act,' he managed to say eventually, though his shoulders still shook. 'Then I realised it wasn't . . .'

'That's nothing,' replied Izzy. 'Think how I felt, not knowing whether he was you . . . or you were him . . .' She thought for a second, then shrugged. 'If you know what I mean.'

'I know what you mean,' he agreed, wiping his eyes with a handful of peach-shaded tissues. 'That was fantastic. I think I love you.'

That had been one half of the fantasy, thought Izzy with a wry smile, but the rest of it appeared to have gone somewhat awry. Joel McGill wasn't supposed to be five feet two, with orange hair the texture of a Brillo pad, tiny round spectacles and the very smallest nose she'd ever seen. Neither had it occurred to her, while she was scouring the audience, to seek out a man wearing a powder-blue Argyll patterned pullover, an orange shirt and the kind of tartan trousers more commonly found on a golf course.

'You don't look like an A&R manager,' she said finally.

'No?' Still smiling, Joel McGill blew his nose with vigour. 'What do I look like?'

Izzy knew what she thought. Instead, tactfully, she said, 'Jack Nicklaus?'

He gave her a look that told her she'd disappointed him. 'Really?'

'OK. A train-spotter,' she confessed with reluctance, and he burst out laughing once more.

'I don't know why you had to make me say it,' Izzy grumbled. 'It isn't exactly enhancing my career prospects, after all.'

'Listen,' he said, leaning forward and stuffing the tissues into the back pocket of his terrible trousers. 'I'm one of the best A&R managers in the business. This means, happily, that I don't need to try and look like one. What's important to me is spotting new talent, assessing its potential and signing it up. Now, I spent a great deal of time yesterday listening to your demo tape, and tonight I've seen you . . . in action, so to speak.'

'Mmm?' said Izzy with extreme caution. Her pulse was racing and her fingernails were digging into her palms.

'And since I liked, very much, what I both heard and saw, why don't you stop grumbling and let me be the one to worry about your career prospects?'

'You mean . . . ?'

'I'm offering you a contract on behalf of MBT Records,' said Joel McGill, with an oddly engaging grin. 'Although there must be, I'm afraid, one proviso.'

Anything, thought Izzy passionately, anything at all. If it were stipulated in the contract, she'd even wear baggy tartan trousers.

Almost speechless with joy and gratitude, the most she could manage to get out was, 'What . . . ?'

'The trick with the toupee,' he informed her, struggling unsuccessfully to keep a straight face. 'Whatever you do, don't try it out on the president of MBT. Not unless you really want to die young.'

Guiltily aware that she should be studying for tomorrow's exam, which was chemistry, Katerina had baked herself a chocolate-fudge cake instead and eaten it while mindlessly watching an hour-long episode of a serial she had never seen before, and which she would certainly never watch again. At least both Gina and Izzy had been out, which meant that neither of them realised she had spent the earlier part of her evening sitting alone in a winebar in Kensington High Street, sipping Coke and waiting for Andrew to turn up. When, after an endless ninety minutes he still hadn't arrived, she had returned home and tried hard not to allow her imagination to run riot. He could be in hospital, he could be dead, Marcy could be in hospital . . . the possibilities had been both endless and agonizing . . .

When the phone shrilled at eleven-fifteen, Katerina and Jericho both jumped. Cake crumbs showered on to the carpet as she raced to answer it.

'Hallo?' she whispered, and this time it was so unmistakably her voice that Andrew didn't need to hesitate.

'Darling, it's me. I'm so sorry, I've been trying to get hold of you, but I'm in the bathroom and Marcy's next door.'

'You're OK?' Her hands were shaking uncontrollably. She slid down the wall, ducking to avoid Jericho's chocolatey kisses, and rested on her heels. 'What's happened?'

'Marcy had a miscarriage yesterday.'

'What!'

'She lost the baby,' Andrew repeated, his tone even. It would be indecent to sound too overjoyed, yet at the same time it was the answer to their unspoken prayers . . .

'Oh, poor Marcy,' breathed Katerina, her palms now clammy with perspiration. At the same time relief flooded through her, because Andrew was all right. 'Is she . . . very upset?'

'Yes,' he said briefly. 'That's why I couldn't leave her. Darling, you understand, don't you. I wanted to see you tonight, but—'

'Sssh.' Unbidden, the image of Andrew and herself in bed flashed through her mind. While she had been losing her virginity, Marcy had lost the baby. Overcome with shame, she said, 'Don't say that. Of course you have to stay with her. Look, I have to go now. Someone's coming home.'

'But—'

Quietly replacing the receiver, cutting him off in midprotest, Katerina realised that she felt sick. She was the Other Woman, and quite suddenly she was no longer sure whether she was equipped to deal with it. Simon had been right; it wasn't clever and it wasn't a game. It was becoming suddenly, frighteningly real.

From her vantage point, she held the phone in her lap and watched Gina – the other Other Woman, if she only knew it – wave a fond goodbye to Ralph.

'Gosh, you startled me.' Gina's eyes were bright. She looked so *happy*.

'Sorry,' said Katerina, rising to her feet and feeling old.

'I was on the phone. So, how did your date with the actor go? I thought you might have invited him in for coffee.'

She had been looking forward to seeing Ralph and out-acting him. Now she was glad she didn't have to.

'I did ask, but he has to be up at five o'clock tomorrow morning.' Gina, blushing slightly, looked happier than ever. Katerina, summoning up a smile, thought, You coward, Ralph.

'But did you have a nice evening?' she prompted. 'Do you think you'll see him again?'

'We had a wonderful evening,' Gina replied proudly. 'And yes, I'm seeing him again. Tomorrow night, as a matter of fact.'

'Tomorrow!' Katerina tried not to look too astonished. 'Good heavens, he must be keen.'

'I know,' said Gina, so dazed with joy that when she tried to hang up her jacket she missed the coat stand altogether. 'It's incredible. We just seem to have so much in common . . .'

Chapter 26

Seduction Rule Number One, thought Vivienne cheerfully as she knocked on Sam's bedroom door: catch your subject naked and unaware.

After a long silence, Sam said, 'Go away,' which wasn't the most promising of starts, but Vivienne had decided that enough was enough. The way they had been carrying on for the past few weeks was plain silly. Smiling to herself, she knocked once more.

'I said . . . go away.'

Rule Number Two, Vivienne reminded herself: offer your subject unimaginable delights.

'I'm making breakfast,' she explained. 'Bacon and mushroom sandwiches . . . but if you'd rather go back to sleep . . .'

There was another long silence. Finally, he grumbled, 'I'm awake now. OK.'

'Such gratitude,' Vivienne replied lightly. 'It'll be ready in ten minutes.'

Moments later, she heard the shower begin to run, as she had known it would. Grinning to herself, she returned to the kitchen and turned the heat under the grill down very low indeed.

The noise of the shower meant that Sam didn't hear the bathroom door click open. Vivienne, revelling in the voyeuristic pleasure of watching him through the frosted glass, slipped out of her robe and moved quietly towards the shower cubicle.

'What the—' spluttered Sam, as flesh encountered flesh.

'Sssh, no need to panic,' Vivienne murmured, behind him. 'I'm a trained lifeguard. You won't drown.'

It was no good; she had caught him out. Before he even had time to protest, he knew he was lost. Vivienne, running her hands over his body with soapy, slippery ease, pressed herself against him. Within seconds Sam was aroused.

'This is crazy,' he sighed, willing himself to ignore the erotic effect of her warm, wet flesh and teasing fingers, and failing absolutely.

'But hygienic,' Vivienne murmured, her breasts sliding tantalizingly against his back, her tongue circling one shoulder-blade. Unable to contain her amusement, she said, 'This must be what you British call Good, Clean Fun.'

Turning finally to face her, acknowledging defeat with good grace, Sam took her in his arms and kissed her. Moments later, with a crooked smile, he said, 'We British call it risking life and limb.'

'Oh well,' Vivienne replied huskily, switching off the shower, 'if you want to be staid and boring, I suppose we'll just have to retreat to the safety of a bed.'

Afterwards, Sam rolled on to his side. 'Well?' he demanded. 'Was that staid and boring?'

Vivienne, so happy she thought she would burst, smiled back at him. 'As you British might say,' she informed him solemnly, 'it was very pleasant indeed . . . jolly well done . . . ahbsolutely mahvellous . . . top notch . . . altogether rahther splendid . . .'

'Good,' he interrupted in brisk tones. 'So, now can I have that bacon sandwich?'

'Oh, Izzy!' cried Vivienne, beside herself with delight. 'This is fantastic . . . Jeez, you really *are* on your way, now!'

Izzy grinned as the chauffeur, who swore his name was George, held open the door of the gleaming, ludicrously elongated limousine. 'The first of my lifetime ambitions,' she explained, running her hands lovingly over the ivory-leather upholstery. 'Even if it is only mine for six hours.'

'What's your second lifetime ambition?' Vivienne demanded, pouncing on the cocktail cabinet.

Izzy winked at the chauffeur. 'Wild sex in the back of a limo.'

'God, count me out. George, you aren't listening to this, are you?'

'No, madam,' replied George, maintaining a straight face.

'So, where are we going?' continued Vivienne, pouring enormous drinks and handing one to Izzy as the huge car purred into life.

'Are you kidding?' Izzy looked pained. 'In this thing, *everywhere*.'

By the time they arrived at The Chelsea Steps it was almost one-thirty and a huge crowd of paparazzi were milling around on the pavement outside. Within seconds, they were swarming around the rented limousine.

'My God,' said Izzy, awestruck. 'I got famous quicker than I thought.'

The photographers' expressions soon changed, however, when George opened the rear door.

'Shit, you aren't Tash Janssen,' exclaimed one with evident disgust.

'Never said I was,' Izzy replied loftily. 'Nincompoop.'

He shrugged and sighed. 'So, who are you? Anybody?'

Ignoring him, Izzy turned her attention to the chauffeur. 'Don't let anyone touch the car, George. We won't be longer than a couple of hours. And no gossiping to nincompoops in the mean time, if you value your job.'

'Very well, madam.' He tipped his cap to her.

The photographer regarded Izzy with suspicion. 'Hey, *are* you somebody?'

In reply, she gave him a pitying half-smile. 'Why don't you ask Tash Janssen if I'm "somebody", OK? He'll be here in five minutes. Maybe he'll tell you.'

The club was absolutely heaving with bodies. Izzy, peering through the crowd, said, 'There's Sam. What do you want to do, be polite and say hallo, or ignore him?'

Vivienne coughed delicately. Her green eyes sparkled. 'Ah well . . . as a matter of fact, you aren't the only one with a bit of good news to celebrate.'

'You mean . . .' Izzy stared at her. 'You and Sam?'

'Oh hey, we aren't getting married or anything,' Vivienne giggled. 'No need to look that stunned.'

'But you . . .'

'Got laid,' supplied Vivienne with characteristic bluntness. She heaved a blissful sigh. 'And it was as great as ever. I mean, really. Sam Sheridan is seriously fantastic in the sack.'

I bet he is, Izzy thought ruefully, but she was able to smile and be pleased for her friend. What she'd never had she couldn't miss, she reminded herself, and even if she didn't happen to believe that particular bit of propaganda, at times like this it came in useful.

'I'm glad,' she said honestly, as Sam made his way towards them. 'But don't forget, I want to keep this recording contract a secret for the time being. He still thinks I'm a dumb female and I want to wait until there's something to really show him . . .'

'Izz, I won't breathe a word,' protested Vivienne. 'I *adore* our secret. Why, just this afternoon he was running you down something rotten and I stuck by you all the way.'

Incredulous, Izzy demanded, 'What was he *saying* about me?'

'Oh . . . something about this guy Tash Janssen coming to the club tonight,' said Vivienne vaguely. 'Sam said that if you saw him you'd turn instant groupie.'

'And what did you say?' Izzy's dark eyebrows had disappeared beneath her hair.

Vivienne winked. 'Why, honeychile,' she drawled teasingly. 'I said no way some rich rock star would get it for nothing. You'd charge!'

So annoyed with Sam that she didn't even trust herself to speak to him, Izzy left them to it and went for a wander. And although she tried hard not to think about her lost opportunity with Sam, not to mention the new and ludicrous pairing of Gina and Ralph, she couldn't help noticing that the rest of the world appeared to be going around in twos.

I don't need a man, she reminded herself crossly. I have a recording contract instead.

But it had been an awfully long time; the days of Ralph and Mike and the happily synchronised subterfuge which had made her life so complete were long gone, and now even Katerina had fallen in love . . .

She had to step aside to avoid a couple with their arms locked adoringly around each other's waists. As she did so, she glanced across and saw Vivienne laughing with Sam, over at the bar. Never mind Gina, thought Izzy with a forlorn attempt at humour quite at odds with her previous high spirits; at this rate it wouldn't be long before *she* was the one carting Jericho around the park in search of men.

As soon as she returned from the loo, where excitement was high and lipsticks and Schwarzenegger-strength hairsprays were being wielded with abandon in anticipation of Tash Janssen's rumoured arrival, Izzy observed the hive of activity around the entrance and realised that he had indeed turned up. Famous though The Chelsea Steps might be for its laid-back, no-fuss policy, and although there were no actual stampedes or hysterical screams of delight, the appearance of one of the world's most outrageous and successful rock stars couldn't help but evoke more than a frisson of interest.

Despite herself, Izzy smiled as freshly lipsticked, miniskirted blondes streamed out of the loo and gravitated towards the dance floor. The DJ, who evidently had a sense of humour, promptly played a record to which it was almost impossible to dance. The blondes, first hesitating then retreating in temporary defeat to the sidelines, pretended they hadn't wanted to dance anyway and shot him looks of icy disdain.

'Hmm,' murmured Vivienne, reappearing at Izzy's side and gazing unashamedly in Tash Janssen's direction. 'I have to admit, he is *disturbingly* gorgeous. If I weren't in love with Sam I might even be tempted to have a go at him myself.'

Izzy watched the Janssen entourage – all male, for now at least – settle themselves around The Chelsea Steps' most coveted table. The singer, with his spiky dark hair, heavily lidded, even darker eyes and thin, tanned face, was casually dressed in a red shirt and black jeans. There was an air about him of deceptive languor, as he picked up his drink and murmured a few words to one of his black-suited minders. When he drained his glass in one go, another appeared before him within seconds.

'Definitely dangerous,' pronounced Vivienne, sounding excited. 'Will you look at that mouth . . .'

Despite herself, Izzy was intrigued; how could a man who wasn't, in truth, *that* good-looking, possess such an extraordinary degree of attraction for so many women? And had that attraction preceded the fame or become unleashed as a result of it? Whatever must it be like to exude such an aura . . . to be recognised by literally millions of people the world over . . . to simply *be* Tash Janssen?

'You aren't drooling,' Vivienne observed, giving her a sharp sideways glance.

Izzy, who had been miles away, murmured absently, 'I'm thinking.'

'Never think,' Vivienne declared, because it was one of her father's favourite sayings. 'Just act.'

Izzy grinned. 'Don't tempt me.'

'Will whatever it is annoy Sam?' Vivienne was looking interested now.

'Oh yes.'

'Will he be angry with me?'

'Nooo . . .'

'In that case,' said Vivienne, smiling with relief and clinking her glass against Izzy's, 'what the hell are you doing, hanging around talking to me? Go for it.'

'I don't believe it,' murmured Sam, twenty minutes later, as the larger of Tash Janssen's minders made his way in a direct line across the dance floor and approached Izzy, now sitting demurely on her own at a small table in the very furthest corner of the club.

'Maybe he's asking her to dance,' suggested Vivienne, doing her best not to laugh. The minder was addressing Izzy now, indicating that she should follow him.

'What *is* she playing at?' Sam had never quite overcome his fear that one evening Izzy – who knew no shame – would burst into song in front of one of his more celebrated guests . . .

Vivienne, reading his thoughts, squeezed his arm. 'No, you cannot go over there,' she admonished in stern tones. 'He invited her, didn't he? She hasn't exactly forced herself upon him . . .'

With some unwillingness, Sam conceded that this was

true. But he still wasn't happy. 'She planned this, somehow,' he said darkly, his eyes narrowing as he watched Tash Janssen rise to his feet and shake Izzy's politely proffered hand. 'I don't know how she did it . . .'

'Oh my,' said Vivienne good-humouredly. 'All this fuss over Izzy. Sweetheart, are you sure you aren't just the teeniest bit jealous?'

'Of course I'm not jealous,' Sam replied evenly. Pausing, he took a sip of his drink. 'I just don't want her to start *singing* . . .'

Chapter 27

At close quarters, Tash Janssen was even more devastating to look at. Izzy, sitting next to him with her hands clasped modestly in her lap, wondered how many times he had enjoyed wild sex in the back of a limo, then hastily abandoned such thoughts in case he was able to read her mind.

'Well,' he announced finally, when he had finished subjecting her to a slow up-and-down scrutiny. 'I have to say that I've had plenty of notes passed to me in my time, but none quite like yours.'

'No?' said Izzy with the utmost politeness. The note, which she had handed over to her favourite barman, now lay on the table in front of them, but Tash Janssen quoted the first sentence without even glancing at it.

'I'm not offering you my body, I don't have blonde hair and I am old enough to be your mother. But I would like to make you the very serious offer of a song which may interest you a great deal.'

'Yes,' Izzy replied simply.

'You aren't old enough to be my mother,' he observed with a crooked smile.

'My only fib,' she conceded, the corners of her own mouth beginning to curl.

'And you're telling me that this song is great?'

'Oh, the greatest.'

'Another . . . fib?'

He was amusing himself. Izzy knew perfectly well that he wasn't taking her seriously. Yet at the same time she sensed that even if he didn't actually believe her, she had captured his interest, temporarily at least.

'This song,' she said mildly, 'is the best.'

Tash Janssen laughed and glanced briefly at his watch. 'Look, are you sure you wouldn't like to change your mind about sleeping with me?'

'It would take *five* minutes . . .' Izzy protested, realizing that the softly-softly approach wasn't working and that she was in danger of losing him.

His eyebrows shot up. 'Excuse me, but that just is not *true* . . .'

'To listen to my song, stupid.'

He raised his hands in relief. 'I thought we were discussing my sexual prowess. OK, OK, why don't you send me a tape, care of my record company? I promise to listen to it.'

'No,' said Izzy, opening her bag, lifting out her copy of the demo tape and flicking it away from him when he reached out to take it from her. 'I have a car waiting outside. Come and listen to it now.'

'I . . . do . . . not . . . *believe* . . . it,' said Sam, through gritted teeth.

Vivienne, beside herself with joy, replied consolingly, 'Now, now. She is an adult, after all.'

'That woman is the second most amoral adult I know.' Sam, glaring at the departing figures, observed that Tash Janssen's hand was resting lightly upon Izzy's shoulder.

'And she's just walked out – practically arm in arm, for God's sake – with the first.'

'Maybe,' suggested Vivienne, ever helpful, 'they've gone to feed his meter.'

Izzy, adoring the expression on the face of the photographer who had earlier doubted her, grinned at Tash Janssen, said, 'Your car or mine?' and took three steps towards her own rented limousine before he could open his mouth. With a shrug, she continued smoothly, 'OK, mine. Thank you, George . . . would it be rude to ask you to wait outside the car for a few minutes? Mr Janssen and I have some private business to discuss.'

'Full of surprises,' remarked Tash, when they were safely inside, protected from prying eyes and lenses by blacked-out windows. Leaning closer to Izzy, he murmured conspiratorially, 'Have you ever done it in the back seat of one of these things?'

'Since before you were born,' replied Izzy with a sigh. Pushing him upright, she went on. 'Look, nobody can hear us now, so you can drop the big rock-star act. Just behave like a normal human being for five minutes and listen to my song.'

He laughed. 'Have you ever thought of becoming a schoolteacher?'

'Sssh.' Izzy fitted the cassette into the tape deck and adjusted the balance for quadraphonic sound.

'Your hands are shaking,' he observed.

'That's because I'm nervous.'

He looked interested. 'You practically kidnapped me. Why should *you* be afraid?'

Turning to face him, her dark eyes huge, she said slowly, 'This is important to me. I'm afraid that you won't take the trouble to listen properly, because you're treating this whole thing as a joke, whereas I'm serious.'

After a moment, he took her hand in his, kissed it, then replaced it with care on the seat beside him. 'Sorry,' he said, 'I'll listen properly. I can be serious, too.'

The opening bars of 'Never, Never' flooded the car and he listened. Izzy watched him listen – with his eyes closed and his long legs stretched out in front of him – and scarcely dared to breathe for the entire four minutes.

When the song ended and he didn't move, she thought for a second that he was asleep. Then, slowly, he opened one eye. 'Play it again.'

'Please,' murmured Izzy, rewinding the tape.

He smiled before closing his eyes once more. 'Please.'

Fifteen minutes later, when 'Never, Never' had finished playing for the fourth time, he sat up and ejected the tape, turning it over in his fingers and looking thoughtful. Since he still hadn't said anything about it, Izzy was by this time almost paralysed with anticipation.

'Well?' she said eventually, and with great difficulty because her tongue was by this time stuck to the roof of her mouth.

'I'm impressed,' he replied, sounding faintly amused. 'But then you knew I'd be impressed, otherwise you wouldn't have gone to all this trouble to drag me out here. What I don't understand is why *you* don't want to sing it.'

'I didn't drag you out here,' she reminded him evenly. 'And I do want to sing it. Very much indeed.'

'Then why offer it to me?'

Izzy took a deep breath, inhaling the scent of leather upholstery, cigars and cologne. 'Because I want us to sing it together.'

He looked stunned. 'A duet?'

'That is, I believe, the technical term for it,' she agreed with a brief smile.

'I don't do duets.'

'Maybe you should. The public likes them. Look at Tom Jones and Cerys Matthews.'

'And?' prompted Tash.

'Bryan Adams and Mel C.'

Tash shot her a wry look. 'Not to mention Kermit and Miss Piggy.'

'George Michael and Aretha Franklin!' Izzy swiftly intercepted him before he could start making fun of her again. 'Oh please . . . the fans *love* that kind of thing.'

'Is that right? And how many fans do *you* have?'

'Approximately seventeen,' said Izzy, deciding that it might be prudent to exclude Toupee-Man from the list. She paused, then added, 'And a dog.'

'I see,' said Tash thoughtfully. 'Is the dog small or large?'

She risked a smile, because he still hadn't actually said no . . . and because he was still here in the car . . . and because she was beginning to think that maybe, just maybe, he might be seriously considering her suggestion. 'Why?' she countered, her expression innocent. 'Is size really important?'

'You tell me,' he countered, lying back and tapping the cassette idly against his denim-clad thigh. Then, turning abruptly to face her and regarding her with shrewd, dark eyes, he said, 'No, tell me how long you've been planning this.'

For a second, Izzy wondered whether he would be more impressed if she said weeks, or months. Maybe if he thought she had written the song specifically with him in mind . . . that it had never even occurred to her that anyone else *could* sing it . . .

But they weren't really the kind of eyes you could lie to, she realised, and the events of the evening were beginning to catch up with her. She simply didn't have the energy left to start improvising now.

'About an hour ago,' she admitted with a small shrug. 'When you arrived at the club.'

Tash was struggling to keep a straight face. 'So, it was a spur-of-the-moment decision, an impulsive gesture. How very flattering.'

'But does that make it a bad idea?' Izzy demanded with a trace of irritation because he was laughing at her now. 'Is your rock star's ego too great to cope with the fact that I didn't write the song *for* you?'

'A little diplomacy never goes amiss,' he replied, deadpan, 'but I daresay I'll recover, in time. Is this really your name?'

He was holding the cassette up to the dim light, his eyes narrowing as he scrutinised the label for the first time. Izzy, caught offguard by the abrupt switch in his train of thought, said crossly, 'Of course it's my bloody name.'

'Hmm.' He paused, apparently lost in thought. The next moment, without even glancing at her, he had reached for her hand once more and raised it to his lips.

The gesture was innocent enough. Its effect, however, was wildly erotic. Izzy, tingling all over, murmured faintly, 'Hmm what?'

'Tash and Van Asch,' he said, breaking into a smile. 'I don't know about you, but it sounds pretty good to me . . .'

Chapter 28

Sam, who didn't enjoy musicals and who had been given a pair of much-coveted tickets to see the latest Andrew Lloyd Webber show, newly opened in the West End, dropped round to Kingsley Grove the following afternoon and offered them to Gina.

Gina adored musicals and was delighted. 'Stay for dinner,' she urged, returning her attention to the mixing bowl of pastry she was in the midst of kneading and inclining her head towards the plate of steak fillets on top of the fridge. '*Boeuf en croûte*, and I'm making far too much, so you really must join us.'

Sam hesitated. 'I only really called by to give you the tickets,' he said, not even allowing himself to wonder where Izzy might be, or whether she had even returned home last night. 'Vivienne's expecting me back at the flat . . .'

'Phone her,' said Gina happily. 'Tell her to come round, too. The more the merrier!'

A moment later he heard a footfall upstairs, and the sound of a bedroom door opening. 'Is that Izzy?'

Gina, now energetically rolling out the pastry, puffed a strand of hair away from her forehead and shook her head. 'I heard her come in at around six this morning, but by the time I got home from work she'd disappeared again. That was Kat you just heard.'

Sam tried hard not to think of Izzy and Tash Janssen in bed together. Instead, turning his attention back to Gina and realizing how much better she had been looking over the past few weeks, he said, 'You're cheerful.'

Gina stopped rolling and smiled at him. 'I am, aren't I?'

At least he could be pleased about that. It was about time Gina had some luck. He tilted his head slightly. 'So?'

'Oh, Sam,' she breathed, wiping her cheek with her forearm and streaking it with flour. 'I've met someone, someone really nice . . . and I know it's far too soon to even think about the future, but he's so *special* . . .'

'I'm glad,' said Sam, getting up from his chair and kissing her unfloured cheek. With mock severity, he added, 'And you're not so bad yourself, Mrs Lawrence, so don't let him think he has some kind of monopoly on specialness.'

Gina shook her head. 'At the moment I still can't believe how lucky I am. And you'll meet him, if you stay for dinner. He's due here at six-thirty.'

'In that case,' said Sam, reaching for the phone, 'how can I refuse? I'll tell Vivienne to pick up some wine on the way over.'

When he had replaced the receiver, he said, 'Now, what can I do to help?'

The doorbell rang. Gina, whose arms were floury up to the elbows, smiled. 'Answer that.'

Since neither Sam nor Gina were aware of Ralph's alarming tendency towards over-punctuality, which Katerina had always maintained was a by-product of the fact that the acting profession was so notoriously insecure, it didn't occur to either of them that the doorbell ringing at five forty-five could have any connection whatsoever with his expected arrival at six-thirty.

Sam, opening the door and recognizing him at once, was only momentarily surprised. 'Oh. Hi,' he said easily, glimpsing a gold bracelet and suppressing a grin. 'Izzy's not here, I'm afraid. Was she expecting you?'

'Er . . .' Ralph's composure had temporarily deserted him. Behind Sam, he could see Gina hovering in the hallway.

'She may be back soon,' Sam continued, cheerfully unaware of the havoc he was creating. 'Why don't you come in and wait?'

'Er . . . er . . .'

'What's going on?' said Gina, her voice unnaturally high. She felt as if someone had switched channels in mid-programme. All the colour had drained from her face.

Sam, who had a good memory for names, stepped aside so that she had an unimpaired view of their visitor. 'It's Ralph, sweetheart. Have you two met before? I was just saying that if he's arranged to meet Izzy here he must have a drink with us while he's waiting.'

Gina stared, first at Ralph, then at Sam. Slowly, wondering whether she might be going mad, she said, 'What are you . . . talking . . . about? Is this a joke?'

Improvisation had never been Ralph's strong point. 'Oh, shit,' he said with feeling.

'What?' demanded Sam, glancing in turn at Gina and realizing that she was on the verge of keeling over.

It was her stricken expression that finally gave it away.

His heart sinking, he echoed beneath his breath, 'Oh, shit.'

Izzy, returning home at seven, found Sam waiting for her in the kitchen, alone. Buoyed up by her day at the head offices of MBT in Mayfair, where she had been introduced by Joel McGill to the company's president, its manager and financial directors and the producer with whom she would be working, she was in tearing spirits. And this evening she was having dinner with Tash.

'Hallo, darling!' she exclaimed as Jericho, scrambling to his feet, hurtled towards her. Then, grinning at Sam and realizing that it was no good, she couldn't keep her wonderful secret from him any longer, she said, 'Hallo, Sam. Guess where I've been?'

Then, as he looked up at her, she saw the cold fury in his eyes. 'You mean apart from that creep's bed?' he spat with contempt. 'I really don't know, Izzy. You could have been anywhere, stirring up any amount of trouble and disrupting any number of innocent lives.'

Izzy, stunned by the unexpectedness of the verbal assault, gazed blankly at him for a second. She'd never seen Sam so angry before. Then she twigged: he meant Tash. Sam had warned her not to approach him and she had ignored the commandment. Rock stars, it seemed, weren't the only ones with big egos . . .

'Not that it's *any* of your business,' she replied crossly, because she had come home bearing glad tidings and now he was spoiling it all, 'but I didn't sleep with Tash Janssen. I have no *intention* of sleeping with him—'

'Of course you don't,' Sam jibed, fuelling the words

with sarcasm. 'Come on, let me guess. You spent last night admiring his art collection!'

'We spent last night talking about music,' Izzy retaliated, a faint smile lifting the corners of her mouth. Heavens, she hadn't dreamed that Sam would react this strongly. He must still care about her, after all . . .

'So, you two were "talking about music",' he continued, his tone dangerously even.

'We had a cup of tea as well,' volunteered Izzy, beginning to enjoy herself now. 'And I ate six chocolate biscuits.'

'Where was Gina?'

'What?'

'Last night,' prompted Sam, moving inexorably in for the kill. 'While you were out. Where was she?'

'You mean *our* Gina?' Izzy, confused by yet another abrupt switch in the conversation, said, 'She wasn't there! She went out to dinner with . . . someone else.'

'And who exactly did she go out to dinner with?'

'Oh, hell!' Izzy, understanding finally what he was saying, closed her eyes in dismay. 'Bloody hell. *Bloody* Ralph . . .'

'Bloody who?' he demanded, suppressing the urge to shake her until her teeth dropped out. Izzy's ability to swan through life absolving herself from all blame was positively breathtaking. 'How the fuck could you stand by and let it happen? You *condoned* it . . .'

'I did not!' Her fingers gripped the edge of the dresser. She was quivering with rage now. 'I told him not to hurt her.'

'And if you'd told her in the first place, she wouldn't be

hurt now. But you chose not to, didn't you? Because it amused you to play along with the charade . . . because it made a good story to tell your friends.' He gestured towards her with disdain. 'You probably told Janssen about it, last night.'

Unable to contain her fury any longer, Izzy picked up the nearest object to hand and hurled it at him. The Victorian china ginger pot, missing him by several feet, crashed in spectacular fashion against the far wall and shattered into a million pieces.

Sam, who hadn't even flinched, sneered derisively. 'Oh, well done. Gina *will* be pleased.'

'I'll replace it,' shouted Izzy.

'Of course you will,' he replied, his tone icy. 'Just as soon as you've managed to persuade her to lend you the money.'

'Stop it,' said Gina quietly, from the doorway. 'Both of you.'

Izzy's eyes promptly filled with tears. 'I'm sorry.'

'It doesn't matter.' Gina, stunned by her reaction – Izzy *never* cried – shook her head. 'Andrew bought it for me last Christmas. I never liked it.'

'I meant . . . Ralph,' sniffed Izzy. 'I wasn't trying to deceive you, although I know I did . . . but you just seemed so happy . . .'

'I know,' said Gina soothingly. 'It wasn't your fault. I was a bit shocked when I realised who he was, but it's hardly the end of the world, is it?'

Sam, outraged by the fact that she was siding with Izzy against him and making such light of the matter, said, 'But you told me how much you liked him. You said—'

'Maybe I did,' Gina intercepted, without looking at him. 'But how upset do you honestly expect me to be? I was married to Andrew for fifteen years. For heaven's sake, I only met Ralph a few days ago.'

Izzy, rummaging blindly in her bag for a tissue and still desperate to make some kind of amends, encountered her purse. The first thing she'd done after leaving MBT's offices had been to rush to the bank and cash a good proportion of her advance cheque. Now, stung by Sam's earlier jibe, she pulled out a fat wad of notes.

'Here's the money I borrowed the other day,' she said rapidly, stuffing them into Gina's startled hands. 'And here's something to replace the pot.' Then, because she didn't have enough cash in her purse to be able to make the ultimate grand gesture and hurl it in Sam's horrible face, she withdrew her cheque book instead and scribbled out a cheque for £1300. Pushing it across the kitchen table towards him, she said, 'That's for Vivienne. Don't worry, it won't bounce.'

As he rose to leave, Sam cast a single, derisive glance in her direction. 'She was right, then,' he said evenly. 'You *do* charge.'

'I don't know why he should have turned on you like that,' said Gina later, while Izzy prepared to go out. 'It's not like Sam at all.'

'Don't apologise on his behalf.' Izzy, concentrating on her mascara, dismissed him with a shrug. 'He's a moody pig and I couldn't care less what he thinks of me. Look, are you quite sure you'll be OK here on your own this evening? Because you can always come along with me.'

Gina laughed. 'I'm sure Tash Janssen would enjoy that. What's the problem – do you think you might need a chaperone?'

'According to Sam,' replied Izzy, glossing her lips and pulling a fearsome face, 'I'll need six.'

When Katerina poked her head around the sitting-room door five minutes later, Izzy was saying, '. . . really am sorry about Ralph, you know.'

'Of course I know,' Gina replied in reassuring tones. 'It was only Sam getting hold of the wrong end of the stick. I know you'd never do anything deliberately to hurt me.'

Katerina, who had been about to announce that she was going over to Simon's house, felt her heart skip a couple of beats. How would Gina feel if she knew that in less than an hour she would be meeting Andrew? Could there be any more deliberately hurtful gesture? Was she really the world's worst bitch, or simply a helpless victim of circumstance?

Abruptly, avoiding Gina's eyes, she said, 'I'm off now.'

'Don't be late home.' Turning, Izzy smiled at her. 'And cheer up, sweetheart. Just think, one more paper tomorrow morning, then that'll be it. Oh, and tell Simon I'm taking the two of you out to dinner tomorrow night, to celebrate. We'll go somewhere splendid!'

Katerina hesitated, then said unhappily, 'I don't know whether Simon . . .'

'I'm taking you *both* out,' repeated Izzy, in firm tones. 'Because you damn well deserve it. And this way I can thank Simon for all the help and hospitality he's given you over the past few weeks. Ask him if there's anywhere in particular he'd like to go, will you, so that I can book the table in advance.'

Chapter 29

Izzy, twisting round in the passenger seat of the dark grey Bentley and watching the electronically controlled gates swing shut behind her, felt a sudden affinity with Little Red Riding Hood. Ahead, just visible through the trees which lined the curving driveway, Stanford Manor loomed multi-turreted and magnificent. Izzy swallowed and tried hard not to look too impressed. Jericho poked his head between the front seats and whimpered. When the car slowed to a halt at the top of the drive, Izzy wrapped his lead around her wrist three times in case Tash kept guard dogs.

There were none in sight, however, when he came out to greet her. Jericho, shamelessly fickle, leapt at once towards him and investigated him with evident delight.

'Your greatest fan, I take it,' Tash observed, patting him. Izzy, realizing how desperately Jericho was moulting, prayed that the car's upholstery wasn't too covered with hairs.

'My chaperone,' she corrected him, shivering suddenly despite the fact that it was still warm. When Tash transferred his attention back to her, she felt her legs begin to tremble of their own accord.

Last night, persuading him to listen to her music and take her seriously had been all-important, and she hadn't allowed herself to even consider how seriously attractive he really was. Now, however, it hit her like a brick. He was stunning. It was official. Several million females, she thought with a brief half-smile, couldn't be wrong.

The driver who had picked her up and brought her to Stanford Manor had, by this time, disappeared. Following Tash and Jericho into the vast, high-ceilinged entrance hall, Izzy admired Tash's tall, athletically proportioned body. This evening, dressed in a pale pink shirt, faded denims and no shoes, and smelling cleanly of Calvin Klein aftershave, he seemed altogether more normal than he had done last night. It was bizarre to think that he owned this great house, not to mention two other *pieds-à-terre* in Paris and New York. It was mind-boggling to think how much money that gravelly, sexy voice had earned him . . .

'How old are you?' she asked, gazing up at the stained-glass windows and at the minstrel's gallery running along three sides of the hall.

Tash cast a sideways glance in her direction. 'Old enough to be your son, according to you.'

'Seriously, I'm interested.'

'Thirty-three.'

Three years younger than me, thought Izzy. 'And you've been married how many times?'

Looking amused, he replied, 'Only twice. Although I do have a tendency to find myself engaged. Every time I buy a pretty girl a ring it turns out she expects me to marry her.'

If anything about Tash Janssen was more famous than his voice, it was his predilection for blondes. Startlingly beautiful, *always* tall, these blondes were famous in turn for their less-than-dazzling intellect. One or two had even been suspected of not yet having come to terms with the complexities of joined-up writing. Izzy couldn't help wondering why someone like Tash, evidently no intellectual slouch himself, should confine himself to bimbos when he could have anyone he chose. 'Maybe you should stick to signed photographs in future,' she suggested absently.

He smiled. 'Maybe. How about you?'

'Heavens, how kind.' Izzy feigned surprise. 'I'd like a motor bike.'

'I'll make a note of it in my diary. Through here.' Opening a carved oak door, he waved her through to the dining room. 'I meant how old are you and how many times have you been married?'

'Thirty-six,' said Izzy. 'And never. I'm not the marrying kind.'

' "Never, Never",' Tash observed drily, pulling a dining chair out for her and ensuring that she was comfortable before seating himself opposite. The table, which would easily have accommodated a rugby team, was covered with a dark blue linen cloth and laid for two people with heavy silver cutlery, glittering crystal goblets and a bottle of Chablis in an ice bucket. Lighted candles, spilling snaky trails of beeswax down their sides, cast an apricot glow over the proceedings.

Izzy placed her forefinger momentarily over the flame of the nearest candle then held it up, blackened, and said, 'Isn't this what happens when you get married?'

He grinned and poured the wine. 'Financially, you mean? Of course it is, if you're me.'

The divorce settlements obtained by his ex-wives were

legendary, yet he didn't seem perturbed.

'Don't you mind?' said Izzy, genuinely interested.

Tash shrugged and replied lazily, 'What the hell, it's only money. And it seems to keep the girls happy.'

'I want to be rich,' said Izzy, with longing.

Deadpan, he replied, 'That's easily achieved. All you need to do is marry and divorce me.'

At that moment another door opened and their dinner was served to them by a brisk, plain, middle-aged woman with the air of a schoolmistress. Izzy, half-expecting to be reminded to eat up all her vegetables, smiled at the woman as the dishes were laid out and received a blank stare in return.

'Mrs Bishop makes it a strict rule to disapprove of my female friends,' Tash explained, when they were alone once more.

'I didn't expect you to live like this.' Izzy shook her head, bemused by the formality of it all. Having imagined wall-to-wall groupies, non-stop music, cans of lager and pinball machines, all this silence and *House & Garden* perfection was unnerving. 'Do you have fun here? Are you *happy*?'

Tash's dark eyebrows arched in surprise. 'You mean has becoming a multi-millionaire ruined my life? Sweetheart, I grew up on a council estate in Neasden with three brothers and two sisters. This is how I can afford to live now. Would *you* be unhappy?'

Izzy, however, still wasn't convinced. Despite the excellence of the food she had lost her appetite. 'I might be,' she replied, pushing her plate to one side. 'Of course, that's something you never find out until it's happened, but I've always been poor and I'm curious. I have fun spending money on things I know I can't afford, like going out for a wonderful meal when I really should be saving the money to pay the gas bill.' She paused, then added helplessly, 'But what do *you* do, when you want to have fun?'

'I can't believe you asked that question,' drawled Tash, his dark eyes glittering with amusement. All pretence at dinner abandoned now, he rose slowly to his feet and held his hand out towards her. 'Come on.'

'What?' Izzy gulped, her stomach leaping helplessly as his fingers curled around hers. 'Where . . . ?'

'You wanted to know what I do when I want to have fun,' he reminded her. 'Come with me and I'll show you.'

The recording studio, situated in what had once been a wine cellar, was a revelation – as far as Izzy was concerned – in every respect. Making the demo tape at the prestigious Glass Studios on the Chelsea Embankment had been exciting, but then she had been the performer, singing when she was instructed to sing and generally doing as she was told, while the producer and sound engineers worked their inscrutable magic in the control room next door.

Now, sitting at the amazingly intricate thirty-two track console and actually being allowed to experiment with the wondrous effects of the midi-synthesiser, a whole new world was opening up to her. Who needed to be able to write music when any notes played on the keyboard were instantly displayed on a computer screen and stored on disc? Who needed to be able to play the drums when at the touch of a button the same keyboard could transform any note into that produced by a snare, a kick-drum, a crash cymbal or a hi-hat? Who *needed* to struggle to emulate the exact degree of reverberation required at the end of a verse, when they had a machine like this, capable of doing it for them?

Even more stunning, however, had been the change in Tash. Gone was the lazy, laid-back demeanour, the air of boredom which she had first observed at The Chelsea Steps. The moment he had pulled up a chair and begun to demonstrate the different functions of the myriad machines before her, he had come properly alive. Making music – this was what gave him pleasure. This was Tash Janssen's idea of fun and for all his earlier double entendres Izzy realised that now if she were to pull off her jeans and top and dance naked around the studio, he would take no notice at all.

'Flick that switch,' he instructed her, so engrossed in the columns of figures on the computer screen that he didn't even realise his fingers were resting on Izzy's knee. Izzy tried hard not to notice, either. Whereas it had been easy to rebuff his good-natured advances yesterday, this abrupt switch to indifference – and the fact that he was no longer *trying* to seduce her – was ridiculously erotic. Pressing the switch he had indicated, she glanced around the room in order to take her mind off his proximity. Each wall was lined with cork tiles of different thicknesses in order to deaden the acoustics and the stone-flagged floor was covered with matting. More inviting was the slightly battered, green velvet sofa positioned against the wall behind them. Apart from the faint whirring of the tape she had set in motion, the room was in total silence.

'Now press play,' said Tash, when the tape had skittered to a halt.

Izzy, entranced by his seriousness, obeyed. Moments later, as the first bars of 'Never, Never' filled the studio, she sat upright and said, 'Oh . . . !'

When the tape ended she gazed at Tash with new respect. 'You did all that from memory.'

He smiled briefly. 'Since you wouldn't let me keep the tape, I didn't have much choice. It isn't exactly the same, but I wanted to experiment with the vocals . . . I'm pretty out of practice as far as this kind of singing's concerned.'

'I knew you could do it,' sighed Izzy. Unaccustomed though he might be to producing anything less than hard-driving, full-tilt rock, that husky voice was wonderfully suited to the slower, gentler pace of 'Never, Never'. Despite herself, she felt a lump form in her throat. She *had* known he could do it, but she hadn't imagined he would do it this well. Now, for the first time, she realised just how much of an effect last night's impulsive introduction could have on her life . . .

Two hours later, dropping the headphones she'd been wearing on to thé desk and rumpling her hair back into some sort of shape, Izzy collapsed on to the sofa. Adrenalin was still bubbling through her veins and it didn't appear to have anywhere to go. Trying not to gaze at Tash's rear view – at the way his jeans clung to his narrow hips as he leaned across the mixing console to close down the computer – she said, 'So, this is what you do when you want to have fun.'

'Mmm.' He had his back to her, but she thought he

was smiling. 'Better than sex, don't you think?'

'That depends on who you're doing it with.'

He was definitely smiling now. 'I thought you didn't want to sleep with me.'

'I didn't want to sleep with the famous Tash Janssen,' she replied carefully. 'But you're different.'

Izzy held her breath as he turned and came to stand before her, then slowly reached out and drew her to her feet. Even more slowly, he traced the curve of her cheek with a forefinger. Hopelessly excited, incapable of concealing her own longing, she was pink-cheeked and trembling.

'We have a business partnership,' he reminded her. 'I don't think it would be a wise move. I really don't think we should risk spoiling that.'

Oh bugger, thought Izzy, not knowing whether to argue the point or give in gracefully. The humiliation of it all! And how Sam would laugh if he ever found out that she had been rejected by none other than Tash Janssen, the most unscrupulous seducer since Valentino.

'Right,' she said bravely, attempting to sound business-like and uncrushed. 'Of course. Look, it's past Jericho's bedtime. I'd better be making a move . . .'

But she didn't move anywhere, because at that moment Tash bent his head and kissed her, slowly, luxuriously and with stunning finesse. It was about the most unbusiness-like kiss she had ever encountered, and her senses reeled. Izzy was now thoroughly confused.

'Just checking,' murmured Tash, glancing over her shoulder and meeting Jericho's calm, unflinching gaze.

'What?'

'That dog of yours. He is one lousy chaperone.'

She looked surprised. 'Of course he is. Would I have brought him along otherwise?'

'I don't know.' Pausing, he slid his hand beneath her hair and idly stroked the sensitive nape of her neck. 'I don't know what you might do.'

Izzy thought she might be in danger of exploding with frustration. Trying not to squirm, she said faintly, 'Look, you said we were business partners. This isn't very fair . . .'

'You said you didn't want to sleep with me,' he reminded her for the second time. Then he smiled. 'Maybe I was lying, too.'

'I wasn't lying,' Izzy protested, wanting him to understand. 'I just changed my mind.'

Suppressing laughter, Tash pulled her towards him once more. 'Well, don't do it again. At least, not for the next couple of hours . . .'

Chapter 30

Tash was a light sleeper. Through half-closed eyes he watched for some time while Izzy crept about the bedroom struggling to locate her clothes in the dark. Finally, he said, 'What on earth are you trying to do?'

'Find my shoes.' Izzy, who had barely slept at all, didn't turn to look at him. She had been lying awake, bitterly regretting her actions, even before he had flung out a bare arm and murmured, 'Anna,' in his sleep. She'd already known she'd made a mistake, but that was the moment when she realised she could no longer stay. She'd behaved just as Sam had predicted and now she was suffering the inevitable consequences. She was nothing but a tart. And where the bloody hell *were* her shoes, anyway?

'You don't have to leave.' Tash sounded amused but made no move towards her. 'Breakfast will be served from eight-thirty onwards. Why don't you just come back to bed and—?'

'No, thanks.' Izzy abruptly intercepted him, sensing that he was humouring her. Just as he must have humoured so many other women in the past, she thought with a surge of shame. 'I'm going home.'

This time he yawned and made a non-committal gesture. 'If that's what you want, OK. Don't say I didn't offer.'

'Don't worry,' she replied evenly, dredging up every last vestige of pride. 'I won't say anything at all.'

Tash smiled to himself as the two figures came into view ahead of him, imprisoned in the twin beams of his headlights. Izzy Van Asch was one hell of a stubborn lady. A barefoot stubborn lady, at that. He was impressed they'd managed to get this far in the twenty minutes or so since they'd left the house.

Slowing to a crawl alongside them, he lowered his window and held out one of her shoes. 'OK, Cinderella, you've made your point. Were you really thinking of walking all the way back to Kensington?'

Since Kensington was over twenty miles away, Izzy certainly was not. As soon as she reached the nearest village – she could have sworn they'd passed one on the way here last night – she was going to find a public callbox and phone for a cab. But the village had mysteriously distanced itself from Tash's isolated home, the soles of her feet were burning with pain and she was *hungry* . . .

'Come on, get in,' said Tash, admiring her spirit. 'Look, poor old Jericho wants a lift, even if you don't.'

Jericho, with characteristic shamelessness, was pressing his nose against the window. Izzy couldn't help smiling at the expression on his face. When Tash opened the car's rear door the dog scrambled on to the back seat with all the grace of an eager groupie.

'I don't turn out at five-thirty in the morning for just anyone, you know,' he remarked as Izzy slid into the passenger seat.

'I'm not just anyone.'

'Of course you aren't. You're a damn sight more bloody-minded than most people I know.'

They had breakfast at an hotel in Windsor, sitting out on the terrace and watching a string of polo ponies setting out on their dawn gallop across the dew-drenched lawns of Windsor Great Park. Jericho, wolfing down sausages and basking in the pale, early morning sunlight, was in heaven. So were the hotel staff, when they realised they had Tash Janssen on the premises.

'I felt cheap,' Izzy explained, feeling immeasurably better after five bacon sandwiches and several cups of strong black coffee.

'Maybe I did, too.' Behind his dark glasses, Tash gave her a mocking grin. 'Hasn't it occurred to you that whenever some woman wonders what it must be like to go to bed with a rock star, I'm the one on the receiving end? They don't want *me*, they just want to screw a celebrity and it's up to me to put in a good performance, otherwise they'll rush out and tell all their friends how hopeless I was.'

Izzy, who hadn't thought of it that way, pinched a grilled mushroom from his plate and said, 'You weren't hopeless, you were very good.'

'Of course I was good!' He raised his eyebrows in mock despair. 'That's because it wouldn't be healthy for my ego if you were to go belting off to the papers screaming, "We were going to record a song together but he was so terrible in bed I couldn't bear to go through with it. I'm going to sing with Des O'Connor instead." '

'Des O'Connor,' breathed Izzy reverently. 'I hadn't thought of him. How *stupid* of me . . .'

Katerina's heart sank when she rounded the corner and saw Andrew waiting for her in his car. It wasn't what she needed right now, but at the same time she wasn't particularly surprised to find him here. Last night had been awful and he hadn't taken it at all well. Katerina wondered whether he'd had as little sleep as she had. The big difference, of course, was that he wasn't due to take a final physics exam in less than half an hour.

'Kat, we have to talk.' Andrew certainly didn't look as if he'd slept. His thin face was almost grey with anxiety and the inside of the car was thick with cigarette smoke. Since a group of Katerina's classmates were meandering past, however, she wasn't about to get involved in a shouting match on the pavement. Pulling the passenger door shut behind her, she said wearily, 'I'm not going to change my mind, Andrew. We can't carry on seeing each other. It's *wrong* and I've been a selfish bitch—'

'But I love you,' he said urgently, trying to take her hand. 'And you love me, so how can it possibly be wrong? Nothing else *matters*.'

'Gina matters.' Katerina closed her eyes. When she opened them again a second later she saw Simon heading towards them, pretending not to look inside the car. 'Marcy does, too. She's just suffered a miscarriage. You should be looking after her.'

She was holding herself rigidly away from him. Andrew, longing to take her into his arms, knew she didn't really mean what she was saying.

'I want to look after you,' he told her, willing her to stop this stupid game. 'Kat, I've never loved anyone as much as I love you.'

Simon, rounding the final corner, swallowed hard when he saw who was waving to him by the school gates. Shit, now what was he supposed to do?

'Simon!' Izzy called out to him, as if he could have failed to notice her. Whoever could miss Izzy Van Asch? he thought, colouring with pleasure at the sight of her even as his mind raced ahead to the immediate problem of preventing her from seeing Kat and Andrew together.

'I had to come and wish Kat good luck for this morning and she hasn't arrived yet,' she explained, her dark eyes alight with amusement. 'I can't believe it – for the very first time in my life I'm early and she's late.'

Simon, crossing his fingers behind his back, said, 'She'll be here any minute now.'

'And how about you? Are you nervous?'

'Uh . . . yes.' That was an understatement. He promptly turned one shade pinker as Izzy gave him a kiss on the cheek.

'Well, don't be. You'll both do brilliantly, I know it. And then there's tonight to look forward to,' she added cheerfully. 'Where have you decided you want to go?'

Simon, who didn't have a clue what she was talking about, hesitated for a second. 'Well, Cambridge is my first choice. Although Mum isn't so keen on the idea of me leaving home.'

Izzy burst out laughing. 'I'm talking about restaurants, not universities. Honestly, that daughter of mine! Didn't she even tell you I'm taking the two of you out to dinner tonight?'

Distracted by the realization that the sleek bronze car parked at the kerbside was the very latest Mercedes, and that the big, ungainly dog peering out of the open window was Jericho, Simon said, 'Um . . . she must have forgotten to mention it.'

'It's Tash Janssen's car.' Izzy, who had followed his gaze, smiled at the expression on his face. Clearly, Kat had kept equally quiet about Tash.

He gulped. 'Really?'

'Really. So, how about this meal tonight, then? Where would *you* like to go?'

Katerina's mother really was amazing, thought Simon. Awestruck, he craned his neck sideways in an effort to catch a casual glimpse of the driver. The tinted windows didn't help, but he was just about able to make out the silhouette of his hero, wearing sunglasses and drumming his fingers idly against the steering wheel.

'I've always wanted to go to Planet Hollywood,' said Simon hopefully, wondering if by some miracle Tash Janssen might be there, too.

Planet Hollywood? Good grief. Awash with disappointment, Izzy said, 'Not Le Gavroche?'

'Anywhere. Anywhere.'

Delighted, she pushed back her hair. 'Le Gavroche it is, then. As long as we can get a table at such short notice. Simon, where *is* Kat?'

Just around the corner, arguing with her lover. Simon, panicking all over again at the thought of the proximity between mother and daughter, muttered hastily, 'Don't worry, she won't be late. Do you really *know* Tash Janssen?'

Izzy paused, wondering where Kat might be. It wasn't likely, but there was always the faint possibility that she might have overslept. 'We're recording a song together,' she replied absently. 'Do you think we should be looking for her?'

'No!' Simon shuddered. 'She's never late. She'll *be* here. Le Gavroche . . . isn't that a bit expensive? Do they serve English food?'

'They serve the *best* food,' declared Izzy, with an expansive gesture. The next moment her gaze slid past Simon and her eyes lit up. 'There she is! Darling . . .'

Katerina wasn't in the mood for hugs and kisses and Walton-type endearments. Behind her, she could hear the tyres of Andrew's car squealing as he made his ill-tempered getaway. Ahead of her stood Izzy, still wearing last night's clothes, looking hopelessly unmotherly in skin-tight jeans and a lacy off-the-shoulder top. Simon, obviously entranced, towered over her and several fellow pupils were lingering on the pavement close to a sporty, metallic-bronze car which Kat just *knew* had to be connected in some way with Izzy.

'Mum, I've got an exam.'

'Of course you have! Sweetheart, I've just been talking to Simon. We're all set for dinner at Le Gavroche, but we couldn't resist coming to wish you luck. Down, Jericho! Kat, you must say hallo to Tash Janssen. Tash, this is my brilliant daughter.'

Izzy, flushed with pride, pulled open the driver's door of the Mercedes and the girls lingering on the pavement gaped. Katerina, desperately on edge after her difficult encounter with Andrew, could scarcely bear to meet the eyes of Tash Janssen. She wished she could murder her mother.

'Say hallo,' prompted Izzy, puzzled by her daughter's lack of enthusiasm. 'We drove all the way over here to see you . . .'

'I didn't ask you to,' Katerina retaliated crossly, realizing she was on the verge of tears. This was all too much, too embarrassing for words. The other girls were giggling like five year olds, pushing each other closer to get a better look at this stupid rock star, and she was the one who would have to put up with their inane questions later. Trust Izzy, she thought bitterly, to turn her A level exams into a bloody circus.

Simon, glancing at his watch, said, 'It's nine o'clock, Kat.'

'We have to go,' she explained brusquely, beginning to edge away.

Disappointed, Izzy gave her a hug. 'Well, good luck, darling. You'll do brilliantly, I know you will.'

Katerina tried not to flinch as her mother kissed her; it was too reminiscent of the way Andrew had tried to put his arms around her just now in the car. 'Don't, Mum,' she said in pained tones. 'Everybody's watching.'

'So what?' declared Izzy, trying to coax a smile out of her and failing absolutely. 'Who cares?'

'I care,' snapped Katerina. Then, more cruelly than she had intended, she added, 'We don't *all* long to be the centre of attention, you know. Not *all* the bloody time.'

Chapter 31

It was no good. By mid-morning, it was glaringly obvious that his inability to concentrate was affecting his work. Even Pam, his secretary, had been moved to enquire whether anything was wrong.

Everything's wrong, Andrew had wanted to shout at her, hating the way her eyebrows rose in polite disbelief as, emphasizing every mistake, she proceeded to read his dictation back to him.

'Maybe you're going down with summer 'flu,' she suggested, not believing for a second that he was really ill. Something was up, and her fertile imagination was at work figuring out what it might be. Three times this week she'd fielded phone calls from Marcy Carpenter, telling her Andrew was in a meeting when in reality he'd slipped out of the office for yet another prolonged 'lunch appointment'. Pam, who spent her own meagre lunch breaks devouring egg-and-cress sandwiches and Mills and Boon romances borrowed from the local library, couldn't help hoping that Andrew and Gina would get back together. Gina had always remembered her birthday, complimented her on her cardigans and been interested enough to ask her how she was, whereas Marcy Carpenter was nothing but a selfish, idle trollop.

'I do have a bit of a headache,' lied Andrew. His headache was persuading Katerina to see reason, making her understand that guilt and a ridiculous sense of obligation towards Gina weren't valid reasons to end their love affair.

Ever practical, Pam said, 'I've got some aspirins in my handbag.'

Gina had always carried aspirins around in her bag. For a fleeting moment Andrew wished she'd swallow a whole tub of them, then she wouldn't be able to stand in the way – however unwittingly – of his own happiness. It was ludicrous, he thought with rising frustration, that Katerina should feel compelled to make such a noble gesture simply to save the feelings of the wife from whom he was separated. Who, after all, could say whether Gina would even *care* . . . ?

'Thanks,' he replied absently, rising to his feet and almost knocking a stack of files to the floor as he did so. 'But I think I'll take a breath of fresh air instead. I'll be back by two if anyone needs to speak to me.'

He was out of the office within seconds. Although it was only eleven forty-five, Pam pulled her packed lunch out of her capacious handbag and settled down to enjoy a few extra chapters of *A Marriage Made in Heaven* by Desiree Bell. She deserved that much at least, she told herself as she bit forcefully into an apple. If Andrew Lawrence couldn't even wish her a happy birthday he needn't expect *her* to slave away over his rotten, incompetent dictation.

Andrew knew vaguely where Gina was working because Katerina had once told him, but he had to use the *Yellow Pages* in order to get the full address. Fired up with enthusiasm – it was so blindingly obvious, he couldn't think why the idea hadn't occurred to him earlier – he drove straight over to Doug Steadman's office and took the stairs two at a time, only pausing for breath when he reached the door at the top of the landing, upon which a small, highly polished plaque announced D. STEADMAN, THEATRICAL AGENT.

'Andrew!' Gina looked up, startled. Automatically, her left hand smoothed her straight, blonde hair, as it always did when she was caught unawares. The fact that she was no longer wearing her wedding ring was, he felt, an encouraging sign.

'I had to see you,' he explained, his eyes bright with purpose, and Gina felt her heart begin to pound. Could it all be over between Andrew and Marcy? Had he come here to ask her to forgive him? Did he really want to come back to her?

'Y-yes?' she stammered, twisting a pencil between her fingers and wishing she'd worn a dress that wasn't four years old. She hadn't had time to blow dry her hair with her customary attention to detail this morning, either. And why, oh why, had she allowed Izzy to bulldoze her into leaving off her wedding ring?

'We have to talk, Gina. About something very important.'

At least Doug was out of the office. An audience would be more than she could cope with, thought Gina faintly, although it certainly hadn't seemed to bother Debra Winger in *An Officer and a Gentleman*.

'OK,' she murmured, reaching out with trembling fingers and taking the phone off the hook. She'd just have to pray that no one came into the office and interrupted them. 'What do we have to talk about?'

Having intended coming straight out with it, Andrew now understood that in order to avoid confusion he must first fill Gina in on one or two other pertinent details.

'Look, the situation with Marcy and me . . . well, it isn't working out. I thought I was in love with her, but I realise now that I was wrong. If I'm honest, it started going wrong almost straight away.'

My God, thought Gina, struggling to contain herself. This is really happening! I can't believe it . . .

'The baby,' she murmured, feeling so light-headed she had to grip the edge of her desk.

Andrew looked momentarily surprised. He'd forgotten she didn't know about that. 'Oh, she lost it.' He dismissed the subject with an airy gesture. 'Miscarriage, a couple of weeks ago. I shouldn't say it, of course, but in some respects it was a bit of a relief, what with the way things were going between us. As soon as she finds herself somewhere to live, Marcy will be moving out of the flat. It was just one of those things, really. I suppose we all make mistakes.'

Oh God, thought Gina. Oh God, he wants me back . . .

'So, that's that out of the way.' Andrew took a deep, steadying breath. 'I had to explain, otherwise you'd have thought I was behaving badly. The thing is, you see, I've met someone else now. And this time it *is* for real. The only problem at the moment is the fact that she thinks you might be upset if you found out about it.'

Gina attempted to smooth her hair, but her arm was so heavy she couldn't lift it. Her entire body felt like lead.

Her heartbeat had slowed to an ominous, funereal pace.

'What?'

'Of course, *I* knew you wouldn't mind,' continued Andrew, adopting a hearty manner. It was quite the best way, he'd decided; if he was forceful enough he could make Gina realise it was the only sensible attitude to take. 'We're practically divorced, after all, but she was still worried.' Leaning forward, he added confidentially, 'I think she's afraid you might never speak to her again, or some such ridiculous thing.'

Gina sat there, paralysed. It was like thinking you'd won an Olympic medal, then being told you were being disqualified through no fault of your own. And in the few mind-numbing seconds following the realization that Andrew was talking about another woman, she had struggled to envisage the stranger – a chic, dark-haired divorcée, possibly – with whom he had fallen in love.

But now . . . now he was making it plain to her that the woman was someone she actually *knew*, and not only was that so much worse than any imaginary stranger, but she couldn't for the life of her even begin to guess who it might be.

Until Andrew, in his eagerness to sort the matter out, said, 'And she'll be moving into my flat, so you don't have to worry about any awkwardness at home.'

It was becoming progressively harder for Gina to breathe. Betrayal hit her like a hammer blow. She couldn't believe it.

'You. You and . . . Izzy . . .' she said faintly.

'*Izzy?*' Andrew, staring at her in amazement, almost laughed. How could anybody get something *so* wrong?

'Do me a favour, old thing! It's not Izzy I'm talking about. It's Kat.'

Izzy, having spent the day with Tash at his record company's headquarters, had discovered how the other half of the music industry really lived. MBT, the label to which she herself had been signed, was a young and thrusting company with a great reputation for fostering promising new talent. By contrast, Stellar Records was quite simply *the* biggest label in the business and it had the headquarters to prove it. Stellar House, situated in Highgate, was as big as a museum and twice as impressive. Open-mouthed, Izzy had followed Tash along endless, record-lined corridors and been introduced to people-who-mattered along the way. Within an hour of their arrival his manager was summoned and faxes started to fly. Meetings were set up between Tash's 'people' and hers. Contracts were drafted over a stupendous lunch. And Izzy was warned in no uncertain terms – on at least five separate occasions – that under no circumstances whatsoever must she either do, say or even think anything which might have a detrimental effect upon Tash Janssen's career. At all costs, his reputation must stay intact.

At this, Tash had cast her a sideways glance and awaited the explosion, but Izzy had thought it so funny she'd simply laughed. 'You mean like letting slip his deepest, darkest, most *shameful* secrets?' she had countered, with a subtle wink in his manager's direction. Harvey Purnell had coughed, straightened his bow tie and replied stiffly, 'I mean precisely that, Miss Van Asch.'

'OK, don't panic,' she replied with a grin. 'I won't

breathe a word about the fact that he knits all his own sweaters. Not to *anyone.*'

'I've heard of bringing your work home with you,' Vivienne grumbled as Sam set the word processor down, 'but this is ridiculous.'

He never seemed to *be* at home these days, she amended fretfully. And now it looked as if even those few precious hours when he was were going to be taken up with yet more boring paperwork.

Sam, however, replied drily, 'Don't sulk. It's for Katerina.'

'Oh yes?'

'She's just finished taking her A levels and I wanted to give her something which would be useful when she starts her medical training. Since we're in the process of replacing our computer system at The Steps, I thought she may as well have this.'

Vivienne softened. Sam was extremely fond of Katerina, who worked hard and appeared to possess so many of the attributes which Izzy – as far as *he* was concerned – sadly lacked. Privately, Vivienne had never before encountered a seventeen-year-old girl who dreamt about logarithms and who seemed to have no interest whatsoever in boys. As far as she was concerned, attractive girls like Katerina weren't meant to devote their teenage lives to serious study. It surely wasn't *natural* . . .

Chapter 32

When they arrived at Kingsley Grove at six-thirty that evening, however, only Gina was there.

'It's a present for Kat,' explained Vivienne with enthusiasm as Sam carried the word processor through to the dining room and placed it carefully on the highly polished table. If he could get it up and running before she returned home, so much the better.

'Katerina doesn't live here any more.'

'What?' Sam straightened and turned to face Gina, who had spoken the words in a tone that was almost nonchalant. 'She was here yesterday.'

'She doesn't live here any more,' repeated Gina with a shrug.

Sam was frowning. Vivienne, hearing the click of the front gate, peered through the dining-room window and said, 'Well it doesn't matter, because she's here now. Quick, Sam – plug it in and make it do something intelligent!'

'Don't plug it in.' As Katerina's key turned in the door, Gina's gaze flickered momentarily towards the fireplace. Hurling her wedding ring into it earlier had given her enormous pleasure. Emptying the contents of Katerina's carefully annotated A level files on top of it and watching the whole lot go up in flames had been even better.

* * *

'So tell me,' she enquired evenly as Katerina entered the room, 'how long have you been screwing my husband?'

Katerina froze. Simon, who was one step behind her, almost fell over.

Shit, I don't believe this, thought Sam.

'Tell me,' Gina repeated with mechanical slowness, 'how long you've been . . . sleeping with him.'

Oh God. Katerina, clinging to the door handle for support, met the steely grey gaze and experienced a surge of nausea. She hadn't wanted this to happen. She hadn't wanted to hurt Gina. She didn't want *anyone* to be hurt . . .

But it had happened and there was no escape. Gina knew. The game was up. She wished she didn't feel so sick.

'Not long,' she replied in a voice that was barely audible. 'A few weeks, that's all. Gina, I'm so sorry—'

'You aren't sorry. You're a lying bitch,' hissed Gina, her grey eyes narrow with hatred. 'A lying, hypocritical, back-stabbing *bitch*.'

Katerina looked as if she was about to pass out. Since Simon was clearly not planning on being any use at all, Vivienne rushed forward and caught her, putting her arm around Katerina's thin waist and guiding her into the nearest chair. Shocked by Gina's venomous outburst, astounded and inwardly enthralled by the revelation, Vivienne was having to make a lightning reappraisal of Izzy's daughter. 'It's OK, it's OK,' she murmured sympathetically. The poor kid was evidently no match for Gina at full throttle, for the moment at least. She needed someone on her side.

'I still can't believe I'm hearing this,' said Sam. Since he knew Katerina rather better than Vivienne, he was even more stunned. Instinctively, however, he moved towards Gina, who had just been through the worst six months of her life and who was now being delivered yet another body blow. Andrew and *Katerina*, for heaven's sake.

Simon, who had been looking forward to Le Gavroche all day, and who had been forced by his mother into wearing his father's best tweed jacket for the occasion, jumped a mile as the front door swung open and shut once more. The next moment he broke into a sweat; Izzy had brought Tash Janssen back with her. Oh God, oh God . . .

'Goodness!' Izzy exclaimed, surveying the frozen tableau before her. '*Hasn't* it gone quiet all of a sudden!' Grinning at Vivienne and pointedly ignoring Sam, she went on cheerfully, 'You must have been talking about me.'

'Mum . . .' It came out as an agonised croak. The expression on Izzy's face changed and in a flash she was at Katerina's side.

'Sweetheart, your exam! Was it awful? It couldn't have been *that* awful, you've worked so hard for it . . .'

'Your daughter isn't upset about her exams,' Gina cut in icily. 'She's upset because I've found out about her sordid affair with my husband.'

Katerina was clinging to Izzy. Sam placed his hand on Gina's arm. From his position in the doorway, Tash let out a low whistle. This was interesting.

'Don't be ridiculous.' Izzy frowned, her gaze shifting

enquiringly from Gina to Vivienne. Was Gina having some kind of breakdown? And if so, why was everyone simply allowing it to happen? How could they stand there and let her hurl accusations at poor Kat when they were so patently untrue?

But everyone *was* letting it happen. And Vivienne, her customary smile now absent, was nodding at her as if silently to confirm that what Gina had said was correct. With mounting unease, Izzy said, 'Come on! Is this some kind of joke? Kat doesn't even *know* Andrew.'

'Oh, she knows him all right.' Gina, shaking slightly, wished someone would pour her a drink. 'She knows him in every sense of the word. Apparently, they're *in love* with each other, and just as soon as he manages to dump Marcy, Katerina's going to be moving in with him. It's all terribly romantic . . .'

Izzy gripped Katerina's hands. Slowly, evenly, she demanded, 'Is this true?'

'No.' Katerina shook her head, pleading with her to understand. Her voice broke as she went on, 'Well, not all of it. I'm not seeing him any more. It's over, now.'

'But you *have* had an affair with him?' Izzy had to make sure she'd got it absolutely right. 'With Andrew Lawrence?'

The picture of misery, Katerina nodded. 'Yes.'

Sam was prepared for almost anything, except what happened next. The slap resounded through the air and Katerina's head jerked backwards, the imprint of Izzy's hand white on her cheek. Even Gina looked appalled.

'How could you have *done* it?' Izzy shrieked, oblivious now to their audience. Her dark eyes were ablaze, her whole body rigid with fury. 'You stupid, callous, cheating little bitch!'

Before she could slap her again, Sam intervened. Izzy, it seemed, had sailed through the last seventeen years without ever having had to deal with the problems traditionally associated with motherhood. Now, however, shocked and appalled by her daughter's lapse – and by the evidence that she was not, after all, perfect – she was unable to control herself.

'OK, OK,' he said, drawing her away as Katerina burst into tears and Vivienne attempted to comfort her. It occurred to him that Izzy's reaction was a touch hypocritical, anyway. She wasn't exactly the greatest example in the world for any daughter to follow.

'It is *not* OK!' yelled Izzy, struggling without success to get free and close to tears herself. 'It's disgusting! We live in this house,' she went on, turning to face Katerina once more and almost choking on the words, 'and you've abused that privilege in the worst way possible. You're nothing but a shameless slut. Oh God . . . I'm so *ashamed* of you . . .'

In the throes of her misery, Katerina had nevertheless assumed that the one person in the world who would understand her situation, and who would automatically defend her, was her mother. As she had supported Izzy through years of unconventional living, subterfuge and chaos, so she had expected comfort and understanding in return. But that hadn't happened. Izzy had let her down. Even more unbelievably, for the first time in her entire life, she had slapped her.

'I'm not a slut,' she shouted back, her long hair

swinging as she jumped to her feet. 'You're the one who sleeps with drug-crazed rock stars, for God's sake. If anyone's a slut, it's you!'

Tash, both amused and faintly bemused by the goings-on, had seconds earlier been thinking he could use a joint right now. At this, he raised one eyebrow and smiled, earning himself a look of undiluted disgust from Sam.

'How dare you lecture me on *my* morals?' Katerina's fists were clenched with fury at her sides as she continued her tirade. 'You've never even behaved like a proper mother! Real mothers listen to their children and look after them. They have real homes. Sometimes they even have husbands. Why couldn't I have a mother like that?' she wailed, dimly aware that she had gone too far, but unable to take it back now. 'Why did I have to get *you*?'

The appalled silence which greeted this final, terrible insult was broken by the drainlike rumbling of Simon's empty stomach. Utterly mortified, he hung his head and mumbled, 'Sorry.' Tash, standing beside him, was once again unable to disguise his amusement.

'You aren't the one who needs to apologise.' Izzy, still shell-shocked, turned to Simon. 'Oh, you poor boy . . . how could Katerina have done this to you? It must be so terrible for you, finding out like this . . .'

Oh God, oh God. Abruptly, Simon found himself embroiled in the very centre of the deception. Crimson-cheeked, he tried to look cheated-on, but Katerina soon put paid to that.

'Let's get everything straight, shall we? Simon is not – and never has been – my boyfriend.' Then, because it didn't matter any more, she added with an air of careless triumph, 'Although he has, of course, been a great alibi.'

Within the space of two seconds flat, poor cuckolded Simon became in-on-it-all-along Simon, partner in deception and now public enemy number two. The expressions on the faces of Izzy and Gina said it all.

Sam, who had known Andrew Lawrence longer than anybody else in the room, wondered what the hell Andrew had thought he was doing. Separated from his wife, currently in the process of dumping his pregnant girlfriend and now involved in an affair with a hopelessly inexperienced teenager. It was sheer madness . . .

Meanwhile, however, somebody had to do something before Izzy and Kat came to real blows. Taking his car keys from his pocket, he said, 'Vivienne, take Kat back to the flat.'

'Andrew's flat?' Gina intercepted in cutting tones. 'Won't it be a little crowded?'

'Stop it.' Sam quelled her with a look, then turned to address Tash. 'Maybe you should leave us to sort this out.'

Two things intrigued Tash. Firstly, Sam Sheridan clearly wasn't too impressed by the fact that he had arrived here with Izzy, making him wonder whether there might not have been something undercover going on between the two of them until very recently. The set-up in this house, he reflected daily, was downright *complicated.*

As for the other item of interest . . .

'I was just leaving,' he drawled, unable to resist the opportunity to say what had apparently not yet occurred to anyone else. Stepping towards Izzy, he kissed her briefly on the mouth. 'Give me a call tomorrow and let me know what you decide.'

Distracted and confused, she said, 'Decide about what?'

'The deal.' Carefully, he pushed a strand of dark hair away from her cheek. 'You signed a contract with Stellar this afternoon, but I'll understand if you don't want to go ahead with it now.'

Izzy was still puzzled. What on earth did that have to do with Andrew Lawrence?

'Your daughter,' explained Tash with a brief, sardonic look in Simon's direction. 'And those touching lyrics of hers. I think we can safely assume, in the light of all this, that she wasn't dreaming of old Roy of the Rovers here when she wrote "Never, Never".'

Chapter 33

'You can stay here with us,' Sam told Katerina the following morning. Having slipped out of the flat at eight-thirty and returned half an hour later with a copy of *Loot*, her black coffee had grown cold beside her as she proceeded to study and circle the small ads. Pale, gripped with determination and refusing to even discuss yesterday's calamitous showdown, she now chewed the top of her felt-tipped pen and shook her head.

'Of course I can't stay. You're the good guys and I'm the social leper. Don't worry, I'll find something in no time.'

'A rat-infested hovel,' Vivienne put in, helping herself to a slice of the toast which Sam had made for Katerina, and which hadn't even been touched. 'Honey, you can't do that. How will you *live*?'

Hollow-eyed from lack of sleep, Katerina shrugged. 'I'll get a job.'

Sam had already offered her money and been politely but firmly turned down. She was every bit as stubborn as her mother, he thought with a trace of despair; the only difference was that Izzy would have pocketed the loan without even blinking.

'Let me phone Izzy,' urged Vivienne, through a mouthful of toast. 'Look, she was upset last night – she'll be over that now. Oh please, let me call her.'

'No.' Bleakly, Katerina recalled the terrible things they had said to each other . . . the slap on the cheek . . . Izzy's reaction when she realised that 'Never, Never' had been written not for Simon, but for Andrew . . . 'I don't want to see her. I *won't* speak to her.'

Vivienne gazed at the girl before her, dressed in an olive-green T-shirt and white shorts and with her long brown legs tucked beneath her on the chair. Until yesterday, she had envied Izzy her easy, uncomplicated relationship with her daughter. Now she couldn't even begin to imagine what her friend might be going through. 'Sweetheart, your mom loves you. She's *worried* about you.'

'Bullshit.' Katerina didn't look up. Dangerously close to tears once more, she said, 'Do you think I haven't worried about *her*? I've supported my mother all my life. This is the very first time I've *ever* needed her to support me . . . and she didn't. She's let me down and I don't think I'll ever forgive her for that. She hates me for what I've done and I hate her back. From now on, she can do what she likes with her stupid men and her stupid music. I don't care any more what kind of a mess she makes of it all.'

'Forget Izzy for the moment,' countered Sam, deciding to risk another outburst. Personally, he thought Andrew deserved castration at the very least. 'What about you and Andrew?'

This time Katerina did look up. He saw the sadness in her eyes, and the determined line of her mouth. 'That's what makes it so ironic,' she replied bitterly. 'I really had finished with him . . . put it all behind me. But now that all this has happened, I may as well carry on seeing him after all.'

'Kat, get back into the car. You aren't even going to *look* at this one.'

It was three-thirty in the afternoon and Sam was beginning to lose patience. Katerina's search for a bedsitter had led them from one unbelievably dreary address to another and the accommodation on offer had been so sordid he could hardly bear it. Still in a belligerent mood, she had initially been reluctant to allow him to accompany her, but he was bloody glad he had, otherwise the chances were she'd have been raped or murdered by now. Even in daylight the buildings were sinister. And now here they were in the depths of the East End outside 14 Finnegan Street, whose windows were cracked and opaque with grime and whose crumbling front wall was holding up a row of bleary-eyed, bottle-wielding tramps.

'It's cheap,' Katerina replied briefly, ignoring him. 'I can afford it.'

Sam couldn't let her go in alone. Locking the car, he put his hand on her shoulder as they approached the front door. 'Look, you really can't live in a place like this, temporarily or otherwise. I don't understand why you won't let me lend you enough money to rent somewhere decent.'

'Oh, please.' Katerina threw him a look of resignation. 'We've been through this before. I happen to know how you feel about lending money to a Van Asch.'

She knocked at the door and read the graffiti sprayed over it. 'Whoever wrote that can't spell.'

'You aren't Izzy,' persisted Sam. 'This isn't the same thing at all.'

'Of course it's the same thing.' She half-smiled. 'I wouldn't be able to pay you back for years.'

'But that doesn't matter!' Exasperated, he reached for her hand. 'Come on, we're leaving. There's no one here.'

As the door began to creak open, an overpowering smell of mould and cats' pee billowed out to meet them.

'Just a quick look,' said Katerina, who had no intention of borrowing so much as a bus fare from Sam Sheridan. 'Come on. Who knows, it might have hidden depths.'

It didn't have hidden depths. The depths were all there on display, from the damp-blackened walls to the hideously matted rug only half-covering bare floorboards. The furniture, such as it was, was unbelievably decrepit, the curtains were too small for the filthy window and the only light was provided by a naked bulb dangling from the ceiling.

When the scrawny landlady offered Katerina the room and she in turn accepted, Sam couldn't even speak. She was doing it deliberately, he now realised, and there was nothing on earth he could do to stop her.

'Well?' he drawled, when they were out of the house. 'Happy now?'

Beneath the calm veneer, Katerina was feeling slightly sick. Nothing seemed real any more. It was as if her body was making the decisions without consulting her brain. Finding work and somewhere to live were just things she had to do.

'Does it matter?' she countered with an offhand gesture. 'At least everyone else will be happy.'

'Oh yes, delirious.' Revving the car's engine and startling the tramps out of their collective stupor, Sam screeched away from the kerb. 'They'll all be thrilled, I'm sure, when they find out where you're going to be living.'

Katerina was gazing abstractedly out of the window. 'It's none of their business, anyway,' she murmured. 'And it's been very kind of you, driving me around like this, but my problems aren't actually anything to do with you, either.'

She was determined to punish herself. More than ever now, Sam longed to confront Andrew and make him realise the extent of the damage he had caused. A mid-life crisis was one thing, he thought irritably, but this was wrecking people's lives.

In response to his phone call, Izzy had arrived at Sam's flat at seven o'clock. Judging by her outfit – a new, black-sequinned dress and ludicrously high heels – she wasn't exactly prostrate with concern for her only daughter.

'She's moved into a bedsitter in Stepney and got herself a job in BurgerBest,' he said shortly. 'She also tells me she isn't going to medical school.'

'So?' countered Izzy, still boiling with resentment towards him and hating the way he was now trying to make *her* feel like a wayward schoolgirl. 'What am I supposed to do about it? Kidnap her and lock her up in a cupboard?'

'How nice to see you taking your parental responsibilities so seriously.' Sarcasm fuelled his own annoyance. Izzy's *laissez-faire* attitude might have worked in the past, but it was the last thing Katerina needed right now.

As if she realised this, Izzy's expression changed. Sinking down on to the arm of the settee, she stopped glaring at him and heaved an enormous sigh. 'OK, OK, of course I'm not happy about it, but there really isn't a great deal I can do to stop her. She's almost eighteen years old and she's been carrying on an affair with a man old enough to be her father, for heaven's sake. Maybe a few weeks in a bedsitter will give her time to think it through.'

'Izzy, this particular bedsitter had to be seen to be believed. It's a health hazard.' Handing her a piece of paper, he said, 'Look, here's the address.'

'No.' She shook her head, refusing to take it. 'I won't do that. I'm not going to approve of what Kat's done.'

'You're making a mistake,' Sam said warningly. 'She needs you.'

Izzy's eyes glittered, her temper flaring once more. 'And you're her long-lost father figure, I suppose,' she retaliated, stung by the criticism. 'Maybe when you've brought up a child of your own, *on* your own, I might listen to your brilliant advice. But until then, I'll do what I – as a parent – think is best. OK?'

He had injured her pride. Too late, Sam realised that if he had urged her to disown Katerina, there was every possibility Izzy would have done the opposite.

'At least keep the address,' he said with resignation. 'And if you should happen to bump into her, try and make her see that she can't give up her place at medical school.'

Izzy cast him a derisive look. Comments like that only

went to prove how little he really knew Katerina. 'She might have said it, but she didn't mean it,' she replied in almost pitying tones. 'Medicine means more to her than anything. It's all she's ever wanted to do.'

'Cut!' yelled the director, and with a gurgle of relief Izzy collapsed into Tash's arms.

'Ever felt overdressed?' he drawled, helping her out of the full-length, dark green velvet coat which clung to her damp body.

'Ever thought of hiring a hit man,' Izzy countered, 'to take care of whichever sadist dreamt up this idea?'

The set, upon which part of the video for 'Never, Never' was being shot, depicted winter in Moscow. In reality, the first week of August was proving to be the hottest of the summer so far and the temperature had rocketed to 90°F in the shade. Izzy simply couldn't understand how forty seconds' worth of video could possibly take seven and a half hours to produce.

'You're looking at your watch again,' Tash observed drily. 'What's the problem? Supposed to be meeting your lover?'

It was a month since Izzy had even seen Sam, yet for some peculiar reason Tash continued to suggest that the two of them were indulging in some clandestine affair. At times he only appeared to be half-joking. Frustrated by the fact that – for once – she was innocent of such a crime yet at the same time touched by this evidence of Tash's own unexpected insecurity, she reached up and kissed the corner of his mouth.

'I told you this morning,' she said patiently, aware of

the fact that the make-up girl and lighting cameraman were eavesdropping behind them. 'There's a house in Wimbledon I'm going to look at. The estate agent's meeting me there at six.'

'What d'you want a house for?' Tash frowned. Over the past weeks, they had spent most of their time together. Nothing had been said . . . no formal arrangements had been made . . . but it had just so happened that a number of Izzy's clothes had gradually taken over one of his wardrobes. The almond-scented shampoo she always used was propped up on his bathroom shelf next to her toothbrush, and several spare pairs of shoes littered his bedroom floor. 'What's wrong with my house?'

'Nothing, except that it *is* your house.' Izzy grinned. It was possibly the most romantic thing he'd said to her, so far. 'I want one of my own.'

'Why?'

'Because I've never had one before. Not a decent one,' she corrected, unscrewing a bottle of lukewarm mineral water and pausing with it halfway to her mouth. 'Besides, it's been over a month now since Kat left. It's time to get that little matter sorted out, and since she can hardly move back to Kingsley Grove I thought I'd get us somewhere neutral.'

Initially attracted to Izzy by her determination and natural independence, Tash reflected now that such qualities had their drawbacks. He wasn't used to being turned down in any shape or form, yet this was what she was doing to him.

'She might not want to live with you,' he retaliated, holding the dark green velvet coat towards her as the director signalled that they were ready to go once more.

'Of course she will,' said Izzy, who didn't doubt it for a minute. There had been an argument, during which they had both said and done things they didn't mean, but now was the time for it to be put behind them and for Katerina to come home. 'She isn't the kind to hold a grudge. By this time tomorrow the whole silly business will be forgotten. And don't look at me like that,' she added, as the snow machines started up and a flurry of polystyrene pips hurled themselves like wasps against her face. 'She's my *daughter*, for heaven's sake. I've known her for years!'

Chapter 34

Katerina felt like a zombie, not like herself at all. Everything was so hideous she no longer stopped to think about it, to consider the awfulness of this new life of hers, because if she did she knew she wouldn't be able to bear it.

But bear it she must, because this was her new life and it was what she deserved. Every day she worked gruelling shifts in BurgerBest, enduring the leers of the customers and the eternal smell of fried onions which clung to her skin and never seemed to wash away completely. Her feet ached, her head spun with the banality of it all and the money was poor. She didn't have the energy, when she returned home each night, to do more than bathe, listen numbly to the transistor radio which was her only luxury and fall into bed.

And all because of Andrew Lawrence; that was the strangest part. Everything happened for a reason, Katerina would remind herself, and Andrew had been hers.

He still loved her, of course, and came round to see her whenever he could, but Marcy was deliberately making things as awkward as possible for him and had made no attempt at all to find herself another flat. Katerina, who hadn't been lying when she'd told Sam she no longer loved Andrew, was half-grateful to Marcy for staying put, relieving her as it did from the necessity of making any further mistakes – which was what she now knew moving in with Andrew would be.

It was all such a muddle, though. Some evenings she found herself looking forward to his visits simply because of the comfort it gave her to know that someone still cared. Luckily, the old dragon of a landlady didn't permit overnight stays so she was spared the difficulty of refusing to allow him to spend the nights with her. But while sex no longer appealed, hugs and sympathy were very much needed. Particularly when she reminded herself that her future no longer lay in medicine, but in chargrilled triple-decker cow-burgers . . .

Katerina had thirty seconds' warning of Izzy's imminent arrival, thanks to Mrs Talmage's passion for curtain-twitching.

'Blimey, there's an 'elluva car pulled up outside,' her landlady reported, peering through the grimy glass while Katerina counted out the week's rent. 'Like somefing outta Dallas . . . 'ere love, come and 'ave a look at this! Some woman wiv a bloody great dog's gettin' out.'

Katerina's hard-earned money disappeared in a flash inside Mrs Talmage's apron pocket. Katerina, glancing through the window, said, 'That's my mother.'

'Never! Wiv a car like that?'

Wearily, Katerina envisaged her rent doubling. Her landlady's pale little eyes were alert with interest, her brain undoubtedly working overtime.

'It isn't her car,' she replied in abrupt tones. 'She's just showing off, as usual. Mrs Talmage, could you tell her I'm not here?'

The pale eyes widened, registering astonishment. 'What, you don't want to see your own mother? Get away wiv you, girl. She's come to visit, and the least you can do is offer her a cup of tea. Tell her you're not 'ere, indeed. I don't know . . .'

'Darling!' cried Izzy, just as Katerina had known she would. 'Come here and give me a great big hug!'

It was absolutely typical of her mother, thought Katerina, to erupt into the room in a swathe of scarves and perfume, wearing way too much make-up and pretending that nothing at all had happened. Added emotional blackmail had been provided, of course, in the form of Jericho, who barked delightedly and leapt up at her in a frenzy of adoration.

But happy as she was to see Jericho again, she had no intention of allowing Izzy to bulldoze her into daughterly submission. When Izzy enveloped her in an embrace she submitted politely but said nothing, concentrating instead on remembering how bitterly her mother had attacked her when she'd needed her most.

'Well, well,' Izzy said, kissing Katerina's cold cheek and gazing around the bedsitting room, with its badly painted walls and dreadful furniture. 'We've lived in some God-awful places in our time, sweetheart, but this has to be the pit to beat all pits. And was that your landlady who answered the door just now? I thought her piggy little eyes were going to drop out of her head when she saw me.'

'Probably because you're wearing false eyelashes,' Katerina observed, easing herself out of her mother's grasp. 'Would you like a cup of tea?'

'What am I, some old great aunt?' Izzy had already spotted the ancient two-ring stove, upon which stood a battered tin kettle. More than anything else, the pitiful sight of those two objects fuelled her determination to get her precious daughter out of this terrible place. 'Sweetheart, you're looking thin . . . you need a splendid meal inside you. Grab some shoes and come with me to Langan's.'

Katerina, who hadn't been eating much at all recently, was almost tempted. Then she shook her head.

'No, thanks.'

'But I've booked a table for eight-thirty,' protested Izzy, her composure beginning to slip. Outwardly cheerful and calm, no one could have guessed at the turmoil she'd been going through. This evening's rapprochement was something she'd been carefully planning for days.

'You can still go.' Katerina, struggling to remain calm herself, wasn't going to fall for emotional blackmail. More brutally than she had intended, she added, 'I'm sure you and Tash will enjoy yourselves there.'

'Oh Kat, don't.' Izzy looked stricken. Fiddling with the emerald-green silk scarf around her neck, she backed away and sat down abruptly on the edge of the unmade single bed. 'Sweetheart, we can't carry on like this. I've missed you so much. We have to talk about it.'

'We've already talked about it,' replied Katerina coldly. 'I know exactly what you think of me, and that's your prerogative. I just don't have to listen to you saying it if I don't want to.'

This wasn't going according to plan at all. Izzy, almost in tears now, wrenched off the stupid false eyelashes so painstakingly applied by the make-up girl earlier. 'Listen,' she pleaded in desperation, 'I understand about Andrew. I won't say a word against him. But Kat, you can't carry on living in this terrible place . . . I came here to tell you I've rented a house in Wimbledon, just for the two of us. We can go back to how we always were before . . .' In a hopeless attempt at humour, because it might win Katerina over, she forced herself to smile and added, 'Only richer, of course.'

Katerina had never seen her mother beg before. For a second she wavered. But it was no good; the damage had been done and it was too late to try and pretend it hadn't.

'We can't go back,' she replied bleakly, ignoring the look of desolation in her mother's eyes. 'Everything's different now. We have our own lives – and you've got the two things you always wanted: success and money.'

Izzy swallowed. Was that really how Kat thought of her?

'What about medical school?' she asked finally, to change the subject. 'Will you be able to cope, living here and commuting to Westminster every day? You won't be able to study and work in the evenings as well.'

Past caring by this time, Katerina went to the door and held it open in the hope that Izzy would take the hint and leave. 'That isn't going to be a problem,' she said, her tone blunt, but at the same time almost casual. 'Because I'm not going to medical school.'

'But—'

'And that isn't a threat, it's the simple truth. They wouldn't accept me now, anyway. You see, I've failed my exams.'

* * *

When Andrew arrived an hour and a half later, Katerina was in bed.

'You've been crying,' he said, putting his arms around her and feeling – as Izzy had done – how thin she had become. 'Angel, you mustn't cry. Everything's going to be all right. Marcy's moving out of the flat on Monday . . . in less than four days we'll be able to be together for the rest of our lives.'

Katerina, the brief outpouring of bitter tears behind her now, gritted her teeth and crawled back beneath the bedclothes. Today, it seemed, was her day for being offered somewhere to live by people she no longer wanted to live with.

But she wasn't up to another argument tonight. What she most needed now after the fraught meeting with Izzy earlier was physical comfort and a bit of tender loving care. And here was Andrew, in his crumpled grey suit, sitting on the edge of her bed and wondering what on earth he could do to cheer her up.

Gazing around the cheerless little room in search of inspiration, he said anxiously, 'How about a nice Chinese takeaway? I could pick up some chicken and pineapple with fried rice . . .?'

It must also be her day, she thought drily, for being offered food she didn't even want to eat.

'I don't want Chinese.' Slowly, almost absent-mindedly, she slid her hand beneath his jacket, running her fingers along the side seam of his shirt. At once, his breathing quickened and the expression in his eyes became hopeful. He understood that the past few weeks hadn't been easy for her, but constantly being rebuffed whenever he made any kind of physical advance hadn't exactly been the greatest ego boost in the world for him, either. They hadn't made love for over six weeks and the strain of wanting Katerina as badly as he did – while in turn having to live with Marcy, who wanted *him* – was beginning to tell.

'No?' Proceeding with caution, in case he was reading too much into the tentative gesture, he held his hand up to her forehead with mock concern. 'You don't want a Chinese takeaway? Shall I phone for the ambulance now?'

Katerina smiled. 'Not just yet.'

'How about an Indian, then? Lamb Passanda? Chicken Tikka and Naan bread?'

With a pang, Katerina remembered that Lamb Passanda was one of Simon's favourite Indian meals. Poor Simon, she hadn't treated him very well either.

But she needed the comfort of Andrew's presence, for now at least. And although she might be taking advantage of him, it wasn't as if she was asking him to do something unspeakably awful. For heaven's sake, it would make him *happy* . . .

'I don't want an Indian takeaway,' said Katerina, loosening his tie and wondering whether she would ever be truly happy again. 'I want you to stay here tonight, with me. I want sex. I want you . . .'

Chapter 35

Since their last meeting hadn't exactly been a raging success, Sam acknowledged Izzy with a cool nod and carried on talking to the Australian actor who was currently wowing audiences in a West End show, and who had turned up at The Chelsea Steps with a particularly fetching little blonde.

Not to be put off, however, Izzy simply stood at his shoulder and waited for the small talk to run out, glancing with disinterest at the underdressed blonde and ignoring the attentions of her companion.

'Did you want to see me?' said Sam eventually, turning and looking mildly surprised. For good measure, he scanned the crowd around them and added, 'Not with your boyfriend tonight?'

'No. And yes, I would like to see you.' Izzy, not in the mood for games, was brief and to the point. 'What time will you be finishing?'

'Four o'clock.' He frowned, sensing that something was amiss. 'Maybe three-thirty. Why, is anything wrong?'

'Yes, there is,' she replied flatly, turning to leave. 'Very wrong indeed.'

The club was still busy when Sam handed over to Toby Madison and left them all to it. Although it was only three-fifteen, Izzy was waiting outside at the wheel of a double-parked Mercedes, drinking Coke from a can and fraying a small tear in the knee of her faded jeans.

Concerned by her obvious low spirits, Sam winked and gave her fingers a brief squeeze as he slid into the passenger seat. 'OK. Your place or mine?'

This earned him the first smile of the evening – just a small one.

'I thought maybe somewhere more neutral,' said Izzy, switching on the ignition. 'Like Bert's.'

Bert had died fifteen years ago, but his son Quentin, who now owned and ran the Chiswick transport café, hadn't let the side down. He still turned out the best and biggest fry-ups in London and nobody ever suggested that the café should be renamed.

If anything was capable of cheering her up, Izzy had decided, it was the steamy, friendly, no-hassle atmosphere of Bert's – which was *always* busy, no matter what time of day or night – and a plate loaded with fried mushrooms, bacon and tomatoes.

Now that the food was in front of her, however, she couldn't for the life of her imagine being able to eat it.

'Look, you were right and I was wrong,' she said eventually, watching Sam stir sugar into his tea. 'That should cheer *you* up, surely.'

'You mean Kat?' He had guessed what this must be about. Izzy was hardly likely to come to him if she was having problems with Tash Janssen.

'I feel so awful,' she blurted out, her dark eyes almost feverishly bright. 'I've never had to try to be a good mother before . . . I've never *needed* to try . . . and now that all this has happened I've been working so hard to do the right thing, but it just gets worse. I stayed away because I thought she needed the time to sort herself out, and it almost killed me to do it. But tonight I went to see her . . . I thought we could put everything behind us . . . and she just wasn't interested. Oh Sam, I think she really does hate me. And now I don't know what else to do.'

'She doesn't hate you,' he said firmly. 'Of course she doesn't. She'll come round sooner or later, she obviously just needs a little more time.'

Much as the Australian actor at The Chelsea Steps had admired Izzy's figure earlier, so a couple of lorry drivers at an adjacent table were eyeing her now with evident appreciation. They looked frankly startled when she began to cry.

'I went to see a h-house in Wimbledon this afternoon,' she explained, between sobs. Wordlessly, Sam handed her a paper napkin as the tears began to plop on to her plate. 'It was a beautiful house, a hundred times better than anything we've ever rented before – apart from Gina's place, of course. I wanted it for the two of us, but Kat refused to even consider it. She won't move. She says she's failed her A levels, so medical school's out of the window. I don't know whether she's trying to punish herself or me and I can't bear to think what she's doing to her life . . .'

'Sssh,' murmured Sam, as her voice wavered. 'You're blaming yourself and you shouldn't.'

'Of course I should,' she wailed, pushing her plate to one side and wiping her cheeks with the napkin. 'It's all my fault.'

The other diners were by this time enthralled. Ignoring

them, Sam got up and made his way around the table, sitting down next to Izzy and putting his arms around her. Accustomed to her noisy, exuberant ways and eternally optimistic attitude towards life, he hadn't imagined her capable of such vulnerability and it touched him more deeply than he could have believed.

For Izzy, the comfort of being listened to by Sam – and of being held by him – was infinitely reassuring. Her desperate concern for Kat was hardly something she could share with Gina, and Tash simply wasn't that interested.

'Will you talk to her?' she begged, clinging to him and breathing in the familiar, delicious scent of his aftershave. 'She doesn't hate you. She might listen . . . take some notice of what you say . . .'

'I'll do my best,' Sam assured her, in turn recalling the last time he had been this close to Izzy. That night at The Chelsea Steps when Vivienne had turned up without warning. Who knew how things might have turned out if Vivienne's journey had been delayed for even a few hours? 'No guarantees, but I'll try. And if you really aren't going to eat any of this food, I think we'd better leave. Who knows what Nigel Dempster would make of this if he were to walk in now.'

Sam drove. Even the shared car journey through the empty streets reminded him of their trips home from The Chelsea Steps, with Izzy balancing boxes of Chinese food on her knees, telling him the terrible jokes she'd heard that night and mimicking with wicked accuracy the more bizarre customers she'd served in the bar.

This time, however, she wasn't laughing.

'It's all such a waste,' she said hopelessly when – to

take her mind off Kat – he asked her how the music thing was going. ' "Never, Never" is being released in eight days' time. I heard it being previewed on the radio yesterday and the DJ tipped it to go to Number One. This morning we recorded an interview for Capital. This afternoon we finished shooting the video and tomorrow we have three more interviews lined up with the music press and the *Mail on Sunday*. It's everything I've ever dreamed of,' she concluded with a dismissive gesture which took in the soft leather upholstery of the Mercedes, 'and this is my car, which is a dream come true in itself, but it doesn't even *mean* anything any more, because Kat isn't here to enjoy it with me. I wanted her to be so *proud* of me . . . and she isn't, so it's all wasted . . .'

They had reached Kingsley Grove. Dawn was breaking, streaking the sky violet, and a milk float clattered along the street as Sam drew to a halt and switched off the ignition.

'I know it isn't easy, but maybe a bit more time is all she needs.' Once again he had to prise Izzy's fingers from the ripped knee of her jeans. The amount of fraying had increased spectacularly. 'I'll go and see her. Talk to her. But she isn't necessarily going to take any notice of what I say.'

Izzy's lower lip trembled and he fought the urge to kiss her.

'She likes you,' she said wistfully. 'And I know she respects your opinions.'

Squeezing her hand, he smiled. 'In that case, I shall make them known to her. And in the mean time, you just have to be patient. Look, when are you moving into your new home? Do you need a hand with any of that?'

Sam was so kind, so thoughtful. Izzy, closing her eyes for an instant as exhaustion swept over her, reflected not for the first time how lucky Vivienne was to have him.

'Thanks, but it's OK.' She shook her head. 'I didn't sign the lease. That house was supposed to be for Kat and me. Now that I know she isn't interested, there's no point in my taking it.'

'Hmm. Well, at least Gina will be pleased.'

Izzy was watching the milk float as it rattled back past them at a sedate ten miles an hour. She wondered whether the milkman, who was whistling and looking cheerful, had a normal happy family and a normal happy life.

'I don't know whether she'll be pleased or not,' she replied slowly. 'But I'm still moving out of Kingsley Grove. Tash has been asking me to go and live with him.'

Sam's heart sank. He'd had no idea the relationship between them had progressed that far. And the man's reputation for bedding and discarding women wasn't exactly encouraging.

'Would that be a wise move?' he said, the tone of his voice indicating his own views on the matter.

Izzy, however, simply shrugged and flicked back her hair with a gesture of defiance. Unconsciously echoing Katerina's explanation for staying with Andrew, she fixed her dark eyes on Sam and replied, 'Does it really matter? It may not last for ever, but who cares? My daughter doesn't want to live with me, so I might as well settle for someone who does.'

Chapter 36

There were mistakes and mistakes, Izzy thought idly a week later. And considering the almost universal disapproval which had greeted her decision to move into Stanford Manor with Tash, the signs so far were that, all in all, it had been a pretty good mistake to make.

'You hardly know each other,' Gina had said, a trifle waspishly, when Izzy had announced her intentions. But Gina, she knew, was more concerned with the fact that she would be left on her own at Kingsley Grove, with only Jericho for company.

'It's bloody stupid,' Sam had remarked dismissively, but that was only because he didn't like Tash and was probably jealous of the fact that Izzy would be living in a house worth almost four million.

Even Doug Steadman had been doubtful. 'If you ask me, pet, you're making a mistake,' he had told her, his forehead creasing with concern. 'Not that your personal life is any of my business, but isn't he going to think you're . . . well, easy?'

At least Vivienne didn't tell her she was making a fool of herself. Vivienne thought it was an absolute scream, a wildly exciting adventure, and Izzy had turned to her with gratitude, ignoring the boring scaremongers and concentrating instead on the fun aspect of the situation. She was going to be wealthy in her own right, successful, famous

. . . and the live-in mistress of one of the most glamorous and desirable men in the world. Who cared if other people thought she was easy? Tash had already had her body; now he would have the pleasure of her cooking, too.

And so far, it *had* been exciting. The prophets of doom might be muttering away to each other behind their hands, but she was enjoying herself, and the novelty of it all had at least partially distracted her from the problem of her estranged daughter.

Yes, there were definite advantages to being a rich man's mistress, Izzy decided, pushing the thought of Kat firmly from her mind and gazing out over the swimming-pool which glittered turquoise in the August sunlight. Having demolished a plateful of smoked-salmon sandwiches – peeling the salmon out of the centres and leaving the bread – she was in the mood for a swim. She was in the mood for Tash, but he was buried in his recording studio, working on ideas for the next album and showing no sign at all of needing a break.

Neither, evidently, did he welcome company during the serious business of song-writing. Izzy, reflecting that it was just as well she hadn't expected an initial honeymoon period to their living together, was finding herself with plenty of time on her hands to explore her new home and make the most of its splendid facilities. But although she was having fun, she was finding it less easy to relax than she'd expected. Topless sunbathing was out of the question because of the silent, unnerving presence of the security guards who roamed the grounds, and who treated her in the kind of distant, off-hand manner which indicated they thought of her as simply one more in a long line of female guests whose name was hardly worth remembering. And despite her best efforts to be friendly, the formidable Mrs Bishop was even less communicative than she had been on the night of her first visit. Attempts at conversation fell on the very stoniest of ground. Any compliments regarding the food were met with an impassive stare. Izzy had even idly contemplated her reaction if she were to lodge a complaint about the cooking, except that there was never anything to complain about. Everything at Stanford Manor was run with pristine efficiency, because that was what Tash wanted and demanded from his staff. And she hadn't managed to catch any of them at it yet, but *someone* was actually screwing the top back on the toothpaste tube in her bathroom . . .

Tash finally emerged outside four hours later, by which time Izzy had swum and dozed off, and – having forgotten to renew the Ambre Solaire – acquired a distinctly pink tinge to her tan.

Adjusting his sunglasses, he surveyed her in sleep, her dark hair spilling around her in glossy abandon, splendid breasts swelling out of her peacock-blue bikini, one hand trailing in the plate of desecrated sandwiches.

Izzy, adorable Izzy, both intrigued and amused him, and an added bonus was the fact that she was about as unlike his usual girlfriends as it was possible to be. Shrewd, sharp-witted and determined to succeed in her chosen career, she was nevertheless touchingly naïve at times. He was particularly entertained by her innocent ideas regarding the music business, and her plans to enjoy the money success would bring into her life.

Fishing an ice cube from the drink in his hand he dropped it into the hollow of her navel and grinned as, with a yelp, she ricocheted into a sitting position.

'Wake up. Mrs Bishop wants to know why you saw fit to massacre her sandwiches. She says unless you eat up every last crumb, she's leaving.'

'Oh God . . . oh, *you!*' Realizing belatedly that he was joking, Izzy sank back against the sunlounger and aimed the ice cube at his crotch. 'That would be too much to hope for,' she grumbled, glancing over her shoulder in case the old dragon was hovering, lurch-like, behind her. Then she examined her ominously rosy chest with dismay. 'And this isn't funny either. Hell, what am I going to look like tomorrow? We've got that photo session and I'm going to have a burnt nose . . . ouch, that *hurts*!'

She squirmed as he ran his fingernails along her collarbone, then smiled because at least he was in good spirits. While Tash would never describe himself as temperamental, she had already discovered his tendency towards moodiness whenever work refused to go well. Life wasn't all roses. Capable of the utmost charm when he chose, several wasted hours in his precious recording studio could change his mood to one of picky, tricky irritation and short temper. Izzy, who couldn't see the point of such irritability – since it didn't solve anything – steadfastly refused to be intimidated and either laughed or ignored him when it happened. But it was undoubtedly nicer, she reflected drily, when it didn't.

'Someone might be watching,' she protested, trying to

wriggle away as Tash began to slide the straps of her bikini away from her sunburnt shoulders.

'So?' He hauled her back before she landed on the plate of sandwiches. 'Would that really be so terrible? Sweetheart, it's half the fun.'

No doubt his past girlfriends had gone along with such suggestions, but Izzy wasn't about to set herself up as a floorshow for the security staff. Rising to her feet, she hooked a finger through one of the belt loops on his jeans and led him uncomplainingly inside. When they reached the bedroom, she slowly unbuttoned his white shirt and murmured, 'This is more fun.'

Afterwards, as he lit a joint and slowly exhaled, Tash said, 'I forgot to tell you. Someone phoned earlier, wanting to speak to you.'

Izzy didn't approve of drugs of any kind, but since he only laughed and called her a prude whenever she tried to tell him of the damage they could do, she no longer bothered. At least it was only marijuana, she consoled herself. It could have been much worse.

'And?' she said, stretching lazily and revelling in the luxury of not having to get up and go to work in either a crowded pub or a smoky, un-air-conditioned club. 'Who was it? Do I have to call them back?'

Tash shook his head. 'Nope. He said he was flying out to the States this afternoon, so I took a message. It was your friend Sam Sheridan.' Aware of the fact that Sam disapproved of his relationship with Izzy, he spoke in faintly mocking tones. 'He just wanted you to know that he'd had a word with Katerina, but that it wasn't a great success.'

'What!' In a flurry of bedclothes, Izzy jerked into a sitting position. 'Why couldn't you tell me earlier? Why on earth didn't you come and find me when he phoned?'

Tash's eyes darkened. He fixed his gaze on the glowing tip of the joint between his fingers. 'I was busy. I didn't know where you were. Look, what's the big deal? The man's a jerk and what he had to say was hardly of earth-shattering importance, anyway.'

Shooting him a look of disdain, Izzy grabbed the phone by the bed and punched out Sam's number. Seconds later, abruptly disconnecting the call, she said, 'Bloody answering machine. Thanks a lot, Tash. My daughter might mean nothing to you, but she *is* important to me.'

And don't we all know it, he thought with resignation, taking a final, long drag before stubbing out the cigarette. Izzy's obsession with Katerina was beyond his comprehension. Rebellion was part of growing up. When he was seventeen years old he'd left home and gone to live in a squat in Bayswater, sharing the icy, unfurnished basement flat with an acid-head and a fifteen-stone transvestite. It hadn't done him any harm, for Christ's sake.

But the marijuana was taking effect and he really couldn't be bothered to get into a fight.

'Angel, calm down,' he said placatingly. 'OK, OK, I'm sorry if I upset you. But I *was* pretty busy when the phone rang . . . and I would have come and found you if Sam had had something more positive to report, of course I would.'

Izzy digested this in silence. Maybe she had reacted too strongly. Tash wasn't being deliberately obstructive, he simply hadn't thought it that important.

'All right,' she said finally, only too well aware herself of the fact that the last thing they needed right now was a major row. The publicity machine was revving up to full throttle; practically every day for the next fortnight they were scheduled for interviews with journalists eager to get the low-down on Tash's latest relationship. 'All right, I'm sorry too. I just can't help worrying about Kat, that's all.'

'No big deal,' he said easily, relieved to have averted the crisis. Sliding out of bed, he strode naked across the room to the vast chest of drawers and took out a slim, matt black jewellery box. 'Here, I was saving this for the day "Never, Never" went to Number One.' With a crooked smile, he dropped it in her lap. Izzy needn't know that the emerald-and-sapphire earrings from Bulgari had been bought for Anna. Splitting up with her three days before her birthday had had its small advantages, after all; he'd never bothered returning them to the shop. 'But maybe you should open it now. Just a little something to cheer you up.'

Kat might not want her but at least Tash did. Overwhelmed by the size and beauty of the stones, and by his thoughtfulness in choosing the kind of earrings he knew she would love, Izzy rose to her knees and slid her arms around his neck. Too moved to speak, she leaned closer and kissed his handsome mouth.

'I'm too old for this,' murmured Tash.

'I'm sure you can cope,' Izzy replied, her lips curving against his as she smiled. 'What the hell, anyway? I'll risk it if you will . . .'

Chapter 37

Later, much later, Gina would come to appreciate the significant part two fingernail-sized slivers of pink tissue paper had played in her life. At the time, however, it didn't even occur to her; she was having far too much trouble keeping a straight face.

The rain was still hammering down outside. It had been the dazzling spectacle of forked lightning against an indigo sky which had drawn her to the window less than two minutes earlier. Doug, hunched in his chair with his ear welded to the phone, glanced up and said hopefully, 'Coffee?' but Gina didn't hear him. In the street below, emerging from a cab and pausing briefly to examine his reflection in the rain-streaked side-mirror was Ralph, whom she hadn't set eyes upon since that humiliating afternoon at Kingsley Grove. All the air seemed suddenly to have been sucked from her lungs. He was one of Doug's most successful clients and she had known she should be geared up to seeing him again, but now that it was happening she was still unprepared. No matter how many times she told herself he didn't mean anything to her, it never quite rang true. Ralph was too charming and attractive ever to be ignored. He was the epitome of *cool* . . .

'With three sugars?' wheedled Doug, who wasn't cool at all. Thanks to Gina's gifts of deodorant and aftershave the aura of BO had dissipated and he no longer smelled anything but sweet, but whenever he was caught in the throes of clinching a deal nothing on earth could prevent those damp patches forming on the underarms of his shirts. Poker, as Izzy had once gravely informed him, was never going to be his forte.

But making coffee would at least give Gina something to do so that she wouldn't have to sit there like a lemon while Ralph made polite conversation and inwardly smirked at her gullibility. Moving away from the window and flicking the switch on the kettle, she began spooning instant coffee into two cups and listened to the rhythmic beat of Ralph's footsteps as he confidently ascended the stairs.

The beige Burberry trenchcoat was rain-spotted but otherwise immaculate, as were – of course – the matching scarf and umbrella. The collar-length blond hair had grown blonder still with the recent addition of expensive and artfully styled streaks. The tan was deeper and smoother than ever. Intimidated by such perfection – as she had known she would be – Gina bent her head to the task of spooning far more sugar than usual into Doug's cup. Since she habitually under-sugared in a vain attempt to reduce his paunch, he would think it was his birthday.

'Doug, how are you?' Ralph, who had in fact taken particular care with his appearance because he was anxious to impress Gina – OK, so he had used her initially to get back at Izzy, but he had rapidly grown to *like* her – stepped forward and shook his agent's pudgy hand with enthusiasm. 'God, what weather! I just called by to let you know that we've finished filming the TV serial. The producers are really pleased with me, and the director has suggested I put myself up for a play he's involved with, so things are on the up. Hallo, Gina,' he added, as if seeing her for the first time. 'You're looking well. Very well. Working for this old slave-driver obviously suits you.'

He was . . . *golden*, thought Gina, forcing a brief smile and attempting to appear unconcerned by his presence.

'Less of the old,' complained Doug, glancing between the two of them and realizing that something was going on. Not always famed for his diplomacy, he nevertheless sensed that a trip to the newsagents around the corner might be in order. 'Hell, I've run out of cigarettes. Gina, make this young man a coffee and keep him entertained until I get back, will you? I'll be five minutes.'

'Fine,' said Ralph.

Help, thought Gina, oh help.

But for once in her life, help was on its way. As the door slammed behind Doug, Ralph settled easily into the client's chair and unwound the cashmere scarf around his neck, and the miracle Gina had been praying for finally happened.

'I wanted to see you again.' He assumed a confidential air, pushing his streaked hair away from his forehead and tilting his head slightly to one side as he studied her. 'You really have bloomed, Gina . . . look, I'm sorry about that misunderstanding we had, but I'm sure we could put it behind us now.'

Gina couldn't speak. If she tried to open her mouth she knew the giggles would erupt. If it had been anyone else, the fact that they had cut themselves while shaving wouldn't even *be* particularly funny, but it was perfect Ralph, the picture of *GQ* sophistication.

With a gulp she gazed, transfixed, at the two torn shreds of pink toilet paper dangling from his throat. Dotted with dried blood, they were an inch and a half apart, which only made them look that much more like a vampire's bite. Exactly on cue, a fresh downpour of rain rattled the windows and forked lightning illuminated the office, causing the lights to flicker in true *Hammer Horror* fashion. As the ensuing roll of thunder shook the building, Gina pressed her lips together and clenched her fists until the nails dug into her palms. The spell had been well and truly broken; no longer perfect, it was now Ralph's turn to look foolish and she was going to make sure she enjoyed every single, wonderful moment . . .

'What's so funny?' he demanded with a trace of suspicion, and she shook her head.

'Nothing . . . nothing. Thunderstorms make me a bit nervous, that's all. Um . . . I can't remember whether you take sugar.'

From the expression on his face she might have been enquiring whether he injected heroin. Ralph took fanatical care of his body.

'Thanks.' Taking the cup, he flashed her a winning smile. Imagining for a moment that his incisors seemed slightly elongated, Gina quelled a further explosion of giggles, and sat back down in her own chair with a bump.

'Am *I* making you nervous?' He spoke gently this time, shaking his head with mock disbelief. The ludicrous shreds of pink toilet paper fluttered in sympathy. 'Sweetheart, there's really no need. Why don't we put the past behind us and try again? I'm free this evening if you'd like to come out with me for dinner.'

'I . . . I'm busy tonight.' With an effort she managed to get the words out. 'Sorry.'

He shook his head once more. Flutter, flutter. 'Oh sweetheart. Don't tell me you're still cross with me.'

'Not . . . cross.' In serious danger of wetting herself, Gina pressed her knees together. 'Just b-busy.'

Ralph shrugged and leaned forward to take a sip of coffee. It was the shrug that finally did it. Absolutely transfixed, Gina watched as one of the dislodged shreds of tissue landed in his cup.

'. . . priceless! So, what did he do? What happened next?'

Gina, who hadn't laughed so much since she was a child, wiped her eyes with a mascara-stained handkerchief. She had an aching stitch in her side. Every time she thought the hysteria was dying down, she only had to envisage the expression on Ralph's face as he'd peered at the alien object floating in his coffee, and it erupted once more.

'He . . . he . . . recognised it!' she gulped, clutching Doug's sturdy arm for support. 'And then of course he realised how stupid he must have looked, and his face went all p-p-purple like an aubergine. I couldn't help it after that, I just burst out laughing and he went even *purpler* . . . then he leapt up, shouted, "You bloody little bitch," and stormed out. I'm afraid your door hinges might never be the same again . . .'

Doug grinned; poor old Ralph. In puncturing his ego, Gina had dealt him the cruellest of blows. He would undoubtedly now find himself a new agent, but Doug didn't even care. How could anyone – particularly someone as imperfect as himself – possibly resist such a wonderful tale? And to see Gina enjoying her much-deserved triumph was a positive delight.

'I suppose I am a bitch,' she continued, her tone unrepentant. 'If it had been anyone else – you, for example – I would have told them straight away, just as you'd tell someone if the label on their sweater was sticking out. But Ralph is so *vain* . . .'

And she was off again, rocking in her chair and clutching her side. Suddenly emboldened by their shared secret and the mood of almost festive celebration, Doug glanced at his watch and said, 'It's five-thirty. Are you really busy this evening, or d'you fancy slipping round to Russell's winebar for a drink?'

Her second dinner invitation in less than an hour. This time Gina didn't even hesitate. 'I think I'd better,' she said with a grin. 'For my own safety. Can you imagine what people will think if they see me giggling to myself all the way home on the tube?'

Over a shared bottle of Beaujolais and succulent ham-and-asparagus quiche in a corner of the dark, crowded winebar, they continued to laugh and shamelessly mock Ralph for his pretentious ways and over-co-ordinated wardrobe.

'But you must have liked him to begin with, otherwise you wouldn't have gone out with him,' ventured Doug finally.

Gina toyed with her glass. 'I suppose so. Well, I was flattered because he seemed so charming and attentive, but he was never really my type. It had just been so long since any man had paid me that amount of interest that I kind of . . . fell for it.'

It was beyond Doug's comprehension why anyone of Gina's calibre should be starved of male attention. As far as he was concerned she was eminently desirable and if he hadn't long ago come to terms with the fact that such women were way out of his league, he would have made his own interest obvious months ago.

'In that case,' he said, eyes twinkling, 'it sounds to me as if you had a narrow escape. Or should I call it a close shave?'

'Oh no,' gasped Gina, almost choking on her wine. 'Don't make me laugh again . . .'

'Really, my dear,' he protested, all innocence. 'Can I help it if I have a razor-sharp wit?'

'Doug . . . !'

'OK, OK. I've stopped. So, tell me, what kind of man *would* be your type?'

Gina thought for a moment. 'Someone as unlike Ralph as possible.'

Doug felt his heart inadvertently quicken. Fingering the frayed cuff of his badly ironed shirt, he experienced a faint – a very faint – surge of hope. Of all the men in all the world, he thought, surely none could possibly be more unlike Ralph Henson than he was.

Chapter 38

In Izzy's experience, throwing a party had always involved working out how much money she couldn't afford to spend, roughly doubling it, then staggering back from the off-licence with enough crates of lager and boxes of wine to ensure that no one could possibly go thirsty. Huge vats of chilli con carne or spaghetti mopped up the alcohol and her rickety but reliable cassette player provided the music. If whichever flat she was living in at the time could comfortably hold thirty guests, she invited fifty and jammed them in willy-nilly because that way they could more speedily get to know each other and have fun. The party continued until the last guest fell asleep and whoever stayed the night helped with the clearing-up the following morning.

Well, that was how it had always been in the old days, thought Izzy drily. Throwing a party at Stanford Manor, however, wasn't going to be like that at all.

But not having to worry about the cost certainly had its advantages. As she adjusted her upwardly mobile, bottle-green lycra skirt, smoothed the strapless green-and-gold sequinned bodice into place and ruffled her hair for the last time in front of the mirror, she could hear the band tuning up downstairs in the main hall, their music punctuated by the stentorian tones of Mrs Bishop as she bullied the outside caterers and made absolutely certain they understood who was boss. The food, it went without saying, would be spectacular, the flow of vintage champagne never-ending and none of the two hundred or so guests need worry about being press-ganged into helping with the washing-up.

By ten o'clock the party was in full swing. 'Never, Never', having entered the top ten the previous week, was expected to go to Number One tomorrow and everyone was celebrating in advance. But it wasn't until the huge front doors swung open and Simon, with Katerina at his side, entered the hall, that Izzy truly began to celebrate.

She was about to rush towards them when Vivienne yanked her unceremoniously back. 'You're supposed to be playing it cool, remember,' she admonished. 'What did Sam tell you? She wants to be treated like an adult. Whatever you do, don't *gush*.'

'I won't.' Izzy, dizzy with delight, determined to be as ungushing as possible. Telephoning Simon and inviting him and Katerina to the party had been a master-stroke. In reasonable tones, she had explained that, although she and Katerina weren't on the best of terms at the present time, there was no earthly reason why they couldn't be civil to each other on a purely social level. Knowing how star-struck Simon was, he had been a foregone conclusion, and she had banked on his powers of persuasion – together with Katerina's deep-seated curiosity – to get her here tonight.

And it had worked, she thought joyfully, making her way towards them. It had really worked . . .

'You made it. I'm so pleased you're both here.' Gosh, it was hard not to gush.

'Simon wanted to come.' Katerina wore a guarded expression, as if she were expecting a more extravagant welcome.

'Well, it's exciting,' said Simon defensively, the colour already rising in his cheeks. Stepping forward, he dropped an awkward kiss on Izzy's cheek. 'And I think it's brilliant, your single doing so well.'

Izzy wondered whether Katerina was wearing jeans and an old, black T-shirt to make a point. Now that she was finally making real money, she ached to shower her daughter with lavish gifts. Instead, taking care to hide her true feelings, she smiled up at Simon and said, 'Thank you. I think it's brilliant, too.'

'Our A level results came through yesterday,' said Katerina abruptly. 'I didn't fail them.'

'Oh darling . . .'

'But the grades are too low for medical school, so I might as well have done.'

'Oh.' Swallowing her disappointment, forcing herself not to react as Kat appeared to want her to, Izzy managed another, slightly wan smile.

'Well, never mind. Look, the band's about to start up again and our eardrums could suffer. Why don't you two head through that archway, get yourself something to eat and drink, and take a look around?'

Simon was already looking. Ogling. This threatened to be the most exciting night of his life and he had already spotted several famous faces, not to mention real bimbos, enthrallingly underdressed.

'There's the drummer with Blur,' he said, his voice hushed with reverence. 'And that girl in the bikini – isn't she Fiona whatsername?'

'For heaven's sake, don't gawp,' said Katerina, determinedly unimpressed. Pushing him in the direction of the bar, she added in a fierce whisper, 'And don't you *dare* ask anyone for their autograph . . .'

'Well done,' said Vivienne approvingly, when Izzy returned to her side. Raising her exceedingly strong vodka and tonic in a semi-salute, she surveyed the departing couple with amusement.

'Poor old Kat, what a muddle. She and Simon actually make a good couple, if only she'd realise it. And if only,' she added as an afterthought, 'poor old Simon could control his unfortunate blushes.'

'Speaking of good couples,' said Izzy, her tone casual, 'why isn't Sam here with you? Does he still disapprove of my being with Tash that much?'

They were making their way out to the floodlit pool. Vivienne, impressively encased in shell-pink satin, undulated like an eel in heels. With a shrug, she replied, 'Who knows? Sam keeps his thoughts pretty much to himself these days. He doesn't ask me what I'm up to any more, and when I tell him, he doesn't even seem to listen. I'm bored to tears and all he says is why don't I get some kind of job. Can you imagine what *that* kind of advice does to someone like *me*?'

Izzy frowned. 'So, what are you going to do?'

'What would any normal human being do? It's practically an invitation to misbehave!' Vivienne tossed back her golden hair and grinned in passing at Tash's drummer, who had quite wickedly dissipated blue eyes. 'Hell, why else would I damn near give myself a hernia trussing myself up in this dress? I'm going to dazzle and delight, honeychile, like it's going out of fashion. This beautiful body is fed up with being ignored . . .' Her voice trailed away for a second, then added, '. . . and I think I may just have spotted the man not to ignore it. Izzy, who *is* that guy over there? The one in the dark blue shirt . . .'

'Oh, Vivienne, what about Sam?' Izzy was beginning to get worried. She clearly meant business.

'Since when did a little jealousy go amiss? And stop changing the subject. Tell me at once who he is, and how much money he earns. This is *definitely* the man for me.'

Izzy didn't think he was, but Vivienne was unstoppable. Refusing even to listen to Izzy's reminder of how very amiss her own love life had gone as a result of the mutual jealousy between Ralph and Mike, she made a beeline for the object of her desire and wasted no time at all introducing herself.

Since Tash was far too busy being chatted up by a rapacious, heavily bleached blonde either to notice or to care what Izzy might be up to, she danced with Benny Dunaway and marvelled – not for the first time – that such an accomplished musician could dance quite so badly. At this rate, her poor feet were in danger of doubling in size.

'Oops, sorry.' Benny, unused to champagne cocktails, looked hopelessly unrepentant. 'Now you know why my wife refuses to dance with me.'

'I don't mind,' said Izzy valiantly, giving him a hug to

prove it. 'If it weren't for you, none of this would have happened. Are you enjoying yourself?'

'Are you kidding? This is how the other half lives.' He flung his arm wide to indicate the splendour of the occasion. 'And from now on, it's how *you're* going to live. You've cracked it, my darling, and I couldn't be more pleased for you.'

She was touched. 'Really?'

'Well, it hasn't exactly done my street-cred any harm.' Benny trod on her toes once more and grinned. 'Did I forget to mention it earlier? The entire fifth year have issued demands for signed photographs. No hurry, tomorrow morning will be soon enough.'

'Nice to know I'm popular with some teenagers,' sighed Izzy, watching out of the corner of her eye as Katerina – sitting temporarily alone in one of the carved stone window-seats – rebuffed the attentions of a pony-tailed youth wielding a chicken leg in one hand and a bottle of Sol in the other.

'Not you,' said Benny cheerfully. 'It's Tash they're interested in, stupid.'

Having been abandoned by Simon, who was deep in conversation with Tash Janssen's bass guitarist, Katerina covertly watched her mother dance first with Benny, then with an horrendously dressed male who had to be Joel McGill. She was clearly enjoying herself in her new home, she thought, somewhat piqued by the fact that Izzy had paid her virtually no attention at all this evening. Everybody seemed to know everybody else. Extraordinary amounts of alcohol were disappearing down throats and several of the guests were on their way to getting stoned. It was certainly a good job Sam hadn't turned up, she thought, glancing in the direction of the pool and observing Vivienne wrapped around a complete stranger in the shadows.

Deciding to explore the rest of the undeniably spectacular house, Kat rested her orange juice on the window-ledge and set off in the opposite direction, away from the crowds and noise, before the jerk with the ponytail could come back and start pestering her again.

'Are you always this, er . . . forward?' asked Terry Pleydell-Pearce, his expression somewhat bemused. 'Not that I'm complaining, you understand, but I wouldn't want you to think I was somebody wealthy or influential, or anything like that.'

'Do I look like the kind of girl who would only be interested in money?' Vivienne protested, genuinely dismayed by the implied slur on her character. She'd practically fallen in love the moment she'd set eyes on this charming, funny, self-deprecating man. The very idea that the attraction might not be mutual filled her with something close to panic.

'Well, yes,' he said, in reply to her question, 'as a matter of fact, you do.'

'OK.' Determined to sweep his objections aside, she changed tack. 'We'll be honest with each other, shall we? I don't make a habit of telling people this, but it really wouldn't matter *how* poor you are, because I have money of my own. Oodles of the stuff. *More* than oodles . . .'

'Stop it. You're scaring me.'

'I'm supposed to be reassuring you!' It came out as a wail. Then he grinned and she realised he had been teasing her. 'Oh, that's not fair.'

'But it *is* scary. When a wealthy, gorgeous Texan blonde shows this much interest in an impoverished, forty-one-year-old widower, it's . . . well, nerve wracking.'

He'd called her gorgeous. Enormously encouraged, Vivienne said gently, 'How awful, your wife dying. Do you have any children?'

'A boy and a girl. Theo and Lydia.'

'And is that why you're so poor? You had to give up your job to raise your kids?' She could have wept; it was all so sad and so noble. This wonderful man, with his kind, careworn eyes and rumpled dark hair had abandoned a career in order to give his young family the love and emotional security they so badly needed . . .

'Good God, no.' Terry burst out laughing. 'Lydia's married with two children and Theo's working as a junior houseman at St Thomas's. When I said I was impoverished, I was speaking relatively. I work as a GP.'

'A medic? So you *can't* be poor,' she countered, her eyes alight with triumph. 'My gynaecologist back home has his own Lear jet.'

'Believe me.' Terry Pleydell-Pearce's expression remained deadpan. 'It isn't like that in this country, particularly if you work for the NHS. Of course, some days I can afford to eat. Others, I simply take a walk through Regent's Park and steal bread from the ducks . . .'

Vivienne's eyes narrowed. 'Forty-one,' she declared accusingly.

'I beg your pardon?'

'You said you were forty-one years old. And your married daughter has *two children?*'

The expression of guilt on his face was an absolute picture. At that moment, Vivienne fell irrevocably in love.

'When a wealthy, gorgeous, Texan mathematical genius shows this much interest in an impoverished forty-one-year-old widower, it's nerve-wracking,' he reminded her. 'But if the impoverished widower happens to be forty-six, it's positively traumatic.'

Moving closer, aching to kiss him, she touched his cheek, 'It needn't be traumatic.'

'And you're taller than me.'

It was the mildest of protests. Slipping out of her heels, she brushed his dry mouth with a trembling forefinger. 'Not any more.'

'I've never met anyone like you before in my life.'

This time, Vivienne smiled. 'I should hope not.'

'So, what happens now?' said Terry Pleydell-Pearce, his voice no longer quite steady.

She raised a delicate eyebrow. 'You're the doctor, doctor. You tell me.'

Chapter 39

'Oh,' said Katerina, coming awake suddenly and realizing that she was being watched.

Tash looked amused. 'It's a talent of mine.'

'What is?'

'Staring at people when they're asleep. Subconsciously, they become aware of it and wake up. Is the party that boring?'

As she struggled into a sitting position he came and sat down on the opposite end of the sofa. Caught off-guard, she replied, 'Of course not. I'm sure it's a very good party. I was just tired, that's all.'

For a fraction of a second, Tash considered offering her a couple of the pills in his shirt pocket, then decided against it. The girl was straight, too straight, and he didn't want to run the risk of being busted, particularly with the next single due for release bearing an anti-drugs message.

'So, what do you think of my games room?' he said instead, gesturing around the huge, candle-lit room to include the pinball machines, snooker and table-tennis tables and giant video screen.

'Impressive.' There was an edge of sarcasm in her voice. 'Look, you don't have to make polite conversation with me. Shouldn't you get back to your guests?'

Tash's dark eyes glittered with amusement. 'It's my

party. I can do whatever I like. Are you always this stroppy?'

'I don't know why you're talking to me,' replied Katerina evenly. 'Unless it's because my mother asked you to. Is *that* why you're here, to give me another lecture?'

He shrugged. 'What you choose to do with your life is nothing to do with me. Now there's line for a song . . .'

Of course he wasn't interested, she realised. If she had agreed to move into the house in Wimbledon, Izzy would be living there with her instead of here with Tash.

For some reason, the thought cheered her. Reaching over, she removed the drink from his hand and took a mouthful to lubricate her sleep-dried tongue. To her surprise it was unadulterated tonic water.

Tash, who had been admiring her slender body, said, 'Do you play snooker?'

For the first time, Katerina smiled. 'Is Steve Davis boring?'

'OK.' Clasping her hand, he hauled her to her feet. 'Rest time over. Game well and truly on.'

'I can play. I didn't say I was any good.'

'No problem.' Tash winked as he began setting up the table. 'I'm a great teacher.'

Vivienne was nowhere to be found. Izzy, who had gone out to the pool in search of her, found herself buttonholed instead by a dippy-looking girl with fuchsia-pink cheeks, matching eyeshadow and the kind of candyfloss hair more commonly found on Barbie dolls. She was wearing an electric-blue rubber dress which emphasized the puppy fat around her midriff, and purple stilettos. Izzy held her breath in order to avoid the reek of Poison.

'You're Izzy Van Asch,' said the girl with a giggle. Holding out her hand, then realizing that a cigarette still burned between her fingers, she said, 'Oops, my mistake. I'm Mirabelle. Hi.'

You certainly are, thought Izzy, glancing around the pool and wondering where Tash had got to. This girl was seriously out of it.

'I saw the video the other night. Great song. Wild,' continued Mirabelle. 'Tash is great, too, isn't he? I know he's a bastard, but I just love him to death. Wild.'

'Hmm.' Izzy couldn't see Kat anywhere, either. 'Have you known him for long?'

Mirabelle smiled, revealing very small white teeth. 'Oh yeah. Nearly seven months now. I'm Donny's girlfriend.'

That figured. Donny, the band's keyboards player, might be musically talented, but he possessed about as many brain cells as the average Webb's lettuce. Izzy, growing increasingly desperate to escape, scanned the poolside once more in search of someone – anyone – she might use as an excuse to escape. Even Mrs Bishop . . .

'Yeah, and I was Anna's best friend,' continued Mirabelle, swaying slightly as she took another drag of her cigarette. 'You know, Tash's girlfriend before you.'

'I know,' replied Izzy carefully. Was this conversation perhaps leading somewhere after all?

'You're ever so much older than her.'

'I know that, too. Look, is there some kind of problem? Do you have something you want to say to me?'

'Well yes, I guess I do.' Mirabelle twirled a strand of candyfloss white hair around her fingers, hiccuped twice and gazed at her, wide-eyed. 'Hey, like, I just wanted you to know, it's cool. No problem at all. As long as you're with Tash, I'll be your best friend too.'

Tash should have called it the fun-and-games room. The first time he had brushed past her on his way around the table, Katerina had given him the benefit of the doubt. Three reds, a pink and a green later, she realised he had other benefits in mind.

'You should splay your fingers more to make a firm bridge,' he said, moving up behind her and reaching forward to correct the angle of her left arm. In doing so, his body came to rest against hers; Katerina felt the gentle pressure of his lean thighs and allowed herself a grim smile.

'That's much better,' he said, when she'd potted the ball. 'You see, all you need is a little guidance.'

All Tash needed, she thought, was a little bromide. But she wasn't about to object yet; it was going to be fun seeing just how far he thought he could go.

She didn't have to wait long to find out. Tash, who had earlier been indulging in some of the excellent coke brought along by Mirabelle, was finding Izzy's daughter increasingly desirable. She had the most gorgeous figure – and the longest legs – he'd seen in years. And as for that glistening, almost waist-length hair . . .

The next moment his arm had snaked around her waist and he was pulling her round to face him. Serious, conker-brown eyes regarded him with heartbreaking intensity.

'My mother could walk in at any minute,' said Katerina in a low voice.

'She'll have to bulldoze the wall down first.' Tash grinned. 'I've locked the door.'

His hands were sliding upwards. The next thing she knew, he had lifted her up on to the snooker table and insinuated his body between her thighs.

'She'd still be hurt if she knew what was going on.'

Tash, who had never understood the female obsession with monogamy, simply shrugged.

'I think we both know how to keep a secret, don't we?'

'But doesn't it worry you,' Katerina persisted, 'that you might be hurting her?'

His dark eyebrows arched in amusement. 'At this precise moment? No.'

'Oh, well . . .' she said slowly, 'in that case, I won't let it worry me that I'm about to hurt you.'

'Aaargh,' grunted Tash, as her right knee shot up, scoring a direct hit. Clutching his groin, he staggered backwards.

Katerina, jumping down from the table and eyeing him with disdain, said, 'Oh, for God's sake, did you seriously think you were *that* irresistible?'

'Shit . . .' groaned Tash, as the pain intensified.

Katerina, who had by this time reached the door and unlocked it, gave him a mock-pitying look. 'Yes, I'd say that just about sums you up,' she declared triumphantly. 'Tash Janssen, despicable little shit. My God, you and my mother deserve each other.'

Izzy was talking to Simon in a corner of the sitting room. Her eyes lit up when she saw Katerina coming towards them. 'Darling, we were beginning to think you'd gone home! Where on earth have you been?'

'Making polite conversation,' replied Katerina briskly. 'It's what you're supposed to do at parties, isn't it? And it's been great fun, but now we are going home.' She patted Simon's back pocket, locating his car keys. 'Ready?'

'Do we have to?' He looked dismayed. The party would go on for hours yet. It seemed almost sacrilegious to leave so soon.

But Katerina was determined. 'Yes, we do.'

'You've enjoyed yourself, though,' Izzy put in eagerly. Despite Kat's abrupt tone, she looked cheerful, almost elated. 'Who were you talking to, someone nice?'

Katerina only just managed to keep a straight face. 'Tash.'

'Oh, I'm so pleased!' Izzy knew she mustn't gush, but it was such encouraging news. She'd always known that Kat and Tash would get on well, once they got to know each other properly. 'Sweetheart, it makes such a difference, knowing that you really like him.'

Katerina savoured the moment. Out of the corner of her eye she glimpsed Tash, now evidently recovered, sliding his arm around the plump brown shoulders of a girl in a blue rubber dress. For a fraction of a second she debated telling Izzy exactly what had gone on in the candle-lit games room, less than fifteen minutes earlier. But then, why should she? Izzy deserved to find out the hard way and it damn well would serve her right for siding against her own daughter when she should have been supporting her.

Katerina, who had endured so much misery in the

past weeks, now revelled in the sensation of her own power.

'Did I say I liked him?' she enquired with exaggerated politeness. 'And is my opinion of Tash Janssen really relevant anyway? I tell you what, Mum. You don't lecture me on my choice in men and I won't lecture you on yours. OK?'

Chapter 40

By four-thirty Izzy was seriously beginning to wilt. Although most of the guests had left, those that remained showed no signs of giving in. Music blared from amplifiers around the pool, people were still dancing and joints were being passed around between unsteady fingers. A well-known actress, currently starring as a nun in a top-rated TV series, was swaying in time with the music and slowly removing her dress to raucous acclaim. Behind her, Tash lay on a white sunlounger, and smiled his deceptively sleepy smile as a slender redhead began to massage his shoulders.

Izzy wished it could all be over. Tired and sober, her head was pounding and her eyes ached. Joel and Benny had long since disappeared, there was no one left she particularly wanted to talk to, and she was having a hard time shaking off the whisky-sodden attentions of a red-faced man who insisted that in real life he was a concert organiser.

'You name it, I've organised 'em,' he declared expansively, reaching for his drink. 'Yeah, all the greats . . . all the biggest venues . . . an' it could be you next, up there on that great big stage. Cute li'l thing like you could have a real future an' I'd be there to look after you, sweetheart . . .'

No longer listening to his drunken ramblings, Izzy

wondered where Vivienne was and hoped her friend had at least enjoyed the party more than she had. Everyone was yelling and applauding the actress as she discarded her camisole top and began to undo her bra. All they needed now was for a member of the paparazzi to leap out of the bushes with a camera.

Idly she watched as Mirabelle, not to be outdone, staggered to her feet and made her way over to Donny.

'Dance with me, baby,' she wheedled, crouching beside him in her high heels. 'Come on, just one little dance with me?'

Donny wasn't interested. 'Nah, dance on your own.'

'But that's no fun,' wailed Mirabelle, clutching his arm as he attempted to open a can of Newcastle Brown. 'Donn*eee*, that's no fun at all. I want to dance with *you*.'

Shaking off her hand, he grabbed the hem of her dress and twanged it. Then he started to laugh. 'Whiney bitch, always moaning. Haven't you seen that film, *Flashdance?*'

'Yes, but . . .'

Reaching for another rubbery handful of the electric-blue dress, he said loudly, 'Well, this is Splashdance,' and twanged again. The next moment, with a shriek, Mirabelle had toppled into the pool.

'Can she swim?' asked Izzy some moments later, when all that had surfaced were bubbles.

Everyone else seemed to find it highly amusing. Amid much laughter, Tash drawled, 'She'll be safe, she's wearing a big enough condom.'

Izzy wasn't so sure. Mirabelle still hadn't risen to the surface and she was far too stoned to be fooling around.

Shaking Donny's shoulder, she repeated urgently, '*Can* she swim?'

But Donny scarcely seemed to be aware of his surroundings. With a vague gesture, he said, 'Hey man, how should I know? How d'you get the lid off this sodding can, anyway?'

The night was warm but cold sweat prickled beneath Izzy's arms as she was gripped by a premonition of doom. All around her, people were still laughing. Nobody was going to make a move to help. The horrible party was turning into a nightmare . . .

Izzy wasn't a strong swimmer but she knew there was no time to waste. Kicking off her shoes, she held her breath and dived in.

The heavily chlorinated water stung her eyes and when she touched the bottom of the pool a jab of pain shot through the sole of her foot, but by some miracle she found Mirabelle almost at once.

Sequins grazed her inner arms as she struggled to grab hold of the inert body, slippery in its rubber casing. Feeling as if her lungs were about to explode, Izzy slid her arms securely around the girl's ribcage and hauled with all her strength. Bizarrely, the water around them was turning cloudy pink like something out of a *Jaws* movie. Kicking her feet, blinking as Mirabelle's candyfloss hair plastered itself against her face, Izzy strained towards the surface of the pool. Strangely, in the dim distance, she could hear people cheering . . .

Only the concert organiser deigned to help. Between the two of them they eventually managed to haul Mirabelle – like a large, ungainly seal – out of the pool.

Gasping for breath, wiping her streaming eyes, Izzy searched for and eventually found a weak pulse, but the girl's chest was ominously still.

'Get an ambulance,' she croaked, tilting the slack head back and pinching Mirabelle's nose. Kneeling over her, she bent her own head and breathed into the cold, rubbery mouth.

'Hey, this is more like it,' yelled an indistinguishable male voice. 'Better than a porno film. Watch out, Tash, you've got competition there.'

Shovelling Mirabelle on to her front, Izzy pressed down on her lungs in a desperate attempt to clear them. This was worse than any nightmare. And although she couldn't see where it was coming from, there seemed to be blood everywhere, mingling with the water from the pool and staining the beige concrete upon which Mirabelle lay.

But finally, just as she was about to give up all hope, Mirabelle's chest heaved and water gushed out of her mouth. With a moan – as the water was followed by vomit – she flailed her arms and struggled to raise her head. Izzy rolled her on to her side so she wouldn't choke and sent up a prayer of thanks as the girl's ribcage rose and fell in something approaching a regular pattern.

'I say,' observed the actress in conversational tones, swaying as she bent to take a closer look. 'That's an awfully good trick.'

Izzy spoke through gritted teeth. 'Did they say how long it would take before the ambulance got here?'

Behind her, Tash said, 'She's OK. Just let her sleep it off. Ambulances screaming up the drive would only give the neighbours something else to complain about, and drowning drug addicts aren't exactly the kind of publicity we need.'

Coughing and spluttering, Mirabelle wiped her mouth with the back of her hand and moaned, 'Where's Donny? I'm c-cold.'

'Get some blankets and call an ambulance,' snapped Izzy, fixing the concert organiser with a steely glare. '*Now.*' Then, still kneeling with Mirabelle's head in her lap, she turned to face Tash and his guests.

'You selfish, stupid . . . bastards – all of you. Is anything more important to you than getting stoned? You're lucky she isn't *dead*, and all you care about is bad publicity. Any one of you could have fallen into that pool . . . and not *one* of you is capable of doing a damn thing to help.'

'Christ, this is all we need,' said Tash lazily. Glancing up at the redhead still massaging his shoulders, he winked and added, 'Don't you just hate moralizing do-gooders? Aren't they *the* most boring people to have at a party?'

Trembling with rage, repulsed by the knowledge that this was her lover speaking – and that she didn't know him at all – Izzy said icily, 'You are the most despicable man I've ever met in my life. You are *pathetic* . . .'

Tash's dark eyes glittered with amusement. 'Ah, but at least I'm not boring.'

At that moment a tall figure stepped out of the shadows and moved swiftly towards Izzy. For a fraction of a second she thought she was hallucinating.

But Sam, who had been listening to the heated exchange for the last thirty seconds – long enough to figure out what was going on – didn't waste any more time. Scooping Mirabelle up into his arms, he said briefly,

'Come on, we'll take her to the hospital in my car.'

'*Oh, when the saints go marching out*,' sang Tash, as they passed him. Izzy, who was limping behind Sam, paused. Beyond words, she turned and slapped his thin face as hard as she could. It wasn't enough, but it was better than nothing at all. If she'd had a gun she would have used it, without so much as a second thought.

It wasn't until she emerged from the casualty cubicle and found Sam waiting outside that she finally managed a weak smile.

'I've just seen myself in a mirror. No wonder they thought I was the patient.'

Sam's expression softened. With her white, mascara-streaked face, dripping wet hair and blood-streaked legs, Izzy had presented a far more convincing picture of an accident victim than half the patients in the waiting room, and she didn't look that much better now. With a glance at her bandaged foot, he held out his arm in order to support her back to the car. 'Does it hurt?'

She pulled a face. 'A bit. There was broken glass in the bottom of the pool and I managed to land on it. Oh Sam, should we be leaving? What about Mirabelle?'

He led her firmly through the double doors. 'They've admitted her for observation just to be on the safe side, but they're pretty certain she'll be OK. And there's no need to look at me like that,' he added with a grin. 'I'm in charge. You're absolutely wiped out and I'm taking you home.'

'Home,' murmured Izzy, her expression doubtful.

They had reached the car. Opening the passenger door

and helping her inside, Sam said briskly, 'My home.'

When they reached the flat, he deposited her on the sofa, threw a large towelling dressing gown down beside her and headed towards the kitchen.

'Change into that while I make the coffee.'

Exhausted though she was, Izzy nevertheless summoned up the energy to make her lie sound convincing. 'I thought Vivienne would be here. She left the party ages ago, saying she was going to have an early night.'

Pausing in the doorway, Sam merely looked amused. 'But not in her bed, it seems. Never mind, Izzy. Nice try.'

By the time he returned with the coffee and a packet of chocolate digestives, however, the shock had begun to set in. Izzy, enveloped in the white towelling robe, was shivering so much the sofa practically vibrated beneath her. She looked so uncharacteristically frail and unhappy that Sam's heart went out to her.

'I suppose you've been looking forward to this,' she said, clasping the mug he offered her between both hands in order not to spill the contents.

'To what?'

'Saying, "I told you so." '

'I *was* looking forward to it,' he said truthfully, 'but it doesn't seem all that relevant now. I'm more concerned with how you're feeling.'

Izzy shrugged, her dark eyes enormous but mercifully dry. 'Lucky, I suppose, to be out of it in one piece. Angry, gullible . . . oh, Sam, how could I have been so *stupid*? When I first met Tash I really thought he was a nice person.'

'That's because he wanted you to think he was.'

She sniffed. 'God, I'm a lousy judge of character. Imagine the damage I could do if I was ever called for jury service.'

Easing his long legs up on to the coffee table and tearing open the packet of biscuits, Sam said evenly, 'Anyone can make a mistake.'

'You never do.'

'I let Vivienne move in with me.'

The signs of Vivienne's occupation were strewn around them. Having absently helped herself to a biscuit she didn't want, the chocolate now melted between her fingers as Izzy gazed at a pair of black-and-gold stilettos occupying a chair, and at the CDs littered like playing cards on the floor beside the stereo. The system had been left switched on, with a half-empty wineglass balanced precariously on top of it. In a small way, it was comforting to know how much Vivienne's untidiness irritated Sam. Maybe he was right, after all.

'But she isn't . . . scary, like Tash. She doesn't get out of her brains on drugs. He doesn't care about anyone or anything . . . he's practically psychopathic. You can't compare them, Sam. Vivienne's only unhappy because you aren't paying her enough attention.'

She was speaking more calmly now, and her teeth had stopped chattering. Lifting a semi-damp tendril of hair from her neck and breathing in the chlorine, Sam shrugged.

'That just proves my point. If I hadn't made the mistake of letting her stay here in the first place, she wouldn't be unhappy now. If Vivienne and I were genuinely happy together, I'd *be* paying attention.'

'It doesn't bother you that she didn't come home tonight?' Izzy still found it hard to believe. In her own mind, they were such a *good* couple.

'I'm relieved.' He paused, then added drily, 'It's easier this way. She can make her own decision, and her pride will still be intact. As you may have noticed, Vivienne has more than her share of pride.'

Izzy was finding it hard not to notice his warm fingers at the base of her neck, idly smoothing back her hair. She shivered uncontrollably and gazed down at the chocolatey mess in her hand.

'What you need is a hot bath and plenty of sleep,' he continued gently and for the first time her eyes filled with tears. What she *most* needed was a real hug, and someone to tell her she wasn't an all-time prize idiot.

To her utter dismay she heard herself saying in a small, pathetic voice, 'You're such a nice person. You used to like me, didn't you, Sam? I wish you hadn't stopped liking me. I . . . I wish you didn't hate me now.'

She didn't get her hug. Taking a deep breath and giving her shoulder a brief, meant-to-be reassuring squeeze, he said, 'Don't be silly, of course I don't hate you,' and rose to his feet.

'I'm sorry,' mumbled Izzy, wiping her eyes and feeling more idiotic than ever.

Sam, continuing to exert almost superhuman self-control, dismissed the apology with a brisk gesture. She was vulnerable, exhausted and deeply upset about Tash. Now was hardly the time to tell Izzy how he really felt about her.

'You've had a traumatic night,' he said with a taut half-smile. 'I'll run you that bath, and then you're going to bed.'

In a hopeless attempt to redeem herself, Izzy said weakly, 'Will you do me a big favour?'

This, thought Sam, was precisely what he was struggling so hard not to do. 'What?'

'Can I have Badedas in it?'

Chapter 41

It wasn't as if they were doing anything *lewd*, but it was still kind of embarrassing being caught on the sofa with the new love of your life, particularly when the person doing the catching was your new love's grown-up son.

'Well, well,' he declared in arch tones, dumping a tartan overnight case on the living-room floor and surveying the cosy scene. Vivienne, whose bare feet had been resting in Terry's lap, leapt guiltily into a sitting position and tried to make her cleavage less prominent.

'Theo, for heaven's sake.' Terry was looking equally discomfited. 'I thought you were working this weekend.'

'Somebody wanted to swap shifts,' replied Theo easily, 'so I thought I'd drop in on my old man, make sure he was OK.' He winked at Vivienne. 'I thought he might be lonely . . . in need of a bit of company . . .'

Theo Pleydell-Pearce, sandy-haired and built like an American football player, had his father's blue eyes and endearing freckles. Deciding to brazen it out – since Terry was clearly too embarrassed to say much at all – Vivienne grinned at him and replied, 'I had exactly the same idea.'

'So, you aren't a patient.' The blue eyes sparkled with amusement. 'For a moment I thought I might be interrupting a reverse housecall.'

'Theo, this is Vivienne Bresnick. We met at a party last night . . .' Floundering for an explanation, Terry pushed his fingers agitatedly through his hair. 'We came back here for coffee . . . we've been talking all night . . .'

'What your father is trying to say,' Vivienne intercepted kindly, 'is that our relationship has not been consummated. Yet.'

Since morning surgery started at nine, Theo drove Vivienne back to Kensington. Above the roar of the ancient MG's engine, as they careered along narrow country lanes with the hood down and the cassette player blaring out Bruce Springsteen, he yelled, 'So, tell me, what exactly *is* going on here?'

'Excuse me?'

'Between you and Dad. It would be simpler if you just told me the truth. Was it a drunken one-off or do you really intend seeing him again?'

Leaning across, she switched off the music. Theo obligingly reduced his speed so that she could speak without shouting.

'Your father is one of the nicest men I've ever met,' said Vivienne carefully. 'And more than anything else in the world, I'd like to continue seeing him.'

He nodded. 'OK. I'm sorry if I've offended you, but you must understand why I needed to ask. Since my mother died, he's had his share of women interested in him, but you aren't exactly . . .'

'I know, I know.' Vivienne had spent the entire night listening to this argument. 'I'm not a country lady in twin set and brogues, with a Labrador at my heels and a shooting-stick up my bum. I've never baked a "scone" – whatever the hell that might be – in my life. But the moment I set eyes on your dad, something . . . clicked. I really like him,' she concluded with a simple gesture. 'And I think he likes me.'

With a sideways glance, Theo took in the clinging, shell-pink satin dress, the expanse of tanned thigh, the astonishing bosom and cascading blonde hair. 'I'm not surprised.'

Vivienne smiled. 'I have a great personality, as well.'

'So I'm beginning to realise,' he admitted wryly. 'What I really can't wait to see are the faces of all those tweedy county ladies, when they find out what kind of competition they're up against.'

Sam, in white cotton trousers and a grey sweatshirt, was stretched out on the sofa surrounded by paperwork when she let herself into the apartment. Vivienne, who hadn't expected him to be up at this time of the morning, hesitated in the doorway before kicking off her shoes and dropping her bag into a chair. Despite the exhilaration of the last twelve hours, she was now gripped by a spasm of self-doubt. Sam was *so* stunningly handsome, so physically perfect, how could she even think of leaving him? Yet she had adored him and it hadn't been enough. Nothing she could do would ever make Sam adore her in return. She had done everything in her power, but the necessary spark simply wasn't there.

He glanced up from his paperwork. 'Good party?'

'It had its moments.' Vivienne pushed her fingers through her tangled, wind-blown hair. Then, with a trace of exasperation, she said, 'Well? Aren't you even going to ask me what I've been doing?'

It was a last-ditch attempt to force some kind of reaction, some shred of jealousy, but all Sam did was glance across at her opened bag and look faintly amused. After pausing to pencil in an alteration, he replied, 'Since your bra is hanging out of your handbag, I think I can probably guess.'

So much for jealousy and belated protestations of love. The pale pink bra was new and expensive but a size too small, and Vivienne had merely removed it in the early hours of the morning in order to be comfortable. She hadn't been unfaithful to Sam, yet he had calmly assumed the opposite and *still* didn't even have the decency to care . . .

'How did you ever get to be so *unfeeling*?' Her voice rose to a wail and at last Sam reacted.

'Ssshh,' he said sharply. 'Izzy's asleep in the spare room. Don't make so much noise.'

Despite everything, Vivienne was instantly diverted. '*Izzy's* here? Why?'

'While you were elsewhere, flinging off your bra and enjoying one of your . . . moments, Izzy realised what a bastard Tash Janssen really is.' Sam, who hadn't been to bed, abbreviated the facts. 'She's left him.'

'And she came here?'

'I brought her back here.'

Vivienne, bewildered, shook her head. 'You mean she phoned you up?'

'I thought you might have wanted a lift home,' said Sam evenly. 'So I drove out there when I'd finished at the club. But you weren't around, and Izzy was.'

At that moment her gaze travelled past him and

fixed upon the green-and-gold sequinned bodice draped damply over the back of a chair. It was recognizably the top Izzy had been wearing earlier.

Still confused, she frowned and said with a trace of suspicion, 'Are you and Izzy having an affair?'

'No.' Sam, looking not in the least put out by the suggestion, shook his head. 'We are not.'

'Hmm.' Overcome suddenly by fatigue, Vivienne turned and headed for the bedroom. 'So that makes none of us. No wonder we're all so bloody fed up.'

'How do I always manage to make such an incredible mess of everything?' said Izzy despairingly, over lunch at Langan's. It was three days since the party, two days since she'd moved back to Kingsley Grove, and the question had been preying on her mind ever since.

'I don't know.' Gina attempted a witticism. 'I suppose some people are just naturally untidy.'

'Ha, ha.' Izzy pulled a face. 'No, I'm being serious. Look what's happened to me over the past few months. A spectacularly failed love affair and an alienated daughter. OK, Kat speaks to me – but only just. We used to have such *fun* together . . .'

'A few months ago,' said Gina spearing a bite-sized piece of chicken breast in tarragon sauce, 'you'd never even seen the inside of a recording studio and you worked in a sleazy club for peanuts. Today you're buying me lunch, having driven me here in your very own Mercedes, and you have a single at Number Two in the charts. All you've ever wanted to be is a success and now you *are* one.'

'Ever heard of sleeping your way to the top?' Izzy retaliated, taking a slurp of wine. 'Everyone treats me as Tash Janssen's sidekick, that's all. Without him, I'd still be a nobody. And I'm hardly a successful mother, for heaven's sake.'

It was a tricky subject. Gina still froze every time Katerina's name was even mentioned. With a shrug, she glanced sideways at the diners at the next table and saw that they were still watching. It was heady stuff, being ogled by two such attractive men, even if most of the attention was going Izzy's way.

'Your daughter's choice of partners is hardly your fault,' she replied stiffly.

'But it's still my concern! Everything's been spoiled and I simply don't know where I've gone wrong. I've never been so miserable in my life. And you,' she continued in accusing tones, 'have never looked better. God knows, I'm glad you couldn't make it to that terrible party, but what's been *happening* with you? Is Ralph back on the scene . . . ?'

Indirectly, Gina supposed, Ralph had been responsible for her new-found sense of well-being. For some reason she had been unable to fathom, she simply had felt better since sending him away with a flea in his ear that stormy afternoon when he had erupted, brimming with self-confidence, into the office. In deflating his ego, she had boosted her own immeasurably, and the relationship between Doug and herself had subsequently improved in leaps and bounds. Almost overnight he had become less of an employer, more of a real friend . . .

For a moment she was almost tempted to tell Izzy that

Doug was taking her to the theatre this evening, but she held her tongue. Izzy would either leap to conclusions and imagine some grand romance or gaze at her with fascinated disbelief, which would spoil everything. It wasn't as if she was going out on some kind of date, after all. She simply enjoyed being with Doug and was able to relax in his undemanding company.

'Ralph is definitely not back on the scene,' she said briskly, finishing her lunch and feeling decidedly in control. 'Credit me with some sense, *please*.'

'I'm the one with no sense.' Izzy gazed gloomily at her own barely touched food. 'I'm an abysmal failure.'

'Excuse me.' The bolder of the two men at the table next to theirs leaned back in his chair and attracted her attention. 'Aren't you Izzy Van Asch?'

Being recognised wasn't turning out to be quite as much fun as she'd imagined, either. It always seemed to happen at the wrong moments. But she forced a gracious smile. 'Yes, I am.'

'We thought so.' He smirked at his friend, then said, 'What's it like then, screwing Tash Janssen?'

Gina cringed and held her breath, waiting to see what would happen next.

Finally, Izzy smiled.

'Terrible,' she replied sweetly. 'His willy's even smaller than yours.'

Disasters, as a rule, came in threes. As far as Doug was concerned, however, they were threatening to run into double figures. The harder he tried, the more things seemed to go wrong.

'I'm sorry,' he said again, pulling out his handkerchief in order to mop his forehead and managing to spill whisky down the front of his jacket as he did so. 'This is the worst play I've ever seen. You can't possibly want to go back inside. Shall we skip the second act and find somewhere to eat instead?'

If this had been a proper date, Gina might have been equally embarrassed by the almost farcical events of the evening. But since it wasn't, she couldn't understand why Doug should be so distraught. It was hardly his fault, after all, that his car should have broken down in Park Lane and needed pushing to the side of the road, just as it wasn't his fault that the new play he had brought her to see was one of the unfunniest comedies ever staged. Since it wasn't a real date it didn't even matter that she had ended up with rain-soaked hair, oil stains on her coat and two broken fingernails. All that mattered was that despite all these setbacks, she was still *enjoying* herself . . .

'We can't leave now!' She looked shocked. 'Mavis is expecting us to go backstage afterwards and congratulate her. The play may not be up to much, but she's acting her heart out on that stage and it's her first big break. The least we can do is tell her how great *she* is.'

Doug didn't understand how she could be so cheerful. Gazing down at his damp jacket, he was further mortified to realise that his new shirt, fresh out of its box, was displaying tell-tale box-shaped creases. He couldn't remember the last time he'd put so much effort into getting ready to go out. Now he was unhappily aware that he still possessed about as much sartorial elegance as a hippo in a mac.

Worse was to come. It seemed impossible to imagine that someone so uptight could fall asleep, but to his utter shame Doug found himself jerking awake halfway through the second act. The noise that had awoken him was his own snoring. Gina, beside him, was in fits of suppressed giggles.

'I'm a lost cause,' he said mournfully, when they had done their duty and visited a stiff-upper-lipped Mavis in her tiny dressing room. Leaving via the stage door, which led out into a narrow side-street, they found that the rain was bucketing down harder than ever, and there wasn't a cab in sight.

'Of course you aren't.' Gina squeezed his arm as they set off up the road. 'You gave the audience their best laugh of the evening for a start. And the really nice thing about awful plays is they do wonders for your appetite . . . look, why don't we try this little Italian place on the left, then we don't have to worry about finding a taxi.'

Doug winced as the slender-hipped waiter whisked past, missing him by millimetres as he disappeared into the kitchen. Moments later the swing doors burst open once more as another waiter shimmied past bearing plates of steaming pasta. Anthony Hopkins, he thought darkly – because someone had once said he looked a bit like him, and because that great actor had always secretly been his hero – would never be dumped at the worst table in the house.

Gina, apparently unperturbed, was engrossed in the menu. 'I'm going to have the *moules marinière*.'

'You'll get food poisoning.' He looked more lugubrious than ever. 'That should round off the evening nicely.'

The meal, in fact, was exquisite. By the time they had finished their strega coffees Doug found himself in imminent danger of actually cheering up, but fate hadn't finished with him yet.

The manager, with a discreet cough, appeared by their table. 'I'm sorry, sir,' he said, not sounding sorry at all, 'but have you some other means of payment? This credit card is out of date.'

'It really doesn't matter,' Gina insisted for the fourth time as they climbed into their taxi. 'You can pay me back tomorrow if it makes you happier, but there's no need to keep apologizing. It could have happened to anyone.'

It wouldn't have happened to Anthony Hopkins, thought Doug with silent despair. Bloody expiry dates, bloody sanctimonious restaurant managers, bloody broken-down cars, bloody, *bloody* rain . . .

Chapter 42

The weather continued to deteriorate. On the third Friday in October, London and the south-east of England cowered in the grip of one of the worst hurricanes of the decade. With Izzy away in Scotland pre-recording a television Hogmanay 'special' and her own television out of action as a result of the power lines going down, Gina decided the only sensible course of action was to have an early night. By the light of a flickering candle she made her way slowly up the stairs, prayed that the tiles wouldn't be ripped from the roof by the blistering storm, and wondered if she'd ever be able to get to sleep.

She was just dozing off an hour and a half later when the phone rang downstairs, jerking her back to wakefulness and instant apprehension. Whoever would be calling at twelve-thirty at night with anything but bad news?

The parquet floor was cold beneath her bare feet. Gina's heart was still hammering as she picked up the receiver. Guardedly, she said, 'Hallo.'

At first she couldn't make out who was on the other end. It was a terrible line, awash with crackles and electronic hisses. Eventually, straining to listen through them, she heard what sounded like uneven sobbing and gulps for breath. Not Izzy, surely not Izzy . . .

'Hallo, who is it?' she said, more loudly this time. The

all-enveloping darkness was eerie and the wind still howled outside.

'Mum,' came a small voice, amid more sobbing. 'Mum, is that you?'

Gina had neither seen nor spoken to Katerina since that nightmare day when she'd learned of her affair with Andrew. Now her grip tightened on the receiver and apprehension gave way to annoyance.

'Your mother isn't here,' she replied coldly. 'She's in Scotland.'

'Wh-what? Where?'

'Edinburgh. She's due back on Monday evening.'

A static-riddled silence ensued. Then, with almost animal anguish, Katerina wailed, 'But I want my mum!'

She sounded in a terrible state. Gina, whose initial instinct had been to slam down the phone, relented slightly and took a deep breath.

'Look, she's left me the number of the hotel, but there's a power cut here and it'll take me a while to find it. Why don't you phone directory enquiries and ask them; she's staying at the Swallow Royal in Edinburgh.'

'I want . . . my . . . mum,' repeated Katerina, her voice choking on the words. 'I . . . want . . .'

'What's the matter? Are you ill?'

'I want my mum.'

She sounded almost demented with grief. Feeling increasingly ill at ease, Gina said, 'Directory Enquiries. The Swallow Royal in Edinburgh. They'll be able to give you the number. But look, Katerina, if you're ill . . .'

The phone went dead. Katerina had hung up on her. With a sigh, Gina replaced the receiver and began to feel her way towards the staircase. Katerina's problems were no concern of hers.

But it was no good. After a second of deliberation she turned back, fumbling in the inky darkness for the notepad next to the phone, upon which Izzy had scrawled the hotel's number. By the time she managed to locate the matches and relight her candle she would be able to speak to Izzy herself, discover what was going on and put her own mind at rest. Then she'd be able to get back to sleep.

Forty minutes later, her teeth chattering with fear as much as cold, Gina edged the car out of the drive and set off up the road at a crawl, wincing as the storm buffeted the sides of the little Golf and sent twigs and leaves hurtling against the windscreen.

The telephone lines to Scotland were down. While she had been ringing Sam's flat and getting no reply, her own phone had gone dead. The hurricane was wreaking havoc everywhere. And although she had tried to tell herself that Katerina deserved everything she got, the sheer anguish in the girl's voice had shaken Gina to the core. Listening to her on the phone, she'd sounded more like seven years old than seventeen, and desperately in need of help. She was suffering, and alone. And Gina knew only too well how *that* felt. Driving across the storm-swept city, she wondered if she'd ever been more scared in her life. The streets were mercifully empty of pedestrians and cars, but the air was thick with swirling leaves and rubbish. When a triangular roadworks sign smashed into the passenger door Gina screamed aloud but kept going. She couldn't give up now. It couldn't be more than a mile to Katerina's bedsitter. Not more than another ten terrifying minutes . . .

She hammered on the front door for what seemed like an eternity, struggling to remain upright against the howling gale and make herself heard above it. Finally, just as she was about to give up, the door opened. Katerina's face, pinched and white, appeared in the narrow gap behind the security chain.

'Oh my God,' she wailed. 'What do *you* want?'

It wasn't quite the welcome Gina had been expecting. Hopelessly on edge after her nightmare journey, she snapped back, 'Charming. Are you going to let me in?'

Katerina's eyes filled with fresh tears. 'Why?'

'Because it's almost two o'clock in the morning and I've driven here to make sure you're all right.' Gina spoke through gritted teeth – so much for genuine concern. 'But if all you're going to be is fucking ungrateful, maybe I'd better just leave.'

Katerina wiped her wet cheeks with the back of her hand and digested these words in silence. She'd never heard Gina swear before.

'OK,' she muttered, because it didn't really matter any more; she no longer cared what happened to her. 'Come in.'

The electricity supply had by this time been restored although Gina almost wished it hadn't. The grim little bedsitting room was an absolute tip and Katerina – normally so fastidious – looked dreadful. Now, gazing defensively around at the mess and twisting her fingers, she said, 'Oh, I'm sorry, isn't this good enough for you? If you'd only let me know you were coming I'd have polished the silver and put on a party frock.'

She looked as if she'd been crying non-stop for a week. Her long hair, normally as clean and shiny as a conker, hung in rats' tails and the dark blue sweater and jeans she wore seemed three sizes too big. The unmade bed in the corner of the room was littered with dozens of sheets of foolscap paper.

'Go on,' taunted Katerina, observing the look of distaste on Gina's face. 'Tell me I've let myself go and it's no more than I deserve.'

There was no heating in the room. With a shiver, Gina replied evenly, 'Well, you've certainly let yourself go.'

'Oh, get *out* of here!' With a howl of grief, Katerina's face crumpled and she turned away. This was too much to bear. 'Just leave me alone . . . I didn't ask you to come here . . . I want my mum . . .'

That final heartfelt cry was too much for Gina to bear. It was what had brought her here in the first place, a poignant echo of the grief she had felt when her own mother had died so many years ago. Without even thinking, she crossed the room and took Katerina's thin, shaking body in her arms.

'Kat, stop it. You can't carry on like this. I'm here because I'm worried about you . . . we care about you . . . and you're going to make yourself ill if you don't let us help.'

Katerina went rigid. For a fraction of a second Gina thought she was going to hit her. Then, falteringly, and with tears still streaming down her face and neck, she turned and clung to her, burying her head against Gina's shoulder.

'I'm sorry, I'm so sorry, I don't know what's the matter with me,' she sobbed hopelessly. 'I thought I was having a nervous breakdown, but people aren't supposed to know when it's happening to them. I've felt horrible for weeks but the last few days have been like a nightmare . . . everything's got worse and worse and I can't do anything any more except cry . . .'

'Sshh,' murmured Gina in soothing tones. Despite her lack of experience with young children, she was finding it easy to treat Katerina as a distraught seven year old. 'Come on, sit down and tell me all about it. Tell me everything, then we can sort it out.'

Katerina, sniffing, still clung to her. 'Do you really not hate me?'

'I'm here, aren't I? Of course I don't.'

'But I've been such a bitch. *I* hate me.'

Gina, tempted to suggest that a bath might improve matters, gave her a hug instead. 'And now you're punishing yourself. Hasn't it even occurred to you that it was just as much Andrew's fault as yours? More even. He was the one who should have known better, after all.'

Something had evidently gone wrong between them. Surprising herself, Gina experienced relief on Katerina's behalf rather than her own. Andrew was weak, whereas Kat had simply been gullible, and she deserved better.

'I hate him,' said Katerina bleakly. 'And now I'm going to tell you something that really *will* make you hate me.'

'What?'

'I think I'm pregnant.'

The seven year old in her arms had vanished. Izzy's daughter was, after all, a near-adult with adult problems.

Gina, her heart sinking, said, 'Have you told him?'

Katerina nodded.

'And?'

'He said, "Oh fucking hell, not again." '

The hurricane had blown itself out by early morning. With the boot of the Golf loaded up with carrier bags of Katerina's belongings, Gina drove her back through the debris-strewn streets to Kingsley Grove, then ran her a very hot bath, threw the dark blue sweater and disreputable jeans straight into the washing-machine and started cooking breakfast.

'I can't believe I'm here.' Katerina, reappearing downstairs forty minutes later in one of Izzy's dazzling silk dressing gowns, gulped down a cup of strong coffee and attacked her bacon and eggs with enthusiasm. 'I can't believe I'm actually enjoying this food . . .'

She may have been lacking personal experience in such matters, but Gina had heard enough tales of woe from pregnant friends in her time to seriously doubt whether Katerina could be similarly afflicted. Coffee and fried food at eight o'clock in the morning was an absolute no-no under such circumstances.

'The phone lines are back in action,' she said, inwardly wincing as Katerina smothered her eggs in tomato ketchup and black pepper. 'I've just checked with the operator. You can phone Izzy as soon as you've finished eating.'

Katerina hesitated, then gave her a tentative smile. 'Mum's busy. I don't want to send her into a panic. Besides, I'm feeling better now.'

'Good.'

'You really think I'm not pregnant?'

Katerina had wound herself up into such a state over the past few weeks that Gina thought it hardly surprising her period hadn't arrived. Having initially said this in order to calm her down, however, she now erred on the side of caution.

'As soon as the chemist opens, I'll go down and pick up one of those tester packs, then we'll know for sure,' she said carefully. It was strange, but nice, to be discussing such a personal matter with Katerina. 'Although you did say you'd taken precautions.'

'Oh yes.' For the first time, and because it was such a relief to have finally confided in someone, Katerina nodded and broke into a grin. 'And it's a known fact,' she added, crossing her fingers and praying that Gina was right, 'that good Mates don't let you down . . .'

Chapter 43

When Izzy arrived back at Kingsley Grove three days later she thought at first she must be hallucinating. As astonishment gave way to delight, however, she carefully didn't ask too many questions and accepted her daughter's return as a much-longed-for miracle.

To her great joy as well, it was as if the past traumatic months hadn't existed. Katerina, bright-eyed and good-tempered, was her old cheerful self. She had also retained her old forthright way with words.

'Who did that to your hair?' she asked in reproving tones and Izzy – who had been marched along to a Mayfair salon by one of MBT's chief stylists – hung her magenta head in shame.

'I know, they said it had to be this colour to show up under the TV lights.'

Katerina was in the process of making a cheese soufflé. Having finished whisking the egg whites, she paused and wiped her hands on a damp cloth. 'The colour's fine. I like beetroot. I meant you let them cut it.'

'It's not cut,' said Izzy defensively, 'it's layered.'

But Katerina was eyeing the end result with disapproval. Izzy and her wild mass of ringlets were part of each other while MBT, it seemed, was attempting to transform her into something altogether more sophisticated. 'I've always cut your hair,' she said. 'I know it better than anyone else. Tell your trendy record company that in future we'll be taking care of that side of things. I'll cut and you dye, just like we've always done before.'

Best of all, though, was discovering that Katerina had made the decision to retake her A levels. When she wasn't cooking – as if that in some way made amends for her past misbehaviour – she spent hours poring over her text books and painstakingly rewriting the notes which Gina had destroyed.

'I still don't know how you did it,' said Izzy gratefully, when she and Gina were alone the following evening. 'I'm almost afraid to ask.'

Jericho, almost certain that Izzy had dropped a Smartie down the back of the sofa, was burrowing frantically among the cushions. Gina hauled him off. 'She just came to her senses in her own time,' she replied, her voice calm. Since there was no sense in rocking the boat she had felt it unnecessary to even mention Katerina's false alarm. Two pregnancy tests had been negative, which was all that mattered, and a trip to her doctor had assured them that as soon as she relaxed and started eating properly once more, her periods would return.

Izzy regarded her with the merest trace of suspicion. 'There must have been more to it than that,' she persisted, but Gina simply shrugged and fondled Jericho's ears.

'We had a man in common. A stupid, weak man, maybe . . . but at least we both knew what the other had been going through. Once she realised that, the rest was easy.'

'Well, hooray for stupid men,' said Izzy, emptying the last of the Smarties into her hand and pretending to ignore the piteous expression in Jericho's eyes. 'But I still don't think you've told me everything.'

Gina grinned. 'Kat and I are members of an exclusive club. Now maybe if *you* were to have an affair with Andrew . . .'

With a yelp of gratitude, Jericho wolfed down an orange Smartie, his favourite colour. Izzy pulled a face. 'Pass.'

'. . . and just so long as you wouldn't be expectin' me to treat you like some great la-di-da duchess, waitin' on you hand and foot and finger at all hours of the day and night . . . I mean, you seem like a nice enough young thing at this moment in time, but let me tell you, some people have a funny old side to their characters when it comes down to it and I wouldn't be puttin' up with any of that kind of nonsense for even so much as one minute . . .'

Izzy, absolutely fascinated, held her breath and said nothing for fear of breaking the spell. Lucille Devlin from Dublin was quite simply the most amazing woman she'd ever met in her life. And she spoke in the longest sentences.

'. . . but if you're agreeable to my terms and you think we might suit each other,' continued Lucille, who didn't appear to need to draw any breath of her own, 'then I'd be happy to keep your house up together for you, seein' as it would give me a break from that no-good miserable old pig of a husband of mine . . . I sing a bit myself, you know, they used to say I had the finest voice in all Ireland, but of course it turned out to be a curse as much as a blessin', for wasn't it how I went and met the old bugger in the first place, me at nineteen years of age singin' in Daley's bar and him proppin' the bloody thing up . . .'

* * *

Izzy, lying in the bath, couldn't understand why she wasn't the happiest woman in the world.

She had Katerina back, as good as new and working like a Trojan to ensure that this time her A level results would be dazzling.

She had the house of her dreams, a splendid four-storey Georgian property in Bloomsbury which she had rented from one of the MBT executives while he and his family spent a year in Los Angeles.

She had her debut solo album in mid-production with the first track from it, entitled 'Kiss', coming out as a single next week.

She had public appearances lined up beyond Christmas, a carrier bag overflowing with fan mail in the corner of her bedroom, the offer of a European tour sponsored by a soft drinks manufacturer . . .

And she had buxom Lucille Devlin, with her tomato-soup-coloured hair, Technicolour clothes and endless capacity for conversation, who was a full-scale entertainment in herself. How could anyone in the company of Lucille possibly fail to be amused? wondered Izzy, drumming her toes moodily against the tap end of the bath. Lucille could cheer up Russia.

But for some reason it wasn't working for *her*. The success she had craved for so long, and which should have been making her so happy, wasn't doing the trick. Public recognition – even in the form of Lucille hoovering like a maniac and singing, '*I want you to kiss me, To know that you've missed me*,' over and over again in her rich Irish contralto – simply wasn't enough to eradicate the leaden sensation in her stomach and the feeling that somehow there should be *more.*

Three hours later, too restless to stay at home and vaguely searching for that elusive 'more', Izzy entered the comforting familiarity of The Chelsea Steps. She was almost certain that Sam, who had recently been over in the States again, was now back. It was silly, she knew, but the longing to see him again had been almost overwhelming. And now that she was here, even her heart was beating a little faster in anticipation . . .

Sam, however, noticed the commotion before realizing that Izzy was the cause of it. Cursing beneath his breath and moving swiftly across the packed dance floor to the smaller bar at the far side of the club, he knew instinctively that the problem involved the two arrogant and mega-rich Argentinians whom he'd had his doubts about from the moment they'd arrived. The Chelsea Steps, famous above all else for the fact that there was never any trouble within its doors, needed this kind of guests like a hole in the head. Sam's blood ran cold as another yell of male outrage reached his ears and he imagined what a hole in a mega-rich Argentinian's head would do for business. All he could do was pray that neither of them was carrying a gun.

When he reached the source of the trouble, arriving just in time to see Izzy land a stinging slap on the younger Argentinian's tanned cheek and deliver a torrent of abuse to the pair of them, Sam cheerfully could have killed her himself. Cutting through the crowd which had gathered around to watch Izzy in action, he grabbed her by the arm and hauled her unceremoniously to one side.

'Calm down,' he said sharply, because Izzy forever seemed to be getting herself embroiled in some fracas or other and it couldn't always be the other person's fault.

'That oily bastard!' Izzy had no intention of calming down. Her dark eyes flashed as she glared at the thin, equally furious Argentinian, now gabbling frantically in his own language. 'He shoved his revolting hand down the front of my dress.'

'What dress?' countered Sam, glancing down at the skimpy apricot-pink creation which clung to every curve and ended at mid-thigh. It seemed to him that the more money Izzy spent on clothes, the less of them there became.

'Oh, so that gives him the right to *grope* me?' she demanded furiously, colour mounting in her cheeks as she realised that he was landing the blame on her. 'Come *on*, Sam! Whose side are you on?'

Sam was so tired he could hardly think straight. The reason he'd had to fly over to New York was because his supposedly dependable manager there had been busted for possession of cocaine. Now, back in London and suffering more badly than usual from jet lag, he had this to contend with. Izzy might not realise it at the moment but she was in danger of jeopardizing the good reputation of The Chelsea Steps.

'I'm on the side of keeping your voice down and letting the other guests enjoy their evening,' he replied evenly, steering her towards a small table and pressing her rigid body into one of the chairs.

'But he *assaulted* me . . .'

'And you are in my club, not a wrestling arena. For heaven's sake, Izzy, if you wanted to make a complaint all you had to do was come and tell me about it, then I could have dealt with the matter quietly.'

Sam could be such a disappointment sometimes. Izzy, who had been so looking forward to seeing him, felt her eyes fill with angry tears. 'You mean I should have *quietly* let them gang rape me—'

'Don't be ridiculous,' he snapped back. 'I'm just saying that it always seems to happen to you, doesn't it? And what do you honestly expect, coming out on your own dressed like some kind of high-class hooker? Anyone's going to think you're looking for attention . . . God knows, all you've ever *wanted* is attention . . . and now that you're becoming well known you're going to have to learn to handle it in the proper manner.'

'Stop it!' shrieked Izzy, unable to bear the unfairness of it all a moment longer. Now, her heart really racing, she wrenched her hand from Sam's patronizing grasp and rose jerkily to her feet. 'I'd rather be groped by greasy perverts than lectured to by a bastard who cares more about his precious club than his friends. And some friend *you* turned out to be,' she added through gritted teeth. 'When I think of all the nice things I told Vivienne about you . . .'

Vivienne. Another problem Sam didn't need right now. Vivienne had been behaving decidedly oddly during the past few weeks. 'You shouldn't have bothered,' he said in abrupt tones as Izzy turned to leave.

'You're telling me,' she hissed with as much sarcasm as

she could muster. 'But don't worry, it was all lies. And she didn't believe me anyway.'

Chapter 44

'I'm miserable,' announced Vivienne when Izzy answered the phone the following morning. 'Come shopping with me.'

'What's Sam been telling you?' Izzy demanded suspiciously, and a noise like a snort greeted her ears.

'Sam who?'

They set out to do some serious damage in and around Bond Street, Vivienne the acknowledged expert and Izzy an enthusiastic newcomer to the art of real spending. South Molton Street was a particularly good starting-point; after twenty minutes in Browns, Izzy realised that she had blown more money on a pink suede skirt and a white cashmere sweater than she used to earn in an entire month. Vivienne, who had been weaned on designer labels and who never wasted any time glancing at price tags, kissed her gold card and became the proud new owner of a coffee-coloured silk dress and matching jacket, three pairs of trousers and a spectacular black-and-bronze sequinned top by a young Japanese designer with an awful lot of 'Ys' in his name.

'Better?' said Izzy two hours later when they stopped at a crowded bistro for a cappuccino and several slices of Amaretto-soaked chocolate-fudge cake. Glancing down at the slippery pile of carrier bags propped against the table legs, she estimated that they must have spent enough money to cover the cost of a holiday in Barbados.

Vivienne lit a cigarette. 'It helps, I suppose. It always helps.' Then she leaned closer. 'But I still haven't told you yet why I was miserable in the first place.'

'That's easy.' Izzy pulled a fearsome face, startling several nearby customers. 'You live with an unspeakable bastard. It'd be enough to make anyone miserable.'

'I love him so much.'

'Oh, Vee.' Izzy's expression softened. 'Do you still? I really thought you were getting over him.'

Vivienne, who had been idly scooping the froth off her cappuccino with a teaspoon, frowned. 'Not Sam, dumbo. I'm talking about Terry.'

'What!' Izzy, jack-knifing forwards, didn't even notice that she'd landed her left breast in the chocolate-fudge cake. 'Who? You haven't told me anything about this!'

Vivienne hadn't told anyone, so afraid had she been of breaking the spell. But now she simply couldn't help it.

'The man I met at Tash's party,' she explained, stubbing out her cigarette and immediately lighting another, even though Terry passionately disapproved of smoking. 'Oh Izzy, he's wonderful. I love him to pieces . . . he's everything I've ever wanted in a man.'

Reluctant though she was to spoil the fairy-tale, Izzy said cautiously, 'You said that about Sam.'

'Yes, but Sam's never loved me back.' Vivienne shook her head, then half-smiled. 'And Terry does.'

'In that case, I don't understand why you aren't deliriously happy. You love this guy, he loves you . . . so the two of you are crazy about each other . . . and you're miserable!' Izzy was seriously confused. Then she said, 'Uh oh, don't tell me – the dreaded M-word.'

'No, he's not married. He's a widower, with two grown-up children. I've met them, I get on well with them, they like me. Hell, even his bloody cat likes me . . .'

By this time almost bursting with frustration, Izzy screeched, 'Then *what*?'

'He won't take me seriously.' For a moment Vivienne looked as if she was about to burst into tears. 'Oh Izzy, it's ridiculous. He says I'm too young, too beautiful and far, far too rich to be interested in someone like him. I've tried telling him until I'm blue in the face that none of those things matter, but he simply refuses to believe me. And what can I do?' She spread her hands in despair, her cigarette almost setting fire to the trousers of a passing waiter. 'I can't make myself *older*.'

Despite Vivienne's tragic expression, Izzy had to smile. She was envisaging the world's first face-lift-in-reverse.

'Maybe if you stopped wearing make-up?' she suggested hopefully.

'I tried that last week. All I did was look ill.'

'And what did he do?'

'Took my blood pressure.'

'My God! Is he a pervert?'

This time, even Vivienne laughed. 'No, a doctor.'

Izzy, relieved to see that she was at last beginning to cheer up, was absolutely fascinated. 'So, what's he like to sleep with?' she said avidly. 'I've always thought the medical profession must be spectacular in bed because they know exactly where everything is . . .'

To her amazement, Vivienne actually blushed. 'He is

spectacular,' she admitted, lowering her voice in order to frustrate the middle-aged couple at the next table who had been frantically eavesdropping for the last ten minutes. 'Although we've only done it twice, so far. He wouldn't for ages, because he said he was afraid of getting too deeply involved, so in the end I had to seduce him.'

This was all too romantic for words. Izzy, breathless with anticipation, said, 'And?'

Vivienne's green eyes sparkled. The blush and the Texan drawl both deepened. 'OK, you guessed right. He knows *exactly* where everything is.'

They were interrupted several minutes later by the arrival of a waiter bearing a bottle of rather good Beaujolais.

'With the compliments of the couple at the next table,' he murmured with a discreet nod in the direction of their neighbours.

'Good heavens.' Izzy swivelled in her chair to take a proper look, and saw that they were about to leave. 'How very kind, but I don't know what we've done to deserve it.'

'You're Izzy Van Asch,' said the woman shyly. 'Our son Giles is absolutely crazy about you. All he ever does is sing "Never, Never", and fill his scrapbook with photos of you from the papers.'

'Gosh.' Absurdly flattered by the compliment and not yet accustomed to the attentions of total strangers, Izzy went even pinker than Vivienne had done earlier. 'I'm so pleased he likes me. How old is your son?'

'Seven.'

When she had scribbled a greeting and a rather ornate

autograph on the back of the menu, the middle-aged man took it, hesitated for a second, then slid a business card on to the table next to the wine. 'Actually,' he said with a diffident smile, 'I hope you won't think us impertinent, but the wine is for your friend as much as you. We'd so much like to know whether everything turns out all right,' he explained, meeting Vivienne's astonished gaze, 'between you and this nice doctor of yours.'

Izzy thought it all terribly funny. 'I know,' she said with a mischievous grin. 'Wouldn't we all!'

'Well, you can't disappoint that nice couple,' she admonished when they were alone once more. Pouring the wine, she added, 'And it isn't really that surprising, the good doctor's reluctance to take you seriously. You are still living with another man, after all.'

'Sam isn't a man, he's a machine.' Vivienne flicked back her blonde hair with new determination. 'And you're right, of course. The time has come to act. I tried my best, but I guess I simply wasn't his kind of woman. He always complained that my only hobby was shopping; I think he needs someone with interests of her own, either a brilliant career or an obsession with mountaineering . . .' She paused, took a sip of Beaujolais, then said a trifle shamefacedly, '. . . something that keeps her too busy to chase after him like a lost puppy. All I ever did was chase Sam, but what he really needs is an independent woman. Somebody he admires enough to chase for himself.'

Chapter 45

After the merry-go-round comings and goings of the past few weeks, Gina found it almost a relief to have the house to herself once more. Arriving home from work to peace and quiet – apart from Jericho's initial volley of welcoming barks – definitely had its advantages.

An even greater luxury was the fact that the bathroom was always empty and the water hot. This evening, having invited Doug round for supper at eight-thirty, she decided to shower first and cook later; that way she wouldn't miss the first showing of Izzy's new video, 'Kiss', on *Top of the Pops* at seven-thirty.

Gina had a terrible singing voice, but since she was alone in the house it didn't matter. '*I want you to kiss me, To know that you've missed me, Like I've missed you and your smile . . .*' she warbled tunelessly, closing her eyes and letting the needles of blissfully hot water bombard her face. Shampoo, cascading down her body, had completely blocked her ears which improved the sound of her singing no end.

It was minutes later before she realised that downstairs the doorbell was ringing and Jericho was going absolutely frantic in his attempt to answer it and discover who was there.

Definitely not Doug, thought Gina, leaping out of the shower and hurriedly half-drying herself before tying her old towelling dressing-gown securely around her waist and running downstairs.

'Who is it?' She had to raise her voice to make herself heard above the noise of Jericho's barking.

'Me.'

Gina froze. For several seconds she was unable to move. Finally, reaching down and grabbing Jericho's collar, she dragged him – whining in outraged protest – into the sitting room and locked him inside.

Returning, opening the front door, she gazed expressionlessly at her visitor. 'What do you want?'

'To see you.' Andrew glanced uneasily over her shoulder, in the direction of the sitting room. 'What on earth was that? Sounds like a pack of werewolves.'

'He'll calm down in a minute. Why do you want to see me?'

Clearly unnerved by his close encounter with Jericho, and shivering as a blast of icy November wind ricocheted around the stone porch, he said, 'Gina, can I come in?'

She led the way into the kitchen, wondering why on earth he had really come here and at the same time marvelling at her own self-control. This was her ex-husband – no, he was still her husband, the divorce hadn't been finalised yet – and she had loved him for over fifteen years. Now, however, it was like coming face to face with a virtual stranger about whom she had heard unpleasant things, and the very idea that they had once been man and wife seemed almost ludicrous.

She guessed that he had come straight from the office; his grey suit was crumpled, his light brown hair uncombed. Realizing that her own hair was still tangled and wet from the shower, Gina marvelled at the fact that her hands remained comfortably in her dressing-gown pockets, and that she felt not the slightest urge to even attempt to make herself look more presentable. If Andrew had been the milkman she would have done so, but he wasn't. He was only her husband . . .

'Well?' she said evenly, sitting down on one of the kitchen chairs.

Andrew took a deep, steadying breath. It wasn't the most promising of welcomes, but he was here now, and he had been rehearsing for this moment all week. He was aware of the fact that he'd behaved badly, but that had all been part of some mystical mid-life crisis, something a lot of men went through, and like all crises it had passed. He now knew that this was where he belonged. And Gina was his wife; she would forgive him . . .

'Darling, I realise how much I must have hurt you. I've behaved like a fool, but it's all behind me now. It's you I love, only you I've ever really loved.' Damn, he hadn't meant it to come out sounding like something from a Noël Coward play. The words, so carefully planned, seemed ridiculous now even to his own ears. Panicking slightly, Andrew took a step towards her. 'No, don't say anything. I'm trying to tell you that all I did was make a terrible mistake and I'm sorry. I don't understand it myself. Marcy and Katerina didn't mean anything to me, not like you! Oh darling, I want us to forget the past year. I want to love you and make you happy again, as happy as you were before . . .'

Gina gazed up at him, dumbfounded. The next moment before she had a chance to realise what was happening,

Andrew had dropped to his knees beside her chair and pulled her into his arms, enveloping her in an embrace so ferocious she could scarcely breathe.

It would have been laughable if she hadn't been too stunned – or too winded – to laugh. Having done his best to destroy not only her own happiness but that of Kat and Marcy as well – and those were only the ones she *knew* about – Andrew seriously seemed to think she still loved him enough to forgive and forget, and welcome him back to married life as if nothing had ever happened.

Meanwhile, he was still here, wrapping himself around her like Sellotape and frantically kissing her exposed shoulder.

Still inwardly marvelling at her ability to remain calm, Gina stole a quick glance at her watch – it was now twenty-five past seven – and murmured, 'You don't know how many times I dreamed of this moment. I prayed so hard that one day you'd come back to me . . . and now at last it's happened. I can hardly believe it.'

'Oh darling.' Andrew, hugging her tighter still, covered her face with triumphant kisses. 'I knew you'd understand. I love you so much.'

Drawing slowly, reluctantly away, trailing her slender fingers down his forearms and giving his hands a gentle squeeze, Gina whispered, 'Do you want to make love to me? Now?'

Andrew quivered with lust. He hadn't had sex for weeks. Wrenching off his tie and scattering shirt buttons across the kitchen floor, he gasped aloud as Gina's fingers moved to his belt buckle and began to unfasten it.

'Oh my God . . . yes, yes . . .'

She had him just where she wanted him. Gina had never felt more powerful in her life. Tilting her head in order to hide her smile, she reached behind her with her free hand and found the short, sharp, serrated knife with which she had planned to slice the tomatoes for the lasagne.

Andrew, opening his eyes with a start as cold metal made unexpected contact with warm flesh, gasped again. When he saw what Gina was holding he moaned aloud in horror.

'That's interesting,' she said in almost conversational tones. 'Your whole body's gone rigid with fear. Well, *nearly* your whole body.' Her smile broadened. 'Of course a certain small part of it remains as disappointing as it ever was. Some things don't change.'

'G-Gina. For G-God's sake . . .'

She could hear his teeth chattering. Idly turning the knife this way and that so that the blade glittered in the light, she glanced at her watch once more. Very nearly seven-thirty.

'It's a good job I'm not a raving lunatic, Andrew,' she told him pleasantly. 'Because a raving lunatic abandoned wife wouldn't hesitate for a second. She'd cut off this troublesome little appendage quicker than you could say . . . well, knife. And many people might applaud her for doing so.' She paused, then shook her head and tossed the knife into the sink out of harm's way. Leaning back in her chair, she said in cheerful tones, 'Luckily for you, I'm not a lunatic. And I wouldn't want to go to prison . . . just imagine the field-day my respectable neighbours would have when they read about it in the papers. So you can put it away now' – with a brief nod in the direction of the petrified acorn, she drew her dressing gown more securely around her and pulled the belt tight – 'and leave. I'm sure you can find your own way out.'

When he had gone, Gina poured herself a large gin and tonic and made her way through to the sitting room to be sullenly greeted by Jericho, who was very put out at having been excluded from all the fun.

'Cheer up, sweetheart,' she consoled him, rubbing his ears and for once allowing him up on to the sofa beside her. 'It was a pretty delicate situation, after all. And you might not have exercised as much self-control as I did.'

With a noisy woof of forgiveness, Jericho attempted to climb on to her lap. Gina waved the remote control at the television in the corner. 'Now shut up and pay attention, Jericho. *Top of the Pops* is about to start, and your favourite singer's on tonight. No, *not* Cilla Black . . .'

Unable to face slicing up those dear little cherry tomatoes, she had abandoned the idea of home-made lasagne and sent Doug out instead to pick up a takeaway from the new Mexican restaurant in Kensington High Street. Not until they had finished eating did she relate what had happened earlier.

'Well, I think it's marvellous,' declared Doug, when she had told him everything. As his face creased into a smile of genuine admiration he wondered how he could ever have thought of her as 'that skinny, nervy, *bossy* broad'. Over the months, Gina had metamorphosed into a calm, elegant woman who knew her own mind and no longer needed to live her life through the kind of men who treated her like dirt and didn't even deserve her. Doug had never been married; he had never even been in love, but he was aware now of skating perilously close to the edge. He knew, too, that he would never treat Gina like dirt.

The chief fly in the ointment, of course, was the fact that he seemed unlikely to ever get the chance to treat her badly or otherwise, since she had shown no signs at all of even recognizing that he *was* a man, in that particular sense of the word.

'I definitely scared him,' she agreed now, with some satisfaction. 'Oh Doug, you should have seen the expression on his face . . . I wish Kat and Izzy could have seen that expression . . . I still can't believe I really did it!'

'You can do anything you want to do.' He was so proud of her. First Ralph, now Andrew. And her elation was contagious; raising his glass of Mexican beer he saluted her, wondering if he dared pluck up the courage to give her a brief, congratulatory kiss. It was what *he* wanted to do more than anything else in the world.

Gina nodded, still smiling to herself. 'You're right. Know what you want and just go for it. That's Izzy's motto and it's worked wonders for her. From now on, I'm going to make sure it works for me.'

It was more than good advice, he thought as she lifted her own glass and clinked it rakishly against his. It was fate. He was here and Andrew wasn't. They were friends, celebrating together, and Gina – in a crimson cashmere sweater and cream linen trousers – had never looked more desirable. He'd even, thankfully, decided against wearing the new burnt-orange shirt which would have clashed so horribly with her red top. It was fate, it *had* to be.

Quickly, seizing the fateful moment and deliberately not giving himself time to back down, he leaned across and aimed for her cheek. Miscalculating slightly, his mouth landed on her chin, just down and to the left of her lower lip. That wasn't right; that was plain silly. Still clutching his beer he shifted position and felt his arm accidentally brush against the cashmere swell of her breast . . . oh God, her actual breast . . . before managing more by luck than judgement to locate her mouth . . .

Gina, astonished for the second time that evening and breathing in the somewhat overpowering scent of the aftershave she had given her boss for his birthday, tried hard not to flinch. Doug was simply pleased for her and proud of the way in which she had dealt with Andrew, she told herself, quelling the urge to dodge out of the way. Besides, it didn't do to flinch at a kiss from a friend, no matter how clumsy and damp it might be.

Having patiently waited for it to end, however, and finding herself still waiting several seconds later, she placed a firm but gentle restraining hand against his shoulder and disentangled herself from his grasp. It was impossible to be annoyed with Doug; he was too inoffensive . . . too *kind* . . . but enough was enough.

'Your drink,' she said kindly, as yet more dampness – icy dampness, this time – invaded her lap. 'Doug, I think you're spilling it.'

So much for fate, thought Doug, passion deflating as he saw how unmoved she was. Was it ever even *remotely* like this for Anthony Hopkins?

'I'm sorry,' he mumbled, his face burning with shame.

The moment of madness had passed; he supposed he should be grateful that at least he had escaped with his private parts intact. 'I'm sorry, it was just—'

'It's nothing at all,' Gina intercepted briskly, realizing that he was about to start apologizing all over again. With a bright smile, she jumped to her feet. 'Really. These trousers are brilliant. Just chuck them in the washing-machine and they come out as good as new, every time.'

Chapter 46

Izzy, practically dead on her feet following eleven gruelling hours in a south London recording studio, took a while to get the gist of what her housekeeper was actually telling her when she returned home at seven in the evening. Lucille, sensing her confusion, poured her an enormous gin and tonic and splashed a couple of inches of Bushmills into a glass in order to keep Izzy company while she drank it.

'He telephoned an hour ago,' she repeated patiently, 'and I told him you were out, but that you'd be back for sure by eight. Well y'see, he sounded such a charming gentleman and I could tell he was disappointed not to be speakin' to you so I happened to mention that you hadn't any plans for the rest of the evening, what with havin' to catch that early flight of yours to Rome tomorrow mornin', and then it occurred to me that maybe the good fellow might want to pop round and see you before you leave.' Pausing momentarily for breath and an invigorating gulp of the Irish whiskey to which only a heathen would add ice, Lucille licked her lips in appreciation. 'Well, he said that would suit him just fine so I told him to turn up at any time after eight-thirty so as to give you a little while to get yourself ready beforehand. Izzy, I'm tellin' you, that man has a beautiful smilin' voice . . . he all but broke my heart, just talkin' to him . . . oh, and I told him not to eat first because he might as well share something here with you.'

The last of the Bushmills disappeared down her throat with a flourish. Izzy watched it go. Then she watched, helplessly, as Lucille rose to her feet and shrugged herself into a vast, banana-yellow cardigan which reached past her knees.

'This charming gentleman,' Izzy ventured weakly, because it seemed that here at last was her chance to speak. 'Er . . . who is he?'

The weather had turned colder. Lucille, pausing in the act of winding a turquoise-and-yellow striped scarf several times around her plump neck, looked surprised. 'To be sure, the fellow didn't give me his name but he said he was a friend of yours so I thought it best to tell him to come on round here anyway. I knew you wouldn't mind, and he did sound awful *nice*.'

It was hard, trying to imagine what kind of male voice would most appeal to Lucille. Izzy didn't know Terry Wogan, so it couldn't be him. But on the other hand there was always Doug . . .

'So, he's coming round for dinner,' she said, realizing that she was hungry. 'OK, fair enough. What are we having to eat?'

'And who exactly is it that you think I am?' This time Lucille's orange eyebrows arched in astonishment. 'Superwoman, maybe? Haven't I spent the entire afternoon workin' me poor fingers to the bone, cleanin' every window in the house and ploughin' me way through that damn great heap of ironing you wanted done so that you could look halfway decent in Rome . . . ?'

Izzy forestalled her. 'There's nothing to eat, then.'

'Sure an' there's plenty to eat,' scolded Lucille, already halfway through the door. 'There's food in the freezer. All it needs is a bit of attention, you lazy article. Heavens above, anyone'd think you didn't know how to cook a simple meal without makin' a pig's ear of the event! What are you, Izzy Van Asch? Completely helpless?'

'You've made a conquest,' said Izzy, rubbing her wet hair with a towel as she led the way into the sitting room. 'My housekeeper is besotted with your voice. Even more strangely, she's under the impression that you're a gentleman.'

Sam, who had been both startled and amused by the impromptu invitation issued to him over the phone by an unknown Irish woman, replied equably, 'It's not that strange. Some people really quite like me.'

'Hmm.' Izzy, who still hadn't properly forgiven him for bawling her out at The Chelsea Steps the other week, cast him a doubtful look. Stung by Lucille's scathing remarks earlier, she had wrestled irritably with a packet of chicken breasts and concocted a casserole of sorts which Doug would have enjoyed. She had a feeling, however, that Sam might laugh at it.

But Sam, who was in a good mood, made himself comfortable on Izzy's new, dark green velvet sofa and grinned up at her.

'OK, misery. Maybe I was too tough on you, so if I really have to apologise, I will. But only if you promise to cheer up.'

'You *were* tough,' Izzy reminded him, assuming an

injured expression, but at the same time inwardly encouraged by such an admission. As far as she could remember, Sam was never in the wrong. She hadn't known he was capable of even pronouncing the word 'apology'.

He shrugged. 'In that case, I'm sorry.'

'Good.'

'So, are we friends again?'

'Could be,' conceded Izzy, beginning to relent.

'In that case, can I ask a personal question?'

Damn. He was going to make fun of her hair, she just knew it. Slowly, she said, 'Mmm?'

'That smell!' exclaimed Sam, gesturing towards the kitchen. 'That *terrible* smell! What on earth is it?'

This time there was no question about it; Sam was right. The indescribably awful casserole tasted every bit as bad as it had smelled. Izzy simply couldn't imagine how some ingredients could be so burnt, while at the same time the vegetables had managed to stay rock-solid raw. Worst of all, having out of sheer desperation blamed the absent Lucille for the disaster, she realised that Sam hadn't been fooled for a moment.

'No, this is one of yours,' he admonished her. As if to prove it, the piece of carrot he'd been attempting to spear ricocheted off his plate and landed in Izzy's lap.

'Definitely one of yours.'

'I have other talents,' she replied crossly, frustrated by such dismal failure. 'Oh, stop trying to *eat* it, Sam, for God's sake. Why don't we just stick to what we know and send out for a pizza?'

He smiled. 'Why don't we open another bottle of wine

instead? I'm supposed to be drowning my sorrows, after all.'

'What sorrows?' demanded Izzy, when they had by mutual consent abandoned the dreadful meal and settled down in front of the fire in the sitting room. Sam was hardly looking distraught; in fact it was ages since she'd seen him in such good spirits.

He threw her a swift sideways glance. 'The Argentinians you assaulted. They're suing the club.'

'*What*?'

Sam burst out laughing. Izzy, realizing that she'd been had, cursed her own gullibility.

'Not fair,' she grumbled. 'I'm flying to Rome tomorrow. Blame it on pre-jet lag.'

'As an excuse, that's even worse than the casserole.'

Sipping her wine, she repeated slowly, 'What sorrows?'

'Well, Vivienne moved out two days ago.'

He still didn't look upset. Bizarrely, she found herself feeling guilty on Vivienne's behalf. She had been the one who had urged her friend to take action, after all.

'Are you upset?'

Sam's eyes glittered with amusement. 'Oh, distraught. My flat's so tidy it looks like a show home. There's room in the wardrobes to hang up my own clothes, the TV isn't constantly tuned to the soaps and I don't have to sleep in the spare bed any more.'

Even Izzy, herself a veteran of so many such crimes, couldn't help smiling. 'If she asks me, I'll have to tell her you were at least a little bit upset.'

He nodded. 'Of course you will. Poor Vivienne. The decision to leave had to be one she made for herself, for the sake of her pride. I'm just glad she finally realised it couldn't go on any longer.'

'You're cruel,' she protested, feeling sorry now for Vivienne.

'No.' Sam, unrepentant, simply grinned. 'I'm free.'

With two-thirds of a bottle of Sancerre inside her, Izzy began to relax. It was comforting, having Sam back as a friend, and nicer still being able to discuss the failure of their respective love affairs in appallingly indiscreet detail.

'I can just see myself at seventy,' she mused, twirling her hair around her fingers and surveying its colour with a lack of enthusiasm. 'I'll be one of those eccentric spinster ladies surrounded by mountains of newspapers and half-empty tins of sliced pineapple. I shall keep a parrot, train it to sing all my old songs, and bore all my visitors rigid by reminiscing about the time I was famous. Kat will be deeply ashamed of me and try to put me into one of those homes for doolally ex-entertainers . . .'

Sam leaned forward to refill her glass. 'And what about me?'

'Oh, easy. You'll be the sergeant-major type, lining up all the bottles in your drinks cabinet, writing pithy letters to *The Times* and terrifying your poor, down-trodden wife. You'll iron all your own shirts because she never manages to get the creases exactly right, and keep terribly well-trained labradors.'

He raised his eyebrows. 'Don't I get any children?'

Izzy had been poking gentle fun at him. Now, thinking about it, her expression grew serious. 'I don't know. Do you want them?'

He would make a brilliant father, yet for some reason

the idea hadn't even occurred to her. It was hard enough trying to imagine the kind of woman he would choose to marry.

'Is that what you want, Sam? A wife and family?'

He grinned, sensing her disbelief. 'Of course I do. Eventually. Why, d'you think I'm on the shelf? A lost cause? Too . . . *old?*'

Izzy hastily shifted position as he made a grab for her bare toes. 'Don't you dare tickle me! And of course you aren't too old. Men never are. It's unfair.'

Sam looked at first amazed, then intrigued. 'What's this, feeling broody?'

'Not *me*, stupid. I meant Gina. All she's ever wanted was a family and her time's practically up. Whereas you could give yourself another thirty years if you wanted. Then all you'd have to do would be to find yourself some nubile young thing in her twenties and start . . . firing away.'

'I wasn't planning on leaving it quite that long,' he protested mildly.

'Yes, but at least you have the option . . . that's what's so unfair.' She paused, then said, 'What an amazingly grown-up conversation we're having! My God, Sam – we'll be discussing pension plans next.'

Sam didn't care what they discussed; he was just glad to be here. Now that she had forgiven him, Izzy was on great form and her new-found success clearly agreed with her. In her dark blue jersey top and leggings she looked more like a 'nubile young thing in her twenties' herself than a thirty-seven-year-old woman with an almost-adult daughter. She might not be able to cook, he thought wryly, but she certainly possessed more than her share of alternative assets.

Gazing across at her now, remembering those few brief moments during the past months when things had so nearly come right between them, he was struck afresh by the irony of the situation. With Vivienne clinging stubbornly on like a burr, he hadn't allowed himself to think about it too deeply, but if he were honest with himself, the attraction he felt towards Izzy was greater than anything he had experienced for any other woman for longer than he could remember. And yet their relationship had been so ludicrously *chaste* . . .

'What?' she demanded now, long-lashed dark eyes narrowing with suspicion. 'You've gone quiet. I hate it when you go quiet. Oh God, is it food poisoning?'

'More likely the thought of trying to discuss pension plans with someone who thinks an investment is a two-hundred-pound silk shirt.' Rising to his feet, he removed the glass of wine from her hand. 'Come on, show me your new home. I haven't seen it yet and I want the full guided tour.'

Chapter 47

As Izzy led him from one room to the next, her sense of shame increased. Being subjected to Katerina's despairing cries of, 'Oh, Mum!' every time she arrived home from a shopping trip with yet more unnecessary purchases was bad enough, but Sam's silent incredulity was even more galling.

It wasn't until she opened the door leading into the old nursery, however, that he finally spoke.

'An exercise cycle. A sunbed. A Nautilus machine. Izzy, this is bloody ridiculous.'

'We've used the sunbed,' she replied defensively. 'It's great.'

'Well, hooray for that. And the rest?'

'I need to be fit. MBT are setting up a European tour for the new year . . .'

'And you've never exercised in your life.' He gave her a pained look. 'Izzy, you're throwing your money away. You're *never* going to use this stuff.'

'I will!' The words sounded unconvincing, even to her own ears.

Sam's expression switched to one of impatience. 'Take it from me,' he said flatly, 'you won't. And you have to understand that you can't carry on like this, spending as fast as you earn. What happens when the supply dries up? What'll you do then?'

'It isn't *going* to dry up.' He meant well, so she kept her temper. ' "Never, Never" was a top-ten hit in seventeen different countries. The cheques just keep coming . . .'

'And you haven't received a tax demand yet.'

'Sam, don't be so boring! "Kiss" is doing brilliantly . . . I don't have to worry about tax bills . . .'

'You're still wasting your money on rubbish.' He spoke more gently this time, and Izzy's shoulders sagged in defeat. He wasn't, after all, telling her anything she hadn't already figured out for herself.

'I know,' she said in a low voice. 'It's stupid, of course it's stupid. I'm beginning to think I'm not cut out for this being-rich business. I'm just not very good at it.'

Touched by the admission, Sam turned to face her. 'Of course you aren't used to it,' he reminded her. 'But you don't have to rush out and spend, spend, spend. It isn't compulsory, you know.'

All at once Izzy's dark eyes filled with tears. 'Of course it is,' she wailed. 'I'm miserable! It *helps*.'

He steered her swiftly out of the depressing room. 'If it helps so much, why are you crying?'

Izzy wiped her eyes with her sleeve. She herself hardly knew the answer to that. Somehow, though, Sam's being here tonight had made her realise just how *empty* she'd been feeling for the past few weeks. Before, she'd blamed it on her problems with Katerina, but Kat had come back and the gnawing, inner emptiness had persisted.

'I don't know.' She shook her head like a child, deeply ashamed of such inexplicable weakness. 'I've got everything I've ever wanted . . . I have no *right* to be miserable

. . . but something still seems to be missing and I don't even know what it is.'

'Or who he is.' Sam, hazarding an unpalatable guess, said slowly, 'It's not Tash Janssen, is it?'

It was some comfort to see her attempting a watery smile.

'*Definitely* not him. Oh hell, I'm just being stupid. Don't take any notice of me.'

It was about the silliest statement she could have made. Even if he'd been carved out of granite he could scarcely have failed to take notice of her.

In an attempt to cheer her up, he gave her a crooked grin. 'You're certainly a lousy tour guide. Come on, let's go back downstairs.'

'I haven't shown you my bedroom.' Izzy was particularly proud of her glamorous, newly redecorated master bedroom with its emerald-green ceiling, crimson wallpaper and lavishly swathed crimson-and-green four-poster bed. Turning left and leading the way along the corridor, she opened the door. 'And now that you're here, you can carry my cases down for me.'

Now that he was here, Sam could think of far more interesting things to do than haul a set of matching luggage around. It wasn't something he'd planned, but Izzy's unhappiness had touched a chord in him, affecting him more deeply than any amount of outright flirtation could ever have done. There had been so many missed opportunities in the past, yet the mutual attraction underlying their chequered, sometimes volatile relationship had always been there . . .

'I haven't been able to get this one closed,' Izzy

explained, anxious to divert his attention from her embarrassing outburst. The last thing Sam needed now was yet another hopeless, whingeing female crying all over him.

Having crammed far too many clothes and at least a dozen pairs of shoes into the largest pale grey suitcase, she had struggled unsuccessfully for some time to fasten the zip. Now, plonking herself down on top of the case and mentally making herself as heavy as possible, she said, 'Come on, Sam – you're the one with the muscles. If you can just do the zip . . .'

He had to crouch down in order to secure the suitcase. Izzy, perched cross-legged on the lid like a fairy on top of a toadstool, gave him an encouraging smile.

Sam leaned back on his heels and took a deep, measured breath.

'Izzy, I think it's about time.'

'Time for what?' She gazed at him, her expression blank, her lips slightly parted.

'Time you stopped being miserable,' said Sam slowly. Her hands were resting on her knees and when he covered them with his own, she didn't move away. 'And I think it's also about time we stopped kidding ourselves. It's still there, isn't it?'

It was a statement rather than a question and Izzy knew at once what he meant. To Sam's great relief she didn't pretend not to.

'Of course it's still there,' she replied in a low voice, her pulse beginning to race. Admitting it to herself, and realizing that Sam still felt the same way as well, was like allowing a great weight to fall from her shoulders. By tacit unspoken agreement, Vivienne's arrival in London and Izzy's own subsequent ill-fated relationship with Tash had put paid to any thought of continuing what had so nearly been started.

Now, however, the obstacles had been smoothed away; there was no reason on earth why it shouldn't happen. Unless . . .

Sensing her hesitation, he said, 'What?'

Izzy pushed her hair away from her face. 'It's been there all this time,' she said hesitantly. 'So, why now? Why tonight in particular?'

At this, Sam had to smile. Then he glanced briefly at the sumptuous four-poster behind her. 'Well, call me an opportunist, but this is the first time you've ever actually invited me into your bedroom. That is, if you don't count the time at Gina's house when you found a spider in your bed and screamed the place down . . .'

It was a good answer, but Izzy had to be sure. 'Look,' she tried again, her expression serious. 'I don't want this to be happening just because I burst into tears and said I was miserable. I don't want you to feel *sorry* for me, Sam.'

'I have never, in my life, felt sorry for you,' he answered truthfully, and she breathed a sigh of relief.

'OK,' said Izzy, this time with a glimmer of amusement. 'I believe you.'

He raised his eyebrows in mock despair. 'I should bloody well hope so.'

'And now I want you to do something else for me.'

'What's that?'

'Oh, Sam.' Awash with anticipation and longing, wondering if he could hear the frantic thudding of her heart against her ribs, she slid down from the suitcase and into his arms. 'Stop wasting time and seduce me . . .'

Afterwards it seemed to Izzy as if everything had happened in slow motion, each stage of the exquisite mutual seduction becoming so miraculously elongated that time no longer held any recognizable meaning.

And when at last he had explored and caressed her naked body until she'd ached to feel him inside her, her wish was fulfilled. As a lover, Sam was more perfect than she had ever dared imagine. No words were necessary because he knew intuitively – almost before she knew it herself – what to do in order to heighten and prolong each magical moment to such a degree that she couldn't have formulated the simplest of words anyway . . . Closing her eyes and giving herself up to the sheer mindless ecstasy of it all, Izzy moved with him, her fingernails raking his shoulders, her parted lips brushing his neck. The moment was approaching and she knew Sam was holding back, waiting for her. It wasn't fair . . . she wanted it to go on for ever . . . but the sensations were spiralling out of control and nothing – not even Sam – could stop them now . . .

'Oh . . . !' cried Izzy, clutching him and almost sobbing with joy.

The next moment, Sam's mouth brushed her ear. 'I've waited so long for this,' he murmured, his body tensing as he pulled her closer still. 'Izzy . . . I love you . . .'

She awoke at six-thirty to find herself wrapped in Sam's arms. Their legs, too, were comfortably entwined. He wasn't asleep.

'I'm hungry,' she said, smiling up at him and revelling in the blissful security of his embrace.

His fingers trailed suggestively across the lower part of her stomach. 'Hmm, me too.'

'For food,' protested Izzy, gasping as he rolled her gently on to her back and began to explore the swell of her breasts with a lazy tongue. Seconds later, she gave in and whispered weakly, 'But maybe I can wait . . .'

This time the lovemaking was slow and languorous, almost dreamlike. Afterwards, Sam said, 'Do you remember what I told you last night?'

'You mean that stuff about how I shouldn't be throwing my money away?' Izzy pulled a face. 'Sam, don't tell me you're going to try and sell me a time-share.'

He gave her bare bottom a reproving pinch. 'Don't be a smart-ass. I'm being serious.'

'Sorry.'

'And I'm talking about three words in particular.'

It didn't take much effort to guess which three he was referring to. Izzy, who had heard those words uttered at such crucial moments before, tended to take them with a wagonload of salt. Ducking the issue, she gazed innocently at Sam and said, 'Three words in particular? Like "Oh God – cellulite"?'

He pinched her again, hard.

'I told you I loved you.'

'It's OK,' she assured him. 'I'm sure it isn't legally binding.'

'If you carry on like this for much longer,' he warned, 'I shall—'

'Tie me to the bedposts with silk stockings and teach me a lesson I'll never forget?'

Sam closed his eyes in mock despair. 'I think I prefer you miserable . . . Can you be serious for one moment?'

'OK.' She nodded, trying to look penitent. 'But only if you promise to make breakfast afterwards. I'm *still* hungry.'

But Sam wasn't to be put off. 'Those three words,' he said simply, gazing down at her. 'I meant them. And it isn't something I make a habit of saying, in case that's what you thought. If you must know, this is a first.'

Izzy's string of one-liners abruptly died in her throat. Her stomach did an ungainly flip-flop and her mouth went dry. Oh God, she thought, he really *was* serious. And while it was possibly the most wonderful thing he could have said, it was also the most terrifying.

Hopelessly unprepared for such a declaration – and so early in the morning too – she said weakly, 'Oh Sam, don't do this. Please.'

Leaning across, he tilted her chin with his hand so that she was forced to look at him. 'Why not?'

'Because it scares me.' It hurt even to say the words. Sam meant so much to her – far more than he could possibly know – but it only made the situation that much more frightening. Tash Janssen had said, 'I love you,' and it hadn't meant a thing. Ralph had said it dozens of times; so had Katerina's father. And what good had it done, what had it ever *achieved?* As far as Izzy was concerned, the fact that Sam could so easily say the same thing when it clearly wasn't true only proved beyond a shadow of a doubt how little such words meant, and how ridiculously gullible she had been in the past to believe them. God, men were such treacherous shits, she thought with renewed sadness. Why couldn't they just treat women honestly? Why did they deliberately have to confuse them?

'What are you talking about?' Sam demanded now, pushing his fingers through his dark blond hair with an impatient gesture. 'Nothing scares you.'

Being fed a line and being stupid enough to fall for it was what scared Izzy. This time she wasn't going to make a fool of herself.

'It doesn't matter,' she said easily. 'No big deal, Sam. I just don't want you to say those things, that's all.'

'*I* wish I hadn't bloody well said them,' he replied with feeling. This wasn't turning out at all as he had expected.

'Yes, well.' Izzy shrugged. 'It only mucks everything up, doesn't it? I mean, let's be honest; after fancying each other for months we've finally . . . done something about it. And I have to say that on my part at least, it lived up to all expectations. It was great – maybe it can even carry on being great – but there's absolutely no need to spoil it by pretending it means more than it really does.'

Sam hadn't been pretending, but he was damned if he was going to say so now, in the light of Izzy's illuminating comments. He had, it seemed, been a good lay and satisfied Izzy's curiosity to boot. But as for anything more . . . well, that would only *spoil* it.

'I'm being sensible,' she continued, bunching the duvet up around her and hugging her knees. 'Realistic. Don't get funny, Sam.'

'Getting funny wasn't exactly uppermost in my mind,' he replied, his expression sardonic.

It was Sam's turn now to avoid Izzy's gaze. Sliding closer, losing half the duvet in the process, she grinned and landed a kiss on his rigid jaw. 'But you're in danger of doing it anyway,' she said between kisses, 'and there's really no need. We aren't having an argument, after all.'

'Hmm.'

He was weakening; she could sense it. Feeling her stomach beginning to rumble, Izzy stretched a little further, manoeuvring the kisses closer to his mouth. 'So, no getting funny,' she murmured in wheedling tones. 'If, on the other hand, you were thinking of getting breakfast . . .'

Despite himself, Sam smiled. 'You're a hard bitch.'

She was almost on top of him now. 'Oh no,' she said, stifling irrepressible laughter. 'I'm a hungry bitch. Forgive me for mentioning something so personal, Sam, but you're the one who's hard.'

Sam was downstairs in the kitchen when Izzy, emerging from the shower, remembered the phone. Having unplugged it last night in order to avoid any untimely interruptions, it occurred to her now that Joel McGill probably would have been trying to get through for the last hour. As soon as she reconnected the bedside phone, it started to ring.

'No need to panic,' said Izzy, balancing the receiver between chin and collarbone as she wriggled into primrose-yellow silk knickers and kicked last night's dark blue jersey top in the general direction of the washing basket. 'I'm awake, packed and ready to go.'

But it wasn't Joel, phoning to bully her out of bed. It was Gina, sounding distinctly odd.

'I've been trying to get hold of you all night,' she said, her tone jerky. In the background, Izzy could hear the clatter of pans and an unearthly wailing noise.

'All night? Gina, where *are* you? It sounds like Whipsnade Zoo.'

There was a pause, then Gina's voice cracked. 'It's worse than a zoo. Oh, Izzy, I need you here. I'm in St Luke's Hospital and nobody will tell me what's going on . . .'

'But why are you there?' Izzy sat down abruptly on the edge of the rumpled bed. 'Gina, don't cry. Has there been some kind of accident?'

'No . . . no accident.' Gina was crying in earnest now. 'Oh God, Izzy . . . I've been trying to phone you all night! I tried to phone Sam, but he wasn't answering, either. Will you come down and find out what's happening . . . ?'

'Of course I will,' said Izzy automatically, her mind racing. 'But, why are you *there*?'

'My eyes.' Gina's reply was barely audible now. 'It's my eyes. I think I'm going . . . blind . . .'

Chapter 48

Up until now Izzy Van Asch had been a model protégée, writing songs practically to order, singing when she was asked to sing, good-naturedly smiling and posing for hours on end during gruelling photographic sessions and interviewing like a dream. Her endless enthusiasm and down-to-earth sense of humour had won Joel McGill over completely, and although no one could call her the most punctual person in the world, she had never let either him – or herself – down.

Until now. Oh, until now. And how he wished he hadn't answered the damn phone.

'Look,' he said, struggling to remain calm and wondering if Izzy had any idea how much damage she could be doing to her career. 'Everything's been arranged. For God's sake, Izzy – you can't do this to me! You can't *not* go to Rome.'

But Izzy, it seemed, wasn't open to persuasion. She was utterly determined.

'I'm sorry, I know I'm mucking everything up,' she replied, her tone even. 'But I have no choice. Gina needs me and I can't let her down.'

Joel, close to despair, said, 'The Italians aren't going to be amused.'

'I know that.' The fourteen-day schedule of TV appearances, concerts and interviews was a hectic one. Izzy was only too well aware of the phenomenal amount of work that had gone into organizing it. She sighed, a deep and sorrowful sigh. 'And I wish I didn't have to do this. But you see, Joel, now that it's happened . . . there's no way in the world I *can* go to Rome.'

St Luke's Hospital, with its intimidating red-brick exterior and endless corridors of pea-soup-green walls and beige linoleum flooring, was about the most depressing building Izzy had ever seen. The antiseptic smell of the place was all-pervading, the lifts positively antique; even the expressions on the faces of the medical staff they passed along the way seemed uncompromisingly grim.

But if she had found her initial impression disturbing, it was nothing compared with the shock of actually entering the ward to which Gina had been allocated. Now the stench became all too recognizably human. Izzy held her breath and gazed around in dismay at the pitiful sight of thirty or so women, none of whom were a day under eighty, either slumped in chairs or lying corpselike in regimented beds. Some were silent, while others mumbled unintelligibly to themselves. One, frenziedly clawing the air above her head, emitted a series of ear-splitting squawks as they passed by. The terrible smell intensified. Another ancient female with wild hair hurled a plastic beaker on to the floor and cackled with laughter as cold tea splattered Izzy's highly polished, sage-green boots. Two young nurses, frantically busy at the far end of the ward with yet another recalcitrant patient, hadn't even noticed their arrival. The place was pitifully understaffed and there wasn't a doctor in sight.

'It's OK,' said Sam, although it clearly wasn't. Tightening his grip on Izzy's arm, concerned for a moment that she might actually pass out, he continued in reassuring tones, 'Look, there's Gina. Second from the end, on the left.'

It was a measure of Gina's deep distress, Izzy felt, that she was no longer even able to cry.

'You're here,' she whispered almost in disbelief when she turned her head and saw them. 'Oh God, you're both here . . .'

'Of course we're here,' said Izzy, in a voice that sounded as if it didn't belong to her. Appalled by Gina's listlessness as much as by her dreadful pallor, she reached for her hand and squeezed it. 'And you mustn't worry any more, because we're going to get this sorted out. But Gina, what *happened* to you?'

Gina knew only too well what had happened to her, but for a long moment she couldn't speak. Gazing helplessly up at Sam, she raised her left arm – her good arm – and curled it around his neck as he bent to kiss her.

'I tried to phone you,' she croaked, her throat constricted and dry. 'Oh Sam, I kept trying and trying, but you were never there . . .'

The portable telephone-box-on-wheels was still there, pushed against the wall. Izzy said quickly, 'I managed to get hold of him just after you rang me. I unplugged my phone last night because I wanted to get some sleep . . . oh Gina, I'm so sorry.'

Realizing that Izzy was on the verge of tears, Sam took over. Pulling up an orange plastic chair, he said firmly,

'Now, tell us everything. From the beginning. Don't miss anything out.'

He was so strong, so in-control. Now that Sam was here, thought Gina, it was almost possible to believe that everything would be all right.

'Yesterday eve-evening, I was late home from the office,' she began, licking parched lips and reaching once more for the security of his hand. 'Doug's away in Manchester for a couple of days, so there was a lot of extra work. Anyway, I got back at around eight o'clock, and fell asleep on the sofa. When I woke up a couple of hours later I thought I was dying – my head felt as if it was about to burst, I couldn't see out of my right eye and I knew I was going to be sick. So I tried to stand up – to get to the bathroom – but it was as if the whole of my right side wasn't there. I just fell on to the floor.' She paused, then added wearily, 'And was sick anyway.'

To her horror, Izzy realised that the hand she had been holding – Gina's right hand – was indeed as floppy and lifeless as a doll's. 'Then what?' she asked, her voice hushed. 'What did you do after that?'

'Dragged myself across the floor to the phone.' Gina closed her eyes briefly. 'I must have looked an idiot. And Jericho was no help, leaping around and thinking it was all some brilliant new game. Anyway, I managed to dial 999 and an ambulance brought me here. They've been poking and prodding me . . . I've got to have tests done today . . . but they won't tell me what's *wrong* with me . . .'

'That's because they haven't carried out the tests yet,' Sam admonished her gently. The smile he gave Gina was reassuring but Izzy sensed how concerned he really was.

And Gina, it seemed, wasn't falling for it either.

'Come off it, Sam,' she said wearily. 'You met my mother how many times? You know how she died.'

'How did she die?' demanded Izzy, when a doctor had finally appeared on the scene. Drawing the curtains around Gina's bed with a flourish, he had banished Izzy and Sam to the cheerless waiting room while he carried out yet another examination. Now, all thought of last night's shared intimacies banished from her mind, she sat rigidly opposite him and searched his face for clues.

Sam hesitated, then said brusquely, 'She had a brain tumour. It was all pretty traumatic. Gina looked after her at home, almost until the end.'

Izzy, stunned by his words, felt her heart begin to race. 'A brain tumour? But what does that have to do with Gina? She can't possibly have a tumour. She's too . . . young!'

'Yes, well.' He didn't bother to contradict her on that score; even Izzy had to recognise the absurdity of such a statement. 'We *don't* know what it is, yet. Until we do, the most important thing is to keep Gina's spirits up as much as possible.'

'In this hell-hole?' As she gestured helplessly in the direction of the doorway, a fresh chorus of squawks greeted their ears. 'What was it you had in mind, Sam? A quick song-and-dance routine?'

'Miss Van Asch, I appreciate the fact that conditions here aren't ideal, but when Mrs Lawrence was admitted last night, no beds were available on the neurological ward. I can assure you, however, that your friend is receiving the best possible care and attention.'

The doctor was overworked, the hospital underfunded. It wasn't his fault, thought Izzy, but that still didn't make it all right.

'I'm sorry,' she said, ignoring the fact that Sam was giving her one of his what-the-hell-do-you-think-you're-doing stares, 'but the best *possible* care isn't good enough. What Gina needs is the best care, full stop. And she certainly isn't getting it on this ward.'

'I can assure you,' said the doctor stiffly, 'that as soon as a neuro bed does become free, Mrs Lawrence will be moved. In the mean time, however, we have no alternative but to keep her here.'

He was trying to intimidate her. Izzy stood her ground. 'We *do* have an alternative,' she insisted. 'Look, Gina needs treatment, I know that. But she should be comfortable as well. She needs peace and quiet . . . and good food . . . and nurses who aren't permanently rushed off their feet . . .'

'I asked her whether she had private medical insurance,' intercepted the doctor, glancing at his watch. 'She doesn't.'

'I know, but I want her moved to a private hospital anyway,' said Izzy flatly. 'I'll pay.'

He cast her a look of doubt. 'We don't know yet what the problem is with Mrs Lawrence. It could be extremely expensive.'

Izzy was glad. At long last she had found something worthwhile to spend her money on. 'I don't care about the expense,' she said. 'It doesn't matter how much it costs. I'll pay.'

Chapter 49

When Gina had first learned that she was being transferred to Cullen Park Hospital in Westminster, she almost wept with gratitude. Not only was it famous for the unrivalled luxuries with which it cosseted its largely star-studded clientele, but also for its exceptional standards of medical care. The Cullen was a good hospital, equipped with all the very latest high-tech machinery. Wealthy patients from all over the world flew in to be treated there. Gina, who had only ever read about it in the newspapers before now, knew that if anyone could cure her, it would be the incomparable medical staff at the Cullen.

If anyone could cure her. That, of course, was the stumbling block. Because it didn't matter how brilliant the staff might be, or how space-age the technology; some illnesses were still incurable. And after two of the longest, most terrifying days of her entire life, nobody was giving her any clues either way. Nobody, it seemed, was prepared to tell her anything which might indicate whether she could expect to live or die. Everybody, on the other hand, smiled a great deal and chatted brightly about any subject under the sun. As long as it wasn't related to her illness . . .

It was, naturally enough, the subject which occupied Gina's every waking thought. Her mother had been fifty-two when her own brain tumour had first manifested itself. The sudden onset of migrainous headaches – blinding pain and vomiting – had been treated with extra-strong painkillers and hearty reassurance from the family doctor, who had talked about the menopause and told her she needed to start taking things easier at her age.

Over the course of the next few months, however, she had metamorphosed from an active, tennis-playing, smiling crossword enthusiast into a frightened, introverted woman at the mercy of bewildering mood changes and slowly deteriorating eyesight. By the time the tumour was finally discovered, it was beyond treatment. The headaches worsened, a creeping paralysis of the left side of her body made day-to-day living increasingly difficult, and the unpredictable changes of mood were replaced by a pathetic eagerness to please, and finally mild euphoria.

It had been heartbreaking for Gina, having to witness the gradual destruction of the mother she adored, struggling to care for her during that last terrible summer. She had done everything she could, bringing her home from the hospital and nursing her at Kingsley Grove, but love hadn't been enough. The malignant growth had been unstoppable, eroding her mother's memory until she was no longer able to understand that her husband had died three years earlier. Most heartbreaking of all, as far as Gina was concerned, had been having to listen to her mother crying out in endless bewilderment, 'Thomas, where *are* you? Help me . . . don't leave me here on my own . . . oh Thomas, I'm so afraid . . . please don't leave me . . .'

Deep down, Gina knew that the similarity between her own symptoms and those of her mother was too great to be merely a coincidence. The battery of tests continued in earnest, but during the breaks between them she was doing her best to prepare herself – mentally at least – for the realization that she, too, had developed a brain tumour.

And she, too, was afraid . . . so terribly, *desperately* afraid . . . of being left to die on her own.

'I've just been given a funny look by one of those nerve-wracking nurses outside,' grumbled Doug, bursting into the room and thrusting a bunch of crumpled pink carnations into Gina's lap. 'I didn't realise we were expected to dress for visiting hour, here.'

Gina, glad of the diversion, smiled up at him. 'Maybe she's just never seen anyone wearing an orange shirt with a maroon suit before.'

'Oh. Is it bad?' Doug looked so crestfallen, she had to bury her nose in the carnations in order to hide her laughter.

'Not bad, just . . . individual. Mmm, these flowers smell gorgeous.'

Wanting to kiss her but unable to summon up the courage, he sat down beside her instead. 'How are you feeling?'

Her ability to keep up a cheerful front still amazed her. Being asked the same question maybe twenty times each day, she had become adept at telling people what they wanted to hear, rather than the less palatable truth. In a way, too, she was ensuring that they would continue to ask. Weeping and wailing, Gina now realised, would only frighten people away.

'Much better,' she replied, running the fingers of her good hand through her freshly shampooed blonde hair. 'They did more tests this morning, stuck electrodes all over my head and took a recording of my brainwaves. One of the nurses washed my hair afterwards.'

'Good, good.' Doug, who had been frantic with worry since returning from Manchester, looked visibly relieved. 'I expect you'll be out of here soon. And you'll need to convalesce for a while before we get you back to work . . .'

Work, that was a joke. But she played along, glancing up at the clock on the wall and nodding as if in agreement. 'You may have to get a temp in, though. For a few weeks or so. Is the office chaotic?'

For a moment he looked flummoxed, having had neither the time nor the inclination to worry about the state of the office. Gina was all that mattered. 'I don't know. Probably. What did they say about the brain scan you had yesterday?'

She swallowed, not wanting to think about it. The doctors, gathered in a cubicle adjacent to the scanning room itself, had conversed in whispers; all she had been able to make out were disjointed mentions of ventricles, white-matter and hemispheres, whatever they might be. As far as she was concerned, their unsmiling faces and covert sidelong glances were of far greater significance than any stupid words.

The awful panic rose in her throat once more. She didn't want to die, alone and unloved . . .

'They didn't say anything.' Her gaze slipped past Doug once more, to the wall clock, which still said four-fifteen. 'Not to me, anyway.'

Her guard had slipped. Doug, glimpsing the bleak expression in her eyes, thought that if there was anything he could do to make her well again . . . anything at all . . . he would do it.

I love you, he thought, willing her to be able to read his mind. He didn't dare speak the words aloud. I love you *so much* . . .

'Is there anything you need?' he said instead, his forehead creasing with concern. 'Anything I can get you?'

Brightening slightly, Gina nodded. Pushing his flowers to one side, she said, 'Thanks, Doug. On your way out, if you could ask Nurse Elson to come and give me a hand.'

'What's the matter?' He looked alarmed. 'Are you feeling ill again?'

'No, no.' She was reaching into her bedside locker now, pulling out her make-up bag. 'I just want her to help me change into a clean nightie. Sam's coming to see me at five and I want to look nice for him. Oh, and if you could pass me that bottle of perfume on top of the chest of drawers over there . . .'

The looks Sam received from the nurses upon his arrival forty minutes later were far from funny. Katerina, who had bumped into him in the plush foyer downstairs, noticed the effect he was having and grinned.

'Don't look now,' she said, tucking the glossy copies of *Vogue* and *Harpers* under her arm and almost having to break into a trot in order to keep up, 'but I think you're about to be offered a bed bath.'

'Hmm.' Sam, unimpressed, quickened his pace.

'Hmm?' mimicked Katerina in admonishing tones.

Having taken a break from studying and spent a long and enjoyable weekend visiting Simon up at Cambridge, she was in high spirits. 'Whatever's the matter with you, then? Now that you've got rid of Vivienne I thought you'd be making the most of being free again. Or,' she added slyly, 'have you realised you miss her, after all?'

'Did I ever tell you how much I loathe smart-aleck teenagers?' countered Sam equably. As far as he was concerned, there was no earthly reason why Kat shouldn't know about Izzy and himself, but Izzy had come over all coy and born-again-virginal and begged him not to breathe a word of their relationship to anyone.

The lift stopped at the third floor. Katerina pulled a face as they got out. 'I'm only interested.'

'You're nosy. Maybe I like to keep my affairs private.'

'And you think I'd run off to the *News of the World*,' she said with good-humoured resignation. 'Sam, I'm the soul of discretion. I'm my mother's daughter, for heaven's sake. I've had enough practice!'

On entering Gina's room they were almost knocked sideways by the overpowering scent of Miss Dior. Katerina observed with inward amusement the way Gina cried out, 'Sam!' before realizing he wasn't alone. 'Oh and you, Kat, how nice,' she amended somewhat less effusively. 'Pull up a couple of chairs and make yourselves comfortable. I can ring for coffee if you'd like some.'

'Relax, you don't have to play party hostess,' Sam told her gently, as he gave her a brief kiss. 'We've come to see how *you* are.'

Katerina, settling back in a pink-and-green upholstered chair which exactly matched the flowery wallpaper, was further entertained by the sight of Gina blushing beneath her careful make-up. Surely there hadn't been something clandestine going on between these two? Not Sam and *Gina* . . . ?

Two days later, the consultant paid her the visit she'd been waiting for. The tests had all been carried out and now he was here to give her his verdict. With her heart pounding, Gina submitted to yet another neurological examination and braced herself for the news.

But the tortuous game, it appeared, wasn't over yet.

'You're a puzzle,' he told her finally, when he'd finished testing what felt like every reflex in her body. 'The good news, of course, is the fact that the paralysis on the right side is lessening, the headaches have stopped and your eyesight's almost back to normal.'

He was wearing an exceedingly well-cut grey suit and a pale pink Armani shirt. I'm a private patient, thought Gina; of course he's going to smile and give me the good news first.

'And the bad news?' she asked, wishing she had Sam here with her now to give her the support she so badly needed.

'I'll be perfectly frank with you, Mrs Lawrence.' The consultant sat on the edge of the bed in order to be frank. The smile was replaced by a professionally serious expression. 'The tests we've been running have shown up an abnormality, but the precise nature of that abnormality isn't clear.'

If she had been an NHS patient, Gina wondered, would he have simply come out with it and said, 'You have a brain tumour and you're going to die'? It was, after all, more or less what they had told her mother all those years ago.

'So, what happens next?' she persisted, having braced herself for the very worst.

'Well, I think that poor old brain of yours needs a while to recuperate.' He flashed dazzlingly white teeth at her and Gina winced. Such jocular remarks were all she needed. 'There's clearly some swelling in the left hemisphere' – reaching across, he lightly tapped the left side of her head for emphasis – 'and until that recedes, we can't really come to any firm conclusions. So what I suggest is that we send you home for a week or two, then get you back here for another scan. By that time, hopefully, you'll be as right as rain!'

'And what if I'm not as right as rain?' she countered with rising anger. This so-called bloody miracle-worker in his flashy designer suit and hand-made shoes was fobbing her off with ridiculous platitudes. She couldn't just sit around and *wait*, for God's sake. She needed to know. *Now.*

'Why don't we cross that hurdle when we come to it?' This time he tried to give her hand a consoling pat, but Gina snatched it away.

'Just tell me,' she said evenly, 'what *you* think is wrong with me.'

'Ah, but the tests are inconclusive. It really isn't possible to . . .'

He was shaking his head. Prevaricating. Fixing him

with a steady gaze, Gina said, 'But you can't assure me that I *don't* have a brain tumour, can you?'

Chapter 50

Katerina, despatched by Lucille to answer the front door, was delighted to see Vivienne standing on the doorstep.

'I was beginning to think we'd never see you again,' she cried, giving her a hug and almost having her eye taken out in the process by an enormous gold earring curved like a scimitar to match Vivienne's flawless cheekbones. 'And I thought that if we *did* ever see you, we wouldn't recognise you. Now that you're a country doctor's lady, aren't you supposed to trudge around in tweed skirts and wellies?'

'Tried it once, didn't like it,' deadpanned Vivienne, glancing down at her cyclamen-pink silk jacket and short black skirt. Then she broke into a grin. 'OK, that's a lie. Thought about it once and couldn't face it. Hell, at least this way the patients have something to gossip about. I figure it brightens their day.'

'We've got a patient whose day could do with a bit of brightening.' Katerina drew her inside, kicking the door shut behind them. 'Come on, I'll break open the gin, if Lucille hasn't got there first. And I warn you, you're going to need it.'

Vivienne was both appalled by the change in Gina, and enchanted by bossy, bustling Lucille who appeared to run the entire household and whose welcome entailed swiping the bottle of Gordon's from Katerina's grasp and all but emptying its contents into two enormous glasses.

'That girl pours terrible small measures,' she declared expansively, above the clatter of ice cubes. 'Not that I'm much of a gin-person myself, ye understand, but I'm willing to join you for decency's sake. And none of this poison for *you*,' she added, swinging round to address Gina. 'It does desperate things, y'know, to the human brain.'

'Hear, hear,' said Vivienne cheerfully, taking her drink and sinking down on to the dark green sofa next to Gina. 'I was so sorry to hear you were sick. Still, it must be great to be out of hospital.'

Gina managed a wan smile. She looked, Vivienne decided, like a stiffly jointed wooden doll.

'Everyone's been very kind. Izzy insisted I stay here until I'm well enough to . . . cope on my own.' Her tone of voice indicated that this was an unlikely prospect. Behind her, Katerina raised her eyebrows in an I-told-you-so manner.

'So, what exactly *was* wrong?' persisted Vivienne, who had only heard the vaguest details from Izzy when she'd phoned and whose curiosity was now thoroughly aroused. It wasn't like Katerina to be so unsympathetic where illness was concerned.

'I have to go back for more tests before they decide whether or not it's worth trying to operate.' Gina's eyes glittered with unshed tears, but she soldiered on. 'Although if the tumour's malignant, they probably won't bother . . .'

Vivienne's eyes widened. 'You have a *tumour?*'

'Not definitely,' said Katerina, with a trace of

impatience. 'Gina, it isn't *definite*.'

'Of course not.' Gina shrugged apologetically and gave Vivienne a brave smile. 'Well, they're ninety per cent sure, but that isn't definite. Did Izzy tell you my mother died of a brain tumour?'

This was awful, unbelievable. Suddenly ashamed of herself for having asked, Vivienne shifted in her seat and said, 'Where is she? Izzy, I mean. I told her I'd be here at seven-thirty . . .'

'Ah,' said Lucille, who evidently wouldn't recognise an emotionally charged atmosphere if it were to leap up and poke her in the eye, 'but she's a crafty article, that one. She told me you were never anywhere you were supposed to be without losing an hour in the process, so she was goin' to take a nice hot bath while she was waitin' for you to turn up late.' She gave Vivienne a great beaming smile. 'It's thinkin' like that, I said to her, that brings down governments and loses wars. And I'm right, aren't I, because she's still wallowing upstairs in the tub and here *you* are, not so late after all, havin' fun and drinkin' all the gin.'

By nine o'clock Izzy and Vivienne had the sitting room to themselves, Gina having retired to bed in order to rest and Katerina having disappeared to do some revision. Lucille had gone home to her much-beleaguered husband.

'Well, I love your housekeeper, but isn't Gina acting kinda weird?' said Vivienne with characteristic bluntness.

Izzy sighed. 'I suppose so. But then I suppose she's entitled to act weird, under the circumstances. It just doesn't make things easier.'

'This place is like *Little Women*,' Vivienne mused, curling her long legs beneath her. 'Ever read that book? You've got Gina doing her impression of saintly Beth, Kat can be Amy . . . hell, your problem is that none of you has a man!'

'Not so long ago we had problems,' Izzy countered drily. 'And they were *all* caused by men. It's a no-win situation.'

Vivienne looked smug. 'I've won.'

'And we aren't totally starved of male company,' said Izzy, glancing at her watch. 'Doug's round here all the time. He won't admit it, but I'm sure he's carrying a secret torch for Gina.'

'Well, hooray for Doug.'

'And there's Sam, too.' Izzy paused, awaiting her reaction. 'He calls round every night to see Gina, usually at around nine-thirty on his way to The Steps. I expect he'll be here soon.'

But all Vivienne did was laugh. 'What are you doing, testing me? To see if I'm well and truly cured? Honey, I can read you like a book!'

No, you can't, thought Izzy with some relief. Vivienne and Sam might not be a couple any more, but she still felt guilty about what had happened between Sam and herself.

'And if I am testing you?' she said cautiously.

'Everything's different now. Like I said, I've won. Hit the good old jackpot. Oh Izzy, it's like a dream come true! Terry's the one for me and now that I've finally managed to convince him I'm not just messing him around, it's got better and better. I'm living with a man who really *wants* me . . .'

'You haven't explained how that came about either,' said Izzy, curious to know how she'd managed it. 'Sam told me you'd moved into an hotel. The next thing I know, you're out of it and into the love-nest.'

'I moved into *the* hotel,' Vivienne corrected her triumphantly. 'The Ritz, to be precise. When poor old Terry heard what the nightly rates are for that place he all but fainted on the spot. At first he tried to persuade me to move into someplace cheaper, but I told him it was either his place or I stayed put. And since he couldn't cope with the idea of being responsible for such *vast* sums of money disappearing by the hour, he had to give in.' She grinned and said, 'The bill for four days at the Ritz came to just over a grand, what with laundry and room service. But in the end, you see, it was a brilliant investment.'

This was the kind of logic with which Izzy happily concurred. It was also the kind that drove Sam to despair. For a moment she almost wished he could be there to hear it; the expression on his face would be miraculous.

'And you're changing the subject, sweetie,' Vivienne continued, fixing her with a shrewd look. '*You* don't have a man in your life and it isn't right. Aren't you meeting hordes of handsome hunks these days, now that you're mixing in the most glittering showbiz circles?'

'Mainly balding, overweight hunks,' said Izzy, wondering if she should tell her now. It was about as good an opportunity as she was likely to get, after all. But the words wouldn't come. She felt her nerve – quite uncharacteristically – slipping away. 'Not that they're all bald,' she amended lightly. 'Some of them have hair. Well, toupees.'

True to her word, Vivienne didn't even flinch when the doorbell rang. Izzy, answering the door, ducked away before Sam could kiss her and pressed herself like a fugitive against the wall.

'It's OK.' He looked amused. 'I don't have a gun.'

'Sshh. Vivienne's here.'

'So?' Totally unfazed, he gave Izzy a kiss anyway. She only managed to squirm frantically out of reach a fraction of a second before Vivienne appeared in the sitting-room doorway.

'Hi, Sam. Come to visit the invalid? Since our hopeless hostess hasn't offered, I was just about to make some coffee. Would you like some?'

It was all so civilised, thought Izzy wonderingly, ten minutes later. She could hardly have believed that there had ever been anything between Vivienne and Sam. Now, with no apparent awkwardness at all, they were chatting away like old friends, the conversation moving effortlessly from the latest gossip at The Chelsea Steps to Sam's about-to-be-divorced neighbours, and then on again to Vivienne's new-found happiness.

'It's so great,' she enthused, green eyes alight with adoration. 'I keep having to pinch myself to make sure it isn't all a dream. And do you know, Terry doesn't even *care* if I leave my shoes in the kitchen, or burn dinner?'

Sam looked startled. 'You actually cook *meals* for him?'

'Are you kidding?' Vivienne burst out laughing. 'We

have a sweet woman in from the village. She does all the cooking; I heat it up.'

'He'll come to his senses. When the novelty wears off.'

'No, he won't,' she replied simply, not even taking offence. 'Because he accepts me, just the way I am. And it isn't a novelty, it's love.'

Gina was sitting up in bed, waiting for him. Holding out her arms for her customary hug, she said, 'You've been downstairs for ages. I was beginning to think you'd forgotten me.'

Sam looked and smelled wonderful. He was wearing a new, dark grey suit, a pink-and-grey striped shirt and her favourite aftershave. She wondered if he had any idea how much his visits meant to her, how very much he had come to mean to her during these last, nightmarish few days. For while Izzy had been brilliant, footing the ludicrously expensive medical bills and insisting she stay in order to be properly looked after, Gina sensed that only Sam truly understood what she was going through. And he really *cared* . . .

'Of course I hadn't forgotten you,' he said, idly turning over the paperback she'd been reading. 'But Vivienne's still down there. I had to sit through the whole happy-ever-after story before I could escape. Oh, for heaven's sake, Gina!' His expression changed as he read the title of the book. 'What are you doing with this?'

'I'm being sensible,' she replied, an aching lump coming to her throat as she realised the extent of his concern. 'We have to face facts, Sam. It's no good pretending everything's fine.'

'*Arranging Your Own Funeral?*' he demanded, staring aghast at the discreet, dark blue lettering of the title and then at Gina's pinched white face. Hurling the book across the room, he said, 'This is ridiculous . . . you shouldn't even be *thinking* about it!'

Gina, who had never seen him so angry before, promptly burst into tears. 'It needs to be done. There are so many things I have to think about! Making a will . . . organizing the service . . . please, Sam, don't look at me like that. I don't want you to be c-cross with me . . .'

Sam, who was seldom at a loss for words, took her into his arms and let her sob. Eventually he said, 'I'm not cross with you. It just doesn't seem right, that's all. I don't think you should be dwelling on what might not even happen.'

His embrace was so warm, so comforting, Gina didn't want it to stop. But she was scared, and exhausted with the effort of putting on a brave face. The fear of what lay ahead was too much for anyone to bear; she couldn't go through it alone.

Gradually, however, she began to feel better. Having heard muted scrabbling sounds at the door moments earlier, she tilted her tear-stained face and saw Jericho crouched at the foot of the bed, wrestling with the paperback.

'You see?' murmured Sam, stroking her hair. 'Even the damn dog agrees with me.'

'I don't know what I'd do without you.' Gina gave him a weak smile.

'You don't have to know. I'm here, aren't I?'

'As if you don't have enough to worry about. Was it

awful, seeing Vivienne again and having to listen to her going on about how happy she is with her new boyfriend?'

'Are you kidding?' Relieved to see that Gina was looking more cheerful, he carefully wiped her eyes with the back of his hand and grinned at her. 'It's the best news I've had all year.'

Chapter 51

'Well, you've certainly got a bit of colour in your cheeks today,' declared Lucille approvingly at eleven-thirty the following morning, as she wielded the vacuum cleaner with some vigour around the bedroom. Prodding Jericho with the nozzle until he let out an indignant yelp, she added cheerfully, 'Looked like a wee ghost, so you did yesterday . . . will you shift yer carcass, you dumb crazy animal . . . I'll tell you now, I said an extra prayer or two before I went to bed last night.'

'Maybe it worked,' suggested Gina, trying not to flinch as Jericho's tail came perilously close to being sucked into the Hoover.

Lucille, however, wasn't about to let the Almighty take all the credit for this particular small miracle. Switching off the machine – to the profound relief of both Gina and Jericho – she tilted her head to one side and said slyly, 'Somethin' surely worked, but since I'm not entirely convinced the good Lord was able to hear my prayers above all the noise of me old man's drunken snores, I'm thinkin' that maybe it has more to do with a certain visitor . . .'

Doug Steadman, Lucille had decided, was a lovely fellow. Deeply appreciative of her ham-and-mustard sandwiches, which comprised more ham than bread, and always willing to regale her with gossip about her favourite old Irish singers, she enjoyed his daily visits immensely. And he was kind, too; this morning he had brought her a dog-eared programme of a Val Doonican concert from the Seventies, signed by the great man himself.

If Doug wasn't so clearly besotted with Gina, Lucille could almost have had a go at him herself.

At the mention of the word 'visitor', however, Gina's thoughts had flown immediately to Sam. Since stating so emphatically last night that Vivienne meant nothing to him at all, her tentative hopes had soared and she had slept well for the first time in a week.

Now, since Izzy's perceptive housekeeper had virtually raised the subject anyway, she decided to take the plunge and say aloud the question that had been buzzing around in her mind ever since she'd woken up.

'OK,' she said, bracing herself. 'Lucille, if *you* really liked a man and knew he liked you in return, but because you were old friends nothing was actually happening . . . well, would you carry on as you were and just hope it might happen naturally? Or do you think it would be better to come out and say something?'

She could feel perspiration prickling the back of her neck. God, it was hard enough even saying this to Lucille . . .

But the housekeeper's broad smile told her all she needed to know.

'Bless you,' declared Lucille triumphantly, feeling almost as if she had engineered the entire fairy-tale herself. 'And there I was, wondering how long it was going to take you to come to your senses! Of course you must tell him. He'll be relieved and delighted to know how you feel, and that's a promise!'

'Are you sure?' said Gina, sagging with relief. 'Really? I wouldn't want him to think I was being . . . well, pushy.'

'Sure, I'm sure,' Lucille replied, her sweeping gesture towards the window encompassing the entire male population of north London. 'Don't three-quarters of them need a bit of a push and a shove to get them started at the best of times? You mark my words, a fine man is a rare enough creature to track down these days. If you're fortunate enough to find one, you have to thank your lucky stars and then hang on to him by your very fingernails.'

'Bugger, bugger and damn!' shrieked Izzy, slamming down the phone just as Gina wandered into the kitchen.

Katerina, who was standing at the stove stirring a great panful of molten chocolate fudge, raised her eyebrows.

'My mother, the celebrated song-writer. Can't you just picture Michael Parkinson introducing her on next week's show? And now ladies and gentlemen, here to give us a rendition of her latest single, "Bugger, bugger and damn", will you please welcome—'

'That was Doug,' snapped Izzy, ignoring her. 'The concert organisers in Rome have just informed him that if I don't get over there tomorrow night they're going to sue the pants off me for breach of contract.'

'Oh, I get it now.' Katerina grinned. 'Bugger, bugger and damn is a firm of solicitors.'

'I could always have you adopted, you know.'

Gina, sitting down at the kitchen table, interceded. 'Is it really so terrible?' she asked cautiously, in case Izzy rounded on her as well. 'I thought you were looking forward to going to Rome.'

Izzy was exhausted. Weeks of working punishing hours in the recording studios had taken more out of her than she'd realised. The dozens of interviews and personal appearances had been mentally draining too, since she always had to guard against saying the wrong thing and permanent perfection didn't come easily, particularly when the subject of Tash Janssen was so often on every interviewer's lips. She was tired of smiling and endlessly being diplomatic. She was tired of working, sometimes until midnight, with her brilliant but unbelievably picky producer. The only thing that hadn't been tiresome had been the prospect of a week in Rome, which was somewhere she'd always longed to visit, but that had had to be cancelled when Gina was taken ill.

And this is all the bloody thanks I get, she thought mutinously. So much for making the great sacrifice and promising to look after the invalid. Here was Gina, sitting opposite her, wearing violet eyeshadow and urging her to bloody well go anyway.

'Don't be cross,' said Gina, bewildered by her obvious irritation. 'I'm trying to help, that's all.'

'You're ill,' replied Izzy bluntly. 'I thought *I* was supposed to be the one trying to help *you*.'

Finally understanding, Gina's face cleared. 'And you have,' she said with genuine gratitude. 'More than you'll ever know. But you've made enough sacrifices already, and you can't possibly let those Italians sue you. I'll be *fine*,' she added persuasively, thinking of Sam but smiling at Izzy. 'Really. It's only going to be for a few days, after all.'

'Ah, but a lot can happen in a few days,' put in Katerina, sighing with pleasure as she tasted the first spoonful of still-warm chocolate fudge.

Izzy, somewhat mollified, said, 'Such as?'

'Mum, I know what you're like with Italians. You could go over there to do the concert and come back married.' Rolling her eyes for emphasis, she added solemnly, 'To a devastatingly attractive Roman solicitor called Buggeri . . .'

The last time she had packed her suitcase for Rome, Sam had ended up making love to her on top of it.

Izzy felt it suitably ironic, therefore, that Gina should have chosen this particular evening and this moment in which to confide her earth-shattering decision.

The difference, of course, was that this time she was having no fun at all.

'. . . so you see, I know it sounds crazy, but I really do love him,' Gina concluded, while Izzy, like an automaton, continued to pack. 'Oh God, it's such a relief to be able to tell you this! But do *you* think I'm crazy?'

Unable to speak for a moment, Izzy shook her head. How could falling in love with Sam Sheridan be crazy, when she'd done the very same thing herself? And how desperately she wished now that she hadn't insisted upon keeping their relationship a secret.

'You really should be using tissue paper,' said Gina, eyeing the haphazard jumble of silks and cottons spilling over the rim of the case. 'It stops things getting creased.'

'Mmm.'

'Everything that's happened, you see, has made me rethink my life. Particularly now that I might not have much of it left.'

'Don't say that,' said Izzy numbly, but this time Gina wasn't being self-pitying.

'I'm just trying to explain,' she went on, willing Izzy to understand. 'Whenever you've wanted something, you've gone out and got it. I've always admired you for that. And here you are, happy and successful . . . you have everything you could possibly want! So I've decided to be like you. I love Sam and he's what *I* want. I would have been too scared to tell him before, but now I know that life's too short to be scared.' She shrugged, with more bravado than she felt. 'The worst he can do, after all, is turn me down.'

Except that he can't, thought Izzy, her expression bleak and her stomach a clenched knot. Because you've got a brain tumour and Sam's practically your dying wish. So he doesn't really have a lot of choice.

Chapter 52

Knowing that she was entirely responsible for her own misery wasn't making Izzy feel any better. Last night she had dreamt that during a fearful confrontation she'd told Gina she couldn't have Sam because he loved *her*. Gina, utterly distraught, had drowned herself in Izzy's weed-choked fish pond and Sam, in turn rounding on Izzy, had icily informed her that Gina was the only woman he'd ever really loved anyway.

It was all very disturbing and she had woken up in floods of tears, only to realise that what actually *had* happened was just as hopeless. Gina had begged for reassurance that she was doing the right thing and all she'd been able to do in return was agree. How, after all, could she deny her friend that last chance of happiness when she had already endured a year of such awful misery and despair?

It would have been so much easier, as well, not to have had to face Sam and pretend that nothing had happened, but even that small luxury had been denied her. By sheer chance, an urgent business meeting had prevented him visiting Gina the previous night and when he'd phoned to explain, she had told him of Izzy's imminent departure. Izzy, consequently, hadn't had any choice in the matter when Gina had happily informed her that Sam would pick her up at nine-thirty the following morning and drive her to the airport himself.

It was an unfairly beautiful November morning too, brightly sunny and glittering with frost like something out of a Disney cartoon. Still haunted by her earlier dream, Izzy gazed silently out of the car's side-window at the dazzling blue-whiteness of Hyde Park and didn't even notice they were slowing down until Sam had brought the car to a full stop.

'What?' she said, startled, as he switched off the ignition.

'My sentiments exactly,' replied Sam, his tone dry. Leaning across her, undoing her seat belt and opening the passenger door, he added, 'Come on, we're going for a walk.'

Anticipating somewhat warmer weather in Rome, Izzy was wearing a pink-and-green striped blazer over a short pink dress. She shivered as an icy blast of air invaded the car, but all Sam did was hand her his own scuffed leather jacket and motion her to get out.

'Why don't you tell me what's wrong?' he said eventually, when she had trudged along beside him in silence for several minutes.

It was the last thing Izzy felt able to do. Instead, she gave him a brittle smile. 'I'm cold.'

'You're playing some kind of game,' he countered, not returning her smile. 'And I want to know what it is. Even more, I'd like to know why you're doing it.'

And I want to tell you, she thought miserably, more than anything else in the world. But I can't, because that would mean betraying Gina's confidence. It wouldn't be fair. Worse than that, it would be downright cruel . . .

'Look,' she said, shoving her hands deep into the pockets of the leather jacket and quickening her pace in order not to have to meet his unnervingly direct gaze, 'I'm really not playing games. I've thought a lot about . . . what happened the other night, and I know now that it was a mistake.'

'Oh, right.' Even though she couldn't see his expression, the sarcasm in Sam's voice was unmistakable. 'Of course it was. The biggest mistake ever. I thought of writing to Clare Rayner myself—'

'Don't start,' she said unhappily. 'I'm trying to explain, that's all, and you aren't making it any easier.'

A hand on her arm stopped her in her tracks. Frosted leaves crunched beneath Izzy's feet as Sam swung her round to face him.

'But I don't want to hear this bullshit. So, why should I make it easier?'

It was unfair. Everything was unfair. Even the fact that Izzy knew her nose and cheeks were red with cold yet Sam's face remained as smooth and brown as a ski instructor's was unfair. Why on earth, she thought with mounting resentment, couldn't he at least go blotchy like everyone else?

'Look,' she said, trying again. 'When it comes to mistakes, I'm an expert. I can spot them a mile off. And I'm fed up with *making* them . . . so for the first time in practically my entire life I'm trying to do the sensible thing instead.'

She stood her ground as Sam stared at her in disbelief.

'Maybe,' he said finally, 'you should define *sensible*.'

This wasn't easy. She hadn't had time to practise. And it had to sound believable . . .

'I don't want to make any more mistakes,' said Izzy, pushing her hair away from her face with a defiant gesture. 'Sam, we're an unmatched pair. Look at how Vivienne drove you up the wall with her untidiness and the way she couldn't cook a meal to save her life . . . I'm *just* like her, only worse! I know that if we even tried to make a go of it we'd end up hating each other. It simply wouldn't work.'

'I think it would.'

'Only because you're being pig-headed,' she retaliated. 'And because you've probably never *been* turned down before.'

'I've certainly never heard such feeble excuses before.' He was almost smiling now. 'Got any more, or was that the entire repertoire?'

'I'm being serious!' Izzy shouted, infuriated by his refusal to believe her. 'We have no future, so what *would* be the point of even pretending we have?'

He raised his eyebrows. 'So that really is all you're worried about? The fact that you can't cook?'

'No.' Slowly, she shook her head. 'We have no future because I'm thirty-seven years old. I have a grown-up daughter and a career that's finally taken off. You want a nice little wife, and children of your own.' She paused, giving the words time to sink in. 'And that's what you should be looking for, Sam. A wife.'

He wasn't smiling now. 'Perhaps that's what I am doing.'

'No, you aren't.' Izzy, who'd had no idea he was this serious, briefly closed her eyes. Gina was all but forgotten by this time. She was no longer making up excuses; this was the unvarnished, unpalatable truth and not even Sam could argue with it. 'I've had my family and it's too late to start again now. I can never give you what you want, Sam. That's all there is to it. I'm just too *old* . . .'

'We don't have to have children,' he said, but the words didn't sound entirely convincing. Izzy, her eyes already watering with the cold, swallowed hard in an effort to dispel the lump in her throat. It was all so terribly sad; here she was, receiving what virtually amounted to a proposal of marriage from the nicest man she had ever known, and there was absolutely no way in the world she could allow him to talk her into saying yes.

'But you'd always want them,' she said miserably. 'And sooner or later you'd resent me for not being able to give you what you wanted. It's no good, Sam; I can't make myself younger and I couldn't bear to be a stop-gap, a temporary diversion until the right woman comes along. You have your life to lead and I have mine, and the next thing I have to do is catch my flight to Rome, before frostbite well and truly sets in. So, if we could just get back to the car . . .'

The scheduled Alitalia flight from Heathrow wasn't as busy in November as it would have been in season. Izzy, thankful to find she had a double seat to herself and praying she wouldn't be recognised, shielded her eyes with sunglasses and wept quietly all the way to Rome. She'd done the right thing . . . the *sensible* thing . . . and it hurt like hell. All she could do now was remind herself that any kind of future with Sam would, in the long run, only result in more pain than even this.

* * *

Despite making a terrific effort to pull herself together, Rome's magnificence and beauty were wasted on her today. Even the maniacal manoeuvres executed by her excitable taxi driver as he zig-zagged and hooted his way across the city failed to dispel her gloom. Izzy, whose eyes were still swollen behind her dark glasses, gazed dismally out at the sunny streets, until the taxi eventually pulled up outside the Hotel Aldrovandi Palace where she would be staying for the next few days.

But her schedule was tight, there was work to be done and she had little time to appreciate the style and splendour of the five-star hotel. A note at reception from the concert organisers informed her that at four o'clock someone would be arriving to take her to the hall for sound checks and rehearsals. As soon as she reached her room, which overlooked the Borghese Gardens in all their glory, she stripped off her clothes and stepped into the shower.

When she emerged from the bathroom fifteen minutes later, Tash was waiting for her.

'I don't believe this,' said Izzy flatly. 'How the hell did you get into my room?'

The seductive smile was so familiar, her departure from his life might never have existed.

'Sweetheart, in Italy I'm a national hero,' he drawled. These pretty little chambermaids will do *anything* for me.'

'I knew an Italian man once,' she retaliated in withering tones, making quite sure the towel wrapped around her body was firmly secured. 'He had no taste either.'

He looked reproachful. 'Izzy. No bitterness, please!

I've come here to make the peace. I've *missed* you.'

She shivered. His words were uncannily similar to Sam's, when he had turned up on her doorstep just a week earlier. And now here was Tash, as dark and dangerous as a panther in his black sweatshirt and jeans, giving her that look of his and so confident of his own irresistibility that it didn't even seem to have occurred to him that she might say no.

'No,' said Izzy, sparing a glance at her watch. 'And if you'll excuse me, I'm in a hurry.'

But all he did was make himself comfortable in one of the plush velvet chairs. 'Of course you are, angel. I'm here to take you to the hall myself. We have a run-through rehearsal at four-fifteen, after all.'

There was something going on. Warily, Izzy said, 'We?'

'Did they forget to tell you?' He raised his dark eyebrows in mock amazement. 'My manager organised it a couple of days ago. I'm the surprise guest. Halfway through the set, you launch into "Never, Never" and after the first verse I appear on stage to tumultuous applause and screams of ecstatic delight from several thousand nubile Italian virgins. We sing, we hug, we kiss . . . we hit the front page of the papers . . . sweetheart, that's show business!'

'No,' repeated Izzy, realizing that he had orchestrated the entire thing. 'I won't do it. I don't want you there.'

'Ah, but the organisers do. And if you refuse now, you'll have two massive lawsuits to contend with.' Tash shrugged, then smiled again. 'Copies of the amended contract were sent to your agent forty-eight hours ago. With his customary inefficiency, no doubt, he forgot to read them. You should get yourself a smart manager, Izzy, if you want to get ahead in this world. If you wanted to, you could even share mine.'

He was loathsome, but he was also right. Izzy, recognising a fait accompli when she heard one, knew that she had no choice but to go along with the revolting, publicity-courting charade. Out of sheer desperation, and to make him realise just how much she despised him, she said quietly, 'How's Mirabelle?'

Tash, however, didn't even flinch.

'Funny you should say that,' he replied in cheerful tones. 'When I saw her yesterday I mentioned the fact that I was flying over here to do a gig with you.' He paused, then added triumphantly, 'She said, "Izzy who?" '

Chapter 53

Sam, unable to quite believe that a day which had begun so dreadfully could get this much worse, was unable to speak. At almost exactly this time last week the room in which he was now trapped had contained an expensive assortment of exercise machines and he had been telling Izzy in no uncertain terms to stop wasting money and get her life into some kind of order.

Today, no exercise equipment remained. Banished to a small box-room on the top floor of the house, it had been replaced by conventional bedroom furniture and an incumbent invalid. Izzy, having taken his advice and refused point-blank even to consider the possibility that they might have a future together, had buggered off to Rome instead in order to further her career.

He, meanwhile, now found himself having to face rather more than just the music.

His sensation of claustrophobia intensified as Gina clutched his hand with thin fingers, forcing him to return his attention to her.

'. . . and I realise that maybe I'm not being fair to you,' she continued rapidly, 'but I'm just not brave enough to go through this by myself. I'm not scared of dying . . . but I *am* scared of dying alone. And that's why I had to tell you how I feel about you. I love you, Sam. And I need to know how you feel about me, because I don't think I'm brave enough to get through it on my own. Good friends aren't enough . . . I need someone who loves me . . . to *be* with me.' She faltered, her eyes brimming with tears, her grip on his hand tightening with the effort of maintaining control. 'Otherwise it would be . . . unbearable . . . I don't honestly know if I could go on . . .'

She was evidently so distraught she hadn't even recognised that what she was inflicting upon him was emotional blackmail. Much as Izzy had done yesterday, Sam appreciated that he was being given absolutely no choice in the matter. It was a fait accompli from which there was no escape, an offer he simply couldn't refuse. As far as Gina was concerned, she was being punished for a crime she hadn't committed and now, without even realizing it, she was punishing him in return. Trapped, he thought bleakly, wasn't the word for it.

But Gina's desperation was genuine enough. She needed him, and he couldn't let her down.

'I'm here,' he said, taking her thin, shuddering body into his arms and feeling her hot tears of relief soak through his shirt front. 'You're not alone. You've got me. You'll always have me . . .'

'Oh, Sam,' wept Gina, clinging to him. 'I love you. I really do.'

'Sshh,' he murmured, rocking her like a baby and forcing himself not to think of Izzy. 'You mustn't cry. I love you too.'

Katerina, busy putting the finishing touches to an essay, looked up and grinned as Sam entered the room.

'I know I'm in love with my word processor,' she said,

leaning back in her chair and offering him a Liquorice Allsort, 'but you really don't need to knock before coming in. Our relationship is purely platonic.'

'Don't talk to me about relationships.' With a shudder, Sam sent up a prayer of thanks that at least Gina didn't expect him to perform in that respect. He could go along with the charade just so far, but anything even remotely sexual would be out of the question.

Intrigued, Katerina said, 'Problems with Vivienne?'

'Worse.' For a moment he was tempted to tell her about Izzy and himself, but he knew he couldn't do that. She would have to know, however, about the farcical situation with Gina.

'Oh my God,' said Katerina finally, when he'd finished. 'I don't know whether to laugh or cry. However are you going to wriggle out of this one?'

He shrugged. 'No way out.'

She gazed at him, genuinely appalled. Sorry as she felt for Gina, she felt sorrier still for Sam. 'She's got you by the short and curlies.'

'Not quite that.' He winced at the unfortunate metaphor. 'But it's bad enough.'

'Maybe next week's brain scan will be OK,' suggested Katerina, not very hopefully. 'If she isn't going to die, you're off the hook.'

The other alternative – that Gina's death would be mercifully swift – hung unspoken in the air between them, too callous to even voice aloud.

'We'll just have to wait and see.' Sam glanced at his watch. 'Hell, I'd better go. I was supposed to be at the club an hour ago.'

Jumping to her feet, Katerina gave him a big hug. 'Poor old you, what a shitty thing to have happen. And just when you'd got yourself free of Vivienne, too.' Drawing away, starting to laugh as she realised that yellow fluff from her mohair sweater had moulted all over his dark blue jacket, she said, 'Look, even my jumper's hopelessly attracted to you! Has it ever occurred to you, Sam, that maybe you're just too irresistible for your own good?'

It was a shame, thought Sam wryly, that Izzy should be the only one who didn't share her views.

'Thanks,' he deadpanned, brushing stubborn crocus-yellow mohair from his lapels. 'That's comforting to know. At least I'm . . . irresistible.'

'Oh, except to me,' Katerina assured him earnestly. 'I'm totally exempt. I don't quite know why,' she added, breaking into a grin, 'but for some weird reason I see you as more of a father figure than a man!'

Struck by this further irony, Sam allowed himself a crooked smile. 'Thanks . . .'

The atmosphere inside the concert hall was amazing. Izzy, pausing for breath and gazing out in wonder at the bobbing, seething mass of the audience as seven thousand Italians applauded wildly and screamed for more, realised that here was the antidote she so desperately needed. It was a magical evening and the crowd loved her. It was all she'd ever worked for, all that really mattered. For while eventually . . . hopefully . . . she would be able to forget Sam, the exhilaration of singing here would remain indelibly imprinted on her memory. She was, at long last, a real success and nobody could take that away from her.

The heat, too, was stifling. Shaking damp tendrils of hair away from her face and undoing another button of the peacock-blue-and-gold shirt which clung to her perspiration-drenched body, she turned and nodded to the band behind her. Dry ice was already billowing from the back of the stage, signalling Tash's impending entrance. In response to her nod, the drummer and sax player moved into the now-famous opening bars of 'Never, Never'. The audience, recognizing the song at once, sent up a roar of approval that almost shook the hundred-year-old building to its foundations.

Izzy, acknowledging their appreciation with a wave, took a small step backwards and smiled. The clouds of dry ice were close behind her now, sliding noiselessly towards the front of the stage. Above and all around her, spots of lilac-and-blue light darted like moonbeams, illuminating her solitary, unmoving figure. The pure, clear notes of the tenor sax soared and a shiver of pleasure snaked down her spine. Taking a deep, measured breath, Izzy lifted her face to the lights, opened her mouth and began to sing.

'Never, never
Understood how
The rest of the world
Felt, until now.
Was I ever, ever
Alive before now?
You showed me how
It could be.'

And then an even greater roar of amazement and delight went up from the audience as, dressed all in black like the devil himself, Tash emerged from the backlit clouds of dry ice and made his way slowly towards Izzy. The unexpectedness of his appearance was almost too much for them to take in; for the first few seconds, when only his silhouette was visible, the crowd weren't certain that it was actually Tash Janssen. But then, when the spotlights finally beamed down on him, they knew for sure and their tumultuous welcome brought the house down. Screams, whistles and frantic applause raised the noise level to new heights. Izzy, who still hadn't turned to look at him, had to concede that the surprise appearance was indeed a master-stroke of planning. Tash might be a bastard, she thought, but he was undoubtedly a clever one.

'*Never, never Understood how,*' sang Tash, behind her. Seemingly startled, she spun around to face him just as his hand slipped around her waist, and the audience erupted once more. Tash, grinning broadly, murmured, '*Mi amore,*' into the microphone, just loud enough for seven thousand pairs of ears to catch the whispered endearment. Then, expertly picking up on the missed beat, he resumed the song. '*Lucky me, lucky world, You're a woman, not a girl.*'

The husky, powerful voice had enraptured every female in the building except Izzy. But this, as he had told her earlier, was show business and she could feign rapture with the best of them.

'. . . *You taught me how To love. And now,*' she sang back, her voice soaring with emotion, '*As long as I have you, You'll al-ways, al-ways Have . . . me . . .*'

It was a triumphant finale. The audience, delirious with joy, simply refused to let them go. The applause went on for ever, reaching new heights when Tash finally signalled the band to lead them into 'Kiss'. Izzy had already sung it alone, but it would be unthinkable now not to repeat it as an encore. Besides which, the audience knew the words so well themselves that when Tash broke off from singing, '*I want you to kiss me, To know that you've missed me*,' in order to kiss Izzy, they could happily carry on without him.

The kiss, when it came, went on far longer than Izzy had anticipated, but since an undignified tussle was out of the question she had little choice other than to keep her mouth resolutely shut and tolerate it while the audience, avid romantics that they were, whistled approval and bombarded the stage with flowers.

'*I want you to kiss me, to know that you've missed me*,' whispered Tash finally, his fingers stroking the nape of her neck beneath her tumbling damp curls, his hips moving imperceptibly against her own. 'And I think you *have* missed me, sweetheart . . .'

The explosion of flashbulbs was dazzling. Izzy, gazing adoringly up at him for the benefit of a thousand cameras, smiled and said, 'If you think that, you really *are* deranged.'

Tash's glance flicked momentarily to her heavy emerald-and-sapphire Bulgari earrings. 'You wouldn't be wearing those if I didn't still mean something to you.'

Izzy fingered her left earlobe. 'I like them.'

'So you bloody well should! They cost nine and a half thousand pounds.' He grinned. 'But what the hell, you were worth it.'

Behind them, the band continued to play the refrain of 'Kiss'. All around them, the concert hall reverberated to the sound of seven thousand word-perfect Italians singing the chorus. Just then, a Cellophane-wrapped bouquet of yellow roses sailed through the air, landing almost at Izzy's feet.

'See?' said Tash, picking them up and presenting them to her. 'They think you're worth it, too.'

With her free hand Izzy swiftly unfastened first one earring, then the other. The next moment, before Tash had time to react, she'd hurled them into the audience.

'You bitch,' he said, the amusement dying in his eyes.

'Not at all,' countered Izzy sweetly. 'These are our fans, Tash. Surely *they're* the ones who are worth it . . . ?'

Chapter 54

In order to escape Gina's claustrophobic attentions, Sam found himself inventing work and arriving at The Chelsea Steps earlier and earlier each evening.

When he let himself into the club at eight-fifteen on Tuesday night, four days after Izzy's departure to Rome, only Sarah, the blonde receptionist, was there before him. Lounging on one of the charcoal-grey curved sofas adjacent to the main bar, she was eating a Mars bar and racing to finish a fat, lurid-looking paperback before work began. She glanced up with some surprise when Sam came in.

'Well, I know why I'm here early,' she said in reproving tones. 'I hate my husband. So, what's your excuse?'

'I hate mine, too.' Sam tipped her feet off the chair opposite, picked up her glass and sniffed it. 'And I like to check up on my staff now and again. Is this straight bourbon?'

Sarah, a teetotaller and life-long Pepsi addict, giggled. Then, remembering something, she said, 'Oh!' and reached for her handbag, rummaging energetically until she unearthed a folded sheet of newspaper. 'I saved this in case you hadn't seen it. It was in this morning's *Express*.'

The Chelsea Steps, with its illustrious clientele, was frequently mentioned in various gossip columns. Taking the clipping, Sam hoped it wasn't a scathing comment upon the fact that one of the minor Royals had been observed leaving the club the other night slightly the worse for wear.

'It's OK, it's not about us,' said Sarah, reading his mind. Pointing to the photograph with a manicured damson-red fingernail, she added, 'You're a friend of Izzy Van Asch, aren't you? I thought you'd like to see it. Looks like she and Tash Janssen are back together again.'

It certainly did. Sam had enough experience to know not to believe everything one might read in the papers, but it was hard not to believe this. The picture, taken at her concert in Rome, showed Izzy with her arms around Tash and an unmistakable expression of triumph on her face. The short accompanying article reported the concert's riotous success and dwelt lasciviously on the apparent resumption of their affair. Tash Janssen, it seemed, had told the avid reporters that their temporary estrangement was now behind them, and that the lyrics of 'Never, Never' had never been more apt. The blissfully happy couple, furthermore, were staying at the Hotel Aldrovandi Palace and were rumoured to be extending their stay . . .

Sam wished he could dismiss the possibility that Izzy and Tash were back together from his mind, but Izzy's unpredictability and notorious lack of judgement where men were concerned made it impossible. And if she was determined to pursue her career, as she had so ruthlessly informed him the other morning, who better to do it with than Tash Janssen?

'I think she's incredible.' Sarah prattled cheerfully on,

craning her neck to take another look at the photograph. 'She's nearly forty years old, but she looks younger than I do. Mind you, Tash Janssen's pretty stunning himself. If they got married, they'd have the most amazing-looking children, don't you think?'

The urge to socialise having temporarily deserted him, Sam remained upstairs in his office until nearly midnight, concentrating instead on a backlog of paperwork.

The phone on his desk finally interrupted him.

'Meredith Scott's here, Sam,' announced Sarah, ringing from reception. 'She's just gone in, but she was asking for you so I told her you'd be down shortly. Was that OK?'

'It rather looks as if it has to be OK,' he replied, his tone brusque. Meredith Scott, one of the few child stars of the Fifties who had made the successful transition to adulthood and even greater stardom, simply wasn't accustomed to rejection in any form. Now based in Hollywood and – handily – married to a plastic surgeon of some repute, she was an intermittent visitor to The Chelsea Steps and a wonderfully bitchy gossip whose innocent violet eyes belied a lethal tongue.

Her presence at the club, however, was good for business and Sam had always found her to be entertaining company. 'Tell Marco to uncork the Veuve Clicquot,' he said into the phone. 'I'll be right down.'

'Darling, it's been simply ages!' cried Meredith, in time-honoured Hollywood fashion. Faultlessly de-bagged eyes sparkled with fun as she studied Sam carefully for a second before raising her face for a kiss. 'And you're looking more gorgeous then ever, I must say. Go on Sam, break my heart and tell me you're married!'

Glancing with amusement at her shapely, astonishingly uplifted breasts, he nodded in the direction of her heart and said, 'Don't panic, it's safe.'

'Well, hooray for that.' Smiling, she reached up and kissed him once more for good measure. 'If nothing else, it does my husband the world of good to know there are still one or two handsome, eligible men on the circuit. Keeps him on his toes, you know . . .'

'He isn't over here with you?' Sam poured the champagne and handed her a glass. Meredith Scott was always good value and his mood was beginning to improve.

She gestured dismissively in the general direction of America. 'Poor man had to stay behind to do a chin-lift on some wizened old ex-president whose wife, I *happen* to know, is about to leave him anyway. I'm here to promote my new film. I have *the* most stultifying series of chat-show appearances lined up . . . I just know I shall fall asleep during one of them . . . so, I thought I'd at least seize the chance to have some fun first. Oh, and to make the most of my last few days as a forty-something. It's my birthday next week, darling . . . the dreaded half-century . . . and my manager's planning the most tremendous party for me. You simply must come!'

Sam grinned. Meredith Scott was fifty-five if she was a day, but who would ever dare to remind her of such an unpalatable fact?

'Of course I will. But tell me about the new film. What's it like?'

The awe-inspiring bosom, only semi-encased in plunging white velvet, heaved. 'An absolute stinker! Every member of the cast hated each other, we all hated the director even more and the storyline's putrid. But when you see me being interviewed on TV, of course, I shall praise the damn thing to the skies and declare it the most wonderful experience of my life.' She paused and took a sip of her drink, then added with a trace of sadness, 'I might not get any awards for acting in this Godawful film, but I deserve an Oscar for promoting it.'

'It certainly sounds as if you need a good party to make up for it.'

But Meredith's eyes had grown misty. 'I think I'd prefer a good man. I do love my husband, Sam, but he isn't here. I don't suppose you'd consider doing the honourable thing? Escort a lonely actress back to her hotel and . . . keep her company?'

When he didn't reply, she said falteringly, 'I'm sorry, but a woman in my position has to be careful. And at least I know I can trust you to be discreet.'

She was staying at the Savoy. When Sam pulled up outside the entrance, he left the ignition running. In the darkness, Meredith managed a half-smile.

'So, this is your discreet way of turning me down?'

The car was filled with the voluptuous scent of her perfume. For a fraction of a second, Sam wondered what it would actually be like to make love to a world-famous sex symbol.

Instead, he took her hand and gave it a squeeze. The fifteen-carat diamond on her wedding finger dug into his palm.

'You're happily married,' he said, his tone gentle. 'And although I've only met your husband a couple of times, I liked him. He's a nice man.'

She nodded. 'And now you're being an honourable one. I suppose you're right, really.'

'You know I'm right.' Leaning across, he planted a swift kiss on her cheek. 'Come on, cheer up. Think of all those Oscar-winning performances you have to give in the next few days.'

With a rueful grin, Meredith said, 'I could have given one for you, tonight. Except I don't think they hand out Oscars for that kind of performance, more's the pity. Hey, now there's an idea for my party! Everyone gets an Oscar . . . Biggest Jerk, Most Repulsive Paunch, Least Believable Toupee, Smallest Willy . . .'

Relieved to see that she had regained her sense of humour, Sam said, 'Am I still invited?'

'Of course! You can be the Greatest Disappointment in Bed.' Tilting her head to one side she added wickedly, 'That's because I couldn't persuade you into one, of course, but nobody else is going to know that.'

The danger period was over. Sam, having successfully negotiated it, raised his dark eyebrows and said, 'What's wrong with Most Honourable Night-Club Manager?'

'No way! It's insults only, at this Oscar party. And that reminds me . . .'

'What?'

'I forgot to ask you earlier, but somebody mentioned

that you were friendly with Izzy Van Asch, and then I saw in the paper this morning that she and Tash Janssen are back together again.'

Sam felt as if he'd been punched in the stomach. His tone carefully neutral, he said, 'Ye . . . es.'

'It's that song of theirs, "Never, Never",' Meredith continued with enthusiasm. 'I just love it so much, I thought how brilliant it would be if they could sing it at my party. My manager's going to contact theirs, but since you already know Izzy Van Asch, I thought you could have a word with her yourself. Will you ask her to ring me, Sam?'

Was he destined to spend the rest of his life, he wondered painfully, listening to people singing Izzy's praises?

'If I see her,' he replied tonelessly, 'I'll tell her. But it isn't certain that I will. And just because we're . . . friends doesn't necessarily mean she'll say yes.'

'Just if, then,' agreed Meredith, her cheerfulness renewed. Gathering her coat around her, she searched in the darkness for the door handle. Then, with a throaty laugh, she added, 'But I have to tell you, Sam, you certainly slipped up there. She's a beautiful girl. What kind of man would ever want to be "just friends" with someone like Izzy Van Asch?'

Katerina and Lucille were gossiping in the kitchen when he arrived at the house the following morning.

'I've seen it,' said Sam wearily, as Katerina waved a copy of yesterday's paper under his nose.

'That total dickhead!' Kat was outraged. 'Honestly, I

sometimes wonder if my mother has more than three brain cells to rub together. I don't know how she can even bear to *speak* to him, let alone . . . ugh!'

Sam, who shared her sentiments entirely, helped himself to a slice of Katerina's heavily buttered toast and marmalade. 'It might not be true.'

'I've been trying to call her at that hotel, but she isn't in her room.' She shot him a dark glance across the table. 'And Tash's phone has been left off the hook. God, if she ever brings him round here, I'm leaving home again.'

Sam's efforts to change the subject were sabotaged at every turn by Lucille, who was intensely interested in the Izzy-Tash affair. 'Such shenanigans,' she said in gleeful tones, deftly appropriating the last slice of toast and demolishing it with relish. 'We'll have Trevor McDonald here on our doorstep before ye know it. Maybe I should be gettin' me perm topped up, just to be on the safe side.'

Katerina looked horrified. 'Why? Don't tell me *you* think Tash Janssen's irresistible as well!'

'Ah, he's not my type,' replied Lucille comfortably. 'The fellow's too skinny by half, if you ask me. But Trevor McDonald, now; I've always had a bit of a sneakin' fancy for that one . . .'

'Did you hear about Izzy?' asked Gina, when Sam went up to her room.

Later, as he was leaving, he encountered Jericho lying outstretched in the hall, toasting his back against the radiator.

At the sight of him, Jericho thumped his tail with half-hearted enthusiasm. 'Are you quite sure there isn't something *you'd* like to ask me?' said Sam drily, bending to stroke his sleek, golden head. 'Like have I seen the piece in the paper about Tash and Izzy?'

Chapter 55

University life evidently agreed with Simon. When he turned up at the house on Friday evening, all smiles and wielding his battered weekend case as easily as if it were a biscuit tin, Katerina was struck afresh by the change in him. He seemed to have grown both in confidence and in stature, and when the irrepressible Lucille insisted upon feeling his biceps and pronounced herself deeply impressed, he took all the attention effortlessly in his stride. Katerina, one of whose favourite pastimes had always been teasing poor Simon until he didn't know whether he was coming or going, was rather startled to discover that she was no longer even capable of making him blush.

'That was brilliant,' he pronounced, having demolished a vast supper of home-made shepherd's pie followed by two helpings of blackberry-and-apple crumble. As befitted a future member of the university's rugby team he patted a cast-iron stomach and drained the glass of Guinness which Lucille had pressed upon him. With a broad wink in her direction, he added, 'I need to keep my strength up, after all.'

He *had* changed, Katerina decided. Not so long ago, she would have been the one passing that kind of faintly suggestive remark and Simon would have been turning scarlet with embarrassment. Now, however, fully in control and at the same time almost flirting – heaven forbid! – with Lucille, he was scarcely recognizable as the awkward fumbling schoolboy with about as much sex appeal as a teddy bear. It was completely ridiculous, but in the face of such an abrupt role-reversal, she realised that if anyone was in any danger at all of blushing, it was her . . .

Determined to nip such a humiliating prospect in the bud, she countered briskly, 'You certainly will need to keep your strength up if you're going to help me with my physics revision.'

But Simon, apparently, had other ideas. Shaking his head, he said, 'You've done enough work. We can do a final run-through tomorrow, if you like, but there's no point in overloading yourself now. I've come down here to give you a break before the exams start next week. Mental relaxation is what you need at this stage. It's a proven fact.'

In the old days, Katerina had always made the decisions and Simon uncomplainingly had gone along with them. Now that he was being masterful, however, all that had changed. And although she would never normally have allowed herself to be dragged within a mile of a cinema premièreing the latest Arnold Schwarzenegger movie, this time she gave it a chance and found to her astonishment and secret dismay that it was really rather entertaining.

The crowded pub in Holborn where a favourite amateur rock band of Simon's was playing was also more fun than she would ever have imagined, having steadfastly refused to accompany him to such unprepossessing venues before now. It was noisy, it was hot and it certainly wasn't a piano concerto by Debussy, but with a half-pint of shandy clutched to her chest, the security of Simon's muscled arm to protect her from the jostling crowd and the infectious enthusiasm of the band themselves, Katerina realised that once again, despite her initial misgivings, she was actually enjoying herself.

It was past midnight before they returned to the house. Having drawn the line at a doner kebab, Katerina switched on the kettle instead and watched Simon wolf his down.

'So, what exactly were you doing tonight?' she asked when the last shreds of salad had been efficiently disposed of. 'Testing me?'

He looked surprised. 'Testing you for what?'

'I don't know.' Deciding that she didn't want a coffee after all, she came and sat down on the sofa next to him. 'I just thought you might be trying to prove something to me.'

Simon broke into a broad grin. 'Have you been reading Sigmund Freud again?'

'No!' Her curiosity was well and truly piqued now. Where was the old Simon, whom she had been able to manipulate so easily and at will? And why was this new Simon seemingly so much more attractive?

Determined to make him blush at least once, Katerina kicked off her flat, black leather pumps and swung her legs across his lap, wriggling her bare toes and giving him a self-deprecating smile. 'I still think I should have been revising, but I've had a great time tonight. Thank you.'

Not only did Simon not blush, but he picked up one of

her feet in order to examine it more closely and said in conversational tones, 'How strange. I'd never noticed before that your middle toes are longer than the big toes. Have they always been like that?'

This was too much. Having long ago become accustomed to his adoration, Katerina couldn't cope with this new-found lack of it. Stung by the implied criticism of her toes, she wrenched the shameful objects smartly away. 'Don't you dare laugh at my feet.'

'I wasn't *laughing*,' replied Simon mildly. 'Merely making an observation.'

'Well, don't.'

The expression in her brown eyes was unmistakable. It took all his self-control not to burst out laughing. He could still scarcely believe that Jessie had been so *right*.

'If you've put this girl on a pedestal, how can you ever expect her to look up to you?' Jessie Charlton, his flatmate's girlfriend, had made it all sound so simple when, one drunken night, Simon had miserably confided in her. 'Of course she's going to treat you like dirt. That's the way it happens, Si. I'm not saying you have to come over all he-man and chauvinistic, because too much of that is a turn-off as well, but it sounds to me as if a bit of table-turning wouldn't go amiss. Try treating this girl as if *she's* the lucky one. Be macho, be enigmatic, be uninterested . . . and before you know it she'll be wondering what on earth *she's* doing wrong . . . Take it from me, Si. You'll end up practically having to fight her off.'

Good old Jessie, he thought with renewed admiration and fondness. He really owed her one for those inspired words of wisdom. All he had to hope now was that he could maintain the façade of disinterest, both mentally and physically . . .

'How about that coffee?' he suggested, still struggling to keep a straight face, and Katerina stomped into the kitchen. Returning to the sitting room two minutes later with mugs of hideously strong instant coffee, she shoved one into his hands and said, 'You've got a girlfriend, haven't you?'

'Hmm?' Simon pretended to be engrossed in his drink, which tasted even more disgusting than it looked. 'No . . . no . . . of course not.'

She shot him an accusing look. 'You must have. You've changed.'

'Well, my hair's longer.'

'Simon, don't be so flippant! What is the *matter* with you?'

He shrugged. 'I'm OK.'

'Oh yes, *you're* OK.' Realizing that she was losing her cool but by this time beyond caring, Katerina landed an ineffectual punch on his shoulder. 'You're *fine*. You're just treating me as if I was something from another planet. You used to *like* me . . .'

Females were funny creatures, thought Simon. His shoulder didn't hurt but he rubbed it anyway.

'I still like you, Kat.'

'You used to *really* like me,' she countered accusingly. 'I suppose you think that since the Andrew thing I'm some kind of fallen woman. I suppose your mother warned you to keep away from me.'

'She said no such thing.' This was chiefly because he had never mentioned 'the Andrew thing' to his family, but now wasn't the time to sound wimpish. 'And I don't think of you as a fallen woman, either,' he added in reassuring tones. 'After all, you're only eighteen.'

Out of sheer desperation Katerina leaned across and kissed him, hard. Then, because hard didn't appear to be working, she softened the kiss, sliding her arms around Simon's neck and moving slowly against him.

He did his very best to think about something else . . . dustbins . . . rugby practice . . . ice-cold showers . . . anything but what Katerina was doing to him with her hands and mouth.

And failed, miserably.

'You do still like me,' murmured Katerina, her warm lips brushing his neck, her body squirming with triumph and pleasure.

'I didn't say I didn't,' he replied reproachfully, breathing in the clean scent of her skin. 'And this isn't fair. It's a purely biological response—'

'Not so long ago, you wanted to give me a practical biology demonstration.'

Simon had never stopped wanting to, but despite the intensity of his desire, some sixth sense warned him that if he gave in now, his new-found advantage would be lost and he'd find himself back at square one. He no longer would be a challenge and Kat would lose interest all over again. So far, Jessie's advice had been spot-on. If, therefore, there was to be any future for this relationship, he absolutely had to remain aloof, macho and . . . oh, hell . . . uninterested . . .

'Actually,' he said, doing his best to shrink away from actual physical contact, 'it was quite some time ago. And you, if you remember, turned me down.'

For the life of her, Katerina couldn't think why. Neither was she able to imagine how she could have failed to notice until now how attractive Simon really was. He might not be what the girls at school would call 'drop-dead gorgeous' – their true heroes, after all, were currently Leonardo DiCaprio and Robbie Williams – but with his straight blond hair, kind face and American football player's strapping physique, Simon was a million times more interesting than the girls' puny real-life boyfriends.

'So now you're turning me down,' she said, her self-confidence in tatters, the disappointment evident in her eyes.

Simon shifted uncomfortably in his seat, willing his erection to subside and only hoping he was doing the right thing. Knowing his luck, he thought wryly, Kat would meet some other boy next week and fall madly in love . . .

Placing all his trust in Jessie Charlton, however, and furtively crossing his fingers at the same time, he said, 'You didn't want to jeopardize our friendship, if you recall. And I realised afterwards that you were right. Far better to be good friends, Kat, without the hassle of all that sex and stuff.'

To his relief, she broke into a grin. 'Sex and stuff. It isn't that terrible, you know.'

Simon didn't know. Deeply shaming though it was, he had yet to discover the delights of actually making love to a real live girl. If his flatmates ever found out, he would die . . .

'Of course it isn't terrible,' he replied easily, giving

Katerina the benefit of his man-of-a-thousand-conquests smile. Little realizing that he was echoing Izzy's argument with Sam – and lying, just as she had done, through his teeth – he added, 'But friendship's more important than sex, every time. And we don't want to spoil that, do we?'

Chapter 56

Izzy, unaware of the furious speculation surrounding her supposed romance with Tash, was both amused and amazed when – upon arriving home on Saturday morning – she found herself on the receiving end of a decidedly severe mother-daughter lecture.

Since Katerina clearly needed to get the talk out of her system, however, she sat obediently on her bed and waited until it was over before saying, 'But darling, I *know* he's a jerk. This silly newspaper article doesn't mean anything at all. I'm really not seeing him again, scout's honour.'

'Oh,' said Katerina, deflating like a balloon. Lamely, she added, 'Well, good.'

'And I haven't married any Italian solicitors either,' continued Izzy, humouring her. 'In fact, as far as I'm concerned, men are off the agenda for the foreseeable future. I'm going to be concentrating on work, work, work.'

'Me too.'

Dying to ask how things were between Sam and Gina, but sensing that something was still bothering Kat, Izzy gestured for her daughter to sit down beside her. Idly playing with her long, sleek brown hair, she said, 'Is everything all right, sweetheart? Simon isn't . . . making a nuisance of himself, is he?'

Katerina leaned against her mother's shoulder, as she had always done when she was a child. 'No. He's taking me to see a rugby match this afternoon.'

'Oh my God, whatever for? You don't like rugby!'

Katerina smiled. Her mother was looking positively indignant. 'I suppose I might change my mind. I've never watched a real match before. It might be fun.'

Curiouser and curiouser, thought Izzy. Tentatively, she said, 'So, things are going well between the two of you?'

Her expression rueful, Katerina replied, 'If you must know, I've decided that I fancy Simon like mad and he's decided we should be just good friends.'

'The nerve of that boy!'

Katerina shrugged. 'But then why should I be any less miserable than anyone else? Mum, I swear there's a jinx on this house . . . this thing with Gina and Sam is so farcical it's embarrassing. There's Doug, *obviously* in love with Gina, mooning around the place like a lost soul.' She paused, ticking the disasters off on her fingers. 'Then there's Simon and myself, of course. You and . . . nobody at all. Lucille and anyone at all, but preferably Trevor McDonald—'

'What?'

'At this very moment,' said Katerina with heavy irony, 'Simon is downstairs in the kitchen being seriously chatted up by our housekeeper. Yesterday morning she had the milkman closeted in there with her for over an hour. And as for Doug, well . . . the poor man just isn't safe when she's around.'

'And Trevor McDonald?'

'It's only a matter of time,' Katerina replied darkly.

'Heavens.' Izzy thought hard for a moment. 'But Jericho's OK?'

Her daughter grinned. 'Oh, Jericho's happy enough.'

'That's something, I suppose.'

'But the next-door neighbours aren't too thrilled. It seems he's been getting on rather too well recently with their labrador bitch. And now she's developed a craving for Mars bars and pickled mackerel.'

Izzy knew within minutes that accepting Vivienne's supposedly impromptu dinner invitation had been a dreadful mistake.

It was sheer desperation that had driven her to say yes in the first place. Back in the recording studios to complete her album, she was able to avoid bumping into Sam during the day, but evenings at home were a nightmare. Unable to cope with the increasingly strained atmosphere, she had leapt at the chance of escape. Just an informal supper and a couple of good bottles of wine, Vivienne had assured her, and an opportunity for her finally to meet Terry Pleydell-Pearce, the most wonderful man in the entire universe.

And if he *was* the most wonderful man in the universe, she thought drily, what on earth was he doing with a sneaky, conniving, traitorous old bag like Vivienne Bresnick?

'It's a set-up,' she announced, her expression bleak. 'Vivienne, how *could* you?'

Vivienne was just glad that Malcolm Forrester had arrived at the cottage first. Judging by Izzy's reaction, she might otherwise have taken one look at the table set for four and walked straight back out.

'What's the big deal?' she countered innocently, taking care to keep her voice down so that neither Terry nor Malcolm, in the next room, could overhear. 'Like I said, it's just a cosy evening with friends . . . no pressure . . . Malcolm's a real nice guy.'

'Hmm.' Izzy, not taken in for a moment, said, 'Well, excuse me if I don't marry him.'

Vivienne, showing off her domestic skills, pressed the start button on the microwave. 'You could do a hell of a lot worse,' she replied lightly. 'He's divorced, charming and a real gentleman. He's nothing like Tash Janssen at all.'

This was certainly true. Putting on a brave face, Izzy admired the cottage, which was enchanting, got to know Terry, who was every bit as nice as Vivienne had promised, and exchanged pleasantries with Malcolm Forrester, who was of all things an obstetrician.

He was also *old*, probably knocking fifty, with silver wings in his dark, swept-back hair, a paisley cravat and an avuncular manner that reminded Izzy of her grandfather. Vivienne, having found real happiness with Terry, had evidently decided that Izzy should broaden her horizons and at least consider a man of similar vintage.

But the excruciatingly polite conversation, which ranged from the latest exhibition at the Tate to the genius of Dizzy Gillespie, only succeeded in making Izzy realise how desperately she missed Sam. The sense of longing, so acute it was almost a physical pain, was showing no signs at all of going away. Every time Malcolm Forrester called her 'my dear Isabel' she found herself imagining the expression on Sam's face if he could only have been there to hear it. His grey eyes, glittering with suppressed amusement, would have locked with hers as they had done so many times at The Chelsea Steps, and later they would have rocked with laughter together over a shared Chinese takeway.

Her appetite by this time had all but disappeared. Uncharacteristically picking at the delicious meal – *boeuf Bourgignon* with fresh asparagus and tiny new potatoes – Izzy listened in silence as Terry and Malcolm swapped 'And-then-she-said' stories about their respective grand-children. Her sense of aloneness increased when she realised that beneath the table, Terry and Vivienne were holding hands. Nor could they keep their eyes off each other for more than a few seconds; with each newly touted example of infant cuteness Terry would glance at Vivienne as if unable to quite convince himself she was still there. Then, his face lighting up once more, he would give her a brief, secret smile . . .

Finally, unable to contain herself a moment longer, Vivienne leapt to her feet and disappeared into the kitchen. Returning with a bottle of champagne, she said, 'OK folks, this was supposed to wait until after the meal but patience was never my forte. Sweetheart, can you get this thing open? I don't want to wreck my nails.'

It wasn't exactly the surprise of the century, but Izzy dutifully assumed a blank expression. While Terry wrestled somewhat inexpertly with the cork, Malcolm said in hearty tones, 'What's all this, then? Do we have something to celebrate?'

Vivienne, her amethyst silk dress shimmering in the

candle-light, let out a squeal of delight as the cork ricocheted off the ceiling and champagne cascaded over Terry's corduroys. When their glasses had eventually been filled, she clung to his arm and raised her own glass in a toast.

'Ladies and gentlemen, we'd like you to be the first to know. Terry and I are going to be married!'

Amid the flurry of congratulations, with hugs and kisses all round, Izzy found herself being forced to submit to a decidedly firm kiss from Malcolm Forrester.

'Marvellous news,' he declared, straightening his cravat and looking smug. 'How about that, Isabel? Isn't it simply the most marvellous news?'

Izzy, fighting the childlike urge to wipe her mouth with her sleeve, said, 'Absolutely splendid news, Malcolm,' and glanced across at Vivienne to see if she, at least, was sharing the joke.

But Vivienne, who had never looked more radiant, hadn't even been listening. 'And of course,' she continued joyfully, 'we'd like the two of you to be godparents . . .'

Izzy stared at her. 'You're *pregnant?*'

'Oh, not yet. But we certainly aren't going to waste any time in that direction.' Pausing, in order to give Terry another hug, she added, 'I'm nearly twenty-eight, after all.'

'But that isn't old,' Izzy protested, turning to Malcolm Forrester for corroboration and feeling hollow inside. 'Twenty-eight isn't *old!*'

But Vivienne had been reading all the books. 'The sooner it happens, the better,' she said simply. 'You weren't even twenty when Katerina was born, but in the baby-making stakes I'd already be classed as an "elderly primagravida". My fertility is decreasing, the chances of complications only increase with every passing year . . . all *sorts* of things could go wrong!'

'Twenty-eight still isn't old,' repeated Izzy stubbornly.

'Good heavens, of course not.' Malcolm Forrester, swooping diplomatically to the rescue, refilled their glasses and adjusted his cravat once more. 'Why, more and more women these days wait until they're in their thirties before starting a family. Professionally, I'm all for it.' To emphasise the point, he gave Izzy the benefit of his best Harley Street smile. Then, in a jocular undertone, he went on, 'Although personally I can't say I envy them. At least you and I have been through that stage and put it well and truly behind us now. We're the lucky ones, my dear Isabel, don't you agree? At our age we simply don't need to worry about that kind of thing any more.'

Chapter 57

Having for the past week and a half been plagued by nightmares in which the second brain scan had shown up a tumour the size of a melon, the reality was almost disappointing. Gina, sitting in the consultant's immaculate grey-and-white office on the fourth floor of the Cullen Park Hospital with Sam beside her, gazed in silence at the reality for several seconds before placing the films carefully back on the desk. Reaching for Sam's hand, inwardly amazed by her ability to remain calm, she said, 'So, what happens now?'

The consultant was no longer smiling. Gliomas – fast-growing malignant tumours formed from the central nervous system's supporting glial cells – weren't funny. And from the appearance of the scan, he had no doubt at all that this was the type of tumour with which Gina Lawrence had been afflicted.

'We operate,' he replied, his tone carefully matter of fact. Experience had taught him that this was the best way to avoid hysterical outpourings of grief. 'The plan is to remove as much of the tumour as possible before commencing radiation therapy. I've already made the necessary arrangements. Surgery is scheduled for nine o'clock tomorrow morning.'

'It *is* a glioma then,' said Gina, only the convulsive tightening of her fingers as she clutched Sam's hand betraying her agony. It was a glioma which had killed her mother.

The consultant hesitated for a second, then nodded. 'I'm afraid that's what it looks like,' he admitted quietly. 'Mrs Lawrence, I wish I could have given you more hopeful news. I really am very sorry indeed.'

The operation the following day went on for three and a half hours. Doug, unable to cope with the interminable waiting, had gone for a walk in the rain. Izzy and Sam, left alone in the waiting room, occupied seats opposite each other and drank endless cups of coffee. Since idle conversation would be too cruelly inappropriate, neither said much. Izzy tried hard not to imagine the surgical procedures being employed in the theatre downstairs. She wondered what Sam was thinking. Then she tried not to think about Sam and how differently things could have turned out if only there hadn't been all those stupid obstacles between them.

'You're fidgeting,' said Sam.

Putting down her cup and jamming her hands into the front pockets of her jeans, she rose to her feet and went over to the window. Outside it was still raining; a sea of multi-coloured umbrellas bobbed in the streets below. Katerina would be finishing her final biology paper around now. Thousands of city workers were taking their lunch break, wondering whether to choose cottage-cheese salad or lasagne and chips. And Doug, umbrella-less and no doubt by this time soaked to the skin, was still out there somewhere, just walking . . .

Wishing she'd gone with him, Izzy said, 'I don't even

know why we're here. There's nothing we can do.'

'Gina wanted us to be here.'

'Yes, but I hate it.' Unable to look at him, she continued to gaze blindly out of the window. 'I feel so *useless*.'

'Don't be so bloody selfish,' Sam replied evenly. 'There are some things in life that even you can't control.'

When the surgeon erupted into the room ninety minutes later, Izzy reached for Doug's hand and found it as clammy as her own.

'Well?' said Sam, only the muscle ticking in his jaw betraying his tension.

'It wasn't a tumour.' The surgeon, his mask still dangling around his neck, beamed at them. 'Quite extraordinary . . . I must say, I haven't seen anything like it in all my years of working. The scan appearances were so typical I'd have bet a year's salary we had a glioma on our hands . . .'

'So, what was it?' Izzy almost shrieked, unable to bear the suspense. 'Is she going to be all right? What *was* it if it wasn't a tumour?'

'It was an angioma,' explained the surgeon in pacifying tones. 'It's a collection of abnormal blood vessels, rather like a bundle of tangled wool. As the vessel walls weaken the likelihood of haemorrhage increases, and that of course can be fatal.' Pausing for effect, he rubbed his hands together and beamed triumphantly once more. 'Happily, we got there first and were able to . . . defuse the time-bomb, as it were! Mrs Lawrence's angioma was very amenable to surgery; I simply tied off the offending vessels and effectively disconnected them from her circulatory system. The operation was a complete success in every respect, and there's no reason at all now why Mrs Lawrence shouldn't enjoy a long and healthy life.'

Izzy promptly burst into tears.

'She isn't going to die,' whispered Doug. Sweating profusely and looking quite dazed, he enveloped her in a mighty bear-hug.

'Thank you,' said Sam, shaking the surgeon's hand.

When the three of them were alone once more, he handed Izzy a clean white handkerchief. 'It's good news,' he said, sounding faintly exasperated. 'There's no need to cry.'

'The bastard,' sobbed Izzy, still clinging to Doug. 'He could have sent someone in here *hours* ago to tell us that.'

'I cut my best friend's hair once, when I was seven years old.' Izzy, her tongue between her teeth, gingerly combed Gina's blonde hair over the shaved area. 'It ended up looking just like this. Her mother belted the living daylights out of me when she saw it.'

'Let me see in the mirror,' said Gina. Turning her head this way and that, she smiled with relief. Now that the dressing was off and the stitches had been removed, her remaining hair fell naturally over the scar, concealing it so well that it hardly showed at all. 'I can't believe it . . . I thought they'd shave my whole head.'

'You look fine,' said Izzy, giving her a hug. 'You *are* fine, thank God. And it's great to have you back home.'

Gina was glad she was looking her best when Sam arrived to see her a couple of hours later.

'More flowers,' she protested, burying her nose in the pale apricot roses and inhaling their delicate scent. 'I'll soon be able to open my own branch of Interflora.'

Sam, looking distinctly edgy, pulled up a chair and sat down. Gina raised a quizzical eyebrow.

'Is something wrong?'

The fact that he had been planning this speech for days didn't make it any easier now, but the words had to be said. And at least, he'd reasoned with himself, he had a legitimate excuse for getting them out of the way sooner rather than later.

'I have to leave for New York tomorrow,' he said without prevarication. 'There are serious problems with the club over there which may take some time to sort out.'

'Sam, that's terrible.' To his profound relief, Gina seemed more concerned for him than for herself. 'What kind of problems?'

'It seems the acting manager has been embezzling the accounts on a major scale, in order to finance his drug habit.' Sam paused, then shrugged. 'Maybe it's my own fault for not keeping a closer eye on the business myself. But the IRS are involved now and it's evidently going to take a while to work out.'

'You poor thing!' she cried sympathetically. 'And with Christmas coming up, too. What rotten luck.'

'Yes, well.' That was the easy part over with. His grey eyes serious, he said, 'Gina, there's something else we have to sort out before I leave. I don't quite know how to say this . . .'

But Gina, the colour rushing to her cheeks, forestalled him. 'Please,' she begged, reaching for his hand. 'You don't have to say it. I know what it is and you really don't have to say anything. It was all a silly mistake on my part . . . I panicked, and you were nice enough to humour me . . . but all that's behind us now and I don't expect . . . expect you to . . .' Stumbling over the words, by this time redder than a beetroot, she silently pleaded for his forgiveness. She was guilty of having put him under the most terrible pressure and, being Sam, he had shouldered it without a word of complaint. All she could hope for now was understanding and absolution.

'. . . I was just so afraid,' she concluded in a whisper. 'Of dying. Alone.'

Sam, scarcely able to believe it had all been so effortlessly sorted out, felt the great weight of responsibility lift from his shoulders. The sense of freedom was indescribable.

'Anyone would have been afraid,' he assured her, lifting her thin hand and kissing it out of sheer relief. 'Considering what you've been through, I think you were amazingly brave. Now all you have to do,' he added solemnly, 'is get on with the really tricky part.'

Gina smiled. 'And that is?'

This time, leaning out of his chair, Sam planted a brief kiss on her cheek. 'My dear Mrs Lawrence,' he said, his expression deadpan, 'living, of course.'

'I don't know how Lucille's going to cope when Gina moves back to Kingsley Grove,' said Katerina drily, ten days later. 'If we aren't careful, she might even defect.'

Izzy, who had been engrossed in the task of dyeing her hair good old Glossy Blackberry, wiped a trail of dark blue dye from her cheek and spun around to gaze at her in surprise.

'What?' she demanded. 'Why on earth should she?'

From her position in the bath, Katerina watched as a shower of inky droplets hit the basin. Hoping that none were also staining the expensive ivory carpet, she soaped her arms and explained patiently, 'Where Gina goes, Doug follows. It just occurred to me that Lucille, in turn, might want to follow Doug.'

'Hell.' Izzy nodded. It made sense. Not normal sense, maybe, but certainly Lucille-type sense.

'Mum, you're dripping.'

But Izzy, lost in thought, barely noticed. 'She mustn't leave. I'll give her a pay rise.'

Katerina grinned. 'She'd prefer Doug, gift-wrapped.'

'Well, she can't have him. Poor Doug . . . all *he* wants is Gina, and she treats him like a piece of old furniture.' She shook her head. 'No, what we need if we're going to hang on to Lucille is some kind of incentive.'

'You mean another man.' Reaching for the bottle of bubble bath, Katerina poured herself a generous extra helping and turned on the hot tap with her toes. 'We don't seem to be doing terribly well at the moment, where men are concerned. No wonder Lucille's fed up. Simon's gone off me, Sam's gone off to the States . . . even the milkman's too scared to ring the doorbell any more. There's nothing else for it, Mum – you'll just have to find yourself a toyboy.'

'Either that,' said Izzy, gloomily surveying the dye-spattered carpet, 'or we start writing begging letters. To Trevor McDonald.'

Chapter 58

Izzy barely had time these days to so much as fill in a Dateline questionnaire, let alone find herself a toyboy. Christmas was approaching, the album was finally nearing completion and the success of 'Kiss' ensured a steady stream of interviews, photo-shoots and public appearances. To her intense frustration, however, being rushed off her feet hadn't succeeded in getting her over Sam.

Absent Sam, still over in New York, occupied her mind at the most inconvenient times. Izzy tried to tell herself that it was only because she didn't have a sex life, but it didn't help. Everyone else was happy – even Doug, still pursuing Gina with dog-like devotion, seemed happy enough in his own way – and it only made her own unhappiness that much harder to bear. Christmas had always been her absolute favourite time of year, but this time she possessed no festive spirit at all. Festive, she thought dismally, was above and beyond the call of duty right now. The only thing she really wanted for Christmas was a decent night's sleep.

Major Reginald Perrett-Dwyer, ex-Grenadier Guards, veteran of the Second World War and regular contributor to the letters column of *The Times*, disapproved of most things. More than almost anything else at all, however, he disapproved of female singers with disreputable lifestyles moving into the house next door to his own and disrupting his own highly ordered existence. Despite maintaining watch from his drawing-room window, he had yet to ascertain who actually *lived* at Number Forty-five and who was merely visiting, but the non-stop comings and goings of so many people – at what seemed like all hours of the day and night – only served to increase his annoyance and send his blood pressure soaring.

'Drug-taking and orgies,' he boomed, slamming down his binoculars and glaring at his poor long-suffering wife. 'Mark my words, Millicent. That's what they're up to in there. If I had my way, I'd launch a dawn raid on that house. These types of people need teaching a lesson . . .'

'I thought they seemed quite pleasant,' protested Millicent Perrett-Dwyer, her eyebrows twitching with anxiety. Personally, she thought it rather exciting to be living next door to a pop star, and Izzy Van Asch couldn't have been nicer when she'd plucked up the courage last week to ring the doorbell and ask to borrow a jar of mustard. Her husband, however, who disapproved passionately of domestic inefficiency, didn't know about this. Just as he didn't know that each time he set out on his brisk morning constitutional his wife furtively turned the wireless from the World Service to Radio One and sang along to the music while tackling the breakfast dishes.

'Nothing but lazy, good-for-nothing vagabonds,' snorted the major, bristling once more as the Van Asch woman herself drew up outside in her flashy German car and ran, long hair flying, into the house. 'Look at that, I ask you! Can't park straight and hasn't even bothered to lock the damn thing. It's an open invitation to car thieves . . .'

'Oh, do come away from the window, dear,' begged his wife, terribly afraid that he was on the verge of making another of his infamous scenes. 'They aren't doing us any harm, after all.'

But scenes, unfortunately, were what made life worth living for Reginald Perrett-Dwyer. 'Harm?' he barked, staring at his wife as if she was quite mad. 'Is your sense of judgement really as poor as your memory, woman? How can you stand there and say they haven't done us any harm, after what that vicious brute did to Bettina!'

Here, thought Izzy, was living proof that not all dogs resembled their owners. The major, gaunt, upright and congenitally stroppy, was still in full flow and showing no sign at all of running out of breath. Bettina, by contrast, rested peacefully at his feet. Plump and sweet-natured, she seemed to tolerate her master's ranting with almost benevolent amusement. Whenever Izzy caught her eye she wagged her tail as if silently apologizing for all the fuss.

'. . . and it is *no* laughing matter!' stormed the major, intercepting Izzy's smile. 'That irresponsible hound of yours has violated an innocent young bitch, and I demand to know what you intend doing about it.'

'Look, I really am very sorry,' said Izzy in soothing tones. 'But are you absolutely sure Jericho's the father?'

The major's agitation reached new heights. 'Of course I'm sure!' he spluttered furiously. 'That animal arrived here six weeks ago. According to the vet, Bettina is five weeks pregnant. No other dog has been near her . . . has *ever* been near her . . . and I take great exception to the fact that you should even suggest otherwise.'

'It was just a—' began Izzy, but he quelled her with a look.

'Maybe such a suggestion is only to be expected from someone of your . . . type,' he concluded heavily. 'But I can assure you, Miss Van Asch, that Bettina has been brought up in a household of the very *highest* moral repute.'

It was deeply ironic, thought Izzy several hours later, that it should have been Major Reginald Perrett-Dwyer who – in effect – had broken the news to her. Until then, it hadn't so much as crossed her mind.

Now that they had been spelt out for her, however, the facts were inescapable. It was six weeks since Jericho had come to board with them.

Six weeks since she and Sam had made love.

More than six weeks since her last period . . .

'Oh, Bettina,' murmured Izzy with resignation, in the privacy of her darkened bedroom. 'Pregnant. You and me both.'

'That's no good,' Gina sighed. 'Doug, stop . . . you're doing it all wrong . . . that doesn't *go* there . . .'

Doug, his forehead creased with concentration, straightened up and took a step backwards. Something went *crack* under his left shoe.

'Oh, brilliant,' said Gina in despairing tones. 'Now you've trodden on the fairy. Well done.'

Just for a moment, he was tempted to tell her to decorate her own bloody tree. What should have been an enjoyable evening was threatening to turn into yet another major disappointment, and he was beginning to tire of them. It was all very well for Gina, lounging on the sofa and barking instructions like some parade-ground sergeant-major, but hanging baubles and draping garlands of tinsel simply wasn't his forte and he was damned if he was going to apologise for that.

'Look, why don't you get Izzy and Kat over here to do this?' he said levelly, stripping the imperfectly hung garlands from the tree and dropping them back into their box. 'Seeing as I'm clearly not up to it.'

Gina, unaware that the worm was on the verge of turning, simply shrugged. 'I suppose I'll have to,' she replied with irritation. 'At least they understand how it's meant to be done. Where are you going?'

'Home.' Doug reached for his jacket.

'But I thought you were staying for supper.' She looked up, startled. 'I've defrosted a chilli.'

But Doug had had enough. Winding his scarf around his neck, he said recklessly, 'I'm eating out tonight.'

'Who with? A client?'

'No. With Lucille Devlin.'

'You'll never guess what,' said Gina when Izzy arrived at Kingsley Grove an hour later. Sounding intrigued and at the same time faintly put out, she went on, 'Doug's gone out to dinner tonight. With Lucille.'

You'll never guess what, thought Izzy, struggling to keep a straight face, but Lucille is at this precise moment in my house, drinking gin and bawling her eyes out over a video rerun of *Ryan's Daughter*.

Then her gaze slid sideways, to the pile of half-written Christmas cards on the coffee table with Gina's address book lying open next to them.

'Why shouldn't they have dinner together?' she said lightly. 'They get on wonderfully well. Doug's an eligible bachelor.'

Gina's mouth narrowed with disapproval. 'And Lucille's a married woman.'

'I'll let you into a secret,' Izzy confided. 'It's a marriage in inverted commas only.'

'Really?'

'Really. Now come on, tell me what you want me to do with this poor naked tree of yours. And I'm going to need the step ladder. Where is it?'

'In the cupboard under the stairs,' replied Gina absently, her mind still occupied by thoughts of Doug and Lucille.

Izzy rolled up the sleeves of her yellow MBT sweatshirt in a businesslike manner and began investigating the glittering contents of the Christmas box. 'I'll make a start here,' she said, lifting out a tangled skein of lilac-and-silver fairy-lights, 'and you can take that chilli out of the oven. I'm hungry.'

The moment Gina was out of the room, Izzy dropped the string of lights and made a grab for the address book on the coffee table. Feeling like a sneak thief, riffling through the pages until she came to S, she breathed a sigh of relief when Sam's New York phone number and address leapt out at her. Hastily, she scribbled them down on the back of an unused Christmas card and stuffed it into the pocket of her jeans. She hadn't decided yet quite *how* she was going to break the news to Sam, but at least she now had the means with which to contact him. Even if it had been necessary, she thought wryly, to do a James Bond and practically *steal* the information from an unsuspecting accomplice . . .

Chapter 59

Having boarded the jumbo jet eight hours earlier buoyed up by determination and a sense of exhilaration at her own daring, Izzy's self-confidence seeped steadily away as the plane came in to land. No longer separated from Sam by the mighty stretch of the Atlantic Ocean, she had effectively sealed her fate. There could be no backing out now. She was here, in person, to see him . . . to tell him that she was pregnant . . . and to gauge his reaction first-hand.

And although it was a distinctly scary prospect, it was really the only way. Writing a letter, she had concluded after the fortieth failed attempt, was beyond her. The words simply wouldn't come. Neither, she realised, would a phone call work. Apart from the fact that she undoubtedly would lose her nerve, burble incoherently and get everything wrong, she wouldn't be able to tell what he was really thinking. She'd witnessed his ability to mime despair while speaking soothingly into the phone too many times to be able to take his words at face value.

No, doing it that way was out of the question. She definitely needed to *be* there, to say the words and gauge his true reaction for herself.

And now I am here, she reminded herself, as the plane approached the runway at JFK and began to engage reverse thrust.

'Nervous?' asked the middle-aged businessman next to

her, having observed her sudden pallor.

Izzy nodded. She had never been so scared in her life.

'You can hold my hand if you like.'

She had to smile. With a brief shake of her head, she replied, 'Thanks, but it's not that kind of nervous.'

Already cloaked with snow, New York had been promised a further blizzard before nightfall. Having retrieved her suitcase – *the* infamous suitcase – and cleared customs without difficulty, Izzy jostled for a cab outside the main terminal.

'Seventeen below zero,' the driver laconically informed her, glancing over his shoulder and looking unimpressed. 'An' it's gonna get worse. Where to, lady?'

Her teeth were chattering so much, she sounded like a typewriter on speed. Struggling to get the words out between shivers and combing frozen fingers through her damp, dishevelled hair, she said, 'C-can you rec-commend a d-decent hotel?'

'Hey lady, I can recommend the Waldorf-Astoria.' He had an accent like the pregnant one in *Cagney and Lacey* and his tone of voice betrayed his exasperation. 'I can *also* recommend the Tokyo Hilton and the Happy Traveller Motel in Milwaukee. Couldya be, like, more specific?'

Smartass, thought Izzy, glaring at the back of his horrible head. And to think that when Vivienne had told her about New York cabbies she'd refused to believe her.

'No problem,' she replied shortly, and with as much sarcasm as she dared muster. 'The Waldorf will do just f-fine.'

* * *

The hotel was more than just fine; it was unbelievably opulent. Upon hearing the price of a room, Izzy very nearly wheeled round and headed back out of the lobby into the street. But the street was awash with grey slush, she desperately needed a hot bath, and there was always the hideous chance that her cab driver might still be outside, waiting to greet her reappearance with a knowing smile . . . Besides, now that she had come this far, what difference did a few hundred dollars more make? She was here on a mission, possibly the most important mission of her life, and she might as well do it in style.

A long scented bath, she concluded, was a great way of putting off something that had to be done but which you weren't looking forward to doing. Izzy stayed submerged as long as possible, gazing at her flat stomach, realizing how it had looked eighteen years ago and envisaging the repeat performance ahead of her. By next summer, taking a bath would mean submerging the rest of her body and watching the water lap against the sides of a smoothly rounded protruding belly the size of a football. Every so often the perfect symmetry would be distorted by a miniature arm or leg kicking out. At other times – rather less pleasurably – an invisible kick would be aimed at her bladder. And the inconveniently positioned bump would make painting her own toenails a virtual impossibility.

The burning question, of course, was whether or not Sam would be there with her, to witness the miraculous changes her body was about to undergo. Would they be a proper couple, like Vivienne and Terry, or had she driven him away when she'd insisted that such a future was out of the question because her career came first, and because she was just too old to start having babies all over again?

But although she would never have chosen for this to happen, she didn't resent the fact that it had. Maybe it was the hormones taking over, but the thought of being thirty-seven years old and accidentally pregnant no longer seemed as alarming in reality as it had in theory. With or without Sam she would cope, just as she had coped all those years ago when Katerina had arrived on the scene.

Biting her lip, Izzy envisaged once more the process of picking up the phone and dialling Sam's number, which she now knew off by heart. It had to be done, before she lost her nerve completely. Although maybe she'd just repaint her toenails first . . .

The phone rang seven times before it was picked up, by which time Izzy had begun to feel quite sick. All she was doing, she reminded herself, was calling Sam to let him know she was in New York to promote 'Kiss', and to suggest they might meet for a drink. It wasn't, after all, as if this was the big one, the moment when she had to take a deep breath and tell him about the baby . . .

But the voice at the other end of the line didn't belong to Sam. Furthermore, it was a female voice, sexy and slow and sounding as if its owner had just been woken up.

Praying that in her agitation she'd got the wrong number, Izzy cleared her throat and said, 'Er . . . is Sam there?'

But the fickle dialling-finger of fate wasn't that kind. The sleepy, sexy voice, sounding unperturbed, replied, 'I'm afraid he isn't, right now. I'm expecting him home in a couple of hours, though. Can I ask him to call you back?'

Oh shit, thought Izzy, feeling sicker than ever. That something like this might happen hadn't even occurred to her. Whoever she was speaking to certainly didn't sound like any kind of domestic hired-help.

'Um. OK.' It was no good, she couldn't chicken out now. Not leaving a message would be downright immature, and maybe there *was* some perfectly innocent explanation for the girl's presence in Sam's apartment.

'Right, I've found a pen,' said the voice at the other end. 'Fire away.'

'Could you tell him that Izzy Van Asch called.' Giving her full name, Izzy felt, made it sound more businesslike. 'I'm in New York, staying at the Waldorf-Astoria in Room 317. If he could phone me as soon as he gets in . . .'

'Room 317, the Waldorf,' repeated the girl. 'Right, got that. I'll pass the message on.'

'Thank you.' Taking the deep breath she hadn't been planning on using so soon, Izzy added, 'I'm sorry if I woke you up.'

'Oh, no problem,' came the good-natured reply. 'It's about time for my bath anyway. Bye.'

The next two hours crawled past. Izzy, who had never felt more alone in her life, alternately flicked through fifty odd channels of atrocious cable television and paced the luxurious hotel room coming up with reason after plausible reason why Sam might have a female staying in his apartment. The only trouble was she didn't believe any of them for more than a single moment.

Gazing out of her fifth-floor window only served to

increase the gnawing sense of loneliness. The snow was falling heavily now, white flakes hurling themselves against the glass and sliding down like tears. Below her, Park Avenue glittered with lights and life as Manhattanites bent on celebrating Christmas thronged the street on their way home from work and out to parties.

Any minute now, thought Izzy as ten o'clock came and went, the phone would ring and she would hear Sam's blissfully familiar voice. Without even needing to be prompted, he would volunteer the information that his secretary – or maybe the sister she'd never known he possessed – had passed on her message, and that he hoped she was dressed and ready to go because he'd booked a table for the two of them at Spago . . .

Except Spago, she belatedly recalled, was in Hollywood and the phone wasn't ringing anyway.

By eleven-thirty it still hadn't rung and jet lag was beginning to set in. Not having slept at all the night before, Izzy fought the urge to do so now, terrified that she might go out like a light and not hear the phone when it did finally ring.

But at the same time, the prospect of escaping into unconsciousness was an enticing one. Exhausted as she was, prolonging both the mental and physical agony wasn't doing her poor fraught body any favours. It had certainly played havoc with her fingernails . . .

'Honey, it's getting late and you still haven't returned those calls,' chided Rosalie Hirsch. The front of her dove-grey silk wrap fell open as she reached across the bed to refill Sam's wineglass. 'Tom wants to know if you can meet him for lunch tomorrow. And Izzy Van-somebody asked you to ring her at the Waldorf as soon as you got in. You really should phone, Sam. It might be important.'

'Hmm.' Sam, admiring the view of Rosalie's cleavage, trailed his hand across her equally exposed thigh. 'I doubt it.'

'You have no conscience,' she protested mildly, holding her breath as the hand moved higher.

'On the contrary.' Pushing her gently back against the pillows, smiling and unrepentant, he said, 'I feel just terrible about not returning those calls. But some things in life are simply more important. Don't you agree . . . ?'

Rosalie genuinely hadn't minded being woken up by the phone four hours earlier. This time, however, the intrusion came at a particularly crucial moment.

But whereas Sam would have let the damn thing carry on ringing, she couldn't ignore it. Grabbing the receiver, intent only upon getting rid of the caller, she gasped, 'Yes?'

'Oh. Is Sam back yet?'

The woman from the Waldorf, thought Rosalie, closing her eyes. With a breathy laugh, she said, 'Uh . . . well . . . he's pretty busy at the moment. Look, I'm sorry . . . oh! . . . but he'll speak to you later . . . OK?'

Disconnecting the call, leaving the phone off the hook this time, she returned her attention to Sam.

'Who was it?' he murmured with some amusement.

'Nobody important,' sighed Rosalie, her toes curling in ecstasy as she arched against him. 'Don't stop, honey . . . oh my God, whatever you do, don't stop now . . . !'

Chapter 60

Doug was up to his ears in paperwork when Gina entered the office.

'Well, this is a surprise,' he said, carefully concealing his delight.

Gina, unaccountably nervous, removed her olive-green beret so that if he wanted to kiss her, he could. But it didn't happen. Instead, perching awkwardly on the chair opposite, she placed a large gift-wrapped parcel on the desk.

'I haven't seen or heard from you for over a week,' she said brightly.

Doug nodded his head in agreement. 'I know.'

'So . . . I thought I'd pop in and see you. See how you were getting on.'

'Fine,' he replied, glancing at his watch and deliberately ignoring the parcel on the desk.

Abruptly, Gina's fragile defences crumbled. She had rehearsed this meeting a dozen times over the last day or so, but Doug evidently hadn't learned his lines. He didn't even seem pleased to see her.

'Look, I'm sorry if I was rude to you the other day,' she blurted out, twisting her fingers together in her lap. 'It was wrong of me, but I just didn't expect you to walk out like that.'

Doug hadn't expected himself to walk out either, but it

appeared to have had the desired effect. Encouraged by her conciliatory tone, he replied evenly, 'There didn't seem much point in staying.'

'I know. I behaved like a spoilt bitch.' Gina looked unhappier than ever. Smoothing her dark green skirt over her knees, she inclined her head in the direction of the parcel. 'And I really am sorry. I didn't know if I'd be seeing you at all over Christmas, so I thought I'd better give you your present now.'

'That's very kind of you,' he replied gravely. 'Thanks.'

'So, what are your plans for Christmas?' Gina had been biting her tongue, willing herself to remain calm, but the words tumbled out anyway. 'Will you be staying in London, do you think, or going away?'

He shrugged. 'I haven't made up my mind yet, although I'll probably stay here. See some friends, you know the kind of thing.'

It was extraordinary, but she'd never noticed before the slight but definite resemblance between Doug and Anthony Hopkins. The eyes were the same, Gina now realised, gazing at him for what seemed like the very first time. And the shape of their mouths was virtually identical . . .

Pulling herself together and struggling to conceal her jealousy, she said, 'I expect you'll be seeing Lucille.'

'I expect so.' Relaxing in his chair, inwardly amazed by the success of his campaign, Doug felt he could afford to be magnanimous. With a brief smile he said, 'And what will you be doing?'

It's my own fault, thought Gina miserably. All he's ever been to me is kind and in return I've treated him like dirt. I deserve this.

'Oh, I'll be fine.' Her voice sounded unnaturally high. 'I'm not quite up to wild parties at the moment, of course . . .'

'What about Christmas Day?'

She didn't even want to *think* about Christmas Day. If she did, she might cry. 'Oh,' she murmured, flapping her hands in a vague gesture of dismissal. 'I'll be fine, really . . .'

Doug, who had never deliberately hurt anyone in his life, found her stoical sadness almost unbearably poignant.

'If you don't have any other plans,' he ventured, clearing his throat, 'maybe we could spend it together. There are plenty of restaurants open on Christmas Day, and we wouldn't have to go anywhere too . . . wild.'

'Really?' Colour flooded Gina's pale cheeks. 'On Christmas Day? You'd have lunch with *me*?'

'Only if you'd like to.' Doug broke into a grin. There, he'd done it. And it hadn't been so difficult after all.

'I'd *love* to,' cried Gina, her eyes glistening and her body sagging with relief. 'I can't think of anything nicer. But you don't need to book a restaurant, I can do all the food and we can spend the day at my house.'

Doug pretended to hesitate. 'Only if you promise not to ask me to decorate your tree.'

'I won't ask you to do anything,' declared Gina joyfully. 'Except be there. That's all that matters, after all.'

'So, you're back,' Lucille observed, having heard the taxi pull up outside and rushed to open the front door. Giving Izzy a shrewd up-and-down, she added, 'And you're lookin' a bit peaky. That jet lag's gone to yer eyes . . . what you need, my girl, is a bowl of hot soup and a good piece of soda bread to mop it up with.'

What Izzy needed was Sam, but she managed a feeble smile and allowed herself to be ushered into the kitchen, where a vat of Lucille's famous soup simmered on the stove.

'There ye go,' exhorted her housekeeper, plonking a brimming bowl in front of her. 'Get that down into yer stomach and you'll start feelin' better in no time at all.'

If only, thought Izzy. Her appetite had deserted her on the other side of the Atlantic, but with Lucille standing guard she had little choice other than at least to try a spoonful of the soup.

'How's Jericho?' she said, glancing in the direction of his empty basket.

Lucille rolled her eyes. 'Love's young dream! He howls outside Bettina's window until he catches a glimpse of her. It's like Romeo and Juliet all over again and it's drivin' the major demented. But I'm more interested in findin' out how *you* are,' she continued, folding her plump arms across her chest and fixing Izzy once more with that unnervingly direct gaze. 'From the desperate look of you, I'm thinkin' that things in New York didn't turn out quite as you'd planned.'

'What?' hedged Izzy, disconcerted by the note of sympathy in her voice. 'It was a business meeting, that's all. It went OK.'

But Lucille wasn't about to be fobbed off. Her eyes softened as she glanced momentarily in the direction of Izzy's stomach. 'Bless you, girl,' she said gently. 'Ye might be able to get away with foolin' some people, but this is an Irish Catholic ye're talkin' to, now. We can spot a pregnant woman at fifty paces.'

'*What?*' Izzy gasped, appalled. Inadvertently gazing down at her still-flat stomach, she cried, 'How? How can you *possibly* tell?'

'Easy,' said Lucille with a modest shrug. 'I found a crumpled-up letter to the fellow himself, when I hoovered under yer bed.'

Having sworn Lucille to secrecy, and so that Christmas at least could be spent in relative peace, Izzy waited until the day after Boxing Day before breaking the news to Kat.

But it had to be done, and although she still leapt a mile each time the phone rang or the doorbell went, there had been no word at all from Sam, not even so much as a Christmas card.

He had, it seemed, made his own decision to put their ill-fated relationship behind him and involve himself with a sensual American girl instead.

She was probably a blonde, Izzy had mournfully concluded, trying hard not to feel jealous. A beautiful, nubile blonde with great teeth, who was utterly devoted to Sam Sheridan and undoubtedly a good ten years younger than herself.

Katerina was stretched out across the sofa watching *The Wizard of Oz* and working her way methodically through a Terry's Chocolate Orange when Izzy sidled into the sitting room.

'Sweetheart,' she began, perching on the arm of the

sofa and listening to her own voice echoing in her ears. 'I've got something to tell you.'

'You're pregnant.'

So much for Lucille's ability to keep a secret, thought Izzy, torn between outrage and relief. Frantically twiddling her hair around her fingers, she said humbly, 'Yes.'

Kat jerked upright. The remaining segments of Chocolate Orange fell to the floor. 'My God, I was joking!'

'Oh.' Izzy twiddled more furiously than ever. 'I wasn't.'

'You're really and truly pregnant?' cried Katerina, her brown eyes wide with horror. 'It's not just a false alarm?'

Izzy shook her head and tried not to listen to Dorothy, on screen, giving the poor old cowardly lion a pep-talk. Right now she understood just how he felt.

'No, it's real.'

'Ugh!' Katerina yelled. 'That's disgusting! Mother, how *could* you?'

'It isn't disgusting,' countered Izzy, appalled by the ferocity of her daughter's reaction. 'I'm sorry, darling, I know this must have come as a bit of a shock to you, but that still doesn't make it disgusting.'

'You're nearly forty.' Katerina, whose face had drained of all colour, felt physically sick. 'You're *supposed* to be old enough to know better. Has it even occurred to you to stop and think how humiliating this is going to be for all of us?'

Much as she would have welcomed it, Izzy hadn't been naïve enough to expect instant understanding and a pledge of undying support. But the sheer selfishness of Kat's attitude was positively breathtaking.

'I haven't *murdered* anyone,' she retaliated, dark eyes

flashing. 'I haven't done anything to even hurt anyone, for heaven's sake! All I'm doing is having a baby . . .'

'Who will be known throughout his or her entire life,' spat Katerina with derision, 'as Tash Janssen's unwanted "love child".' She shuddered once more at the hideous thought. 'Poor little bastard, what a label. Of all the unsuitable men in the *world*—'

Izzy stared at her, open-mouthed in astonishment. 'Kat, listen . . .'

But Katerina, misinterpreting her expression and looking more appalled than ever, shouted, 'Oh no, don't tell me you're going to marry him. *Please* don't tell me that.'

Not knowing whether to laugh or cry, Izzy could only shake her head. 'Sweetheart, I'm not going to marry anyone, least of all Tash Janssen. He isn't the father.'

'He's *not*?' Now it was Katerina's turn to look dumbstruck. 'Then who the bloody hell is? Oh Mum, don't tell me you had a Roman fling after all!'

'No.'

Outrage had given way to curiosity. To Izzy's profound relief, Kat's main objection appeared to have been to the thought of Tash Janssen's imagined involvement.

'Go on then,' prompted Kat, her voice calm. 'I'm not going to play twenty questions. Just tell me who it is.'

Izzy held her breath. 'Sam.'

'What? It can't be. You haven't slept with him!'

'Isn't a mother allowed to have some secrets from her daughter?' she protested, struggling to keep a straight face.

'So, you did sleep with him? I mean, you *are* sleeping

with him?' Katerina corrected herself. Gazing accusingly at her mother she said, 'OK, just how long has this secret affair been going on?'

By the time Izzy had finished explaining the whole sorry tale, Dorothy was waking up back in her own bed in Kansas and wondering whether or not it had all been a dream.

'. . . so I caught the first flight out of New York the following morning,' she concluded with a shrug, 'and decided that was that. I was the one, after all, who told Sam to find himself another woman so I can't really blame him for going ahead and doing it. It wasn't great fun, realizing that I'd effectively shot myself in the foot, but it isn't the end of the world, either.'

'Oh, Mum.' Katerina hugged her. 'You know what you are, don't you?'

'Hopeless.'

Eyeing her with affectionate despair, Katerina said, 'If the cap fits . . .'

'Oh, the cap fitted all right.' Izzy's mouth began to twitch. 'It's just that the stupid thing had a hole in it.'

Chapter 61

'You'll have to speak up, it's a bad line,' shouted Simon, in Cambridge. Half-covering the receiver with his hand, he said, 'Stop it, Claire.'

'Who's Claire?' demanded Katerina, bridling.

'Nobody. Sorry, what did you say just now? For a moment I could have sworn you'd said Doug and Gina were getting married.'

'They are!' Katerina started to laugh. 'Isn't it amazing? Apparently Gina's divorce was finalised last week. She realised she was madly in love with Doug, and was terrified that Lucille would snatch him away . . . so she proposed to him in the office the very next morning. Oh Simon, it's so funny and so sweet, they're going around like a couple of moonstruck teenagers!'

The trouble with Kat, thought Simon with a trace of exasperation, was that she never seemed to regard herself as a teenager. And what was so funny, after all, about being moonstruck? He'd been crazy about *her* for years.

'So, when's the wedding?' he said, above the crackle of interference on the line.

'That's what I'm ringing about. It's fixed for next weekend, and you're invited. You will be able to come, won't you?' Katerina paused, then added fretfully, 'Who *is* Claire?'

'I told you, nobody. And of course I'll come.'

'For the whole weekend?'

He grinned. 'Yeah, all right. I suppose I can manage that. I'll get to your house at around six on Friday evening. Look, I have to go now . . . we're on our way out to a party. Bye, Kat.'

Replacing the receiver with an air of triumph, he pushed up the sleeves of his crumpled rugby shirt and rejoined the poker game currently in progress at the kitchen table. His two flatmates raised quizzical eyebrows as he shuffled, then rapidly dealt the cards.

'What party's this then?' said Kenny Bishop, pinching the last digestive biscuit.

'And who the bloody hell,' demanded Jeff Seale, 'is Claire?'

Izzy, amazed and delighted by the news and happily taking full credit for having introduced Gina and Doug in the first place, had insisted upon being allowed to pay for the reception.

Gina almost fainted when she realised how much it was all going to cost.

'We can't let you do that,' she protested, horrified. 'Izzy, no! All we were planning to do was take over the private dining room at Cino's restaurant in Kensington. We'd all have a wonderful meal and nobody would need to go bankrupt. Why can't we just go there?'

'Because if I don't spend my money on important things like wedding receptions,' replied Izzy firmly, 'I'll only fritter it away on silly inessentials like sunbeds and tax demands.'

'It looks gorgeous,' said Gina longingly, clutching the

glossy brochure. 'But it's awfully extravagant.'

'So am I.' Izzy grinned. 'And for heaven's sake stop arguing. It's too late now, anyway. I've booked it.'

'Gosh.' Gina squirmed with gratitude and pleasure. Her eyes bright, she added, 'And I'm phoning Sam tonight to see if he can come to the wedding. Just wait until *he* hears about this.'

For Izzy, who had wanted so desperately to be looking her best when she saw Sam again for the first time in three months, the almost inaudible pop of the button breaking free at her waist was the final insult.

Her heart was in her mouth as he made his way across the Register Office's crowded waiting room towards her.

This is unfair, she thought miserably. Sam, *of course*, was immaculately dressed in a dark suit and white shirt. Tall, handsome and still possessing that indefinable charisma which marked him out from other men – and which other women found so hard to resist – he had never looked better. New York, and the love of a younger woman, evidently suited him. Izzy, wishing that she could melt into the wall behind her, tried to take comfort from the fact that at least he hadn't brought her along with him, but somehow even that didn't help.

'Hallo, Izzy.' His brief, polite smile didn't reach his eyes. 'You're looking . . .' He hesitated. Izzy, who knew exactly how she was looking, winced.

'Wet,' she supplied flippantly, deciding that it was the only way to play it. With a nod in the direction of the window, at the torrential rain outside, she went on, 'It was sunny when we left the house, so I didn't even bring a coat, let alone an umbrella. Kat was furious with me . . . she spent thirty minutes putting my hair up this morning and by the time we arrived here I looked like a half-drowned rat, so it all had to come down again. And I managed to ladder a stocking as I was getting out of the car,' she concluded defiantly, before he had a chance to point it out to her himself. 'So all in all, I'm a complete mess.'

'I was going to say you were looking well,' observed Sam mildly. 'But if you'd rather I didn't . . .'

When people said, 'well', in Izzy's experience, they almost invariably meant fat. Horribly conscious of the fact that she had, in the past fortnight, put on almost half a stone and praying that he wouldn't spot the popped-off skirt button at her feet, she sucked in her stomach and hurriedly changed the subject.

'Did Kat tell you she'd got top grades in her exams and been offered a place at medical school?'

Sam nodded. 'You must be very proud of her.'

'And Gina . . . what about Gina?' Izzy feverishly rattled on. 'Can you *believe* she and Doug are actually getting married?'

'These things do happen,' he observed, his tone dry.

'Oh, you don't know about Jericho, either! He's—'

Sam, interrupting her in mid-flow, placed a hand briefly on the damp velvet sleeve of her jacket. 'The registrar's calling us in now. We'd better not keep him waiting. You'll have to tell me about Jericho later.'

'Right.' Flustered by his obvious lack of interest, Izzy pushed her fingers through her still-damp hair. 'Yes, of course.'

'And Izzy . . .'

'Yes?'

The thickly lashed grey eyes remained absolutely expressionless. 'There's a pearl button on the floor by your left foot. I think it must belong to you.'

The reception, held at the Laugharne Hotel in Mayfair, was a splendid affair. Gina, looking more radiant than ever since becoming Mrs Douglas Steadman two hours earlier, threw her arms around Izzy and whispered, 'This is the happiest day of my life. And none of it would have happened if it hadn't been for you.'

'It was nothing,' quipped Izzy. Away from Sam, it was at least easier to behave normally. 'I just happened to be riding my motor bike down the right street at the right time . . .'

'And that's not all,' Vivienne chimed in. 'Think about it . . . if she hadn't invited me to that party at Tash Janssen's place, I would never have met Terry.' Rolling her emerald eyes in soulful fashion, she tightened her grip on his hand. 'And I would've spent the rest of my life a miserable spinster.'

'Like me, you mean,' Izzy suggested with a wry smile.

'Oh yes, you're a fine example of a miserable spinster,' drawled Vivienne. 'On our way here we passed an advertising hoarding with your picture plastered all over it, promoting the new album. It said, "Experience Izzy Van Asch's Kiss," and someone had sprayed underneath it, "Yes please." '

'I'm still a spinster.' For a terrible moment, tears pricked her eyelids.

'Bullshit,' Vivienne declared fondly. 'You could have any man you wanted.' Then, turning to Terry and planting a noisy, fuchsia-pink kiss on his cheek, she added, 'Except, of course, this one.'

'Who's Claire?' demanded Katerina. Simon, forking up smoked salmon and deciding that it definitely had the edge on tinned, hid his smile.

'You keep asking me that,' he complained good-naturedly. 'And I keep telling you, she's nobody.'

'I don't believe you.'

'Why not?'

'Because she must be your girlfriend.'

'And if she is?' Cocking his head to one side, he studied her beautiful, mutinous profile. 'Would you be jealous?'

Katerina wasn't eating. Having demolished a bread roll with agitated fingers, she was now reduced to rolling the dough into pellets.

'Of course I'd be bloody jealous,' she muttered, her cheeks burning with shame. 'I don't even know her, and I hate her.'

Bingo, thought Simon, breaking into a grin. Putting down his fork, he took her trembling hand in his and said, 'In that case, maybe it's just as well she really doesn't exist.'

It was weak and pathetic of her, Izzy knew, but after four solid hours of being relentlessly cheerful she needed a break. Her mouth ached from smiling, her new high heels pinched like crab claws and her stupid skirt – even without its button – was still far too tight. It was hard work socializing without the aid of champagne and harder still avoiding Sam without making the distance between them seem obvious. Other people's happiness, Izzy ruefully concluded, wasn't catching at all. It was making her downright miserable.

Chapter 62

'What are you doing in here?'

Sam's voice made her jump. Izzy, who had been curled up in the corner of a Wedgwood-blue sofa in the otherwise deserted hotel sitting-room for the last twenty minutes, felt her stomach do its familiar ungainly flip-flop.

Avoiding you of course, she thought. But since she couldn't very well say so, she replied shortly, 'Nothing. Having a rest.'

With an inward sigh, Sam realised that this wasn't going to be easy. Discussing anything of any real importance with Izzy had *never* been easy and the signals she was sending out at this moment were unpromising to say the least.

But he was damned if he was going to give up without having even tried. Not when he'd come this far . . .

'You haven't told me about Jericho,' he reminded her, nudging her feet out of the way and making himself comfortable on the sofa next to her.

Oh God, thought Izzy, close to despair, not more polite conversation.

'It isn't exactly the most riveting gossip in the world,' she said with a dismissive shrug. 'He got some poor bitch pregnant, that's all. She gave birth to three puppies last week.'

'Hmm. It sounded more riveting the way Katerina told it.'

Izzy glared at him. 'If you already knew, why did you bother to ask me?'

'Well, we've already discussed the weather . . .'

He was almost-but-not-quite smiling. Realizing that he was making fun of her, she snapped back, 'Don't patronize me.'

'Don't sulk then,' Sam replied easily. 'Izzy, look. It doesn't have to be like this. I thought we were supposed to be friends, at least.'

The more *reasonable* he was, the more she hated it. Childishly, she said, 'Real friends send Christmas cards.'

He started to laugh. 'You didn't send me one.'

'Only because you didn't send me one first.'

'Izzy, is that *really* what this is all about?' Rising to his feet, taking out his wallet, he said, 'Would you like me to go out to the shops and buy you a Christmas card now?'

'Oh, shut up!' she howled, determined not to smile. He had always been able to *do* this to her and she needed so badly to remain in control . . .

But Sam had crossed to the mantelpiece, upon which was stacked a sheaf of the glossy brochures extolling the delights of the Laugharne Hotel. Removing the top from his pen he sat down beside her once more, wrote 'Happy Christmas, Izzy' across the front of one of the brochures, then opened it up and scrawled on the inside page, 'With all my love, Sam.' 'There,' he said, his expression deadpan once more. 'Better?'

But it wasn't better. Izzy, awash with jealousy and realizing that she was once again in danger of bursting into tears, muttered, 'You can't put that. You mustn't put "*all* my love". What would your girlfriend think?'

'My girlfriend.' Sam paused, giving the matter some thought. Then he said, 'What girlfriend?'

Izzy flushed. She was sailing close to the wind now, but the urge to say it . . . and the masochistic need to know what Miss America was really like . . . was irresistible.

'I'd heard you'd got one,' she said, her heart hammering against her ribs, but her tone carefully casual. 'Is she nice?'

But Sam no longer appeared to be listening. Instead, having removed the impromptu greetings card from Izzy's grasp, he was scrawling an additional line below his name.

Barely able to contain her impatience, Izzy repeated, 'Sam. Is she nice?'

'Who?'

'You know damn well who!'

He sighed and handed her the card. 'I can't imagine where you've been getting this highly dubious information from, but there *is* no girlfriend. If you must know, I've been shamefully celibate for the last three months. Now, come on, open your Christmas card and read the last line.'

It said, 'PS Why don't you stop arguing and just say you'll marry me?'

The words swam on the page as Izzy's eyes filled with tears, but this time she made no effort to hold them back. Sam was telling her everything she'd wanted to hear. The trouble was, he was *lying* . . .

'I spoke to her on the phone,' she said, her voice barely above a whisper. 'I phoned you and she was there at your apartment. Sam, I realise that she never did pass on the message for you to ring me back, so you can't be blamed for that. But the second time I phoned, you were there in bed with her. The two of you were . . . together. So please don't try and pretend you've been celibate for three months because I *heard* you . . . and I can't bear the fact that you're telling me lies!'

Sam was silent for several seconds. Finally, he said, 'Which number did you ring?'

'Oh, shut up,' wailed Izzy. 'It was *your* number.'

He reeled it off. When she nodded – because for some ridiculous reason it had remained indelibly imprinted on her mind – he smiled.

'That's where I used to live,' said Sam gently. 'I sold it eight weeks ago. To a TV producer called Sam Hirsch.'

Izzy stopped crying. She stopped breathing. She couldn't remember how to breathe . . . When she was able to speak, she said, 'Are you sure?'

His dark eyebrows lifted. 'Well, I'm fairly sure. And I used the money from the sale of the apartment to pay off the debts at the club . . . But if you wanted to double-check, you could always phone the Hirsches and ask them yourself.'

Every detail of the nightmare thirty-hour trip to New York was hurtling through Izzy's mind: sixteen hours of flying, that beastly cab driver, the sheer torture of sitting in her hotel room waiting for the phone to ring, and then the ensuing anguish . . .

'Oh, Sam,' she said weakly, gazing at him in exasperation, 'why didn't you *tell* anyone you'd moved?'

'I did,' he replied with mock indignation. 'When I sent Gina a Christmas card I gave her my new number and address. All you had to do was ask her.'

'I flew all that way for nothing.'

'You mean you were *in* New York when you called me?'

Izzy closed her eyes for a moment, unable to believe this was really happening. She nodded.

'Well, this is encouraging news.' Intrigued, Sam said, 'Does this mean you actually wanted to see me?'

'Maybe.' Her tone was cautious, but the corners of her mouth were beginning to twitch. 'Oh bloody hell, Sam! Do I have to spell it out? Yes, I flew to New York because I wanted to see you and managed to make a complete idiot of myself in the process. There, I've said it. Are you happy now?'

'Maybe,' he mimicked gently, grinning and pulling her at long last into his arms. 'Although I'll be a lot happier when you've said you'll marry me.'

Izzy's lower lip was starting to tremble again. He kissed it, very briefly, then drew back and gazed into her brown eyes, his expression this time deadly serious.

'I mean it, Izzy. I've had three months to think about it, and it's the only answer. I don't want anybody else. I can't imagine *ever* wanting anyone else. I know now you were trying to be sensible when you told me I'd want children of my own, but that's simply no longer an issue. *I* know I'd rather be married to you and not have children, than marry somebody else and . . .' He shrugged, dismissing the argument. 'Well, it would be totally pointless.'

'Oh.' Suffused with love, Izzy clung to him. In a moment, when she was able to think coherently once more, she would break the news to him that Mother Nature had decreed a change of plan.

But Sam's arms, around her waist, were making a

voyage of discovery of their own.

'Your zip's undone,' he said, looking perplexed and glancing down at her short, topaz-yellow velvet skirt. 'What's the matter, are you ill?'

'We . . . ll,' Izzy began, but at that moment the door to the blue-and-white sitting room flew open.

'There you are,' declared Katerina accusingly. 'For heaven's sake, you two! I've been looking *everywhere* for you.'

It wasn't the most well timed of interruptions. Izzy, struggling to pull herself together, said, 'Why, is something the matter?'

'Of course not.' Advancing towards them, Katerina held out a sealed brown envelope. 'We wondered where you were, that's all. Doug's only just remembered that he was supposed to give this to Sam, so I offered to deliver it.'

'Looks like one of my tax demands,' joked Izzy feebly. Then, glimpsing the loopy, uneven scrawl on the front of the envelope, she said in surprise, 'That's Lucille's writing.'

Katerina winked at Sam. 'Lucky old you, then. It's probably an indecent proposition. Now that Doug's out of the picture she's fixing her sights on the next best thing.'

'Thanks,' said Sam drily, tearing open the envelope and removing a once-crumpled, now flattened-out sheet of paper. Then he frowned. 'But Lucille didn't write this.'

With a shriek, Izzy made a lunge for it. 'You mustn't read that!' she yelled, struggling to wrench the half-finished letter from his grasp. 'It's mine! I was just about to *tell* you—'

'It says Dear Sam,' he pointed out, effortlessly fending

her off and skimming the contents in seconds. Then, his expression changing, he turned his gaze back to Izzy.

'Is this true?'

Trust Lucille, she thought, to take matters blithely into her own meddling Irish hands. Carefully keeping a straight face, she said, 'Maybe.'

Oblivious to the presence of his future stepdaughter, Sam dropped the letter to the floor and pulled Izzy into his arms. This time the kiss he gave her wasn't brief.

'Young love,' said Katerina cheerfully. Unembarrassed, she perched on the edge of the coffee table and waited patiently for the grown-ups to finish. Sam, she decided, had evidently taken notice of the advertising posters exhorting him to Experience Izzy Van Asch's Kiss.

'OK,' she said eventually, fixing Sam with a determined gaze. 'This is all very well, but before it goes any further there's something I really must ask you.'

'What's that?' said Sam, his expression suitably deferential. Hidden from Katerina's view, his left hand was surreptitiously exploring the gaping zip at the back of Izzy's skirt.

'I need to know,' said Katerina slowly, 'whether or not your intentions towards my mother are honourable.'

The One You Really Want

Jill Mansell

Nancy can't quite believe it when her Christmas present from her husband turns out to be a lawnmower. She knows for a fact that Jonathan's been spending a *lot* of money on jewellery. So who's got the diamonds?

Nancy's best friend, Carmen, gave up on romance when she lost her adored husband. What Carmen really needs is a man to wake her up – but choosing the right one isn't going to be easy.

Mia's just arrived in London to live with her dad. Once she's met the potential stepmother-from-hell he's dating, she's determined to play Cupid – but her wayward arrows are just as likely to cause chaos as to ease the path of true love . . .

Acclaim for Jill Mansell's novels:

'Delightfully scurrilous, unpredictable and utterly entertaining' *Daily Record*

'A delightful reworking of the Romeo and Juliet story set in the English countryside. An ideal Valentine's read' *Daily Express*

'A sure-fire bestseller from the queen of chicklit' *Heat*

0 7553 0488 8 (A format)

0 7553 3250 4 (B format)

Falling for You

Jill Mansell

NHS specs, unfortunate hair and wonky teeth were the curse of Maddy Harvey's teenage years. Thankfully she's blossomed since then.

But when she meets Kerr McKinnon one starry summer's night . . . well, that's when the problems really start. Because everyone in Ashcombe knows what happened eleven years ago and her mother, Marcella, would rather tear that family to pieces with her bare hands than see Maddy with a McKinnon.

And, OK, maybe Marcella isn't her real mother, but Maddy owes her so much. How can she possibly go against Marcella's wishes? It's Romeo and Juliet all over again. Quick, hide those sharp knives and that little bottle of poison . . .

Acclaim for Jill Mansell's novels:

'A romantic romp full of larger than life characters' *Express*

'A sure-fire bestseller from the queen of chicklit' *Heat*

'An exciting read about love, friendship and sweet revenge – fabulously fun' *Home & Life*

0 7553 0485 3 (A format)

0 7553 3626 8 (B format)

headline
review